SHOOT TO KILL

A bloody shoot-out at St Pancras Eurostar terminal sparks off a major international incident – but affects Carlyle on a much more personal level. When French gangster Tuco Martinez threatens Carlyle's wife and daughter, the inspector has to call on the resources and skills of family man and drug dealer Dominic Silver to try and see him off. But Dom won't do all the dirty work and so Carlyle has to go into hiding. Cut off from his home turf, Carlyle struggles to cope with the situation. Meanwhile, back in London, the charismatic mayor, Christian Holyrod, is spiralling out of control...

MAA

WITHDRAWN

SHOOT TO KILL

by

James Craig

Magna Large Print Books
Long Preston, North Yorkshire,
BD23 4ND, England.

British Library Cataloguing in Publication Data.

Craig, James
    Shoot to kill.

    A catalogue record of this book is
    available from the British Library

    ISBN   978-0-7505-4242-5

First published in 2014 by Constable

Published in Large Print 2016 by arrangement with
Little, Brown Book Group

Magna Large Print is an imprint of Library Magna Books Ltd.

Printed and bound in Great Britain by
T.J. (International) Ltd., Cornwall, PL28 8RW

ACKNOWLEDGEMENTS

This is the seventh John Carlyle novel. Thanks for help in getting it over the line go to Michael Doggart and Chris McVeigh at 451, as well as Krystyna Green, Rob Nichols, Martin Palmer, Clive Hebard, Joan Deitch and all of the team at Constable & Robinson.

Thanks for their help and support go to Michael Webster, Will Baldwin-Charles and Ryszard Bublik.

As always, the greatest thanks are reserved for Catherine and Cate. This book, like all the others, is for them.

'When you have to shoot, shoot, don't talk.'

Tuco Ramirez, *The Good, the Bad and the Ugly*

Il ne faut pas vendre la peau de l'ours avant de l'avoir tué.

French proverb

ONE

'Inspector Carlyle?'

Shit. He could see the door and, beyond it, the real world. Life going on outside this asylum, waiting for him to jump right in and disappear. All he had to do was keep walking.

'Inspector!'

John Carlyle hesitated, cursing as he did so. He should have taken the back exit.

'INSPECTOR!'

Gritting his teeth, Carlyle tried to fix the approximation of a smile onto his face as he wheeled around and said, 'Yes?'

Angie Middleton, one of the newer desk sergeants, waved a sheet of A5 paper at him, a standard-issue worried look on her face. A massive black woman, she was sporting the kind of look that she normally reserved for times when the canteen had prematurely run out of her favourite roast beef and Yorkshire pudding. It suggested despair, laced with the slightest threat of impending violence.

Carlyle stopped about a foot from the desk in the hope that he could still make a getaway. 'What is it?'

'We've had a report of a suspicious package,' she said, suddenly lowering her voice. She thrust the note towards him.

But I'm off the clock, he thought wearily. 'Yes?'

he repeated, making no effort to take it from her. A suspicious package in London was about as suspicious as a pigeon in Trafalgar Square. And probably a lot less dangerous.

'It's in your building,' Middleton added somewhat belatedly, her voice now barely a whisper.

The inspector tensed. 'Winter Garden House?'

Winter Garden House, where he lived with his wife and daughter, was a 1960s block of flats in the north-east corner of Covent Garden, near to Holborn tube. A mixture of owned and rented properties, its inhabitants mainly consisted of low- and middle-income families, and others who qualified for social housing. The idea that anyone would want to try and blow it up was, quite frankly, ludicrous. But that was the thing about the so-called 'war on terror' – no one ever sought to deploy the weapon of common sense.

Angie nodded. 'Yeah.'

Grabbing the piece of paper, he turned and hurried towards the exit, quickly scanning the details of the call as he did so. 'EOD are on their way,' Angie shouted after him. The Met's Explosive Ordnance Disposal Unit was a group of ex-Army officers called to deal with suspected Improvised Explosive Devices. In the aftermath of an explosion, they were also called to the scene, in order to determine its cause. 'They should be there in about five or six minutes.'

Great, thought Carlyle as he lengthened his stride. *The whole bloody circus is about to descend on us. It just gets better.*

Outside, the cold night air invigorated him. Once across Agar Street, he called his wife's

10

mobile. As always when he really needed to speak to her, it went straight to voicemail. Frustrated, he left a terse message: 'Helen; it's me. If you get this before I see you, either stay in the flat or don't go home until I call back. Nothing to panic about, it'll be sorted within the next ten minutes.' Ending the call, he dialled up his home number and listened to it ring. Stepping off the pavement in Bedford Street, he was almost mown down by a black taxi. Carlyle jumped backwards in fright as the cab came to a sharp halt in a line of traffic. 'Stupid fucker!' he hissed, giving the back wheel a kick as he manoeuvred his way around it. 'Watch where you're fucking going!'

As he came round the driver's side, the cabbie stuck his head out of the window. 'Did you kick my fucking cab, you tosser?' he snarled, threatening to get out and give Carlyle a good kicking of his own. He was a big bastard and the inspector had no doubt that he would be on the receiving end of a serious pasting if he stood his ground. Without the time or the inclination to do so, he lengthened his stride. Running down Maiden Lane, with the driver's curses falling behind him, he groaned as he heard the robotic message on the home voicemail finally kick in. 'Can't you just answer the bloody phone for once?' Without leaving a message, he pulled up his daughter's mobile number. Third time lucky – Alice picked up on the fourth ring.

'Hi, Dad!' she said cheerily. Some kind of pop music was playing in the background and Carlyle caught laughter and a couple of words from an unfamiliar voice.

'Where are you?' Carlyle demanded.

There was a pause. 'I'm at Olivia's,' Alice said warily, suspecting a trick question.

Ignoring the hostility in her voice, he ploughed on. 'Who?'

'She's a friend at school. Not in my class, though. I'm having a sleepover.'

That's a result, he thought. 'Oh.'

'It was all agreed with Mum. I told you about it the other night.'

'Yes, yes,' Carlyle said hastily. He had no recollection of the conversation but he was happy that she was safe and sound. 'Just checking. You have a great time. I'll see you tomorrow.'

'Yes ... Dad,' she said, the suspicion now replaced by embarrassment.

'I love you,' he said, as he slalomed round an old woman edging her way along the road with the aid of a Zimmer frame.

'Yes, Dad!' Alice laughed, ending the call.

It took him another couple of minutes to jog up Drury Lane, past the Freemasons' Hall and into Macklin Street. Outside Winter Garden House, more than a little out of breath, he listened to the approaching sirens. The Bomb Squad hadn't arrived yet but they couldn't be more than a couple of minutes away, even accounting for London's impossible traffic. Punching in the entry code to the front door of the building, he stepped inside and headed for the lift. For once, it looked like it was working. Protocol said he should take the stairs but it was ten floors up, and getting up there under his own steam was out of the question. Also, he didn't have the time.

'Hold the door!' he shouted at an anorexic blonde woman who was just getting in the lift with her shopping. The woman did as she was told and soon they were heading upwards at a steady if not exactly rapid pace. For once the smell of ammonia did not assault his nostrils and he let the woman and her shopping get off at the seventh floor, proceeding alone to the tenth, three floors below his own flat.

Getting out of the lift, he turned right and made his way to number 20, home of Harry Ripley. Now in his eighties, Harry had lived in Winter Garden House since it had been built. He had no kids and, as far as Carlyle knew, no other family.

There were three doors on the landing. All were firmly closed. This high up, there was no noise from the street; the only sound was that of the leather soles of his shoes on the smooth concrete floor, and the whistling wind outside. Stopping at Harry's front door, the inspector bowed his head and listened. Hearing nothing beyond the wind, he banged on the door with his palm. After a few seconds he banged again, harder this time.

'Harry! It's John Carlyle! Open the door.' He ran his tongue along his teeth. A large glass of Jameson's would go down a treat right now.

'HARRY! OPEN THE BLOODY DOOR!'

'All right, all right,' from somewhere came a tired, crotchety and rather fragile voice. 'There's no need to shout.'

Suddenly disorientated, Carlyle looked around. There was nobody there. 'Harry?'

'I'm here.'

Looking down, Carlyle realized that the old man was talking through the letterbox. *Give me strength,* he thought, trying to hold back an urge to wring the old codger's neck. 'Open the door.'

'No,' Harry said firmly. 'The bomb!'

Maybe he would kill the old bastard, after all. 'What bloody bomb?'

Harry cackled. 'What kind of policeman are you? It's at your bloody feet.'

'Eh?' Carlyle looked down. Next to his feet on the doormat was a small brown cardboard box that had been left next to the front door of the flat. *Ten out of ten for observation, Inspector,* he said wryly to himself.

'I opened the door and saw it there,' the old man explained, 'so I shut it again and called the police.'

Carlyle frowned. 'And what makes you think it's a bomb?'

'They're all over the place,' Harry panted, 'I saw it on the news. There's a whatdyacallit ... a terror alert thingy. Bloody nutters trying to blow everything up. Those Al ... kayeeda folk, they're everywhere. They should be deported, the lot of them. Send 'em back to where they came from.'

That would be the provinces, then.

'You've got to stay alert,' the old man protested. 'I wouldn't stand there. You don't want to get blown to smithereens.'

'Yeah, yeah.' Carlyle took a step backwards and peered at the box. There was some writing on it but he couldn't make it out. *You really need to get your eyes tested,* he thought, and vowed to make an appointment at his local opticians as soon as possible. Less reluctant to bow to the inevitable than her husband, Helen had been there a few months earlier to get a pair of reading glasses. Now she spent half of her life wandering round the flat trying to find the damn things and accusing him of misplacing them. It drove him mad.

Squatting down, he carefully lifted up the box and brought it closer to his face so that he could make out what it said.

Unbelievable.

Carlyle did a double-take.

Un-fucking-believable.

Bursting out laughing, he said, 'Harry?'

'Yeah?'

'Did you order anything from Amazon recently?'

TWO

Dino Mottram finished his Suntory Whisky Cappuccino and signalled to a nearby waiter that he would like an espresso. Watching the last of his directors unsteadily leave the in-house private dining facility next to the main restaurant floor of Nobu London on Old Park Lane, he grunted his displeasure. 'Fitzroy is pissed – again.'

Dropping his napkin on the table, the soon to be ex-Mayor of London Christian Holyrod, watched one of the waiters scuttle over and take the elderly gent by the arm before he had the chance to walk into a broom cupboard. He then let out a small groan of pleasure and patted his ever-expanding stomach. 'Well,' he said, 'you did put on an excellent lunch. And not just the wine; the Beef Tenderloin was excellent.'

'That's no excuse for over-indulging.' Mottram shook his silver head sadly. 'I just hope he doesn't go back to the office and grope his secretary.'

Holyrod narrowed his eyes against the glare from the skylight atrium. 'How very 1950s,' he drawled.

'I'm not joking,' Dino said tersely. 'We had to pay tens of thousands in compensation to the last one when he dropped his trousers in her office and asked for a blow job.'

'Not ideal.'

'No. The old bugger claimed he was having some kind of flashback to his days in the Diplomatic Service in Africa. Ridiculous. Anyway, I've told the new girl that if he does it again, just to kick him between the legs and run.'

'Good advice.'

'I'll get him pensioned off as soon as I can,' said Dino. 'Monty Fitzroy pinpoints exactly why we need fresh blood like you to drag us kicking and screaming into the twenty-first century.'

Christian Holyrod smiled.

'I am genuinely delighted that we have got you at last.' The older man gripped him firmly by the arm. 'The Hero of Helmand residing in the boardroom of Entomophagous Industries – what a coup!'

Holyrod bit his lip. Introduced to Dino Mottram only six weeks earlier, he'd only joined Entomophagous Industries on a whim, largely because of the name. Entomophagy – from the Greek *éntomos* or 'insect', and *ph gein*, 'to eat' – meaning 'insect

16

eating', had tickled his fancy. That, and the six hundred thousand pounds per annum for three days' work a month. He tried to affect something approaching humility. 'Helmand ... that was quite a while ago now.'

Mottram jabbed a meaty finger into the space between them, his green eyes gleaming with passion. 'It wasn't that long ago. Anyway, the time doesn't matter. What matters is that you did it.'

'I suppose so,' Holyrod agreed, although it seemed that his Army days were several lifetimes ago.

'A *Boy's Own* story made flesh,' Mottram beamed. 'One of Britain's best soldiers – and then a stellar political career to boot.'

'You are too kind,' said Holyrod, grimacing slightly. The reality was that if his political career had indeed been 'stellar', or anything like it, he wouldn't be here now, touting himself around the business world, looking to earn some proper cash for once in his life. As Mayor, he had been Prime Minister Edgar Carlton's natural successor. But somehow, despite all the polls, Carlton had scraped a second election win and appeared to have every intention of holding on to the real political power at Number Ten for as long as possible. For Holyrod, well into a second term as Mayor, there was nowhere to go. No one was surprised when he announced that he would not stand for a third term. If, as the saying goes, all political careers end in failure, at least he had avoided failing on the biggest stage. Now, however, he had to earn a living. 'I'm looking forward to getting started.'

'Yes, yes,' Mottram agreed, nodding vigorously.

'I'm afraid that I don't really know much about the company and what it does.'

'Don't worry about that.' Mottram gestured towards the door. 'Half of that lot have been on the board for years and they haven't got a clue either. The trick is never to admit to your ignorance. You know what they say: *never apologize, never explain* and all that.'

'Even so, I need to get up to speed with what it is you – we – do.'

Mottram's espresso appeared and he took a noisy sip. 'We do lots of things,' he said airily. 'Cars, property, natural resources – it's a real old-fashioned conglomerate. We even own a football club.'

Holyrod made a face. 'Football's not really my thing.'

'You surprise me.'

'Why?'

'You know what they say,' Dino smiled. 'Sport is really nothing more than war without the shooting.'

'And what,' Holyrod said, 'is the point of that?'

Dino gave him a quizzical look. 'So you're really not into sport?'

Holyrod pondered the question for a moment. 'I'll watch a bit of rugby now and again, maybe go to Twickenham for the odd international, but I can't say that I follow football. It is all so totally ... base.'

'Don't worry, I won't make you go to any of the games.' Dino sighed. 'We're not having a great season. Then again, we rarely do. What we do have, though, is Gavin Swann.'

Even the Mayor couldn't have gone through life without coming across Swann, a regular on the front pages of the tabloids for reasons that had nothing to do with his sporting prowess. 'Now him,' Holyrod nodded, eager to show willing to his new boss, 'I have heard of. More for what he's got up to off the pitch, though.'

Dino smiled wanly. 'He seems to have put the gambling and prostitutes behind him and have become a proper family man – or he will be soon. Now all he needs to do is score some goals. Apparently, he has helped sell almost half a million replica shirts in the last couple of years. And when he is not fit enough to play, which is fairly often, we can always pack him off to Taiwan or Singapore to open another of our themed restaurants.'

'Do you – we – make any money out of it all?' Holyrod asked.

'Some. Not as much as we should. Swann's agent bleeds us dry. He agreed a new contract less than a year ago and already wants to renegotiate. Every time he does that, he raises the bar for all the others. It's a never-ending cycle.'

Holyrod frowned. 'Why don't you just tell him to get lost?'

'If only it were that easy. Agents are a real pain in the arse. They contribute to football's prune-juice effect – the money comes in at the top and goes straight out of the bottom. We manage to grab some of it on the way down, but only a little.'

'So why not just sell the club?'

Dino smiled ruefully. 'Two reasons. First, and most important, we'd lose a packet. We paid far too much for the bloody thing in the first place,

I'm ashamed to say.'

'And the second?'

'The second is that if we hold on long enough, we might *make* a packet. Hope springs eternal.'

That doesn't seem like much of a plan, Holyrod thought.

'People are always saying the bubble is going to burst, but the whole thing just keeps getting bigger and bigger. Compare Gavin Swann with the Queen,' Dino continued. 'Twenty-five years ago, the Queen's Christmas Day speech was watched by twenty-eight million people in the UK. This Christmas she'll be lucky to get a quarter of that. And the only way for the Royals is down. Even the new lot. Mark my words, in a few years they wouldn't even be able to get their own reality TV show. We make a few of those as well, by the way.'

'Oh?'

'Yeah. Nothing you've ever heard of. Hell, nothing *I've* ever heard of. Anyway, as I was saying, as the Royals have fallen, football has risen: more than twenty-three million people in Britain saw Gavin break his foot at the last World Cup – *at two o'clock in the morning!*' Dino's eyes misted over. 'It is a monster that generates unbelievable wealth ... and we can grab a piece of it.'

We'll see, thought Holyrod.

'It would help if – off the pitch, at least – Gavin were a bit more like David Beckham and a bit less like Diego Maradona.'

'Mm,' said Holyrod, not really sure what Dino meant.

'Anyway,' Dino continued, 'it's probably best not to spend too much time thinking about it all or it will drive you round the bend. In terms of the numbers, sport is only a small part of our Group. There are lots of things in the portfolio that are currently more lucrative – and less likely to make you want to blow your brains out. I'll arrange some kind of induction.'

'That would be great.' Glancing at his watch, Holyrod got to his feet. 'Thank you for an excellent lunch. Let's hope we can build on all your good work.'

Dino Mottram showed no sign of wanting to move from where he was. 'I'm sure,' he said, looking up at his newest recruit, 'that we are going to go and do great things together.'

'Fantastic!'

'And more importantly,' Dino added, with a cheeky glint in his eye, 'make some serious amounts of cash.'

THREE

'Can I touch it?'

'What?'

'Is it real?'

Scowling, Sergeant Alison Roche looked down at the boy who had sidled up to her at the Eurostar terminal in London's St Pancras station. He was a scruffy-looking kid but well dressed; maybe ten or eleven with frizzy hair and a cheeky expression on his face.

'I am Sidney,' he told her.

Looking the kid up and down, Roche said nothing. He was wearing a pristine pair of blue and white Adidas sneakers, a pair of baggy stonewashed jeans and a grey T-shirt with a picture of a Dalek on it in red, under the legend *EXTERMINATE*. In his left hand was a half-eaten king-size Mars Bar.

'That's my name,' the boy persisted. His English was precise but with a clear trace of an accent. Presumably, he was French.

Roche cleared her throat. 'Go away,' she growled.

Standing his ground, Sidney looked thoughtfully at the Heckler & Koch MP5 in Roche's hands, waiting for another question to pop into his head. 'Have you ever fired it?' he asked finally.

Roche felt an overwhelming urge to give him a hard slap round the back of the head. Instead, she took a deep breath. 'Bugger off!'

'Have you?' Sidney persisted.

'Of course I've fired it, you stupid little sod,' she hissed. 'Now clear off.' Thoroughly exasperated, she scanned the heaving station concourse, looking for any sign of someone who was responsible for this annoying kid. People were rushing around in all directions – the usual frenetic scene you got at any mainline terminus – but no one seemed to be looking for Sidney. *Bloody parents,* Roche thought with the righteous anger of someone who had never had any offspring of their own. *They shouldn't be allowed to have children if they can't look after them.*

Sidney stuck the last of the Mars Bar into his mouth before extending an arm and letting the wrapper flutter to the floor.

Roche gestured angrily at the litter with the toe of her boot. 'Pick that up!'

Happy to have gotten a rise out of the female copper, the kid grinned, revealing a mouth full of chocolate and caramel. 'Are you going to arrest me?' he asked, making no move to pick up his rubbish.

No, thought Roche, *but a bullet in the foot might encourage you to lose the attitude.* Subconsciously checking that the safety on the Heckler & Koch MP5 was on, she felt her finger tighten around the trigger and realized that she'd been holding her breath. Exhaling at length, she took a step away from the boy. *Get a grip,* she told herself. Shaking out some of the tension in her shoulders, she made a mental note not to recall this little episode the next time she was called for a session with the departmental shrink. Suddenly, she saw a middle-aged woman in a paisley kaftan waddle towards them, a look of concern etched into her face.

About fucking time.

'Sidney,' the woman squawked, *'viens ici!'*

'Maman...' the boy sighed, slumping his shoulders in the exasperated fashion of children the world over.

The woman grabbed her child by the arm and pulled him towards her with a force that seemed to Roche somewhat excessive. Catching the mother's eye, Roche saw a look of horror cross her pudgy face. *'Attention, chéri,'* she whispered theatrically. *'Elle est armée.'*

'I know,' Sidney said in English. He beamed. 'It's cool.'

23

'*Tu m'emmerdes à la fin,* Sidney.' The woman dragged him away, Roche glaring at her as she went. If she didn't like the son, she liked the mother even less. *We're supposed to be here to protect you,* she reflected, *and you look at us like we're shit.* Bending down, she picked up the discarded Mars Bar wrapper and tossed it on to a nearby café table.

Sitting at the table, Commissaire de Police Jean-Pierre Grumbach sipped his espresso and gave her a rueful shrug. 'Another happy member of the public goes about her business.'

Roche felt like screaming. She was more than ten hours into a fourteen-hour shift, and for almost all of that time she had been babysitting the Frenchman and his colleague, Lieutenant Ginette Vincendeau, along with their prisoner, a sallow youth called Alain Costello. 'In France,' she replied stiffly, 'I suppose the police are universally loved?'

'No, no.' Shaking his head, Grumbach sat back in his metal chair. He was a tall, elegant man, with a thick head of grey hair and laughter lines around his eyes, which looked good on his tanned face. In a black, single-breasted Christian Dior suit and a crisp white shirt, open at the neck, he looked less like a policeman than some kind of high-end businessman. Irritatingly, he had been hitting on her all day. Roche might have been more receptive to his flirting if it wasn't for the fact that it was so shameless – that, and the fact that they were still on the clock. 'There it is just the same. They need us, but they hate us. Or, at least, they want us kept out of sight, along with the bad guys.'

24

'It's true,' Vincendeau nodded. Slumped over a cappuccino, she sat opposite Grumbach; a short, dark woman, dressed in jeans and a sweatshirt. Her SIG Pro SP2009 was clearly visible, peeking out from a shoulder-holster under her leather jacket. 'But people in England are still not so used to seeing cops with guns.'

'They should be by now,' Roche shrugged. 'We're at airports, stations, even shopping centres. SO15 patrol the streets every day.'

'That's one thing I didn't understand,' Vincendeau said, gesturing at her prisoner. 'Why did the Counter Terrorism Command Unit grab this one?'

'The whole thing was a big mistake,' Grumbach said, reaching across the table and gently punching Alain Costello on the shoulder. 'They picked him up by accident. Funny, huh?'

Costello grunted but didn't look up from the game – which Roche recognized as *Grand Theft Auto: Liberty City Stories* – that he was playing on his PSP console. In handcuffs.

Roche felt embarrassment mingle with her frustration. It was true that the whole thing had been a bit of a cock-up. If SO15 hadn't mistaken Costello for a suspected North African terrorist by the name of Mehdi Zerdab, Roche would have had nothing to do with him. As it turned out, he was only a low-level drug dealer, albeit high on the wanted list of the Préfecture de Police. To be fair, it was a relatively easy mistake to have made. The distinction between drug smugglers and terrorists was becoming more blurred all the time. In the last month alone, SO15 had seized seven machine guns and more than a dozen automatic pistols from terror suspects with well-documented connections to the illegal drugs industry. It was a symbiotic relationship that both sides were increasingly happy to exploit: the terrorist groups gained cash and the traffickers, protection. Smugglers carrying cannabis, cocaine, ecstasy and heroin were known to transport weapons on behalf of their business partners.

Forty-eight hours earlier, following a tip-off, SO15 had picked Costello up in a raid on a Brixton flat. The place was supposed to be home to a terrorist cell. Instead of the anticipated haul of Jihadi propaganda and homemade explosives, however, the police found twelve kilos of cocaine, twenty thousand Euros in cash – and Costello. The little runt had been caught trying to flee through a bedroom window, having stopped to rescue his games console on the way.

They removed him to Stockwell Road police station for processing. Deprived of his games console, Costello refused to say a word, declining even to ask for a lawyer. However, once his fingerprints had been fed into the Interpol database, the authorities found more than enough information to be going on with. Given there were three warrants out for his arrest in France (one for attempted murder), plus two in Belgium and one in Holland, there was clearly going to be a queue of people waiting to take him off SO15's hands.

Less than two hours later, Grumbach and Vincendeau had been dispatched from Paris to take him home to the cell waiting for him in the Maison d'Arrêt de la Santé in the 14th *arrondissement*.

'Why do you let him play that?' Roche asked, keen to change the subject.

'Keeps him quiet,' Vincendeau sighed. 'Just like taking your kid on a trip.'

Bored with the conversation, Roche watched Sidney and his mother return to their place in the queue for the next train to Paris. She glanced up at the departures board above their heads. It told her that Eurostar 9042 to Gare du Nord should be boarding in about twenty minutes. Departure: 16.52. Surely it was time to be making a move.

Grumbach followed Roche's gaze. 'Don't worry,' he smiled, placing a hand on her forearm. 'We've got plenty of time.'

'She's right,' said Vincendeau gruffly. *'Allez!* Let's get going.' Getting to her feet, she scanned the lines of passengers waiting to go through passport control and scowled. 'We should never have come this way anyway. All this "hiding in plain sight" business of yours, Jean-Pierre.' She shot Roche a knowing look and raised her eyebrows.

'We're not hiding,' Grumbach objected, gesturing at his demitasse. 'I just wanted to have a decent cup of coffee before we get on the damn train.'

FOUR

When Carlyle finally got home, Helen was in the bath, the remnants of a Big Blue seaweed ball from Lush fizzing about in the water. Giving her a kiss on the forehead, he quickly pulled off his

27

clothes and joined her in the warm, salty water. Splashing his face, he leaned back against the taps and smiled.

Looking at her, his mind flashed back to their recent health scare. Helen had been identified as a possible carrier of a faulty gene called BRCA2, which meant an increased risk of breast and ovarian cancer. For several weeks, their lives had been turned upside down. Then the test came back negative and the whole thing disappeared in an instant. *How different would life have been, if the result had been positive?* He quickly shook the thought from his brain. They'd had a lucky break; it was pointless to brood on it. Life had almost instantly returned to normal, and now, it was as if the whole drama had never happened.

He shifted in the water, trying to get comfortable.

'Hey, if you're going to annoy me, you can get right back out again.'

'You didn't get my message then?' Carlyle asked, changing the subject.

'No. Why?'

'Bomb scare.' Remembering that Alice was out for the night, he felt a tiny tingle of anticipation. 'Harry downstairs thought that Osama bin Laden was trying to take him out. He really is beginning to lose his marbles.'

Helen's eyes widened. 'What?'

Carlyle explained what had happened. 'Literally, the Bomb Disposal guys ran all the way up to the tenth floor to find Harry holding a box of Jim Reeves CDs and a biography of Harold Macmillan. They were *not* best pleased.'

'I bet they weren't,' Helen laughed, carefully getting to her feet.

He watched the water drip off her buttocks. 'They wanted to arrest him for wasting police time.'

'That seems a bit much,' she said, wrapping a towel tightly around her waist.

'I made them see sense in the end.'

'Well done.' Helen stepped out of the bath and reached for a second towel, draping it over her shoulders. 'Seeing as we have some time to ourselves, I thought we might go and see a film tonight – unless you have other ideas?'

Carlyle just grinned.

She blushed slightly. 'John!'

'A film would be great,' he said, pulling out the plug.

'Come on then. There's something on at the Renoir that I thought we could go and see. It starts in forty-five minutes. Maybe get a bite to eat afterwards.'

'Sounds good.' Standing up, he made a grab for her towel. 'That gives us plenty of time for what I had in mind.'

Watching the two French officers head slowly towards the first-class barrier with their prisoner, Roche tried to shake the stiffness out of her legs, gaining only momentary relief. Sniffing her shirt, she caught a whiff of the accumulated body odour and let out a little groan. When she got home she was going to have a long, hot bath and a glass or three of chilled Sauvignon Blanc. Then she might put on one of the anti-stress DVDs that everyone in SO15 had been given by the Met's Chief Medical Officer.

Closing her eyes for a nanosecond she pictured herself in the perfumed water. It was a reverie that was over before it had begun. First came the sound of gunfire, rapid and precise: one, two, three. It sounded like a handgun of some description.

Roche opened her eyes and tried to focus.

Then the screaming started.

People were fleeing in all directions, the panic so loud that she almost couldn't make out the next shots: four, five, six.

The radio clipped to the breast pocket of her jacket exploded with the chatter of competing voices.

A woman with an outsized paper cup walked straight into her, sending a caramel latte all down the front of Roche's uniform. Without saying anything, Roche pushed her out of the way. Raising the MP5 to her shoulder, she began walking steadily towards the gunfire.

Breathe. Just breathe. Fucking breathe! Roche shook her head angrily.

'Stop talking to yourself,' she hissed. Her heart felt as if it were about to jackhammer out of her sodden shirt.

'Find a target.'

Amidst the chaos, she could see that Vincendeau was down, blood already spreading across the floor from behind her head, her weapon still in its holster. Standing in the mess, apparently oblivious to the chaos, Costello was still hunched over his PSP. Looking five yards past him, she could see the shooters. Leaning in to her weapon, she barked into her radio: 'I have two ... three targets.'

There was a crackle of static, but no reply.

'I have...' *Fuck it – move!*

Two males, dressed in combat pants, sneakers and hooded sweat-tops with no obvious branding. Both were wearing the kind of rubber masks you get in joke shops. As Roche tried to work out who they were supposed to be, another volley of fire into the ceiling brought more screams. Knots of people were cowering on the concourse while others dashed for the exit. Over the PA system came a strangely seductive female voice: *Can Mr Black please report to the station manager's office? Mr Black to the station manager's office. Thank you.*

The code for a Level One Emergency Incident.

Roche felt the acidic taste of vomit rising in her throat and swallowed hard. Where the hell was Grumbach? She answered her own question almost immediately as a clump of passengers scattered and she almost tripped over the Commissaire. He was sitting on his backside as if he needed a rest from all the excitement. The look on his face was completely blank. The round that had gone right between his eyes suggested it wouldn't be changing any time soon.

Roche regained her footing. 'Fuck! We have two officers down!' she shouted into the radio.

There were lots of voices but no one was talking to her.

She felt the sweat rolling down the side of her face. The gunmen were already making their escape through the glass exit doors. It was too late to get a shot off. Costello, however, was

31

barely five yards in front of her. 'Stop.' It was less of an order than a croak. Coughing up as much spit as her parched throat would allow, she tried again.

'Stop! Police!'

Still focused on his game, Costello turned and gave her a mocking smile. Then he began walking away.

Where the fucking hell was everybody? Roche wondered. In the distance, she could hear sirens. 'STOP!' she screamed at the top of her lungs. 'POLICE! PUT YOUR HANDS IN THE AIR OR I WILL SHOOT.'

Costello broke into a casual jog.

'Fuck, fuck, fuck.' At this distance, a two-second burst from the MP5 would cut him in half. Suspect shot in the back while trying to escape; she could hear all the jokes already. And what if she were to hit an innocent bystander? Fuck it. A corrosive hatred for the bastards who were making her do this welled up inside her. Closing her eyes, she squeezed the trigger.

Nothing.

Oh sweet fucking Jesus!

Roche's brain felt like it was going into meltdown. *The safety. The fucking safety.* With trembling fingers, she flicked it off and took aim again. But this time, Costello was gone.

FIVE

Standing on the steps of the Brunswick Centre, a Grade II listed modernist brutalist residential-cum-shopping centre in Bloomsbury, Carlyle looked in the direction of St Pancras station, which lay a couple of blocks to the north. A police car flashed past on Hunter Street, quickly followed by an ambulance, then another. Sirens seemed to be converging from all directions. Helen appeared at his shoulder and slipped her arm though his. She followed his gaze. 'Something up?'

'Looks like it.' Carlyle felt a familiar frisson of excitement rush through him. Another police Range Rover raced through a zebra crossing, almost taking out a woman pushing a buggy. 'Something is most definitely up.' Feeling her stiffen at the prospect of him bolting and leaving her to watch the film on her own, he kissed her gently on the lips. 'But it's not my problem.' His mobile began vibrating in the breast pocket of his jacket.

'Are you sure?' she asked doubtfully.

'Quite sure,' he said, pulling out the phone and carefully switching it off.

Roche watched Chief Inspector Cass Wadham, her boss at SO15, step gingerly past the covered body of Ginette Vincendeau and head in her direction. 'So now they're all here,' the sergeant mumbled under her breath. 'The bloody cavalry –

at last!' Before giving up, she had counted almost fifty officers in the otherwise almost deserted station. With the forensics guys, medics, firemen and others working on the scene, the number was well over a hundred. Outside, she was vaguely aware of frantic noise and activity. The inevitable television crews had started to arrive and a set of floodlights had been switched on, illuminating the vast hall in a grainy, pearlescent light, further adding to the unreality of the scene.

The adrenaline rush was wearing off and Roche felt ravenously hungry. Next to her foot, an aluminium chair had been knocked over in the stampede to get away from the gunmen. Pulling it upright, she carefully placed her weapon on the seat. Stepping over to an abandoned concession stall, Roche pulled a half-litre bottle of Diet Coke from a fridge, unscrewed the top and took a long drink.

'I hope you are not looting, Sergeant.' The voice behind her was clipped and tense, just like the Chief Inspector herself.

'Of course not.' Without turning round, Roche fished a two-pound coin out of her pocket and placed it behind the counter, next to the cash register. Then she let Wadham – a scrawny blonde in her mid-thirties who looked like the uniform was the only thing holding her body together – make a show of giving her a careful once-over.

When she'd seen all she needed, the Chief Inspector turned away. 'Bloody mess,' she said in her cut-glass accent. 'Terrible.' Shaking her head at the scene in front of them, she gazed to the heavens in search of some kind of inspiration.

Makes one wish one had joined the Foreign Office instead, doesn't it? Roche thought snidely.

'Absolutely ruddy frightful.'

'Yes.' Roche took another swig of her Coke. Over Wadham's shoulder, she could make out six bodies. Who were the other four? She felt a sudden spasm in her guts that young Sidney, the cheeky litter lout, might be one of them.

'What happened?'

'They started shooting,' Roche said quietly, the fizzy drink already beginning to make her feel sick. 'I saw two gunmen. They escaped, along with the prisoner.'

'Internal Investigations Command will want to speak to you this evening,' said Wadham primly.

Roche nodded.

'And you will be required to see Dr Wolf tomorrow.'

'Yes, ma'am,' said Roche wearily. This was her first fatal shooting but she knew the standard operating procedure. After IIC came the shrink. She really needed that bottle of Sauvignon Blanc now.

The Renoir was one of his favourite cinemas, along with the Lumière on St Martin's Lane before it closed back in 1997. Helen had introduced him to both, getting him interested in 'arthouse' movies back in the days before they were married, long before their daughter Alice was born. In the 1980s and early 90s, she would take him to see French films like *Betty Blue* and *Les Amants du Pont-Neuf*. Maybe that was one of the reasons he had married her. It was just a small one, one among many. It was a nice thought, but it was a long way down the list. The primary reason was that she had let him. There were times when he still marvelled at that.

Carlyle would watch just about anything. Unlike Helen, he needed the subtitles. But he enjoyed the films all the same. Indeed, once he cottoned on to the fact that 'arthouse' did not preclude sex or violence, and often demanded lashings of both, he was quite happy to sit back and enjoy.

Standing in front of the Renoir, Carlyle thought about that time. Early-afternoon matinées in an empty cinema. Perfect. Perfect and long gone. Now, the Lumière had been turned into a gym. At least the Renoir was still there. He looked up at the films listed above the entrance. None of the titles meant anything to him, but that didn't matter. 'What are we going to see?' he asked, pulling her close.

'*Alice in the Cities*,' Helen smiled.

He looked at her blankly.

'It's a Wim Wenders road movie.'

'Sounds good,' Carlyle nodded. 'Let's go.'

'This stuff's not bad.' Olivia Blackman sucked down on the small joint and offered it to Alice Carlyle.

'Nah.' Alice shook her head. 'I've had enough.' She felt sluggish. The latest Lady Gaga CD was playing in the background but she tried to ignore it. Having spent the last five years listening to her dad's CD collection, she was more into The Clash than whatever was currently flavour of the month. Right on cue, 'Guns of Brixton' started

36

playing in her head and she smiled to herself.

'Suit yourself.' Flopping down on her bed, Olivia took another drag and began coughing.

'Don't your parents mind?' Alice asked, climbing into her sleeping bag on the floor.

'What,' Olivia asked once she'd finally got the coughing under control, 'about me smoking dope?'

'Yeah,' Alice said. 'Mine are really pissed off about it.'

'Big surprise,' Olivia observed. 'Your father *is* a cop, for God's sake.' She rested the spliff on an ashtray on the bedside table. 'What do you expect?'

Alice shrugged. 'It's not like they didn't do stuff themselves, like, when they were young.'

Olivia pushed herself up onto her elbows. 'Being a parent means being a hypocrite, that's what my mum says, anyway.'

'But your parents, they let you do what you want.'

'I wish!' Olivia took another toke and rolled her eyes to the ceiling. 'They won't let Ryan stay over, for one thing.'

'Mm.' Alice felt herself blush slightly. Her experience of boyfriends wasn't great and it wasn't something she wanted to discuss.

'I think they just ignore it,' Olivia continued, 'at least my dad does. He's travelling a lot of the time, so I guess it's not his problem.'

'And your mum?'

'Ha!' Olivia collapsed back on to the bed, throwing out her arms, as if she was being crucified. 'She absolutely *needs* me to do drugs.'

Confused, Alice sat up. 'Eh?'

'My dear mama,' Olivia simpered, 'is none other than Lucy Pulse.' She raised her eyebrows as if this explained everything.

Alice frowned. 'But I thought her name was Andrea Blackman?'

'It *is*. Lucy Pulse is her pen name. She writes a monthly column in *The Times* called "My Teenager Hell". It's a thinly fictionalized account of life with me and my brothers.' She lifted her wrist to her forehead in a dramatic pose. 'You know, saintly parents locked in an endless struggle with their wretched offspring with nothing but a bottle of Gordon's, a DVD box set and a packet of Benson & Hedges for comfort.'

'Oh.' Alice thought about it all for a minute. A nasty thought entered her head. 'Am I in it?'

'Hardly,' Olivia laughed. 'Although I'm sure if you manage to vomit down the stairs or something, you'll get an honourable mention in the next one. She's on deadline and I heard her moaning on the phone the other day that she had nothing to write about.'

'But why does she do it?'

'Who knows?' Olivia said. 'It's not for the money, which she says is a pittance. I guess she needs the attention and doesn't have anything else to write about.' She started to giggle. 'Sometimes I feel like I'm under *sooo* much pressure to perform. All that my lovely brothers do is play World of Warcaft and masturbate, sometimes at the same time.'

'Gross! That's too much information.'

'It's not enough to keep a column going. If it

wasn't for yours truly smoking dope, getting into trouble at school and chasing boys, she would be totally fucked.'

Alice was beginning to see Olivia's mum in a whole new light. 'Why doesn't she just make it up?'

'She does, a lot of the time. But she needs to be able to claim it's broadly based on real life; otherwise, no more column.' Olivia picked up a diary from next to the ashtray. Inside was a collection of newspaper cuttings. Flicking through the pages, she found the one she was looking for. *'The aim of the column is to offer a scrupulously honest picture of family life. At the same time, inevitably, some incidents are partly fictionalized, some details have to be carefully rearranged and some characters become composites, to conceal the identity of our children...'*

'Your mother said that?'

'Yeah,' Alice nodded. 'About a month ago, not long after she was outed by another newspaper.'

'Don't you mind?'

'Nah.' Olivia closed the diary and tossed it onto the carpet by the side of the bed. 'Who cares about some shitty newspaper column? Certainly no one at our school. The good thing is that the paper's website is behind a pay wall, so no one will go and look at it online. Only a total idiot would pay to read the rubbish my mum writes.'

'That's something, I suppose.'

'I wish she hadn't done one about my first period, though,' Olivia groaned. 'And I've told her that Ryan is, like, totally off-limits, but I know that cow will write something about him anyway, just to embarrass me. I think she probably fancies him herself.'

'Urgh!' Alice stuck her head back inside the sleeping bag. *Fictionalized ... rearranged ... composites.* She made a vow that she would be very careful around Olivia's mum from now on.

SIX

Tomorrow's special was to be Shepherd's Pie with chips and peas. All for the heavily subsidised price of just £2.99. For another £1.50 you could also have Bakewell tart with custard. Standing in front of a large whiteboard in the basement canteen of Charing Cross police station, a tiny, grey-haired dinner lady wrote up the details in large capital letters in bright red marker pen. When she had finished, the woman admired her penmanship, carefully replaced the cap on the marker then disappeared back behind the serving counter, which had been cleared for the night. Feeling more than a little peckish, Commander Carole Simpson scanned the vending machine in the corner. A Bounty Bar stared enticingly back at her. Disappointed with the amount of effort it took to abstain, she turned to John Carlyle, watching with a certain amount of envy as the inspector happily munched on an apple.

'Where did all these people come from?' she whispered.

'Well,' he whispered back, 'if you ask for volunteers to raid a strip club, what did you expect?'

40

He gestured at the expectant crowd of officers. 'I could have sold tickets for this gig.'

'We didn't ask for volunteers,' Simpson said tetchily. She looked relaxed after a week's holiday on safari in South Africa but, back on the job, he could already see the stress building up, starting to seep out of the corners of her eyes and her mouth. A mere couple of days back in wet and cheerless London had already taken their toll.

Standing next to his boss, Carlyle looked almost spectral by comparison. As befitted a man who was unwilling to take any unnecessary risks with his health, he had not exposed himself to any serious sun for years, if not decades. 'You might as well have done,' he mumbled.

'Don't start, John, for God's sake!' she hissed.

You sound like my wife, Carlyle thought. Realizing that was not an idea he wanted to pursue any further, he killed it quickly and concentrated on his job. 'What am I supposed to do with this lot?' He had counted almost thirty uniforms standing around joking and laughing, waiting for the fun to start. At most, he reckoned he needed eight.

Ignoring the question, Simpson looked at her watch and muttered, 'I'm going to be late for dinner.'

Carlyle wondered what he was going to have for his own tea; probably just a couple of fried eggs on toast and – assuming that Alice hadn't already emptied the packet – a handful of Jaffa Cakes. He was not the kind of bloke who felt the need to extend himself in the kitchen. 'Going anywhere nice?' he asked.

'Maze.' Simpson mentioned the name of a famous chef, almost instantly regretting her shameless name-dropping.

'Nice,' Carlyle murmured. He had never heard of the place but he knew it would be expensive.

'It will be,' said Simpson through gritted teeth, 'if I ever get there.'

Carlyle grinned. 'How is the new boyfriend?'

Did he imagine it, or did she redden just a little? 'He's fine,' she said quietly. 'Thank you for asking.'

Carlyle thought about prolonging her embarrassment and decided, for once, that discretion was the better part of valour. Then his mouth overrode his brain, as it was wont to do, and the grin became a smirk. 'I saw you both in the paper last week, in *ES* magazine.'

'Ah yes.' Simpson stared at the floor. She was definitely blushing now.

'At the *Harper's Bazaar* Women of the Year Awards, if I remember correctly,' he went on, after a moment's contemplation, 'in association with Estée Lauder.'

Simpson gave him a crooked smile. 'My, Inspector,' she said coolly, 'what a good memory you have.'

'I find that it's very handy in my line of work.'

'Not that I was up for an award, of course,' she said hastily. 'I only went along because ... Dino got an invite.'

'Of course,' Carlyle nodded. For reasons that he couldn't now recall, he had cut the photo and associated caption out of the magazine and stuck it on to the door of the fridge at home. Simpson looking very glamorous in a knee-length navy dress, smiling at the camera on the arm of Dino

Mottram, an old-style entrepreneur, ten years or more her senior. Was he in line to become Mr Carole Simpson number two? Carlyle wondered idly. He was rather embarrassed to admit it – even to himself – but he rather hoped so.

If anyone deserved a bit of domestic bliss it was Carole Simpson. Simpson's first husband, Joshua Hunt, had died of cancer a few years earlier, following a spell in prison. Joshua, an insider-dealing City spiv, had managed to make his wife a widow and crater her career prospects at the same time. Before the wheels had come off her home life, Simpson had worked her way through the ranks of the Metropolitan with determination and, to the inspector's mind, a rather unpleasant efficiency. Carlyle knew that Simpson had harboured hopes of rising still further, perhaps as far as Assistant or even Deputy Commissioner. But having a crook for a husband ended all that. When Joshua was arrested and sent to trial, the press, of course, had a field day. Although not involved in any wrong-doing herself, Simpson came under considerable pressure to resign and walk away, in order to spare the Force any further embarrassment. When she refused, Simpson was effectively blackballed by those higher up and was told in no uncertain terms that there would be no more promotions. It was even suggested that, if she was to hang around, her pension might be under threat. Refusing to buckle, she simply got on with her job, showing a quiet dignity that Carlyle, never previously one of her greatest allies, had not seen before.

In the face of widespread hostility from her

fellow officers, Carlyle had been mightily impressed by the Commander's continued commitment to the job in the difficult years that followed. Always the type of man to trust his own judgement, Carlyle had ignored the gossip and the backstabbing. He had been amazed and delighted to find in the humbled Simpson a true friend and colleague. Indeed, she had saved his bacon on more than one occasion when other bosses would have happily hung him out to dry. As a result of their rapprochement, he would be the last person in the Met to begrudge his boss another shot at domestic happiness. He put a gentle hand on her shoulder. 'And how were the Laurent Perrier champagne and Russian Standard Vodka cocktails?'

'John,' she frowned, looking slightly worried now, 'are you stalking me?'

Now it was his turn to feel embarrassed. 'No, no,' he said innocently. 'It was Helen who pointed it out to me.' The lie was smooth and simple. 'She likes to keep up with how the other half live.'

Simpson moved away from him. 'I very much doubt that,' she said, in a voice not totally devoid of a sharp edge, 'and if you continue baiting me, I might just take it up with your wife directly.'

'Fair enough,' said Carlyle, somewhat contritely, knowing that, not for the first time, he had pushed the joke too far. It was time to get back to the matter in hand. 'Did you know,' he pointed out, 'that the number of lap-dancing clubs in Britain has grown more than tenfold in the last decade?'

Simpson gave him a look that said: *my, you are a repository of useless information.* 'Is that so?'

'Three hundred new lap-dancing clubs have opened; at the same time, more than a hundred and sixty police stations have closed.'

'Is there a correlation?'

'No idea,' Carlyle said. 'But that's the kind of country we've become: more strip clubs, betting shops and nightclubs; fewer cop shops, post offices and swimming pools.'

'Fascinating,' Simpson yawned.

'Interesting factual information,' Carlyle said, rather miffed.

'Look at it this way, John,' Simpson said. 'Would you rather raid a strip club or a swimming pool?'

Carlyle thought about it for a moment. 'I was never really into swimming.'

Simpson sighed, 'Shall we just get on with it?'

'Yes.'

'You've got to get rid of most of this lot.'

'Okay.'

Simpson looked around the room once again in the vain hope that some of the uniforms might have disappeared. 'Christ! There are even bloody PCSOs here,' she snorted, failing to keep her irritation in check.

Carlyle glanced at the trio of pimply boys in the corner under a poster that proclaimed the Met's slogan: *Working together for a safer London.* As slogans went, it was not hugely inspiring; the inspector thought it was long overdue a change. His preference would be for something a bit more thought-provoking, along the lines of: *London – it's bloody safe, so stop moaning and enjoy it.* It was not an idea he had shared with the PR department.

One of the pimply boys in the corner said

something and the other two began sniggering. Carlyle tutted. 'Where do we bloody get them from?'

'You tell me,' Simpson grumbled.

Police Community Support Officers, known as 'plastic policemen', were volunteers who were universally disliked by 'proper' officers. Always given the lowest and the grubbiest jobs, they had about as much chance of being allowed to take part in a stripper hunt as Carlyle had of making Chief Inspector.

After a short pause, Carlyle banged the empty mug on a nearby table. 'Okay, you lot!' he shouted, taking a couple of steps forward. 'Listen up. I don't need all of you tonight.'

A groan went up from the back.

Carlyle stared at the ceiling. 'So,' he said airily, 'thank you all for coming. Your ... enthusiasm is gratefully acknowledged,' he allowed himself a cheesy grin, 'and I hope that it can be sustained into some of this evening's other duties.' Out of the corner of his eye, he saw the PCSOs slip out of the door, knowing that they would be the first to be dismissed. Turning his attention to a burly, middle-aged man at the front of the group, Carlyle took another step forward, lowering his voice to a normal level. 'Sergeant Bishop, choose half-a-dozen officers for this job and let the others go back upstairs.' He nodded at Simpson. 'Then the Commander will give us a briefing.'

Bishop shot him a look that said *thanks a lot* but restricted himself to a curt, 'Yes, sir!' before turning to sort the wheat from the chaff.

SEVEN

While they were waiting for Bishop to pick his team, Carlyle moved back to stand by Simpson's shoulder. 'By the way,' he asked, 'when am I getting *my* new sergeant?'

Simpson smiled. 'It should be next week.'

'Are you going to tell me who it is?'

Simpson's smile widened. 'In due course, Inspector.'

Don't yank my chain, Carlyle thought. 'Why not now?'

'No.'

Carlyle gave a disgusted shake of the head. 'C'mon!'

'No. It can be a surprise.'

'I don't do bloody surprises...' he sulked.

'That is the thing about you, John,' Simpson said, adopting a tone of mock seriousness. 'You have absolutely no patience.'

So what? he thought. *Where's the virtue in being patient?* 'That's not true,' he lied.

'John,' she sighed, 'I don't know anyone in the whole of the Met – in the whole of bloody London – with less patience than you.'

'Fair enough.' Carlyle was not prepared to argue the point any further. He would find out who his new sidekick was soon enough.

'Rest assured, you are getting someone good,' said Simpson, leaning back on a table. 'So try not

47

to lose this one.'

'I haven't "lost" anyone yet,' Carlyle protested.

Simpson gave him a curious sideways glance. 'This will be your third sergeant in almost as many years.'

'That's hardly my fault, is it?'

Simpson raised her eyes to the heavens but said nothing.

'Alison Roche left because she wanted to go to SO15,' Carlyle said defensively. 'And before that, Joe Szyszkowski was, as you well know, murdered.'

Realizing that she had hit a raw nerve, Simpson moved the conversation on. 'How is Roche getting on?'

'After the gunfight at the OK Corral, you mean? I think she's all right. She'll be the first to admit that she didn't exactly cover herself in glory, but she's gone back to work.'

'Good for her,' said Simpson with some feeling.

'Didn't throw a sickie,' Carlyle added. Both of them knew that it would have been all too easy for Roche to claim that she was suffering from some form of stress-related illness and avoid returning to duty. If, as legend had it, American cops ate their guns, their British counterparts liked to hide under the duvet. Each day, up and down the country, thousands of police officers were either off or on severely reduced duties as a result of stress. Doubtless, many of them had a case but Carlyle, like Simpson, strongly suspected that many did not. Either way, the result was an annual bill to the taxpayer of something like a quarter of a billion pounds.

'Maybe there is something useful in the Chief

Medical Officer's anti-stress DVDs after all,' Simpson quipped.

'Maybe,' said Carlyle doubtfully.

'And she's seeing the shrink?'

'Yeah,' Carlyle nodded. 'It's hardly optional. She's still got IIC crawling all over her and she'll have to take her lumps at the disciplinary hearing. Under the circumstances, you have to show willing in the psychobabble department. She's seeing my friend Dr Wolf, so that will be a big help.'

'And you?' Simpson asked. 'Are you still...'

'I am continuing with my regular sessions,' Carlyle said, keen to avoid his boss's probing. His sessions with Wolf were now down to one a quarter. Carlyle had bracketed them in the same category as his trips to see the dental hygienist. Routine care and maintenance: just another box to tick in order to keep other people happy and in work. 'I'm sure that Roche will be fine. She is very robust.'

Taking the hint, Simpson changed the subject. 'Any leads yet on the guys who were responsible for the attack at St Pancras?'

Carlyle let out a long sigh. 'Nope.'

Simpson grimaced. 'And the guy who was being transported back to La Santé?'

'Alain Costello?' Carlyle shook his head. 'Nah. He's still in the wind.'

'Do you think he's back in France?'

'You would assume so.' Over her shoulder, Carlyle saw Bishop signal that he had picked his team. Six constables and two WPCs, none of whom Carlyle knew particularly well, stood to attention while their disappointed colleagues

49

slunk off.

'Fine,' said Simpson, stepping forward and addressing her audience. 'Right! Thank you, everyone. Tonight we are going to be paying a visit to Everton's Gentleman's Club on Parker Street.' The young men before her were grinning like Cheshire cats while the women restricted themselves to the occasional grim-faced nod. Simpson took a sheet of paper from her jacket pocket and unfolded it. Then she pulled a glasses case from her bag. Opening it, she took out a pair of Prada black metal full-rimmed spectacles and slipped them on.

Carlyle, who had never seen her wear specs before, tried not to stare. *Christ*, he groaned silently, *we're all going blind.*

Clearing her throat, Simpson paused to ensure that she had everyone's full attention. 'This is part of a London-wide clamp-down on strip clubs and lap-dancing venues that has been organized under the auspices of the Home Office. Across the capital, more than a dozen locations are being targeted tonight, including three of Westminster's twenty-seven establishments and two of the nine in Camden. It is important to remember that Everton's is a legally licensed club. We are not trying to close it down. What we *are* looking for are people who are employed illegally. Everyone working there needs to provide a name, address, and a valid I.D. Anyone without any valid documentation will be brought back here.' Looking up from the sheet of paper, she paused to scan the eager faces. 'Is that understood?'

Carlyle idly wondered what would go wrong

tonight. Something invariably did on these sort of outings.

'I realize,' Simpson continued, 'that this is a rather exotic assignment.' She smiled as a couple of the officers laughed. 'No pun intended. But everyone has to be polite and professional.' The laughter died down and, finally, even the male constables tried to look serious. 'Also, remember, no walkie talkies tonight. Has everyone got their mobiles?'

Another chorus of moans went round the room and Carlyle recalled the memo that had come round the previous week, decreeing that officers should send texts on their own phones, rather than speak on their official police radios, in order to save money. It appeared that the Met was spending millions using a privately run emergency services communications network, with penalty costs of two pounds a *second* whenever it went over its agreed limit. On the other hand, you could send a thousand texts for just four pence. No wonder the bean counters wanted the change. It was amateurish but it made financial sense.

As the noise died down, one wag waved a battered-looking Nokia handset at the Commander. 'Can I claim the cost of the texts back on expenses?'

'Talk to HR,' Simpson told him.

'Good luck,' Carlyle growled.

'Finally,' Simpson said, moving briskly on, 'be advised that there will be a video crew accompanying you to film the raid.'

'What?' Standing behind the Commander, Carlyle bit his lip. 'That doesn't sound good.'

Simpson, not wanting to get caught up in another pointless argument with her subordinate, stole a glance at her watch. 'They are producing a video for the Mayor's website about his campaign to clean up London.'

You could have told me, Carlyle thought. 'The Mayor's website?' he echoed. There was no love lost between Carlyle and the Mayor, Christian Holyrod. Their paths had crossed several times before and the result was usually unhappiness for all concerned. Now, according to what he read in the papers, Holyrod was planning to cash in his chips and trade 'public service' for some lucrative private directorships. Carlyle hoped that meant the bastard would never be heard of again, at least by him. 'Why does *he* care?' he moaned. 'It's not like he's running for re-election, thank God. He'll be out of the job later this year.'

Simpson gave him an *as if I could give a monkey's* shrug.

'We're policemen, for fuck's sake,' he continued, warming to his theme, 'not some bloody multi-media ... content provider.' Was that how these type of people described themselves? He wasn't sure but it would be close enough.

'Look at it this way,' Simpson said sweetly. 'As long as you're polite, don't assault anyone or ogle the strippers too much, what have you got to worry about?'

Carlyle looked at the other male officers in the group. The enthusiasm was draining from their faces. They were all thinking the same thing: *why would we have volunteered for this if it wasn't for the perks?*

Simpson also knew what was floating through their brains. 'Remember – keep it all above board tonight,' she ordered as she began making her way towards the door. 'Do not forget that this is the twenty-first century. That means twenty-first-century policing, twenty-first-century rules and, above all, twenty-first-century scrutiny. I want you all to bloody well behave out there.'

'Okay.' Carlyle clapped his hands together. 'Let's go. You heard what the Commander said. Be polite. No swearing. And,' he snapped, 'remember to fucking *smile*.' Feeling put upon, he watched Simpson disappear down the corridor. 'I hope you have a nice meal,' he mumbled, unhappily, to himself.

Dinner had been worth waiting for. The roasted Muntjac deer, crushed celeriac, chestnuts, red cabbage and spiced chocolate jus had been delightful and she had also allowed herself the indulgence of the Kentish strawberry and elderflower cheesecake, with black pepper crème fraîche.

'Enjoyable?' The crafty glint in Dino Mottram's eyes suggested that they could well be breaking out the Viagra Professional tonight.

Carole Simpson squirmed involuntarily in her seat. After a drought of more than two years, sex with Dino was still fun but, for an old guy, he still seemed to have a lot to prove. Tonight she would insist on going on top – since the alternative was to be pounded remorselessly into the mattress by a man possessed. That or she'd plonk him on the sofa with one of his favourite porn DVDs while she relaxed in a long, hot bath.

She took a mouthful of the Crianza 2004 and sighed happily. 'Delicious.'

Dino looked around for a waiter. 'We should get going, I've got a busy day tomorrow.'

'Me too,' Simpson told him. Maybe the red pills could stay in the bottle tonight.

Dino poured the last of the wine into his glass as the maitre d' appeared with the bill. 'I had lunch with the Mayor today.'

Simpson tensed up at the mention of the M-word. Holyrod and his cronies had presided over the steady politicization of the Metropolitan Police in recent years – something that she objected to both in principle and in practice. Although she had started out as an active supporter, she now considered the Mayor a vain and ineffective man who had no use for public office other than as a vehicle for his endless self-promotion. 'Holyrod?'

Dino gave her an *of course* look. 'Interesting man.'

'Yes, he is,' Simpson nodded. 'I've come across him a few times.'

Dino raised an eyebrow as he took a sip of his wine. 'Oh?'

'He's the Mayor,' Simpson shrugged. 'He gets involved in policing.'

'Well,' said Dino, 'he's getting involved in my world too. He's joining the Board of Entomophagous Industries as a non-executive director.'

'Snouts in the trough time.'

Displeased by her response, Dino made an effort to mishear what she had said. 'I'm sorry?'

'He needs to make some money.'

Dino smiled blandly. 'Don't we all?'

You certainly don't, Simpson thought. Her mind alighted on a quote she'd read recently from some contemporary thinker: *in poor countries, officials receive explicit bribes; in the west, they get the sophisticated, implicit, unspoken promise to work for large corporations.*

'He's certainly not coming cheap,' Dino mused.

Simpson drained her glass. 'I hope you get your money's worth,' she said tartly.

Dino, bristling at Simpson's chill tone, gave her an angry stare 'You think that it's a mistake?'

'Dino...' Reaching across the table, she patted him gently on the arm; for a captain of industry, he could be incredibly thin-skinned at times. 'You know that's not something I would have a view on.'

He took her hand in his, lacing his fingers through hers. 'But I'm asking your opinion.'

'Unlike you,' she said sweetly, pushing her chair away from the table, 'I don't feel the need to have an opinion on absolutely everything.'

'Yes,' he replied, 'but you do have one on our Mayor, don't you?'

Simpson thought about it for a moment. 'Holyrod was a soldier,' she said finally. 'By common acclaim, a good one. Just because you're good at one thing doesn't mean you'll be good at others.'

Dino nodded his agreement. 'Most people aren't good at anything.'

'Quite. Christian Holyrod always struck me as a bit of a fish out of water as a politician. God knows what he'll be like as a businessman.'

'Don't worry,' Dino said coolly, 'the bar's not

set very high. I'll sort him out.' He gave her a searching look. 'As you know, I always get my money's worth.'

EIGHT

Corporal Adrian Gasparino tapped the toe of his boot against the low mud wall in time to the tune of Bleeding Through's 'Love Lost in a Hail of Gunfire', which was pounding through the headphones of his iPod Nano. Reaching up into the shade, he plucked a fat white grape from the vine above his head, popped it into his mouth and crushed it between his teeth. Sharp and juicy, it tasted good, so he snapped off a couple more, crushing them mechanically between his teeth.

'Hey! Leave those alone.' Sergeant Spencer Spanner appeared at his shoulder, poking him gently on the arm with the barrel of his SA80 assault rifle. 'Those aren't any old grapes; they're *terrorist* grapes.'

'They're good,' grinned Gasparino, taking another.

Taking a handful for himself, Spanner stuck them in his mouth and chewed. 'Mm. Not as good as Tesco's.'

'Cheaper though.'

'Whatever,' Spanner shrugged, tiring of the chat. With his SA80, he pointed at the buildings behind the wall, on the far side of the compound. 'Let's go!' he shouted at the line of soldiers strung out behind them. 'Another day at the office beckons. Watch where you put your fucking feet.'

'Okay.' Gasparino smiled as Metallica's 'Nothing Else Matters' took over the task of numbing his brain. He scanned the dense orchard littered with mines and other ordnance which concealed the irrigation canals used by the Taliban to move freely under the noses of the coalition troops.

'A chess game,' was how their Commander had described it in an interview with CNN a few months earlier, 'played with bullets and IEDs.'

A chess game? Like fuck. Gasparino glanced at the ground a metre in front of him in a half-hearted attempt to identify anything suspicious. Not only was it a waste of time, it only made him feel worse about his situation. Your best hope was that, if you did get blown up, the IED was sufficiently powerful to blast you to smithereens, so that small parts of your body were scattered to the four winds before you even had a chance to realize what had happened. Far better that than losing your legs and bleeding in agony while watching the confused, helpless expressions on the faces of your mates.

'Your *best* hope.' A familiar feeling of the pointlessness of what they were doing engulfed Gasparino. Every day was the same. It was truly remarkable how nothing ever changed. They had about as much chance of pacifying the country as he had of becoming Prime Minister. An estimated 25,000 Taliban fighters kept 140,000 coalition troops, plus the ANA and Afghan police, at bay. The bogus body counts – the US Army claimed to have killed 952 Taliban and captured 2,469 in the last three months – fooled no one. 'On average,' said one commander, 'we're killing three to five mid-level enemy leaders.' *Well,* thought Gasparino, enraged by the corruption and fecklessness of the Afghan government, *there are plenty more where they came from.*

Not quite twenty-six years old, Gasparino was already on his fifth tour of duty. After three trips to Iraq, this, his second in Afghanistan, would be his last. For him, the war ended here, in the area known as the Devil's Playground. He had promised Justine, his heavily pregnant wife, that he would leave the Army and get a civilian job.

Time was quickly running out on Gasparino's Army career. In little over a week, the Duke of Lancaster's Regiment were due to turn over their stretch of the Arghandab River Valley, sixty miles from the Pakistan border, to their American replacements from 2-508th Parachute Infantry. The Brits and the Americans were currently patrolling together as part of the handover process. In the pre-dawn twilight, twenty-eight soldiers had left their combat outpost a mile away, heading for the Taliban-controlled vineyards and pomegranate orchards. In the abandoned compound they would wait to engage the enemy as they did almost every day with monotonous regularity.

As he watched his comrades take up their positions around the compound, he idly wondered what he would do in civvy street. Nothing ever came to mind. With a single GSCE in woodwork to his name, Gasparino was not exactly well equipped to deal with the so-called 'real world'. He had never had a hankering to do anything in particular; that's why he had joined the bloody Army in the first place. The situation vexed him but there was no point in worrying now; it was something he would just have to deal with next month, when he would be back in England for good.

Alain Costello scratched his belly. 'I need some new games,' he told his father down the phone.

Je m'en fous, Tuco Martinez thought angrily. Not for the first time in recent days, he wondered what had happened to Alain's mother, a night-club singer from Toulouse who had run off with her 'business manager' (read pimp) less than a year after their child had been born.

She had really put one over him. He felt an overwhelming desire to give the bitch a slap for lying to him about her birth control.

And for giving him the clap.

And for stealing 240,000 francs from him – at a time when that sum was still worth something. If it wasn't for the fact that he was sure she was long since dead, he would have hunted her down and killed her.

On the other hand, she was the only woman who had managed to give him a son. It drove him insane. Disappointment or not, Alain was his only hope for handing the business down to the next generation.

'I'm bored,' Alain complained. 'I need to get something good, like *God of War: Ghost of Sparta.'*

Tuco shook his head. *What did people do before computer games?* Wandering around all day like zombies; these things were worse than drugs. He sincerely hoped that the boy was just winding him up. The alternative – that he was just stupid – was something that he refused to contemplate. 'Enough with the games!' he barked.

'It's totally boring here,' the boy whined. 'I want to come home.'

Tuco sighed. Looking out through the open windows, past the terrace towards the cool blue of the Mediterranean, he tried to work out where the sea ended and the sky began. It was a view he could stare at for hours on end without getting bored; one of the few things in life that made him feel calm. *'Tu dois rester là-bas pour le moment,'* he told his son.

'Fuck. *C'est trop banal ici. Je crève d'ennui et il pleut sans cesse.'*

Tuco allowed himself a little laugh. He knew what the kid meant. He didn't like going to London himself. It was a total shithole. But it was a shithole full of customers. He was in business, so you had to respect that. The market was always right: you had to follow the money. *Aucune question.*

Traditionally, outside of France, Tuco had always lacked what business analysts called 'critical mass'. London was waiting for him like a big, fat whore, her legs wide open. The problem was, his dick was just too small to give her a proper seeing-to. He needed more sales, growing revenues if he was to become a player and take the business to the next level. That meant finding a serious local business partner, someone with a successful track record and a good reputation. After a couple of expensive false starts, Tuco was optimistic that he had finally found that man.

He suddenly caught sight of one of the hookers he'd brought down from Paris for the weekend strolling towards the pool. Black as ebony, she wore a fetching canary-yellow bra but was naked from the waist down. 'Look,' he said to Alain, his voice thickening. 'You have to stay where you are for a while. I need some time to sort this out.'

'But–'

'No buts,' Tuco snapped. 'Just keep out of sight. I will speak to my – our – business partner in London. He will make sure you are well looked after. I'll even ask him to get you some more games.' Before the boy could complain any further, Tuco ended the call. Tossing the handset onto a nearby sofa, he headed for the pool.

The temperature was well on the way to a humid 100 degrees. Sitting in the dust, with his back resting against the outside wall of an empty hut, Adrian Gasparino took a mouthful of water from his bottle and thought about Justine back home in Worthing. Hopefully she would be getting a good night's sleep around now. He hadn't spoken to her for a few days. She was due to have a scan of the baby this week but he couldn't remember which day. Gasparino wanted a boy. Justine hadn't been convinced that they were ready to start a family, but couldn't go through with an abortion and he had talked her round. They could have a boy now and then a girl later, once he had sorted himself out with a decent job. Maybe a third one a little later down the line.

Perfect.

From behind his Oakley M Frames, he watched as one of the Americans, a sergeant called Anthony Withers, strolled over, placed his M-16 carefully against the wall and dropped heavily onto the ground beside him.

Gasparino offered up a palm and they exchanged a high-five. Withers was one of the few Americans who had shown any interest in fraternizing with the Brits. He had taught Gasparino and a few of the other guys how to play poker – taking them for a tidy sum in the process – and generally had shown an interest in learning from their experiences in the Arghandab, unlike most of his comrades who, it seemed, just wanted to work out, smoke dope and listen to thrash metal. They seemed more hostile to the Brits than the Talibs.

With his regulation buzz cut and beefy features, Withers was a squat guy from Hartford, Connecticut. Gasparino had tried to imagine where that was on a map. Somewhere near New York? He had no idea. Withers had told him that Hartford had once been the 'insurance capital of the world' but now it was number three on the list of America's Top Ten 'dead cities' – former business hubs which had been left behind by the global economy in recent decades.

'A good place to get out of,' Gasparino had mused, for want of anything else to say.

'Absolutely,' Withers grinned. 'That's why I'm here.'

'It's just the same in England.'

'Yeah?'

'Lots of places like that. Lots of dead towns and cities. Probably just about everywhere's dead, apart from London.'

'Ever been?'

'To London?' Gasparino shook his head. 'Nah. Too big. Too many people. Too noisy. Too dirty. Too expensive. Not for me.'

They sat together in companionable silence for a while, listening to the sound of sporadic small-arms fire in the middle-distance. After a while, Withers took a bottle of water from his pack, drank half of it and poured the rest over his head. 'How's it going with you Brits?'

Gasparino shrugged. 'It's going.'

Withers smacked him on the shoulder. 'Chin up, my man. It's another day closer to going home.'

Gasparino smiled. 'Yes, indeed.'

'Thing is,' Withers stared into the middle distance, 'as soon as you get home, you wanna get back.'

'Tell me about it.' The realization that he would miss all this – seriously miss it – was like a nervous ache in his stomach. Gasparino hoped that the baby would make that feeling go away, or at least give him something else to think about and make it more manageable.

Withers rubbed the heel of his left boot into the dirt. 'I mean, this shit can be boring, but when it's exciting, it's really fucking exciting.' He turned to Gasparino. 'Know what I mean?'

'I do.'

'It's a great fucking buzz.'

'Yeah,' Gasparino said almost wistfully.

Withers took a packet of Camel cigarettes from his jacket pocket, offering one to Gasparino, who refused.

Withers pulled a cigarette from the pack with his teeth, lit it and took a deep drag. 'So,' he said, exhaling the smoke through his nose, 'will you be coming back?'

'Me? Nope.' Gasparino shook his head. 'This really is my last time.'

'Yeah?'

'Yeah.'

'You're not coming back?'

'That is correct. I'm not coming back.'

Grinning, Withers sucked down another mouthful of smoke. 'Wanna have a little bet on that?'

NINE

Men, couples, singles, groups – all welcome!

Carlyle read the sign and yawned. It was late and he was of the firm belief that he should have been in bed hours ago. Everton's Gentleman's Club was maybe a two-minute walk from his flat and he felt a strong temptation to keep on walking. Inside, the inevitable commotion had kicked up as the police went in and started asking people to prove their identities. Almost immediately, a couple of customers slipped out, middle-aged businessmen, eyes glued to the pavement, the looks on their faces suggesting a mixture of frustration and embarrassment. After watching them slink round the corner and disappear into the hustle and bustle of Kingsway, the inspector turned his gaze to the girl standing in the doorway. She was wearing a lime-green Puffa jacket over a white blouse, with the shortest skirt he had ever seen showing off her black suspenders to good effect, as well as the goosebumps on her thighs. In her Ferrari-red stilettos, she still only came up to his chin.

'ID?' he asked.

Shivering against the cold, she shook her head.

'No papers?'

'No understand,' she lied lazily, making no effort to try and be convincing, in an accent that suggested she came from somewhere east of the Danube. Belatedly, he thought that maybe they should have brought a translator.

'Where are you from?' he said slowly, sounding like an English tourist abroad.

Wiping her nose on the sleeve of her jacket, she took a tentative step towards him, glancing quickly inside. 'Caledonian Road.'

For fuck's sake, Carlyle thought, *why do I bother?* He took a pile of flyers from her hand. 'You go inside,' he said slowly, gesturing with his thumb, 'and get something that proves who you are. Passport, driver's licence, something like that...'

Still shivering, she stood her ground.

'Show it to one of the officers,' Carlyle continued. *And put some proper clothes on,* he thought. 'Now!'

Reluctantly, the girl finally went into the club. Even more reluctantly, Carlyle followed her. Inside, the place was almost empty. A couple of punters sat at their tables, drinking in silent amusement as the police went about their business. The sound system had been turned down to a respectable level and the house lights had been turned up, allowing him to appreciate the full splendour of Everton's somewhat gothic decor.

Carlyle looked at the Harlequin Contour pattern wallpaper in brown and salmon pink and tutted. 'Surely this kind of stuff went out of fashion in the 1970s,' he quipped, gesturing at the wallpaper, to a small, pretty WPC standing by the bar.

'I wouldn't know, sir,' the girl deadpanned. 'I wasn't born then.'

Ignoring the mischievous twinkle in the WPC's eye, the inspector turned his attention to the matter in hand. It appeared that Sergeant Bishop had divided the staff into 'talent' and the rest. Along one wall, a group of gentlemen – oversized bouncers and undersized barmen – had been lined up while Bishop and a couple of the other WPCs went through their documents. On the other side of the room, a larger group of officers were slowly processing the strippers, none of whom were wearing more than a G-string and heels.

Trying not to make his gawping too obvious, Carlyle scanned the latter line, making random notes in his head as he did so. There were two black girls, two white and one Asian. All had effortlessly adopted the kind of generic bored-hostile look that Carlyle saw day in, day out from just about every member of the public that came into contact with the police.

When the Asian girl, who had the best, most natural-looking figure, caught Carlyle staring at her chest, he quickly looked away, feeling himself blush as he did so. His gaze turned to the far end of the room, where the small stage, lifted barely six inches off the ground, was empty.

'Get on with it!' shouted one of the punters, a stocky young guy in a suit, as he slammed an empty beer schooner down on the table.

Bishop stepped towards the guy's table. 'Shut it,' he warned, 'or you'll be under arrest.'

A look of indignation flashed across the young man's face. 'For what?' he said belligerently.

'Oh, I'll think of something,' Bishop growled.

Carlyle smiled. He liked the sergeant's style. Bishop was a relatively new arrival from some station out east; the Isle of Dogs' loss would be Charing Cross's gain. He wondered about asking Simpson to assign Bishop to work with him on a more regular basis. That decision, however, had already been made.

Not knowing when to stay schtum, the man was about to talk himself into a cell when there was an almighty commotion from the back of the stage. One of the officers, a young PC called Lea, came sprawling through a doorway, holding his nose as blood poured from it. 'I've been hit!' he groaned, stumbling over the edge of the stage and falling flat on his face. The laughter that rolled round the room was quickly followed by gasps of amazement as a raven-haired Amazon followed the hapless Lea through the door. Easily six foot tall, she was completely naked apart from a pair of incredibly high stilettoes.

Those look very classy, thought Carlyle, impressed. *And she's gone to town with the Philips Ladyshave*. A true professional.

In her hand, the woman had some kind of cosh. With an angry flourish, she brandished it at Lea. 'C'mon, you bastard!' she screamed, in what

67

seemed to Carlyle to be some kind of American accent. 'Come and get another thrashing.' Whimpering, Lea sought refuge under a nearby table.

Finally tearing his eyes away, Carlyle looked at his troops. Those that weren't mesmerized were drooling. 'Okay,' he sighed, gesturing to Bishop, 'that's enough. Take them all in. We'll sort this out at the station.' Swivelling on his heel, he walked straight into a man in a baseball cap with a large video camera on his shoulder. 'Who the fucking hell are you?' he barked.

The guy readjusted his cap and kept filming. 'Danny Craven, Scattered Flowers Productions.'

'What?'

Keeping his eye glued to the viewfinder, Craven pulled a crumpled business card from the back pocket of his jeans and thrust it towards Carlyle. 'Content providers for the Mayor's website.'

Reluctantly taking the card, the inspector weighed it in his hand as if it was a piece of desiccated dog shit. Several thoughts passed through his mind, none of them pleasant. 'Fuck that,' he said, striding towards the door. 'Sergeant Bishop! You can arrest this stupid fucker as well.'

'Sure thing,' said Bishop with a smile.

Sticking to his task, Craven went in for a close-up on the belligerent stripper.

'Good man!' Carlyle shoved Craven's card into his jacket pocket. Over his shoulder, he gave the troops a regal wave. 'I'll see you back at Agar Street.' *After,* he said to himself, *I've had a decent kip.*

Another day, another dollar. Wiping the sweat

from his brow, Adrian Gasparino watched as a small contingent of Afghan National Army soldiers entered the compound, looking like a bunch of schoolkids on a day out. As far as he knew, they hadn't been expecting any ANA, but that didn't mean much – they had a habit of just showing up.

Given that the ANA were usually quite good at arriving in places where there wasn't going to be any fighting, he was happy enough to see them. Maybe this would be a quiet day at the office for all of them. He counted a dozen of them as they stood aimlessly in a group about twenty feet from where he was sitting. None of them looked older than about fourteen; they were small, stick-thin, their uniforms several sizes too big, with hollow cheeks and dead eyes. Gasparino sighed. The idea that the coalition forces could train these boys to take the place of professional soldiers was just another of the fantasies you had to believe in if you were to try and convince yourself that this was a war worth fighting and that the billions of dollars' of weapons, equipment and aid thrown at the locals had been money well spent.

The British Prime Minister, a feckless ex-public schoolboy by the name of Edgar Carlton, had recently said that the 10,000 British troops in Afghanistan could start withdrawing from as early as next year. British commanders were under ever-greater pressure to talk up the ANA and its ability to take over responsibility for security in the country. The 146,000 trained 'Afghan warriors' had to be praised at all times. Gasparino had been particularly amused by the comments of the Commanding Officer of Task Force Helmand

Brigade Advisory Group at one press conference: 'They are brave in the fight. They are willing to tackle the insurgents head on and they are astute and shrewd in their judgement when they are dealing with the local population.'

If the embedded hacks had taken the comments at face value, the soldiers had been somewhat more sceptical. 'Bollocks,' had been the sergeant's mumbled response. 'I wouldn't want those bastards watching my back.'

Most of the ANA soldiers carried M-16 assault rifles, although Gasparino noticed a couple carried AK-74s, weapons left over from the days when the Soviets had been fighting here. One of them had a 7.62mm, M240 machine gun slung over his shoulder. All of them looked jumpy, although that was the usual state for members of the ANA. Gasparino noticed that a couple of them were holding hands, 'man love' being Standard Operating Procedure in the ANA. He shook his head, mumbling the local Afghan saying to himself: *Women are for children, boys are for pleasure.* It was accepted that many Pashtun men were *bacha baz* – 'boy players'. Like his colleagues, Gasparino had been shocked by the tradition of Afghan men taking boys, some as young as eight or nine, as lovers. In Kandahar, on an earlier tour, he had been to a dance party where boys of around nine dressed up as girls, with make-up and bells on their feet, performing for leering middle-aged men who threw money at them before whisking them off for sex. One of the unit's translators, Rahmatullah, had explained to him that it was down to Islamic law. Women – covered from head to foot –

are invisible and unapproachable. It is commonly accepted that Afghan men cannot talk to an unrelated woman until *after* they have proposed marriage. 'How can you fall in love if you can't see her face?' Rahmatullah asked. 'We can see the boys, so we can tell which ones are beautiful.'

'But,' Gasparino frowned, 'doesn't Islamic law also forbid homosexuality?'

'We don't love them,' Rahmatullah shrugged, 'we just have sex with them.'

'Bloody hell!' Gasparino laughed nervously. 'You make it sound like the Catholic Church.'

Rahmatullah gave him a confused look.

'Never mind.'

'Are you after a boy yourself?'

'Er, no thanks.' Gasparino felt himself blush violently as he beat a hasty retreat back to the camp.

It was a conversation that Gasparino had played over in his head many times. However you looked at it, the set-up was basically institutionalized child abuse. He was all for religious tolerance, but couldn't get past the fact that many aspects of the treatment of children and women here were just plain wrong. He thought about what his own family life would be like – a world away from this – and felt more confused than ever about what he was supposed to be doing here. The whole situation made him hugely uneasy – but he had no idea what he could do about it.

He watched as one of the sergeants, Spencer Spanner, wandered over to the ANA's commanding officer, a lieutenant who was still too young to be able to grow a proper beard, shook hands and started talking. There was the usual gesturing and waving, head-scratching and grinning as Spanner explained about the day's operation and tried to get to the bottom of just what exactly it was that the ANA were up to. Gasparino felt a wave of nostalgia wash over him. Spanner was a great bloke; he would miss him, back in England. Closing his eyes, his mind wandered to the shower he would have back at camp. After that he would try and call Justine, leaving it as late as possible, in case today was the date of her scan.

TEN

The receptionist had disappeared without a trace. Sitting in the empty waiting room, with nothing on the off-white walls, Roche looked around for something to read. But there were no pamphlets, no magazines to browse, not so much as a copy of yesterday's *Standard* or today's *Metro*. The idea was that you just sat there and contemplated your fate.

What was Dr Wolf's first name? She had no idea and, somewhat disappointingly for a police officer, no real curiosity either. Wolf was not someone she saw as 'helping' her situation; rather he was just another part of the bureaucratic maze that she had to negotiate, in order to continue with her professional life.

The question of the guy's name fluttered across her brain as she was trying to focus on other, more important things. Or maybe less important things. Different things. Alison Roche had seen the psychiatrist, once before and once after her arrival in SO15. Those had been routine meetings. This, most definitely, was not.

Roche fretted about not calling Carlyle ahead of her visit. She knew that the inspector had been sent to see this guy too. A couple of years ago, Commander Simpson had insisted on Carlyle getting some 'help' when his run-in with SO15 and Mossad had spiralled out of control. Roche had even busted him out of a session one time; inventing an 'emergency' that allowed the pair of them to escape to a nearby café.

Even now, the thought of the inspector being made to sit through an hour of Dr Wolf's painful extended silences made her laugh. Carlyle was easily the most shrink-proof person she had ever met: he just didn't do introspection – that was something they had in common.

All the same, maybe he could've given her some tips on how to handle the session; how to take control, keep Wolf at arms' length. *Fail to prepare,* the saying went, *and prepare to fail.* Maybe, after the massacre at St Pancras, she wanted to fail.

After a while, the door to Wolf's office opened. The shrink popped out his head and beckoned her inside. The room itself was small and cosy. Littered with family photos and books, it had a lived-in look that Wolf had doubtless striven hard to create. There being no couch, Roche took a seat in one of the two armchairs in front of the battered wooden desk. From the bay window behind the desk came the remaining dregs of the afternoon gloom, along with the reassuring hum of rush-hour traffic. Illumination came from a freestanding floor lamp in the corner, its light falling across a framed poster for *The Wild Bunch*.

Roche cleared her throat. *Better get on with it,* she thought. 'Good evening, Doctor.'

'Good evening to you, Sergeant Roche,' Wolf replied, somewhat uncertainly, as he slipped into the chair behind the desk. Opening a hardback A4 notebook, he flicked through the pages until he came to the notes he was looking for. Running an index finger down the page, he scanned them carefully.

Waiting patiently, Roche looked Wolf up and down. In a grey, open-neck shirt, he was a short, wizened man of indeterminate age, with watery blue eyes and long grey hair, tied back into a rather unfortunate ponytail. Sometimes he wore a wedding band. Today it was absent. Otherwise, she noticed no differences from her last visit.

After what seemed like several minutes, Wolf closed his notebook and looked up. 'So,' he smiled, then said in an accent that Roche had never been able to place, 'how are we today?'

'I am okay,' said Roche, careful to sit up straight in her seat.

'I see that you have gone back to work,' Wolf said evenly.

'Like I said,' Roche replied, 'I feel fine. I saw no reason to stay away. I think it is good to get back to being busy.'

Wolf leaned across the desk. 'But you are not able to carry a gun.'

'No,' Roche said calmly. 'Given what happened, there will need to be an investigation before I can do that.'

The shrink raised his eyebrows. 'How does that make you feel?'

Ha! thought Roche. *I saw that one coming.* A tight smile spread across her lips. 'It makes me feel that I am going through a proper and professional process that will help me return to my full range of duties in due course.'

Sighing, Wolf sat back in his chair and folded his arms. 'Tell me about what happened when you lost the prisoner.'

Christian Holyrod took a sniff of his half-full tumbler of Auchentoshan Three Wood and let out a purr of pleasure. Allowing the blackcurrant, orange, plum and raisin aroma to fill his nostrils, he took a healthy mouthful of the Lowland single malt. The oaky sweetness covered his tongue and he swallowed slowly. Sitting forward in his chair, the Mayor pulled up the video file that had just arrived in the inbox of his private email account and hit Play. As the interior of Everton's Gentleman's Club filled the 17-inch screen he took another mouthful of whisky and carefully placed the glass on his desk next to the laptop. Slipping on his telephone headset, he quickly dialled the number of Abigail Slater with one hand while fumbling with his fly with the other.

She picked up immediately, even before he had time to find his member. 'I'm in a meeting,' she whispered.

Distracted by the black woman straddling the pole on the screen in front of him, he could only manage a grunt.

'Christian?'

Finally releasing his tool, Holyrod began massaging himself. 'I was just...' A blonde girl had arrived on the stage and proceeded to stick her face between her colleague's buttocks. Squeezing the tip of his penis between the thumb and forefinger of his right hand, the Mayor began to pant. He hadn't realized just how horny he was; this was going to be a sixty-second job, at most.

'Christian?' his mistress said crossly, her voice rising as she became more angry. 'Are you all right?'

Just when he thought he was going to reach *la petite mort,* the fake lesbians disappeared and the screen went blank. 'Shit!'

'Christian!'

For some reason, she sounded like his mother. It was not a mental image he wanted right at this moment and he tried to shake it from his mind. Happily, the screen burst back into life with an image of the naked Amazon haranguing a cowering police officer.

'Hello?'

The more annoyed Abigail sounded, the more aroused he became. 'I was just wondering,' he groaned, 'what kind of underwear you've got on.'

'For God's sake,' she breathed, lowering her voice to less than a whisper, 'you're not playing with yourself again, are you?'

The Amazon was astride the policeman now, hitting him repeatedly over the head with what looked like an outsized albino truncheon.

'Good God!'

As he teetered on the point of no return, Holy-rod watched in horror as the camera jerked up and away from the action. For a couple of seconds he was treated to a series of shots of Everton's ceiling. Then a face filled the screen. As it came into focus, Holyrod let his erection slip from his hand. 'Holy shit!' he hissed, trying not to fall from his chair. 'What the fuck are *you* doing there?'

'Thanks.' Carlyle took the mug from his wife and gave her a quick peck on the forehead. Alice had already left for school and they had the flat to themselves. Taking a couple of hasty gulps of peppermint tea, he poured the rest down the sink.

'In a hurry?' Helen asked.

'I've got to get going,' he replied. 'See how the great strip-club round-up is going.'

She gave him a stern look. 'I hope you're not going back there.' Helen had been deeply unim-pressed by his tale of the raid on Everton's. Al-though she trusted her husband, she saw no need to have him put needlessly in the way of tempt-ation. For that reason, the Vice Squad had never appeared on Carlyle's CV.

'No, no,' he said hurriedly, trying not to sound too defensive. 'I'm off to the station.'

'Good,' she said, reaching up on to her toes and giving him a kiss on the lips. 'I'll see you later.'

Standing on the pavement, the inspector watched a group of four white guys unload the back of an open-topped lorry on the opposite side of the street. They were fitting out what had been Il Buffone, the café that Carlyle would visit most days for his breakfast. The owner, Marcello Aversa, would have a double macchiato and outsized raisin Danish on the table in front of him almost before Carlyle had slipped into the back booth where he liked to sit, contemplating the day ahead under a crumbling poster of the 1984 Juventus scudetto winning squad, the team of Trapattoni and Platini, higher beings from a different time. With Marcello retired, Carlyle knew that the place would never be the same. But a man still had to eat and he was prepared to give the new establishment a go.

Slowly, a couple of the men began lifting the new sign into place above the front door. Carlyle's jaw dropped. 'You're fucking kidding!' he wailed. 'A kebab shop?' One of the men gave him a dirty look. Carlyle glared back at him before turning on his heel and heading quickly in the direction of Holborn tube, his stomach grumbling noisily. Ten minutes later, he was sitting in the basement of Cornwell & Black Opticians, trying to guess the blurred letters that were being flashed up on the screen in front of him.

'Your eyes are fine, Inspector.' Denzil Taleb swivelled on his stool and scribbled some notes in Carlyle's file. 'You are just a bit short-sighted.'

Carlyle grunted the most reluctant of acknowledgements.

Denzil, a small, wiry man in his sixties, sporting a pair of thick black Prada frames which kept slipping down his nose, smiled happily, safe in the knowledge that there would never be a lack of demand for his services. 'We all need glasses as we get older, it's just a fact of life.' Sliding off the stool, he moved to the door. 'Let's go upstairs and find a nice pair for you.'

Extracting himself from the examination chair, Carlyle followed. Ten minutes later, he had chosen a pair of half-rimmed, gunmetal grey Police frames. Effortlessly relieving him of £300, Denzil cheerily informed the inspector that his new glasses would be ready the next day.

'How is your wife getting on with her reading spectacles?' Denzil asked, as he walked Carlyle out.

'Fine,' the inspector smiled wanly, still feeling the pain in his Visa card. He didn't have the heart to tell the optician that Helen had lost her glasses again.

'Pass on my regards,' Denzil said, giving him a gentle pat on the back. 'We'll let both of you know when it's time for your regular examinations.'

Great, Carlyle reflected; *something else to relieve us of our cash*. He shook the optician's outstretched hand. 'Thanks,' he said insincerely. 'I'll see you tomorrow.'

Belatedly realizing that they were a long way from home turf, Dominic Silver watched the silver-haired gentleman standing next to him flick off the safety on the Italian pistol that nestled all too comfortably in his right hand. Taking a deep breath, he glanced over at the impassive face of Gideon Spanner. Sticking his hands into the back pockets of his Firetrap jeans, Spanner gave the slightest of shrugs. All they could do was indulge their host.

In front of them stood three guys – teenagers, Dom guessed – in regulation hoodies and sweat pants. All three had been relieved of their shoes and socks. And beaten, badly beaten. One had his left eye almost completely closed by a massive shiner. Another had blood still spilling from his left ear. Indeed, it looked as if the ear had been half-sliced off. Silver was mesmerized by it, even as he wanted to look away. As the forlorn trio stood, heads bowed, shifting from foot to filthy foot on the cold, clammy concrete floor, he wondered how much of this show was for his benefit. Maybe about half, he concluded. There would be others who were meant to get the message as well. Dom sighed; he wasn't a fan of violence. Invariably, he had found it to be unnecessary, if not counter-productive. But, in the business that he was in, he knew that it was often unavoidable.

The barrel of the gun was pointed casually at the middle hoodie. *'Lorsque vous devez tirer, tirez – n'en parlez pas.'*

Silver and Spanner exchanged another look.

The old man with the gun glanced over at Silver. 'Do you speak French, Dominic?'

Silver smiled apologetically. 'I'm afraid not. You know what it's like in England, we're all useless at languages.'

'It's understandable,' the man sighed. 'English is the international business language, after all. If everyone else has to learn your language, why should you bother learning theirs?'

Dom shrugged. 'People are lazy.'

'I suppose they are.' Squeezing the trigger, the man shot the middle hoodie in the face, before dispatching his squealing comrades in similar fashion with a minimum of fuss.

Whoa! Dom held his ground as a pool of blood began moving steadily towards him.

Carefully putting the safety back on, the man tossed the semi-automatic to one of his henchmen.

'*Un deuxième tour pour chacun,*' he growled, '*juste pour être sûr.*' Then 'Get rid of them,' he snapped. Then, placing a hand on Dominic's arm, he steered him towards the exit. 'Now that little problem has been dealt with,' he said, 'I think it's time for some lunch.'

'What the hell is that?' Carlyle picked up the A4-sized transparent plastic evidence bag from Angie Middleton's desk and lifted it up to the light. Inside was a slim white cylinder, maybe seven inches long and a couple of inches in girth, rounded at one end. It looked like a quarter-sized light sabre, except that it had a wind-up mechanism at one end and was attached to a nylon harness.

'It's called the Earth Angel,' the desk sergeant smirked.

Carlyle made a face that suggested he was none the wiser.

'It's the world's first green vibrator.'

Blushing slightly, Carlyle looked swiftly over his shoulder to check that no one was eavesdropping on their conversation. He needn't have worried. It wasn't yet eight in the morning and the place was deserted. 'Is the colour relevant?'

'Green as in "environmentally friendly", Inspector.'

'Oh, right. And what exactly is a "green" vibrator?'

Middleton pointed at the wind-up mechanism. 'It doesn't use batteries; you crank it up by hand. The guy who invented it said he was worried about climate change.'

'Aren't we all,' nodded Carlyle. Personally, he couldn't really give a toss about global warming. Given his experience of dealing with the human race, he assumed that whatever was being done about it was bound to be too little, too late. If we all ended up drowning, it would be our own stupid fault. He handed the bag back to the sergeant. 'Is it any good?'

Middleton gave him a bemused look. 'How would I know? It's not mine.'

'No?' Carlyle teased.

'No.' Middleton's face broke into a sly grin. 'I'm more of a Rampant Rabbit girl myself.'

Now Carlyle felt himself go properly red. 'That's good to know,' he coughed.

'That,' Middleton explained, gesturing at the device again, 'is evidence. It was what that stripper used to bash Lea over the head with.' She picked a sheet of paper from the desk and scanned it carefully. 'Or, as Sergeant Bishop has so beautifully described it in his report: *the assailant brandished the rigid feminine pleasure device above her head and advanced on the officer in a threatening manner, proceeding to strike him about the head on multiple occasions.*'

Carlyle laughed heartily. 'Was it wound up at the time?'

'That,' Middleton chuckled, 'is not recorded for posterity.'

'Anyway,' said Carlyle, feeling his eyes welling up with mirth, 'I thought that a "rigid feminine

82

pleasure device" was a name for a credit card, not a sex toy.'

'Very good, Inspector,' Middleton guffawed, 'very good. We are on form today, aren't we?'

'Thank you, thank you.'

'For once.'

'Hey, hey,' Carlyle protested, 'less of that. I get stereotyped enough as it is round here.'

Middleton reached over and squeezed him on the arm. 'You're not stereotyped, Inspector,' she crooned. 'You're just a grumpy old sod, who manages to come out with the occasional funny one-liner.'

Carlyle shook his head. 'So young, yet so insightful.'

'Thank you, sir!' Middleton gave him a fake salute. 'It's all the training they give us these days.'

'How is Constable Lea, by the way?' Carlyle asked, once they had finished laughing, trying to fake some concern for his injured colleague.

'They took him up to A&E at UCH to get a couple of stitches. He'll be fine.'

Carlyle nodded. The wound would be healed in a week; being clobbered by a naked lap dancer wielding a dildo would take considerably longer to live down. 'And the stripper?'

Middleton jerked a thumb towards the cells. 'She's downstairs.'

'Got some clothes on?'

'Yeah.'

Shame, thought Carlyle. 'What about the video guy?'

Middleton looked at her worksheet. 'Mr ... Craven? Bishop let him go without charge.'

Fuck, thought Carlyle.

'He wasn't very happy, all the same. Shouting about police brutality, infringement of his civil liberties. All the usual stuff.'

'Did we give him his camera back?'

'Yeah.'

'Jolly good.'

'Apparently he left at three a.m., promising to give you a starring role in his film. Everyone's desperate to check out the internet.'

'I bet they are,' Carlyle said bitterly.

'You might be on the Mayor's website already.'

'I'll go and have a look,' Carlyle replied, heading for the lifts.

ELEVEN

Adrian Gasparino was shaken from his reverie by the sound of gunfire, heavy calibre. It was close. Very fucking close. Then the wall above his head exploded and shards of baked mud landed on his head as his brain tried to engage.

It took him another moment to realize the firing was coming from inside the compound. Clutching his SA80, he threw out a hand to grab the American, Withers. 'C'mon!' he hissed. 'Move!' There was no response. Turning towards the American, he realized that the sergeant had taken a round in the chest. He wouldn't be going anywhere.

'Bollocks!' As the ground started exploding at his feet, Gasparino's survival instinct finally kicked in. Snaking to the left, he threw himself through the doorway of the hut. Inside, in the sweaty gloom, he kept his head firmly on the ground, his eyes equally firmly shut, listening to his heart beating so fast that he thought it would have to burst right out of his chest. The shots kept coming but none of them seemed aimed at him. Gasparino could hear a range of different weapons now as the coalition troops engaged in the firefight.

How long he stayed like that, he couldn't say. Finally, he lifted his head half an inch off the ground, opened his eyes and peered out, just in time to see the ANA guy with the M240 take two shots to the head and crumple to the ground. From the four corners of the compound, coalition soldiers swarmed over their erstwhile allies, disarming them and pushing them to the ground, screaming at them to get their hands over their heads. Quickly, with a minimum of fuss, the boys did what they were told. Following them down, Gasparino's gaze fell on the three ANA soldiers who had been caught in the crossfire. Then he saw the body of Sergeant Spencer Spanner, lying at a crazy angle, his head stuck under his right arm, a pool of blood already drying in the dirt. The medics weren't making any effort to revive him.

'Oh, fuck!'

Stifling a sob, Gasparino struggled to his feet. As he did so, he felt a searing pain in his left leg. Looking down, he saw the blood dripping onto his boot and realized that his war would be finishing even earlier than expected.

Sitting at his desk on the third floor of the police

station, Carlyle surreptitiously Googled 'Mayor of London'. Christian Holyrod's official site came top of the list of searches and he clicked on it. The front page was full of the usual politician's guff about how the Mayor was probably solely responsible for improving everything to do with the capital, for London's inhabitants and visitors to the city.

'Oh yeah?' Carlyle looked at the photo of Holyrod, in thoughtful repose, above a list of his aims to deliver a cleaner city, safer streets, better transport and good quality affordable housing.

Nothing about closing down strip clubs then. Carlyle clicked on the link that said *Mayoral Webcasts* and was confronted by a menu of videos with appealing titles such as *GLA Intelligence Seminar. Visualizing London; London Waste and Recycling Board Meeting* and *Representation Hearing on Southall Gas Works Site*. Resisting the temptation to peek at any of those, Carlyle chose the video at the top of the list. Entitled *Cleaning Up London: Working with the Police*, it had been added to the site earlier that morning. With a heavy heart, he opened up Windows Media Player, sat back in his chair and waited for the 3:12 video to start. Over a breathless commentary explaining 'the Mayor's plan' to crack down on illegals working in London, he watched some shots of Sergeant Bishop leading the other uniforms into Everton's. Once the action moved inside, so many of the shots had to be heavily pixilated that it was impossible to work out what precisely was going on.

Carlyle let the video run for another minute or so but it was just about unwatchable. 'Your tax money at work,' he mumbled angrily to himself. Relieved, he was just about to close it down, when the video cut to a familiar face – a *very* familiar face. The bastard film-maker had indeed given him a starring role in the Mayor's poxy video. Worse, the bloody thing had been cut to show him running around like Inspector sodding Clouseau.

'Oh, fuck!' Carlyle groaned. Never mind PC bloody Lea, *he* was never going to live this down. The inspector pulled the video-maker's card out of his pocket and stared at it for ten seconds. 'Well, Mr Danny Craven of Scattered Flowers Productions,' he growled, 'I'll be seeing you.'

Sitting in an otherwise deserted pizza restaurant on Allée de Coubron, Dominic Silver picked at his salad. Seeing three boys shot in the face had done nothing for his appetite, but business etiquette demanded that he had to make the effort. Taking a long drink of San Pellegrino, he politely declined a refill from the two-thirds full bottle of Domaine d'Aussières 2008 sitting on the table.

'What?' the old man frowned. 'You don't drink?' At the table he looked tired and fragile. With the gun in his hand, he had looked ten years younger – twenty when he was pulling the trigger.

Dominic said politely, 'As a rule, not during the day. And rarely when I'm conducting business.'

'I can respect that,' the man nodded, tucking in to his plate of *cavatappi* pasta with hot-spiced beef.

Dominic dropped his fork onto his plate. 'What did you say to those boys?'

Chewing thoughtfully, Tuco Martinez gave the impression of having to dig deep into his memory in order to recall the morning's events, even though they were barely an hour old. 'Ah yes,' he said finally, waving his wine glass as if he was about to make a toast. 'I told them that when you have to shoot, shoot. Don't talk.' He let out a harsh laugh. 'Good advice for them to take to the grave.'

Dominic looked at him blankly.

'You like Westerns?' Martinez enquired.

'Cowboy movies? John Wayne?'

'Yeah.'

'They don't really make them any more, do they?'

'No, they don't. Not like the old days.'

Dom smiled. 'It's all gangster movies these days.'

'Ha! We're just too popular for our own good,' Tuco joked.

'So,' Dom tried to pull the old fella back on to some kind of track, 'when you have to shoot...'

'It's a line from the film *The Good, the Bad and the Ugly*,' the man explained, taking a mouthful of wine. 'From my namesake, the Eli Wallach character.'

Dominic thought about it for a moment. He liked spaghetti westerns well enough, but he couldn't remember anything about that one other than the title and the fact that Clint Eastwood was in it. Mind you, if he remembered rightly, Clint Eastwood was in most of them. 'It's a great line,' he said limply.

'Damn right!' His host nodded vehemently. 'Excellent advice. If only those useless bastards in Hollywood would pay attention now and again.'

Dom frowned. How did they get on to a rant about the movie business?

'I always hate it,' the old guy continued, 'at the end of a film when the bad guy keeps talking away, unravelling the plot, and gives the good guy time to wriggle off the hook and save the fucking day. Just shoot the bastard, I say. You can explain everything to his corpse. Let the bad guy win for once – everyone would be cheering in the cinema!'

Everyone's a critic, Dom thought sadly. 'This guy, he had your name?'

'Tuco Ramirez,' the man laughed. *'The Good, the Bad and the Ugly* was my dad's favourite film, and Tuco, played by Eli Wallach, was his favourite character. We used to watch it all the time. That's how I got my name. I was his *little Tuco.'*

'I see,' said Dominic, smiling weakly. *Fucking hell,* he thought, *I'm going into business with a psycho granddad named after a crazy character in a cowboy flick.* He felt a bitter pang of regret seep through his stomach, and gave himself a silent warning: *Better keep your wits about you on this one, old chum.*

'It's not my real family name, obviously,' the old man explained.

'No.'

'I think of it more as my stage name, if you like.'

Dom took a deep breath and forced a smile on to his face. 'Yes.'

'Then there's my nickname, the Samurai,' Tuco said cheerily. 'That comes from another movie entirely.'

'Oh, really?' Inside, Dom groaned as Tuco talked him through his other moniker.

Finishing his little spiel, Tuco took another

89

mouthful of wine. 'Good idea, don't you think?'

'Well...'

'Don't you have one? You could be, I dunno – The Professor.'

'I don't think–'

'You should try it,' Taco insisted.

Dom made a show of thinking about the stupid idea for a few seconds. 'I think it might be a bit late for me,' he replied finally. 'I reckon I would find it difficult to have more than one name. It might make me a bit schiz ... confused.'

Taco Martinez looked him carefully up and down. 'You are wondering about my little show this morning?'

'I try never to pry into other people's business,' Silver murmured, not meeting the older man's gaze.

Placing his wine glass on the table, Tuco patted the corners of his mouth with a napkin. 'That's a very sensible attitude,' he said. 'But maybe not one that can be sustained when you are standing in the basement of a parking garage in Clichy-sous-Bois, trying not to get the diseased blood of some cretin on your shoes.'

Dominic lifted the glass of sparkling water to his lips. Looking over the rim he thought that maybe his dining companion did look a bit like Eli Wallach. You could see a similarity if you wanted to, rather like people who saw the image of the Madonna in a potato or a weeping Jesus in a pool of oil on the road. 'You were making a point,' he said evenly. 'I understand that.'

Martinez raised a salt and pepper eyebrow. His eyes were hazelnut brown, hard and threatening.

'Oh? And what was the point that I was making?'

Dominic smiled wanly. Tuco Martinez, all bollocks and bluster, was exactly the kind of business partner he thought that he'd successfully left behind. Sipping his wine, Martinez waited patiently for an answer.

'You were demonstrating to me that no one fucks you over,' Dominic said quietly.

'That's right!' Martinez banged a fist down on the white tablecloth. 'Those idiots,' he gestured outside, 'they thought they could steal from me. Well, now they know differently.'

'I have never–'

'I know, I know,' Tuco waved away Dominic's protest with an impatient flick of the hand. 'But it is always best to have clarity at the beginning of a relationship, don't you think?'

Dominic nodded. Glancing at his watch, he still harboured hopes of catching the Eurostar early enough to be home in time for dinner. 'I would agree with that one hundred per cent.'

'In London,' Tuco continued, 'they say that you are not the biggest but you are one of the best.'

'Thank you.'

'Or *were* one of the best,' Tuco chortled. 'You are in semi-retirement.'

Suddenly feeling the need for a drink, Dominic reached across the table and grasped the bottle of red wine before filling his glass. 'You can't retire in our game, can you?' He took a long drink and immediately poured some more wine into his glass.

'No, that's very true.' Raising his own glass, Martinez gave a toast. 'Here's to our new business partnership and to no more lessons in car parks!'

'Yes, indeed,' Dominic agreed over the clinking of glasses.

Tuco lifted his glass to his lips. 'They were stupid. You would have done the same.'

Dominic raised his eyebrows. 'That's not really my style.'

'Something similar,' Tuco grinned. 'I am sure we have similar instincts.'

What was the use of arguing with the fellow? Dom conceded the point. 'True.'

Finally, it was time for something to eat. With the demise of his regular haunt, Il Buffone, Carlyle had found a new home from home at the Box Café on Henrietta Street. Barely a minute from the police station, just down from the piazza, it was cheap and, more often than not, relatively free of tourists. By now, the Ukrainian owner, Myron Sabo, knew Carlyle well enough to make his coffee scalding hot and not to bother him with too much chitchat. Since Myron was not known for his love of conversation, that was not too much of a problem. His pastries fell considerably short of the standard set by Marcello at Il Buffone but Carlyle was not the kind of man who wasted his time striving for perfection, not even when it came to cakes, so Myron's establishment was more than good enough. Given that it was as near as dammit lunchtime, he ordered a latte and a large slice of apple strudel and, plucking a dog-eared copy of *The Times* from the rack by the till, he took a seat at the back. After a quick check to reassure himself that the raid on Everton's hadn't made it into the home news section, he flipped to the back pages to scan the all-important sports news. Inside, a full two pages had been devoted to the latest contract wrangle involving bad boy superstar Gavin Swann.

'Two hundred grand.' Myron appeared at the table, coffee in one hand, strudel in the other. He shook his head. 'A bloody week!' In slow motion, he placed the latte onto the table, still managing to spill a good portion of the murky brown liquid into the saucer. 'After tax!'

Shocked by the Ukrainian's sudden outburst, Carlyle grabbed the plate containing the cake before he dropped it. It was a generous slice of strudel by any measure and he didn't want to lose it. Or, more to the point, he didn't want to have to embarrass himself by picking it off the floor and then eating it. 'I know,' he said, once the plate had been carefully placed on the table, 'it's a complete joke. How can any footballer be worth that?'

For a few moments, both men contemplated the absurdity of the situation.

'How can anyone be worth that?' Myron wondered sadly.

'Quite,' said Carlyle. Closing the paper, he folded it in half and handed it back to Myron, signalling that the time for talking was over. Using the teaspoon from his saucer, he began a steady, determined assault on his cake.

Once the strudel was a happy memory, Carlyle's thoughts turned to his 'to do' list for the day. He still had to interview the stripper who had assaulted PC Lea and wasn't looking forward to it. Off the job, strippers were usually dull and unappealing creatures and quite mouthy with it. This one, having refused to plead guilty to a charge of aggravated assault, was bound to be a pain in the arse. Still, it had to be done. Finishing his coffee, he had almost worked himself up to going to work when his mobile went off.

He looked at the screen. No number came up, but as it was his 'private' phone, it could only be one of a small number of potential callers. The Nokia 2330 was one of the cheapest pay-as-you-go models currently on the market. Carlyle had bought it for cash and he topped it up for cash at random newsagents well away from his usual haunts. He didn't flash it around and gave the number out to very few people. Even then, he changed both the phone and the sim card every three or four months. He knew well enough that this didn't guarantee complete secrecy, but it meant that no one was checking his calls as a matter of routine. It gave him some privacy, and for that the hassle and cost was worth it.

'Yes?'

'Inspector?'

Recognizing the voice immediately, Carlyle smiled. 'How are you, William?'

'Fine, I'm fine.' Over the years, William Wallace had been one of his more useful contacts.

'What's going on?'

'I've got something for you.'

Carlyle's smile grew wider. 'Okay...'

'But you have to come to me.'

'Where?'

Wallace gave him an address in East London.

'Hold on,' said Carlyle, gesturing to Myron for a pen and a piece of paper. The café-owner quickly obliged. 'Give that to me again.' This time he scribbled down the address. 'Thanks. I'll be there in about an hour.' Ending the call, he fished a handful of change out of his pocket and paid his bill. Then, happy to have an excuse for not going directly back to the station, he headed out into the damp, grey day.

TWELVE

'Clichy-sous-Bois is the most notorious suburb in Paris.'

'Mm. Looks a bit like Tower Hamlets to me.'

'The government couldn't care less.'

'They tend not to, in my experience.'

'That's right!' Warming to his theme, Tuco Martinez waved in the direction of the tower blocks in the distance. 'Poor housing, chronic poverty and rampant unemployment, we have it all. Rioting and looting are the local pastimes. Life here is supposed to be nasty, brutish and short. If I didn't conform to the stereotype of the vengeful crime boss, the little bastards would eat me alive. But that's not the whole story. We do a lot for the people around here.'

Ah yes, the pusher turned social champion. The world was full of drug dealers who saw themselves as Robin Hood-type figures. It was not an unfamiliar line in bullshit, but one Dominic Silver had always tried to avoid himself. The fact was he sold illegal drugs, pure and simple, and didn't feel the need to dress it up with any under-graduate sociology spiel.

His story was an unusual one, but not especially earth-shattering. Having trained as a junior officer, Silver had quit the Metropolitan Police after the brutal Miners' Strike of the early 1980s. Over the following decades, he had built up a multi-million-pound business, becoming some-thing of a legend in police circles in the process. The son of a policeman, the nephew of a police-man, he was the archetypal good boy turned bad, but with an honesty and a style that gleaned a little goodwill from even the most hard-nosed copper. Now, even after more than thirty years, there was still a little part of Dom that was 'one of us' in the eyes of many officers of a certain age.

At his peak, during the course of the first decade of the new century, he had reached maybe the third or fourth tier of narcotics entrepreneurs in the capital. This was not a bad place to be, reason-ably comfortable, avoiding the problems facing those above and below him. His operation was turning over millions of pounds each year, with clients including a swathe of minor celebrities and newer entries in *Who's Who*, rather than City bar-row boys or benefit losers. He even had a couple of corporate clients, who bought on account.

It was a good gig. In an industry crying out for quality management, Dom stood out. If there were dozens of mid-level dealers in London, there was only one Dom. Independent. Cautious. Dis-creet. *Sensible*.

Above all, Dominic Silver was a family man. He'd been with his common-law wife, Eva Hollander, for more than twenty-five years. They had four kids; a fifth, Marina, had been diagnosed with Type I Cockayne Syndrome, a rare genetic disorder characterized by an appearance of premature ageing, which led to her death at just six years old.

The combination of family trauma and the ongoing financial crisis had hit Dom and his business interests hard. Business school had shown him how to build up a portfolio of assets and diversify risk. A couple of years ago, drugs probably accounted for less than 40 per cent of Dom's income. But a series of unfortunate investments had slashed his net worth from almost £50 million to less than £20 million. That sum would be enough for most people, but not for Dom. The amount of money in the bank was his way of keeping score – and this was a game that wasn't going to finish until he had won. Despite Eva's objections, he decided to return, full-time, to the day job. Even the drug-dealing business wasn't as lucrative as it had been in previous years, but it still paid the bills. So it was time to forge new partnerships; partnerships with people like Tuco Martinez.

'This place,' said Tuco, waking Dom from his reverie, 'is only twelve kilometres from the centre of Paris.'

Dom shrugged.

'But there are people here who have never been there in their lives. They have never seen the Eiffel Tower, for real, or the Arc de Triomphe or anything else. There is only one bus out of here – it goes to the airport for the people who work as cleaners at Charles de Gaulle – and no Metro. And the politicians!' He let out a snort of derision. 'They wring their hands but do nothing.'

'It's the same everywhere,' said Silver, pushing his chair back from the table. 'Politicians are less than useless.'

Tuco nodded sadly.

'Now,' said Dom, getting to his feet, 'back to business. We have some things to sort out before I leave Paris.'

Chief Inspector Cass Wadham eyed the warrant card and the Glock 26 on the desk in front of her before looking up at Roche.

'The IIC report has concluded that you can return to full active service,' she said, clearly not impressed by the decision.

Clasping her hands together, Roche nodded but said nothing, resisting the temptation to reach across the table and grab her things.

'You will, of course,' the Chief Inspector continued, 'have to carry on seeing Dr Wolf. There will be regular assessments and additional weapons training. Is that clear?'

'Yes.'

Wadham looked her up and down. 'Personally, I question whether it's too early. However, given the recent personnel cuts and the high rates of absenteeism we are currently experiencing...'

Well, thought Roche, *thank you for the vote of confidence.* Getting to her feet, she waited patiently for Wadham to hand over the weapon and her ID. Then she turned on her heel and left without another word.

'They may take our lives,' Carlyle cackled, 'but they'll never take our freeeeeDOM!'

William Wallace shook his head. 'Inspector,' he laughed, 'how many times have I told you? You need to find a new joke.'

Carlyle held up a hand. 'I know, I know. I'm sorry.' He took a mouthful of Jameson's whiskey and swallowed greedily. 'I should know better. But you've got to admit it's a strange name.'

Sir William Wallace was a thirteenth-century Scottish knight, made famous in popular culture for his portrayal by Mel Gibson in the film *Braveheart*. *Mr* William Wallace, sitting across the table from Carlyle in the Reliance pub on Old Street, was a thirty-something albino Yardie, originally from the Rose Town west Kingston ghetto in Jamaica.

'If it makes things easier for you,' Wallace said, 'you can call me Will.' A good two inches over six foot tall, he was whippet thin with high cheekbones, pale grey eyes and a tightly cropped bleached-blond afro. After more than a decade in London, he sounded like most of the city's other eight million inhabitants, an undefined native with an undefined accent.

Wallace had known Carlyle for most of his time in London. Framed for a murder he didn't commit, Carlyle had championed his case, saving him from both incarceration and extradition by going in front of the judge and presenting evidence that his fellow officers had somehow 'lost'. Wallace walked. The killer was never caught. Several colleagues – not to mention the victim's family – would never forgive Carlyle. Wallace, however, managed to find his way onto the straight and narrow, developing a career in the music industry, first as a studio engineer, then as a producer. He was now the co-owner of the Rose Town studio in Shoreditch, along with a discreet business angel, who had invested in the project as a favour to Carlyle. The inspector, pleased if rather bemused to have found himself in the role of successful social worker, had not sought anything in return. But Wallace, it seemed, felt obliged to provide the odd piece of information that came his way.

'Okay.' Carlyle extended a hand and they shook.

Wallace took a slug from his bottle of Peroni. 'My parents had no idea about the name and I've never watched that Mel Gibson film.'

'Neither have I.' As a second-generation Scot, Carlyle was conscious of, if not particularly inter-ested in, his roots. There was a lingering anti-Englishness that came with the territory, but first, last and always, he was a Londoner. London was where his parents had escaped to when there were no opportunities for personal development in post-war Glasgow. London was where he had been born; it was where he had lived all his life. It had given him everything and he was suitably grateful. 'You know that he was killed near here?'

Wallace frowned. 'Who?'

'Your namesake. The Scottish terrorist. When the English caught him he was brought down to London, tried–'

'Found guilty.'

'Of course. This is 1305 we're talking about, after all. Wallace was stripped naked and dragged through the city at the heels of a horse to Smithfield. He was strangled by hanging but released while he was still alive. Then he was eviscerated, and his bowels were burned in front of his face. Then he was beheaded, castrated, and cut into quarters.'

Wallace finished his beer and shivered. 'Nice.'

'His head was placed on a pike on London Bridge. Then they took the body parts on tour. His limbs were out on show in Stirling, Berwick, Newcastle and Aberdeen.' Carlyle finished his drink and signalled that he was going back to the bar for another round. On his return, he handed Wallace his Peroni and took another mouthful of whiskey, vowing that this one would be the last. He took a relaxed view of drinking on duty but he never overdid it. 'So,' he said, 'thanks for the call. What did you want to talk about?'

Wallace took a sip of beer. 'It's about that guy.'

Carlyle emptied his glass. He had a nice buzz going and felt the pleasing warmth of the Jameson's on the back of his throat. 'What guy?'

'The guy who escaped from St Pancras, after the shoot-out.'

Carlyle sat up and leaned across the table. 'The French guy?'

Wallace nodded. 'Yeah – him. I know where he is.'

'What am I going to do about my boy?' Playing with his wine glass, Tuco kept his gaze on the table.

Not my problem. 'Where is he now?' Silver asked.

'He's staying at a safe house in London.' Tuco looked up. 'I want you to get him back to Paris.'

'That,' Dominic sighed, 'is not going to be easy. After what happened at the Eurostar terminal...'

Tuco held up a hand. 'I know, I know. It was not handled well.'

'That's some understatement,' Dom said bluntly. 'People have died. The police in London will not just let that go.'

'He should have been more careful.'

'Yes,' Dom agreed, 'he should.' Idiots like Alain Costello really pissed him off. On the other hand, it was the very fact that they were idiots that gave him a considerable competitive advantage. There was no way he was going to put himself at risk by getting involved. The boy would have to fend for himself. 'I'll see what I can do,' he said grudgingly.

'Thank you,' Tuco said, reaching across the table and slapping him on the shoulder. 'I knew that I could depend on you. This will cement our working relationship.'

Or kill it before it has begun, Dom mused.

THIRTEEN

'How reliable is the information?'

'It's reliable enough. It's a very good source. And he has actually seen the guy. The location is the home of a known drug dealer.'

There was a pause. 'Why are you telling me?' Alison Roche asked finally.

You know why. 'I thought that you'd want to know.'

Another pause. 'I'll get SO15 on it.'

'Okay. Keep me posted.'

'Will do.'

Now it was Carlyle's turn to pause. He wanted to end the call, but didn't. 'How are you doing?'

'Fine,' said Roche dully, like a monosyllabic teenager. Even when they'd been working out of Charing Cross, Carlyle was not really the kind of guy to show much interest in her private life or her mental state, and that was the way she liked it. Now that they didn't work together, there was even less reason to share.

'I hear the IIC gave you a clean bill of health.'

'Yeah.'

Carlyle ploughed on. 'I also hear we're sharing the same shrink.'

'Wolf?' Roche let out a shrill laugh. 'He's useless. Look, thanks for the info. I'll give you a call when I know what's happening. Speak later.' The line went dead before he had the chance to say anything else. For a moment, he looked blankly at the handset before dropping it in his pocket and heading off in search of a bus that could take him in the direction of the station.

Carole Simpson gazed at the solid gold crown, thought to belong to a high-ranking nomadic woman more than twenty centuries earlier. The champagne glass in her hand was empty and she felt both light-headed and weary. The special viewing of the surviving treasures from the National Museum of Afghanistan came at the end of a long day. Pulling Dino Mottram close, she slipped her arm through his.

Smiling, he bent over and kissed her on the cheek.

'Dino,' she whispered, 'how long do we have to stay?'

His furrowed brow gave her all the answer she needed. Entomophagous Industries had spent more than twenty thousand pounds sponsoring this evening's reception and, true to form, Dino was determined to get his money's worth. Realizing that she would be on her feet for a while yet, Simpson felt even more tired. This time, she made no effort to conceal the boredom as she returned her gaze to the crown.

Stepping into interview room B3 in the basement of Charing Cross police station, Carlyle nodded to the WPC, indicating that she could leave. Dropping the thin file onto the desk, he pulled up a chair and sat down. Flipping open the file, he scanned the three sheets of paper inside before eyeing the tired-looking woman sitting opposite him dressed in a T-shirt and sweat pants. 'Well, Christina,' he began, 'that was quite a show you put on for us at Everton's.'

Christina O'Brien shrugged. 'I was high. Some guy came chasing after me. How was I supposed to know he was a police officer?'

Carlyle pushed out his lower lip, indicating thought. 'Because he was wearing a uniform?'

'I told you,' she said in an increasingly affected, mid-Atlantic drawl. 'I was high.'

Carlyle slipped into bureaucratic mode. 'PC Lea, the officer you assaulted, will make a full recovery.'

'Great.' Christina's face brightened considerably. If it didn't manage to make her pretty, at least she didn't look quite so hard. 'So, can I get out of here?'

'That is not going to be possible,' Carlyle replied. 'You have been charged with Actual Bodily Harm. Given that the assault was witnessed by numerous police officers and was also recorded on camera, I think it's reasonable to assume that you will be convicted.'

Christina raised her eyes to the ceiling. 'Oh, man.'

'If I were you, I would just plead guilty.'

She thought about this for a moment. 'Will I get sent to jail?'

'Probably. Or, given that you're a US citizen, they might just deport you.'

'Fuck.' Sitting back in her chair, she folded her arms.

Carlyle closed the file.

Christina eyed the miniature camera hanging from the ceiling in the corner of the room. Leaning across the table, she lowered her voice. 'Is that thing on?'

Carlyle turned to check the red blinking light below the lens. 'Looks like it.'

'Can you turn it off?'

'No,' Carlyle lied.

Christina ran her tongue across her top lip. 'I give great head,' she whispered, 'truly re-mark-able. Switch that thing off and I'll do you right here. Make this thing go away and you can come and see me in Everton's any time.'

Carlyle jumped to his feet before he could start

105

seriously contemplating the offer. 'Thanks,' he mumbled, 'but I think I'll pass.'

Throwing herself back in the chair, Christina banged on the table in frustration. 'Fucking English faggot!'

Carlyle felt a flash of anger in his chest. *Don't call me fucking English!* Grabbing his file, he quickly slipped out of the door.

The exhibition's curator, an elegant man in his late fifties with the outsized moniker of Simpson Salvador St John, stepped in front of the shimmering crown. 'Ladies and gentlemen,' he said, addressing the small group, 'this is our star attraction, one of the world's most beautiful and priceless objects. At the time, it was the ultimate accessory, flat-packed for easy transport in the first century AD.'

'How much is it worth?' asked a man hovering at his shoulder.

St John tried not to show his frustration at the vulgarity of the question. 'Like many of the other items in this exhibition,' he said patiently, 'its value is incalculable. It was discovered by Soviet archaeologists in 1978 in an elite nomadic cemetery and has never been shown in Britain before.' He gestured across the exhibition floor, the sweep of his arm taking in a dazzling array of classical sculptures, gold jewellery, carved ivory and enamelled Roman glass. 'Most of these pieces are unique in terms of the information they give about ancient trading patterns and Afghanistan's relationship with the outside world at the time.'

Another of the guests began to say something, but St John, in no mood for any more banality, ploughed on with his prepared spiel. 'At the heart of the Silk Road, Afghanistan linked the great trading routes of ancient Iran, Central Asia, India and China, and the more distant cultures of Greece and Rome. The country's unique location resulted in a legacy of extraordinarily rare objects, which reveal its rich and diverse past. Nearly lost during the years of civil war and later Taliban rule, these precious objects were bravely hidden in 1989 by officials from the National Museum of Afghanistan, to save them from destruction. They were kept hidden until 2004, after the fall of the Taliban and the election of the new government. We should salute the courage of the Afghan officials who risked their lives in order to safeguard the treasure.'

'Hear, hear,' Dino murmured, finally steering Simpson away from the group.

'It really is an amazing collection,' Simpson said, trying to sound grateful for the invite.

'I know,' Dino agreed. 'But they say that everything will go back to the National Museum of Afghanistan in Kabul, so God knows what might happen to it.' He shrugged his shoulders. 'Anyway, let's go and get some dinner.'

Sitting in one of the first-class carriages on the Eurostar, heading for home, Dominic Silver looked across the table at Gideon Spanner, who was staring vacantly out the window. For years, Dom had assumed that Gideon was suffering from some kind of post-traumatic stress disorder from his time in the Army. Now, he had come to the view that he was just a very closed-off guy,

107

with the enviable ability to switch himself on and off. In the car park in Clichy-sous-Bois with Tuco the gunslinger, Gideon had been totally alert. Now he was resting; on standby mode.

Gesturing to the service assistant for another glass of wine, Dom pulled out his mobile and called home.

Eva picked up on the third ring. 'Is everything okay?' He could clearly hear the mixture of irritation and concern in her voice and vowed not to rise to it.

'It's fine,' he said calmly, 'we're on our way back. How are the kids?'

'A handful,' she sighed, 'as usual.'

He looked at the clock on the screen of his phone. 'I should be home about nine.'

'Do you want some dinner when you get in?'

'No, it's all right. I'll eat on the train.'

'Okay. See you soon.' She ended the call, letting him know that she was still pissed off with his Parisian adventure. *Keeping me on my toes,* Dom reflected. *Always keeping me on my toes.*

He had barely slipped his handset back into his jacket pocket when the sound of Motörhead's 'Ace of Spades' came from the other side of the table. Gideon looked blankly at his crotch before fishing an iPhone out of his pocket. He stared at the screen for what seemed like an eternity before taking the call.

'Yeah?'

The service assistant arrived with another small plastic bottle of wine and handed it to Dom, who nodded his thanks.

'I'm on my way back,' said Gideon to his caller.

Unscrewing the top, Dom emptied two-thirds of the bottle into his glass, conscious of Gideon eyeing him intently as he did so.

'Uhuh ... when?... Okay, okay, I will come straight there when I get into London.'

Dom sipped his wine. He was getting a nice buzz going now. He smiled as Gideon ended the call. 'Anything important?'

For a moment, Gideon looked bemused by the question. 'My brother,' he said finally.

Dom shifted uneasily in his seat. He didn't know Gideon had a brother. In fact, he didn't know anything about Gideon's family at all.

'He's dead.'

'What?' Almost dropping his wine glass, Dom sent most of his Merlot down his shirt.

'Shot in Kandahar by a Talib in an ANA uniform. Some Taliban infiltrated the Afghan army. Turned up at a compound where Spencer and his team were waiting to engage the enemy and opened fire.' He thrust a hopeless hand towards the unchanging gloom of the passing French countryside. 'Game over.'

Dom gulped down the rest of his wine before he spilled any more. 'Jesus!'

'Apparently,' Gideon said tonelessly, 'Spencer's killer was a serving member of the army, rather than an insurgent disguised as a soldier, as if that makes any difference. There is no way the Afghans can pick up rogue officers. The Americans just want to get out as quickly as possible. Just like us. The areas that the Taliban don't control already, they will do soon enough.'

Dom had long since given up paying any attention to the news about Afghanistan; it was just a basket case, a medieval country living on the edge of extinction. 'Is there anything I can do?' he asked, feeling like a useless prick for even asking the question.

Gideon frowned. 'Nah. I'll take care of it.' As the train headed into the tunnel, he stared unseeingly at his reflection in the window.

Relieved that the conversation was over, Dom sat back in his seat and closed his eyes. As he listened to the carriages move effortlessly under the Channel, taking him back to his more than charmed life, he suddenly realized that that had been – by some considerable distance – the longest personal conversation he'd had with Gideon in all the years they'd been working together.

FOURTEEN

Waiting to collect her coat, Simpson felt a hand on her shoulder. Turning, she found herself looking at a familiar face.

'Good evening, Commander.'

She gave him a thin smile. 'Good evening, Mr Mayor.'

Dino appeared from the gents, still zipping up his fly. 'Christian!' he said cheerily, slapping Holyrod on the back. 'I'm glad you could make it.' He handed his ticket over to the waiting coat-check girl while gesturing at Simpson. 'Do you know Commander Carole Simpson?'

'Yes, indeed,' Holyrod said politely. 'We go back quite a long way.'

Dino's eyes widened. 'Oh, really?'

'My former husband,' she said, the smile now frozen on her face, 'was a supporter when the mayor first ran for election.'

'Ah,' Dino nodded. Realizing that he had strayed onto a sensitive subject, he collected the waiting coats from the counter and began helping Simpson into her camel-hair jacket. 'As you know, Christian has just agreed to join my Board,' he said, 'which is a major coup for us.'

'I'm sure it is,' said Simpson without any enthusiasm as she buttoned herself up.

'Dino is too kind,' Holyrod said smoothly. 'I have a lot of learning to do if I am to get up to speed with the business.'

'Well,' said Simpson, 'good luck with that.' Pulling her belt tight, she watched with some irritation as Dino struggled into his Ralph Lauren trench-coat. 'I hope you enjoy the exhibition, Mr Mayor. The pieces on display really are quite incredible.'

'I'm looking forward to it,' Holyrod beamed, edging closer. 'But there was something I was meaning to ask you about as well.'

Dino gave her a quizzical look.

Simpson's heart sank. Not only had she been embarrassed by the antics of her insider-dealing husband, she had been embarrassed by the political company that he had kept. And now, with hindsight, she was even more embarrassed to admit that she had been a fellow traveller; a fellow traveller to the point where, arguably, she had overstepped the mark in disclosing to Holyrod details of an investigation in which he personally had been involved. As it happened, her indiscretion had not affected the outcome of the case; but it could have done and that thought still rankled. Still, she had learned an important lesson. Her dealings with politicians were, she had hoped, all long in the past. That was most definitely where she wanted to keep them.

Holyrod let his voice drop until it was barely audible over the background hubbub. 'It concerns my favourite policeman.'

John bloody Carlyle. Simpson felt a sour twinge in her gut. The Commander's relationship with her subordinate had improved immeasurably over recent years, but that did not preclude her from having an acute awareness of his somewhat severe shortcomings. The inspector was the kind of man who had a chip on both shoulders, along with the innate ability to piss off important people, especially the Mayor. On more than one occasion, Simpson had been caught in the middle when the pair had clashed. Whereas Carlyle seemed to revel in the conflict, she herself found it wearisome and futile.

'There's an issue in relation to—'

Simpson stopped him. 'I am aware of the situation. Why don't you call me in the morning?'

Holyrod was about to reply when an imperious figure appeared at his shoulder. At well over six feet, Abigail Slater towered over Simpson. She was wearing a Moschino twill blazer over a pearl blouse with the top three buttons undone, giving more than a glimpse of an ample décolletage. Dino's mouth fell open. Resisting the urge to elbow her partner in the ribs, Simpson gave Holyrod a sly smile. 'Is your wife not coming this evening?' she asked maliciously.

Catching her tone, Dino closed his mouth and, taking her arm, began manoeuvring the Commander towards the exit. 'We're off to dinner,' he said, injecting a note of false cheer into his voice.

'I will call you in the morning,' Holyrod said grimly as Simpson walked away.

'What a bitch,' Slater sneered, loudly enough for Simpson to hear.

'Forget it,' Holyrod snapped, pulling her in the opposite direction. 'Let's go and see the bloody exhibition.'

The squaddie drained his pint of Spitfire Ale and banged it down on the table. 'They're almost here.'

Not looking up from his bottle of Foster's, Adrian Gasparino grunted noncommittally. He was freezing cold in his dress uniform and trying to ignore the dull ache from his crippled leg.

'Aren't you going to come out and watch it?' Not waiting for an answer, the squaddie was already out of the door and into the crowd, a few hundred strong that lined the main street in Wootton Bassett, the small Wiltshire town through which dead soldiers were driven on their way to the John Radcliffe Hospital in Oxford.

Gasparino looked up at the television screen set high on the wall. One of the news channels was showing live images of the scene outside. Over the pictures, a newsreader's voice said: '*Since they began more than three years ago, there have been 149 repatriation ceremonies for 346 personnel. The rate has been increasing, with 34 ceremonies for 86 soldiers so far this year.'*

A perky blonde presenter was running up and down the street interviewing anyone in a uniform. Everyone used the same words – 'tragedy' and 'bravery' – the excited chatter only stopping when the hearses finally hove into view. There were six bodies being repatriated today. One of them belonged to Spencer Spanner. Gasparino kept his eyes on the screen as they passed by outside. As the last one disappeared, he finished his beer and went back to the bar.

Fed up with waiting for his wife to make a comment, Carlyle picked up his new spectacles and waved them in front of his face.

'What do you think?'

'They make you look different,' Helen smirked.

'At least I haven't lost them yet,' Carlyle replied, miffed that she couldn't come up with something more positive to say about his new look.

Reaching across the sofa, Helen took the frames from his hand. Placing them carefully on his face, she gave him an affectionate kiss on the lips. 'They look good. With the grey hair, you are on the way to looking really quite distinguished.'

'Getting old,' Carlyle said sadly.

'We're all getting old,' Helen retorted. 'No need to get all gloomy about it.' She gestured at the television. On the screen were pictures of Union Jack-draped coffins being unloaded from an RAF plane. 'There's a lot worse could happen to you. Those kids were only in their twenties. It seems

114

like they're coming home almost every day now.'

'I know.'

The news report turned to a series of vox pops with people who had turned out to watch the bodies return home. 'I'm here to pay my respects,' said one woman, carrying a baby. 'They're all heroes.'

Carlyle shook his head. 'What kind of person takes a young kid to something like that?'

Helen made a face. 'It has clearly become a bit of a tradition. A day out for people.'

'I'm sure it makes the poor buggers in the coffins feel a whole lot better,' said Carlyle grumpily.

A stern-looking chap in uniform appeared on the screen under the title Lieutenant-General Sir Kelvin Frank. 'There is a greater infatuation with the military,' he announced, staring into the camera in a rather disconcerting fashion, 'than at any other stage of recent history. Much of it is pretty mawkish – what you might call recreational grief ... Diana ... Graceland-type stuff. It's just an extension of the vapid celebrity culture that is corroding our country and doesn't do anyone any good.'

Carlyle gave a small cheer. 'At last,' he said, gesturing at the screen, 'someone's talking some bloody sense. Why do we let ourselves wallow in all this sentimentality? You tell 'em, General!'

'Alice came back with something from school yesterday,' Helen said. 'They're doing a sponsored walk for Help for Heroes and Veterans Aid.'

Carlyle looked at her uncomprehendingly.

'They're charities aimed at helping ex-servicemen get back into civilian life.'

'Isn't that the government's job?' Carlyle asked. Holding up his hand, he corrected himself immediately. 'Sorry, that was a remarkably stupid thing to say. Good for Alice. How much is she looking to raise?'

'A minimum of two hundred quid. She's really up for it.'

'Good for her,' Carlyle repeated, quietly wondering how much he would have to stump up himself. 'What does she think of it all?'

'Dunno,' Helen replied. 'I think she buys into the basic idea that the soldiers are heroes, but doesn't have much of an understanding – if any at all – about what they're actually fighting for.'

'Same as everyone else then,' Carlyle quipped. 'I'd better see if I can dig out an old Stranglers CD for her to listen to.'

Leaping off the sofa, he began singing the first verse of 'No More Heroes' in his best Jean-Jacques Burnel accent. Raising her eyes to the ceiling, Helen picked up the remote and raised the volume on the TV.

Standing in the mud in the Royal British Legion Wootton Bassett Field of Remembrance, Gasparino shivered. He had eaten nothing for more than twenty-four hours and the beer had gone to his head. Looking around, he saw a smattering of people, small knots of families wandering among the rows of tiny crosses pressed into the turf. A sharp blast of wind blew across the field. Looking up at the slate-grey sky, he breathed in deeply, trying to clear his head. In his hand, he was holding a six-inch wooden cross, the legend *Sergeant*

Spencer Spanner written in blue biro across the tip. Dropping on to his good knee, Gasparino drove the cross into the ground until he was sure it was safely secured. His injured leg flared with pain as he struggled to his feet. Stepping away from the cross, he felt the first rain of the day on his uncovered head.

'Sorry, mate,' he said, choked.

Keeping his gaze on the ground, he headed for the road.

The inspector sat in the familiar surroundings of Simpson's office in Paddington Green police station. Aside from the basic office furniture, the place was empty. The only personal touch – a photo of Simpson's husband – had been removed years earlier, around the time the latter had been arrested for fraud. Carlyle waited patiently while she signed some papers. After a few moments, she tossed the biro onto the desk and looked up.

There was a pause while she did a double-take.

'When did you...?'

Carlyle shuffled uncomfortably in his seat. 'The other day.'

Simpson tried not to grin. 'They make you look different.'

A familiar sense of being persecuted stabbed Carlyle in the chest. 'That's exactly what Helen said.'

Simpson nodded.

'There's nothing wrong with my eyes,' he added, somewhat defensively. 'Everyone needs specs in the end.'

'Quite,' Simpson agreed, gesturing to her own

glasses case lying on the desk. 'Anyway, you know what this is about.'

Carlyle cringed. 'The Mayor's website: have you seen the video?'

Simpson shook her head.

'You must be about the only person in the Met who hasn't.' Carlyle grinned. 'I have a starring role.'

Simpson picked up a mug of steaming peppermint tea from her desk and took a sip. 'Why couldn't you just do what you were told?' Carlyle made to say something but she cut him off. 'For once, just execute my order. Not create another bloody drama that gets the Mayor's back up.'

Carlyle's grin got wider.

'You bloody enjoy it!' Simpson slammed her mug down on the desk, spilling tea over her newly signed letters. 'Shit!'

Carlyle struggled to suppress a laugh.

Simpson could tell there was no point in trying to clean up the mess. The letters would have to be redone. 'The problem is that you just like making trouble,' she complained. 'What on earth was the point of arresting that cameraman?'

Carlyle spread his arms wide in what he hoped was a conciliatory fashion. 'What was the point of arresting anyone? How many illegal aliens did we actually catch?'

Simpson glared at the inspector. They both knew the answer to that: zero.

Carlyle ploughed on. 'One stripper arrested for assault – an assault that only happened because we turned up – and thousands of pounds' worth of police time wasted. And all for what? So we could

118

make some fancy video for the Mayor's website.'

'The Mayor–'

'The Mayor,' Carlyle said angrily, 'can go fuck himself. It's not like he's going to be in the job for much longer anyway.'

Simpson thought about mentioning Holyrod's new job with Dino's company but decided against it. 'He'll still be an important man,' she said lamely.

'We'll see,' Carlyle snorted.

'What about the woman that assaulted your constable?'

'PC Lea? She's an American citizen by the name of Christina O'Brien. I expect that she'll be deported. Bishop's dealing with it, unless my new guy turns up, sharpish.'

'That was the other thing I wanted to talk to you about,' said Simpson, opening a desk drawer and pulling out a thin file. She handed it to Carlyle, careful to avoid the pool of tea on the table. 'He starts on Monday. Here are the details.'

'Thanks.' Sitting back in his chair, Carlyle flicked through the contents. 'Umar Sligo,' he frowned. 'What kind of a name is that?'

'Fucking shit!' Alain Costello threw his PSP at the wall in frustration. *Merde alors!'*

He had been playing the same game for weeks and had to get to a store to buy something new or his head felt like it would explode. No one would be looking for him now. His father Tuco was being a total arsehole. If Tuco had made more of an effort, Alain could have been home by now. Well, fuck him. Grabbing his puffer jacket, he headed for the door.

'Hey! Where you going?' Salvatore, the minder Taco had instructed to look after him, stuck his head out of the kitchen door. In his hand was a ham and cheese sandwich. Frowning, he took a large bite. Alain swore to himself; all the fat fuck ever did was eat.

'I'm going out.'

'But...' Salvatore struggled to chew and talk at the same time. 'Tuco–'

'Fuck Tuco,' Alain whined. 'I need some new games.'

Salvatore shoved the remainder of the sandwich into his gaping maw and wiped his hands on his Kings of Leon T-shirt. 'Tell me what you want. I'll go and get them.'

'I want to go out.'

'But the police...'

'There are no police,' Alain scoffed. 'Everyone thinks I have left the country.'

Salvatore looked doubtful. 'Hold on,' he said finally. 'I'll come with you.'

FIFTEEN

Feeling weary, Adrian Gasparino turned into the driveway of number 47 Hobart Street and walked down the side of the house. Placing his rucksack against the wall, he gently pressed down on the handle and pushed open the back door. Stepping into the kitchen, he gazed upon the pile of dirty plates in the sink and breathed in the familiar, stale cooking smells that always filled the tiny space. Closing his eyes he tried to feel something. Over the ticking of the clock on the wall came the sound of children laughing from the garden next door.

The door that led into the living room was ajar. From behind it he heard a noise – a grunt – followed by what sounded like a slap and an indistinct male voice. Gasparino stepped carefully to the door and pushed it open another couple of inches. His eyes moved to the large mirror hanging on the far wall, which gave him a view of the end of the L-shaped room. Biting his lip, he watched Justine, naked, on her hands and knees, her bump almost touching the carpet, move her legs apart for a man he had never seen before. Equally naked, the man slipped his engorged penis between her buttocks and thrust vigorously.

Justine fell forwards on to the carpet, passing wind noisily as she did so. 'Hey!' she complained over her shoulder. 'Not there! That's the wrong hole!'

Laughing, the man slapped her on the arse and pulled her back up into a kneeling position.

Gasparino was amazed by the size of her breasts. They were twice as large as he remembered them, banging either side of her belly, blue veins standing out against her off-white skin.

'Take it gently,' she whispered. 'Don't hurt me.'

Moving back inside her, the man grasped her by the hips and began grinding slowly against her rear. Gasparino waited for him to look up and see that he was being watched, but, concentrating hard on the matter in hand, he never did.

He noticed a large blue teddy bear sitting on the sofa, watching the engaged pair with an air of amused detachment.

Maybe it's a boy, thought Gasparino.

The man's thrusts got faster.

'Oh, fuck,' Justine groaned.

Stepping back into the kitchen, Gasparino went out of the back door. Picking up his bag, he moved quietly out of the drive and began walking back down the road in the direction he had come.

Roche sat at the first-floor window of an empty house on the other side of St Paul Street, sipping a cup of tea that she'd bought from a café round the corner. She hated surveillance work and would far rather have gone straight in and searched the place that Carlyle had been told Alain Costello was hiding out in. But the powers-that-be had decided they should wait. Two weeks earlier, the Met had mistakenly raided a wedding party in Bethnal Green, thinking it was a terrorist cell. There could be no more fuck-ups, for a while at least. Finishing her tea, she tossed the polystyrene cup into the corner of the room as two men came out of the target address. Both were wearing hoodies under their jackets, obscuring their faces.

The radio burst into life. *'Do we engage?'*

'Shit!' Roche grabbed the Vanguard binoculars at her feet. But the pair were on the street now, walking away from her. Then she saw the PSP console in the hand of the guy nearest to her. 'It's him,' she mumbled to herself.

'Do we engage?'

Ignoring the radio, Roche grabbed her Glock 26 and raced down the stairs. Out on the street she checked in both directions. Apart from the two hoodies and the two constables in an unmarked Range Rover twenty yards away, it was empty. Her targets were moving slowly down the far side of the street. In a couple of minutes, they would be on a busy main road and things would be far harder to control. Roche knew that she had to act now. Slipping between a couple of parked cars, she began jogging down the middle of the road, her gun at her side. They were less than fifteen yards in front of her now and she was closing quickly. Stepping on to the pavement, feeling her heart pounding in her chest, she raised the Glock.

'Stop! Police! I am armed and I have the authority to shoot.'

Flicking an imaginary piece of lint from the sleeve of her blouse, Sandy Carroll took another mouthful of Verdicchio and wondered if they should order another bottle. She was beginning to feel pleasantly light-headed but knew that it would take a couple more glasses before she was getting the full effect of the alcohol. Putting the glass back on the table, she picked listlessly at her *pollo pancetta*. She didn't normally eat this early and her appetite was lacking. The clock over the front door edged towards five fifteen. The Pizza Express just up from the Royal Opera House was already noisily full. Indeed, a queue of people waiting for a table was beginning to snake down the street; the usual collection of families, pre-theatre diners and tourists exhausted by a day spent trudging around

Covent Garden's crowded, tacky piazza.

Sandy watched the waiters and waitresses flit from table to table, trying to get the current occupants served and out of the door as quickly as possible in order to accommodate those hovering outside. It crossed her mind that there must be dozens, if not hundreds, of other restaurants within a five- or ten-minute walk of Bow Street. For that matter, there were probably quite a few other Pizza Express restaurants nearby as well. Why stand on the pavement waiting to get into this one? Sandy wouldn't be seen dead queuing to get into anywhere, never mind a pizza restaurant.

A waiter, a small, thin bearded bloke who looked Italian, or maybe Turkish, swooped on their table, picked up the bottle of wine and refilled her glass. Sandy gave him a curt nod, refusing to return his cheeky smile. She'd just completed a tough afternoon's shopping and wanted to get pissed without anyone hitting on or otherwise hassling her.

'How is your food?' the waiter asked in lightly accented English.

'It's fine,' Sandy mumbled, carefully avoiding any kind of eye-contact that might be misconstrued. Waiters were most definitely not her type. 'Thank you,' she added, almost as an afterthought.

'Excellent – enjoy!' Still smiling, the waiter placed the three-quarters empty bottle on the table and danced off. *Must make your mouth hurt, that job,* Sandy thought, *what with having to smile all the bloody time.*

Over the general hubbub of the restaurant, the oh-so-familiar sound of 'Parachute' by the nation's former sweetheart, Cheryl Cole, started bubbling up from under the table. With a squawk of delight, Sandy's dining companion, Kelly Kellaway, reached down and pulled her iPhone from her tote bag. Taking another mouthful of wine, Sandy watched as Kelly opened a text message and, cackling with glee, quickly tapped in a reply.

'Who was that?'

'Drink up,' Kelly ordered, signalling to the waiter for the bill. 'I'll get this. We're off.'

Sandy frowned. It wasn't like Kelly to pay the whole bill. 'Where are we going?'

Without saying anything, Kelly handed Sandy the iPhone. Then, taking her purse from the bag, she fished out two twenties and a ten and dropped them on the table with a flourish.

Sandy stared at the message on the screen. The texter's ID just said *Gavin*. The message read, *I'm at the Garden Hotel. Come on over.* She looked at her friend and asked, 'Who's Gavin?'

Kelly snorted with laughter. 'Are you kidding?' The waiter appeared with the bill, scooped up the cash and scuttled off to get some change. Dumping the last of the wine into her glass, Kelly drained it in one. 'Come on,' she said, getting to her feet, smoothing down the front of her Markus Lupfer camouflage knitted dress, a purchase from their most recent trip to Harvey Nichols the week before. 'Let's get going.'

'Is this an agency job?'

'No, it bloody isn't.' Kelly stuck her hands on her hips and pouted like a three year old before her face broke into a grin. 'It's top secret.' The waiter returned with the change on a little tray but Kelly just left it there. Pulling her bag over her shoulder, she began manoeuvring her way between the nearby tables, heading for the exit.

Sandy hesitated. She was tired. She wasn't in the mood. Today was supposed to be a day off. More to the point, she was wearing a fairly grungy pair of M&S knickers and a bra that didn't match. If she'd known what Kelly had in mind, she'd have worn her Agent Provocateur Cendrillon Playsuit – that always went down a treat with the punters.

'Come *on!*' Kelly shouted over her shoulder, already halfway to the door. 'He's waiting.'

With a sigh, Sandy hefted the bags of shopping piled around her feet. Getting up, she realized that not only was she not really dressed for the occasion, but she didn't have any condoms on her. That might limit her bedroom options somewhat. Terrified of catching something nasty, she didn't allow anyone to go bareback, not even a Premier League footballer. Not even Gavin bloody Swann.

'Stop! Police! I am armed and I have the authority to shoot.'

'*Merde!*' As Salvatore took off down the street like a scalded cat, Alain Costello turned to face the woman with the Glock. Recognizing her as the cop from St Pancras, he smiled insolently.

'Stop,' Roche repeated as she moved carefully towards him. 'Put your hands in the air!' She was little more than five yards away when an old woman pushing a shopping trolley started to cross the road. She did a double-take when she saw Roche's gun and let out a high-pitched scream. Laughing, Costello took his opportunity to turn and run.

After spending a minute or so flicking through Umar Sligo's file, Carlyle tossed it back onto Simpson's desk. While he was reading, the Commander's PA had speedily mopped up the spilled tea and removed the soaked letters, but he was still careful to avoid the remaining damp patch.

'What do you think?' Simpson asked. And seeing his expression: 'You could at least show a little enthusiasm,' she scolded. 'I think he'll be good.'

Carlyle shifted in his seat. 'We'll see.' With an Irish father and a Pakistani mother, Umar was living, breathing proof of the benefits of the multi-cultural society. Kassim Darwish Grammar School for Boys, South Manchester *(The true measure of a good education is to explore the limitations of your knowledge)* had been followed by a first-class degree from the University of Manchester in Politics and Criminology. After joining the Greater Manchester Police, he had been rapidly promoted, becoming one of the youngest sergeants on the force at the age of barely twenty-three.

'John,' she instructed him. 'Make an effort.'

'I will,' he protested. 'Of course I will.'

'I will be keeping an eye on the pair of you.'

'Fine,' said Carlyle, getting to his feet. 'Let's see how it goes.'

After many years of working together, Simpson understood Carlyle's idiosyncrasies better than anyone else on the Force. Giving him a quizzical look, she decided to quit while she thought she was ahead. 'Good,' she said primly. 'He'll be with you tomorrow.'

Roche sounded more than a little pissed. 'I can't believe we've lost Costello again,' she wailed.

Carlyle's heart sank. He didn't like these type of conversations and wished he'd let the call go to voicemail. Taking a deep breath, he tried to sound supportive. 'Under the circumstances, it doesn't sound like you could have done much differently. And now we know for sure that he's still in the country.'

'The bloody granny had a heart attack!'

'At least you didn't shoot her,' Carlyle laughed.

Roche mumbled something incomprehensible.

'Look,' Carlyle said firmly, 'get some sleep. I'll go back to my guy and see if he can give us another lead.'

'Okay,' she said, starting to sound tearful.

'Get some rest,' Carlyle repeated. 'We'll talk tomorrow.' Ending the call, he phoned William Wallace. The Yardie answered almost immediately.

'Mr Wallace?'

'Mr Carlyle!' Wallace too sounded somewhat inebriated. There was a party going on in the background. 'Hold on a sec.'

Carlyle waited while Wallace moved somewhere quieter.

'What can I do for you?'

'The address you gave me was good.'

'I told you,' Wallace said, sounding pleased.

'But the guy has done a runner.' Carlyle didn't go into details.

Wallace let out a low whistle. 'You mean you lost him *again?*'

Carlyle chose not to rise to the bait. 'I was

wondering if you might have any thoughts about where he might be now?'

'The guy he was staying with,' Wallace lowered his voice a notch, 'is called Salvatore Razzi. Nice enough bloke, but a bit of a slob. I happen to know that he also owns a place out west.' Wallace gave Carlyle an address in Notting Hill.

'Hold on, hold on. I need to write it down.' After some considerable fumbling, Carlyle found a sandwich receipt and a pen in his jacket pocket. 'Give me that again.'

Wallace repeated the address.

'Thanks, William.'

'No problem.'

Carlyle ended the call and dropped his phone into his pocket. Hopefully, it would be a case of third time lucky.

SIXTEEN

The Garden Hotel was located on St Martin's Lane, a five-minute walk from the restaurant, just to the north of Trafalgar Square. It was the kind of high-end Central London location that attracted A-listers and all the hangers-on and 'support-service' providers that, inevitably, came with them. The girls had hung out at the Garden and its famous Light Bar many times before; they were both known to the chief concierge, Alex Miles, who had a 'gentleman's agreement' with their agency.

As they walked in, Miles was not at the desk.

Sandy recognized one of his sidekicks, a thin, sour-faced woman named Jenny Thompson, who caught her eye, giving a slight nod of acknowledgement as the girls headed for the bank of three lifts at the back of the lobby.

The place was heaving and all of the lifts were busy, stopping at every floor as they slowly made their way down to ground level. 'Where are we going?' Sandy whispered as they waited.

Kelly didn't look up as she tapped away at the screen of her iPhone. 'Top floor, penthouse suite.'

Finally, a lift arrived. The doors pinged open and a procession of guests streamed out, all of them dressed up ready to hit the West End on a Saturday night. Getting into the lift, the girls were joined by an Arab man in his thirties, along with two women, covered from head to toe in black burkas.

'Not a great look,' Kelly giggled as the doors closed.

'They wear the sexiest lingerie under those things,' Sandy breathed, scowling at the man as he shamelessly ogled her chest.

The Arabs got out on the third floor and the girls rode the rest of the way to the top in silence. When the lift opened, they found themselves in a short corridor, with only one door. After taking a moment to compose herself, Kelly knocked loudly on the door and took a half-step backwards. Sticking back her shoulders, she looked her friend up and down. 'Just follow my lead,' she whispered. 'Let me do the talking.'

Sandy nodded meekly.

'Don't worry,' Kelly grinned. 'If past experience is anything to go by, this is only going to take ten minutes. Fifteen tops. Then we'll go and have a few drinks.'

At least they should have some decent vodka in the mini-bar, Sandy thought.

After a few moments, they heard the lock disengage and the door was jerked open. Giggling, they stepped inside.

Susie McCarthy gripped her mug so tightly it looked as though it might be crushed between her fingers. 'You should think about contacting your family.'

'Mm.' Adrian Gasparino looked past the earnest young social worker and out across the River Thames. Sitting in the canteen of New Belvedere House, a hostel for homeless ex-servicemen in Limehouse, East London, his mind wandered back to the image of Justine on her knees on the living-room carpet. Shaking the memory from his head, he smiled sadly. 'It's nice here. I was lucky to find it.'

'Yes, you were,' Susie agreed brightly.

How old are you? Gasparino wondered. *Older than me? What skills and experience do you have that you can use to help me with my problems?*

'The great thing about the New Belvedere,' Susie continued, dropping into what sounded like an oft-repeated spiel, 'is that it's a safe environment. We are only small compared to something like the Royal British Legion, but our aim is to become the most dynamic driver when it comes to repaying the debt of honour that we owe our troops.'

131

'Ah yes,' Gasparino nodded. Suddenly the room felt very stuffy. He had an overwhelming desire to step outside and feel the wind blast his face. 'Thanks for the tea,' he said, getting to his feet.

'Where are you going?' Susie asked as he slipped his rucksack over his shoulder.

'I just fancy a walk.'

She gestured at his bag with her mug. 'With all your stuff?'

Gasparino shrugged. 'I travel light.'

She looked at him doubtfully. 'Where will you go?'

'Not far. Maybe we could have another talk tomorrow.'

She shook her head. 'I have a day off tomorrow.'

'I see,' Gasparino smiled. 'Maybe later then.' He turned towards the door. 'Have a nice day off.'

'I will,' she said happily. 'Thank you.'

Helen handed Carlyle a cup of green tea and then began rummaging in her bag. 'There's something you should see,' she said, pulling out a copy of *The Times*.

'Yeah?' Sipping his tea, Carlyle waited patiently while she found the relevant page and folded the paper in half.

'Here.'

Scanning the article, he frowned. 'What makes parents pack their sons off to Eton?'

'No.' Retrieving the paper from her idiot husband, Helen pointed him to the story below the fold: *MY TEENAGER HELL*. Thrusting the paper back at him, she hissed: 'The bitch has written about Alice in her column.'

Carlyle quickly scanned the article. Helen had underlined a paragraph that said: *Jemima came for a sleepover last week. The girls just lock themselves in the bedroom and smoke dope all night. Somewhere round about two in the morning comes the not unfamiliar sound of retching from the bathroom.* He looked at the by-line. 'Who is Lucy Pulse?'

'It's Andrea bloody Blackman.' The blank look on Carlyle's face told her that he was none the wiser. 'Olivia's mum.'

'And "Jemima" is Alice?'

'Yes. The woman has used her in one of her tawdry little columns.'

'What does Alice think?' Carlyle asked.

'I think it's bloody hilarious,' said Alice, sticking her head round the kitchen door. 'Olivia's mortified, though. And she has to put up with this kind of stuff all the time.'

'Poor kid,' Carlyle clucked. 'Imagine having your life turned into a newspaper column. That must be tough.'

'But did you go over there to smoke dope and be sick?' Helen asked.

Alice stepped into the kitchen. Not for the first time, she had borrowed his Clash T-shirt. 'Nah. We only smoked a little. No one puked up. Olivia's mum has to exaggerate things to make her stories more interesting.'

'What will they say at school?'

'For God's sake, Mum,' Alice pouted, 'no one pays any attention to that rubbish.' She gave her dad a shameless wink. 'Anyway, my grades have been really good recently.'

'Yes,' Helen admitted, 'but–'

Alice cut her off. 'Even the Headmaster said "well done" the other day.'

'Long may it continue,' said Carlyle with feeling. A couple of years earlier, Carlyle and Helen had been summoned to Dr Terence Myers's office after Alice had been suspended for possession of cannabis. At the time, Carlyle had been both surprised and relieved that his daughter had only got a suspension. All the same, he was in no hurry to repeat the experience.

'*And,*' Alice squealed, 'I'm giving up the drugs. It's all getting a bit boring.'

Giving them up? Carlyle thought suspiciously. 'I hadn't even started them at your age,' he grumbled.

'It's a different world today, Dad,' Alice told him. 'Kids grow up quicker. I'm probably already as mature as you were when you were nineteen, or even twenty.'

Fucking hell, thought Carlyle, *that's a result. Let's just hope she doesn't change her mind again next week.*

'I'd say you're already more mature than he was when he was thirty,' Helen grinned, giving Carlyle a dig in the ribs, 'at least.'

'As if.' He gave them both a hurt look.

Alice did a little jig of delight. 'Face facts, old man.'

'Old man?' Carlyle echoed. 'In that case, maybe you can let me have my T-shirt back.'

'I don't know about that,' Alice said, beating a hasty retreat towards the safety of her bedroom.

'Thank you, *Jemima,*' he shouted after her. 'Make sure it's washed and ironed – inside out – when you're finished with it.'

'Leave the kid alone,' Helen admonished him. 'You don't need to iron a T-shirt.'

'But it is The Clash,' Carlyle reminded her. 'You have to show some respect.'

Helen, always more of a Paul Weller devotee, was less than convinced. 'Yeah, right.'

'Seriously. That T-shirt is vintage.'

'Just like you,' Helen couldn't resist saying.

'It cost me a tenner from Camden market thirty years ago.'

'And the rest.'

'Anyway. It's irreplaceable. It needs to be properly looked after.'

'It's just a bloody T-shirt. You can probably get a new one on the internet.' With that, Helen padded off into the living room. After adding some more hot water to his tea, Carlyle followed her. Lowering himself onto the sofa, he rested his head on her shoulder and lifted his feet on to the coffee table.

On the TV was a story about the arrest of a dozen men on suspicion of the commission, preparation or instigation of an act of terrorism in the UK. A serious-looking blonde reporter Carlyle didn't recognize stood in front of a fluttering police tape on a suburban South London street and began speaking live to camera: 'Searches at several London properties began after the arrests, with detectives and forensics experts looking for any scientific evidence of materials that could be used to make explosives. The counter-terrorism operation targeting some of those arrested had been under way for some time, and is described as "significant". At least some of those arrested are believed to have been under surveillance.'

135

'That doesn't tell you much, does it?' Carlyle mused.

A familiar face appeared next to the blonde. Metropolitan Police Assistant Commissioner Quentin Collymore was the country's leading anti-terrorism officer. He began explaining how the raids were launched to take action in order to protect the public. 'This,' he said carefully, 'is a large-scale, pre-planned and intelligence-led operation involving several forces. The operation is in its early stages, so we are unable to go into detail at this time about the suspected offences. We know we face a real and serious threat from terrorism and I would like to thank the police and security service for working to keep our country safe.'

'Sounds like bollocks to me,' Helen scoffed. Somewhat more of a liberal than her husband, she had always been rather bolshie when it came to what she considered the 'political' areas of Carlyle's work.

'They have clearly got something,' Carlyle said gently, not wanting to have the same conversation for the millionth time.

'But we'll never know, will we?' she countered.

'We might, we might not,' Carlyle said. 'That's just the way it is. These guys could be doing a great job, they could be doing a shit job – you're right, we'll never know. But you're not going to put it to the test and then find some nutters from Stoke, or Bradford or Blackburn or wherever, are able to waltz down here and blow us to smithereens.'

'You're beginning to sound like Harry Ripley,' Helen teased.

'We should build a big wall round the M25 to

136

keep all these fucking people out,' Carlyle opined, warming to his theme.

'You could have a word with your mate Christian Holyrod,' his wife smirked. 'They could deport you back to Scotland while they're at it.'

'Me?' Carlyle folded his arms in mock indignation. 'I'm as much of a Londoner as you are.' They both knew that wasn't true. Helen's family had been Londoners, born and bred. Carlyle's parents had only arrived from Glasgow in the 1950s, heading south as de-industrialization and long-term decline kicked in at home.

Helen kissed him on the head. 'Speaking of Harry,' she said, changing the subject, 'I saw him a couple of days ago. He's beginning to look really quite frail.'

Carlyle scratched his armpit. 'That's hardly surprising, given his age.'

'I just hope that he can stay at home. I said I'd see about trying to get the council to give him more help.'

'Good luck with that,' Carlyle snorted. 'With the budget cuts, he'll be lucky to keep what he's got.'

SEVENTEEN

Kicking off her shoes, Sandy dropped her bags on a chair in the corner. Ignoring Gavin Swann lying on the bed, scratching his balls, a half-empty bottle of beer in his free hand, she went straight to the mini-bar and pulled out a couple of miniatures of vodka. She waved them at Kelly, who shook her head. 'Maybe after.'

'Suit yourself,' Sandy mumbled. Unscrewing both caps, she chugged them down, one after the other. In front of her, Sky Sports News was playing on the TV with the sound down. On the rolling ticker at the bottom of the screen, the news flashed up that star striker Gavin Swann was expected to be out of the game for up to a month with a groin strain. She tried to remember the name of the team he played for but the vodka had left her mind a complete blank. Football was so boring. It was unbelievable that blokes got so worked up about it; the whole thing was a joke. At the thought of it, she let out a quiet laugh.

Kelly gave her a quizzical look. 'What's so funny?'

'Oh, nothing,' Sandy replied. Beginning to feel happily pissed, she watched Kelly crawl onto the bed. Looking like a scared kid, Swann sat up, spilling beer over his crotch in the process.

'Mm.' Kelly grinned. Pulling back her hair, porn-star style, she dropped her head towards his groin and began licking it off. 'I love Beck's...'

'*What?*' Alain Costello said irritably. How could he concentrate on *Dead Space 4* when Tuco wouldn't shut the fuck up?

'Do you want to spend the next twenty years in prison?' Tuco repeated in French. 'Are you deliberately trying to get arrested?'

Alain glanced at the handset sitting next to him and shook his head.

'Well?' the old man demanded, his voice sounding even more pained over the speakerphone.

'Je vais me faire arrêter si tu me laisses ici dans cette bordelle.'

'Tu aurais dû être plus prudent.' Sitting in the elegant Rococo calm of his fifth-floor duplex apartment on the Rue Frédéric Bastiat near the Champs Elysées Tuco angrily paused the DVD he was watching on his state of the art equipment. The frozen screen captured Forest Whitaker in blank close-up. Approaching the end of *Ghost Dog: The Way of the Samurai,* the eponymous assassin was about to meet his inevitable fate. It was a film Tuco had seen dozens of times, but he still resented having to interrupt it in order to lecture his infuriating son. 'The way of the Samurai,' Tuco whispered to himself, 'is found in death.'

'Salvatore has disappeared,' whined Alain. 'Where is your man?'

The fucking boy wouldn't even let him mumble in peace. 'What?'

'Your new business associate here in London – why has he not come to help me?'

Because he's no fool, Tuco thought. *He doesn't want a moron like you dragging him down.* 'He said he would try to help.'

'Why hasn't he turned up, then, eh?'

'These things take time.'

'Have you told him about what happened to your last business partner here?'

'Tais toi!' Tuco exploded. 'Now is not the time. Just stay where you are and I will let you know when we have a plan to get you back.'

All he got in response was a series of bleeps from Alain's computer console. Dropping the phone, he restarted the movie. 'Meditation on inevitable death should be performed daily,' he said grimly. 'Every day without fail, the Samurai should consider himself as dead. *This* is the way of the Samurai.'

Fully erect now, Swann caught Sandy's eye and blushed violently. Sandy was surprised by how – well, troll-like – he looked. Lots of body hair but already going bald on top; no real muscle definition, which surprised her, given that the guy was supposed to be, like, a major athlete. And a flat, featureless face that only a mother – or a hooker – could love. Yet this was a guy earning two hundred grand *a week*, two hundred and fifty, according to some papers. If that didn't make you wet, well, there was no two ways about it, you were in the wrong game.

'The Candypants girls,' he mumbled.

Kelly let out a harsh laugh. 'Hardly. Those slags are not in our league.' Sitting back on her haunches, she pulled her dress over her head. Surprised to see that she was naked underneath, Sandy had another mini panic-attack about the quality of her underwear. Swann's penis quivered in anticipation, pre-cum glistening on the tip.

'We're the *fuck-your-brains-out* girls.' Kelly pulled her bag onto the bed. Unzipping a side pocket, she took out a Trojan Magnum, pulling open the foil wrapper with her teeth. Signalling for Sandy to join her, she carefully unrolled the condom over Swann's penis. 'I'd give you some more oral,' she grinned, 'but I don't think you would be able to handle it.'

Swann grunted something that might have been agreement. Tossing the empty vodka miniatures in the direction of the waste bin, Sandy slipped onto the bed next to Kelly, who had lowered herself onto Swann and was moving her pelvis slowly in an anti-clockwise direction. Immediately, she felt Swann's stubby fingers between her legs and Kelly's tongue in her ear. She shrugged off the tongue but let the hand stay where it was.

'So,' Kelly laughed sexily, tickling Swann's balls with her free hand, 'have you ever had a threesome before?'

Sandy wouldn't have thought that it was possible but Swann went even redder. His head looked like it had just been boiled in a pot. All he needed was an apple in his mouth and he could have been served on a platter at a banquet. 'Er, no.'

Pulling off the Trojan, Gavin Swann knotted it and chucked it on to the carpet. According to the alarm clock on the table by the bed, he had held out for just over twelve minutes before collapsing, spent, on the bed. The whole thing had lasted about eleven minutes and twenty seconds longer than Sandy would have imagined. Kelly had called it just right.

Reaching across the bed, Swann picked up the phone next to the radio alarm and called down to the concierge's desk.

'Nick? Hi, it's ... yeah, yeah,' he looked over at the girls and blushed again slightly, 'they were good, yeah. Look, Nick, can you send one of your boys out to get me some fags? Twenty Marlboro, yeah. Great. I'll pay 'em when they bring them

141

up. Thanks.' Ending the call, Swann got up from the bed and disappeared into the bathroom. For several minutes the girls were treated to the sound of the young man's prolonged bowel movement.

'Oh my God!' Sandy whispered, as another satisfied grunt bounced off the bathroom tiles.

Kelly raised her eyes to the ceiling. 'Just be grateful he actually uses a toilet. One girl was telling me about a guy who wanted to do a shit on her chest.'

'No!' Sandy covered her mouth in shock horror. Way back, in the far recesses of her brain, there was the slightest realization that she should be feeling disgusted, rather than just titillated.

'Yes,' said Kelly, shimmying into her knickers, 'and he wouldn't even pay for it.'

They heard the sound of the toilet flushing, followed immediately by a knock on the door.

'Gavin,' Kelly shouted. 'Your cigs are here!'

Emerging from the bathroom, Swann took a bathrobe from the closet and pulled it on before opening the door. Accepting the Marlboro from the bellboy, he stepped back into the vestibule, picked up a small, navy-coloured Nike holdall that was sitting on the floor, next to a pair of trainers. Dropping the bag on the table, he unzipped a side pocket and pulled out a fistful of fifty-pound notes. Sandy watched as he counted out four and stepped back to the door.

'You gave that guy two hundred quid for a packet of cigarettes?' she asked as he reappeared.

Swann looked at her blankly, as if he was struggling to remember who she was. Ignoring the question, he ripped the cellophane off the packet and stuck a cigarette between his teeth. 'Got a light?'

Kelly dug into her bag, pulled out a packet of matches and passed them to him.

'Ta.' Lighting the smoke, Swann sucked it down greedily. Exhaling, he went over to the mini-bar and removed another bottle of beer. Flicking off the top with a bottle-opener, he chugged down half of the beer before letting out a satisfied burp. 'Good times.'

Kelly was starting to get pissed off. 'I need a drink.'

Swann gestured at the mini-bar. 'Help yourself.'

Stepping past him, Kelly knelt down and looked inside. After a moment, she scowled at Sandy. 'You drank all the sodding vodka.'

Collecting up her bags, ready to go, Sandy shrugged.

'Get a drink in the bar downstairs,' Swann said. Reaching back into the holdall, he counted out another wad of fifties and handed them to Kelly.

'Ta,' she said, smiling.

Swann looked from one girl to the other. 'And remember to keep your mouths shut.'

Kelly placed a hand on his arm. 'Don't worry, sweetie,' she said. 'We'd never talk to the newspapers, would we, Sandy?'

Wondering just how much a newspaper would pay for her story, Sandy hastily agreed.

'You'd better fucking not,' Swann hissed. 'My missus would kill me.'

You should have thought about that earlier, Sandy thought. She was trying to remember the name of the guy who sold all the kiss-and-tell stories to the tabloids... Frank – Frank Something? The name wouldn't come. No matter, Kelly would know. She probably had the number in her mobile already.

'Your wife,' Kelly enquired sweetly, 'has she had the baby yet?'

Swann looked at the floor. 'Next month,' he mumbled. 'On the ninth.'

'Is that the due date?' Sandy asked.

'Suppose so,' Swann yawned. 'That's when she's booked in for the C-section.'

'Oh.' Feeling woozy, Sandy tried to smile at Swann as she headed towards the door. His robe had fallen open and she noticed that his penis had shrunk to the point where it was almost invisible. 'Don't worry,' she cooed, nodding at Kelly, 'only total slappers go to the papers. We're not like that.'

Downstairs, Sandy began to feel better. Sitting in the Light Bar, she looked around, scanning the room carefully for a sign of any celebrities. Disappointed not to see any familiar faces, she sucked a mouthful of her Good Time Girl cocktail – Finlandia mango vodka blended with fresh mango and passion-fruit purées, passion-fruit syrup, and organic vanilla ice cream, served straight up.

'A bit quiet in here, isn't it?' she said.

Kelly glanced towards the bar and shrugged. 'It's still early.' She took a hit of her Cinnamon Mule – cinnamon infused with ten-cane rum, shaken with limes and fresh ginger and topped with ginger beer – and leaned towards her friend, lowering her voice slightly. 'And we've just shagged Gavin Swann.'

You've just shagged him, Sandy thought tartly. *I*

144

just gave him a bit of hand relief and let him stick his fingers up my arsehole. 'How much did he give you?'

Kelly took another mouthful of her drink. 'A grand.'

'Nice.'

Kelly frowned. 'It won't even pay off my credit-card bill. And I owe my mum another five hundred for a phone bill she paid for me.'

Sandy wondered what had happened to her share but, knowing that it wasn't worth the hassle to argue, she kept her mouth shut.

'I'm sick of being bloody skint,' Kelly moaned, plonking her glass down on the table so hard that Sandy was worried it might break.

Sandy gestured back towards the hotel lobby. 'Maybe you could go back up and do him again.'

'Don't be stupid,' Kelly laughed, 'it'll take him hours to be able to get it up again.'

'He could take something.'

'I don't think so. Anyway, he'll probably be asleep by now.'

Taking another sip of her cocktail, Sandy eyed her friend carefully. 'Would you ever, like – you know – go to the papers?'

'Nah. Gavin would go mad. His wife would kill him. You heard him, she's something like eight-and-a-half months' pregnant.'

'She forgave him last time,' Sandy pointed out. 'When he was in the papers for shagging the secretary of his Singaporean fan club on a pre-season tour. And the time before that.'

'I know,' Kelly said, 'but this time, with a kid on the way, you'd have thought...'

'But you deserve something, don't you?' said

145

Sandy, quickly changing tack.

'I suppose.'

'The papers deal with this kind of thing all the time. They would do it tastefully. And they'd pay. There's that guy who sells all the stories.'

'Frank Maxwell,' Kelly said brightly. 'I met him once. Seemed like a decent guy.'

'We could give him a call.'

'Maybe,' said Kelly thoughtfully, as if the idea had never before crossed her mind. She gestured at a passing waiter, signalling for him to bring them a couple more cocktails. 'Just to get his input.'

'Makes sense,' Sandy smiled, 'to see what he thinks.'

EIGHTEEN

'What do you think of Alice's plan to give up dope?'

Carlyle scratched his chin. 'You can only hope.'

'I was thinking I might take her to Liberia.'

For a moment, Carlyle was thrown by the change of subject. 'What?'

'I need to go out there in a couple of months and thought it might be good for Alice to come along.' Helen helped run a medical aid charity called Avalon. Set up by three British doctors back in the 1980s, it now worked in more than twenty countries around the world.

Images of child soldiers with AK47s and

machetes flitted through Carlyle's brain. 'Is it safe?'

Helen gave an exasperated grunt. 'Of course it's safe. Liberia is one of Africa's good news stories.'

All things are relative, he thought, waiting for the lecture to begin.

'The numbers are improving, but it is still shocking. The maternal mortality rate is still among the highest in the world at 994 deaths per 100,000 births. In Britain it is twelve. The death rate for under-fives over there is fourteen per cent. In Britain it is nought point six per cent.'

Statistics, statistics, bloody statistics. 'But it's safe?' he repeated.

'I wouldn't take her if it wasn't.'

'Have you spoken to her about it?'

'Yeah. She seems quite up for it. Not least because it would mean a week out of school.'

'How much is it going to cost?'

'Not much. Just her flight, basically. Mine will be covered by work.' She gave him a sly grin. 'You can come too if you want.'

'Mm, got to run.' He gave her a kiss on the forehead, already moving for the door. 'I'll have a think about it.'

'Welcome to London.'

Umar Sligo smiled but said nothing.

It was their first day together and the inspector was trying not to pre-judge his new colleague. The initial signs, however, were not promising. The new boy appeared young, good-looking and enthusiastic; just looking at him made Carlyle feel weary to his bones.

They were standing in the empty front room of a Georgian terraced house on Great Percy Street, just down from Kings Cross. On the bare wooden floorboards lay a machete and an empty can of Carlsberg lager. Under their feet, technicians were removing 'skunk' cannabis plants estimated to be worth more than a million pounds that had been found growing in the basement.

'What I don't understand,' said Umar, 'is how a Scotland Yard Deputy Assistant Commissioner can afford to have a place like this as an investment property?'

Carlyle thrust his hands in his pockets. 'He's got a rich wife apparently.'

'Nice.'

'He's completely straight. Been on the job more than thirty years. Started off as a beat constable in Southwark. They live somewhere in Surrey now. The wife rented the place out through an online letting agent to a British man who provided proof of identity and bank details. The neighbours had complained about the noise, on and off, but the clincher was the £50,000 electricity bill.'

'I bet he feels like a bit of a berk,' Umar laughed.

'The Deputy Assistant Commissioner?' Carlyle asked. 'Yeah, well, he should, shouldn't he?'

'Mm.'

'It's tough at the top,' the inspector mused. 'So they tell me.'

'It's not that uncommon, though. Police in England and Wales uncover about twenty cannabis factories every day, and last year officers and customs seized a million-and-a-half plants worth about two hundred million pounds.'

Carlyle gave his new sidekick a funny look. 'Did you swallow a copy of the *Economist* or something?'

'No,' Umar said defensively. 'It's just one of those things you pick up.'

A uniform appeared from the hallway. 'Inspector?'

Carlyle recognized the constable. 'Lea!' he grinned. 'Good to see you back on duty. How's the head wound?'

PC Lea smiled sheepishly and looked at the floor. 'Fine, thank you. They took the stitches out last week.'

'What happened?' Umar asked.

Lea started blushing violently. 'There are some reporters outside,' he said hastily, ignoring the question. 'They're looking for a quote.'

Carlyle glanced at Umar. 'Tell them we're all looking forward to getting high tonight.'

A confused look spread across the young constable's face. 'Inspector?'

Carlyle held up a hand. 'Only joking. Only joking. Tell them: *The police were called to a report of a disturbance in a property on Great Percy Street. The property was found to house a cannabis factory. There have been no immediate arrests, and enquiries continue.* That's more than enough to be going on with.'

'Okay,' said Lea, moving off.

Gesturing to his sergeant that it was time to leave, Carlyle followed him to the door. 'Speak to the neighbours,' he said brusquely. 'I'm going back to the station.'

On the wall was a sheet of A4 paper, headed, in outsized, bold type, *Frank Maxwell's Guide to Becoming Famous*. Sitting in front of the great man's desk, Sandy Carroll read down the list, butterflies dancing in her stomach:

1. Appear on a reality series
2. Enter a talent show
3. Be abysmal on a talent show
4. Gain fame by association
5. Date a celebrity
6. Flaunt your body
7. Date a member of the Royal Family
8. Make a home sex video
9. Be a success on YouTube
10. Be in the right place at the right time

Underneath the poster was a sideboard cluttered with photographs: Frank Maxwell with Bruce Forsyth, Frank with Simon Cowell, Frank with Victoria Beckham, Frank with some black guy whom Sandy didn't recognize.

Kelly elbowed her in the ribs. 'He's here,' she whispered.

Frank Maxwell breezed into the room, steaming mug of tea in hand, PA in tow. He saw Sandy looking at the photos and smiled. 'That's the PM,' he said pointing at the black guy, before dropping into the oversized chair behind his desk. 'Edgar Carlton. Nice guy.'

'PM?' Sandy frowned.

'Yes,' said Frank, placing his mug onto a copy of the *Sun* lying on the desk. 'The Prime Minister.'

Kelly elbowed her again.

'Oh,' said Sandy, embarrassed. 'I've heard of him, I think.'

Frank exchanged a glance with the PA, a camp-looking guy in his twenties in a grubby blue T-shirt and torn jeans, who stood at the corner of the desk, pen and notepad in hand, ready to take notes. 'So,' Maxwell said, leaning across the table, clasping his hands together, his dull green eyes fixing them with a careful stare, 'what can I do for you two ladies?' He was a short man with well-barbered silver hair and a serious expression. He looked trim, in good shape for his age which, Sandy guessed, had to be somewhere in his early-to-mid sixties.

Sandy opened her mouth but nothing came out.

'Well,' Kelly piped up, launching into an explanation of their encounter with Gavin Swann.

A massive grin broke out on the PA's face and he began scribbling furiously.

After a few moments, Frank held up a hand. 'I get the picture,' he said. 'Sorry, but I don't have much time this morning.' He looked from one girl to another. 'You know that bloke who was accused of hiring a hitman to kill his wife on their honeymoon in Thailand?'

'Yes,' the girls lied in unison.

'I've got to take him to do some media interviews in...' he lifted his left wrist in front of his nose and peered at his steel Rolex Oyster Perpetual Submariner, 'about forty-five minutes.' He shook his head. 'Terrible situation. Truly terrible. To lose your wife like that ... and then be accused of such a vile crime.'

The girls looked at him blankly.

151

Sitting back in his chair, Frank raised his arms to the heavens. 'He's totally innocent, of course. And the good news is that we're winning in the court of public opinion. Anyway, you want to do a kiss and tell – am I right?'

The girls nodded.

'Fine.' Frank gestured towards the PA. 'Brian here will sort out all the details. When is your next liaison?'

'There isn't–' Sandy started.

'Next week,' Kelly cut her off.

Frank nodded thoughtfully. 'Good. Good. That gives us time to get everything in place.'

Kelly squirmed in her seat with excitement. 'How much will we get?'

Frank smiled. 'That depends. We need pictures, video, text messages ... then I can make the calls to the newspaper editors. We'll have another meeting next week.' The phone on his desk started ringing. Waving goodbye to his newest clients, he picked it up on the second ring.

'*Darling...*'

Getting to their feet, the girls shuffled silently to the door.

'What the fuck are you doing here?'

'Nice to see you too, Inspector,' Abigail Slater smiled. She introduced the man sitting next to her in the second-floor meeting room of Charing Cross police station. 'This is Clive Martin, my client.'

The inspector looked the cheery-looking pensioner up and down. The man was somewhere between his late sixties and early seventies, and his trademark silver mullet shone under the strip-lighting. Martin was a local celebrity if ever there was one; Carlyle knew exactly who he was but chose to say nothing.

'Mr Martin,' Slater explained patiently, 'is the owner of Everton's Gentleman's Club, along with various other ... entertainment venues in and around Central London.' Sitting next to her client, the lawyer was an imperious figure. At over six foot tall, with curves in all the right places, Slater looked as if she would be perfectly at home in one of Martin's clubs. Even dressed ultra-conservatively, in a navy business suit with a pink blouse, buttoned all the way to the neck, she exuded an aggressive sexuality that made Carlyle feel uncomfortable.

'We are here to make a formal complaint about your illegal raid on Everton's.'

'Ah,' Carlyle said. 'So the Catholic Legal Network is representing smut kings now, is it?' he asked, making a reference to their last professional meeting, when Slater had represented a paedophile priest by the name of Father Francis McGowan. Justice – in Carlyle's book, at least – had finally been done when McGowan had taken a leap off a church roof, but not before Slater and the CLN had tried to destroy the inspector's career.

'This has nothing to do with the CLN,' Slater said tartly.

Martin gazed at Carlyle, his eyes sparkling with mischief. 'Are you a prude, Inspector?'

Maybe I'll just book the pair of them for wasting police time, Carlyle thought.

153

'These days, we're all in the sex industry,' Martin opined. 'Everyone who sells clothes, music, movies, whatever – we are all sex people, like it or not.'

'Anyway,' said Slater, putting a hand on her client's shoulder, 'the point of this meeting is to make a formal complaint and to notify you that we will be looking to recover damages for loss of earnings.'

'You've got to be kidding,' Carlyle snorted. 'One of my officers was assaulted.'

'Whose fault was that?' Martin chirruped.

Cursing himself for having had the stupidity to ever walk into the room, Carlyle took a deep breath. 'Look,' he said, wagging an angry finger at Slater, 'if you want to go and moan to someone about the alleged infringement of your client's "rights", go and complain to your boyfriend. This was an initiative from the Mayor's office. Maybe after your next fuck, you can get him to talk you through it.'

Sitting up in her chair, a look of grim fury settled on Slater's face.

Carlyle then got to his feet. 'If you want to make a complaint, the desk sergeant will help you fill out a form.' He looked down at Martin. 'I presume you are a pragmatic businessman.'

'Of course,' Martin said smoothly.

'Good,' said Carlyle. 'In that case, do not waste my time again. Or I might just make it my business to come and visit all of your establishments on a regular basis.' Shoving his chair out of the way, he stormed out of the room and headed back upstairs.

NINETEEN

It was already standing room only in the tiny first-floor bar of the Chandos pub, just north of Trafalgar Square. David Guetta's 'Who's That Chick?' was blasting out of a couple of tiny speakers hanging from the ceiling while an Arsenal game played mutely on a TV screen on the far wall. Carlyle felt a trickle of sweat run down his back as he watched a middle-aged man in a pinstripe suit glare angrily at Umar as the young sergeant brushed past him, carelessly knocking a quarter of an inch of London Pride from the pint.

'Sorry, mate,' Umar said breezily, annoying the commuter even more. Taking a sip from his glass of Jameson's whiskey, Carlyle stepped over and shrugged apologetically.

'Sorry, but this is a private event.'

The man was about to protest when an enormous cheer went up. Turning to greet the new arrival, Carlyle joined in the applause as PC Lea appeared at the top of the stairs. Embarrassed, the constable did a small bow, soaking up the cheers of the twenty or so colleagues who were all now waving Earth Angel vibrators above their heads.

Carlyle watched with a certain sympathy as the commuter beat a hasty retreat downstairs. Then he turned to Umar and grinned. 'Where the bloody hell did all those come from?'

'There was a sale at the Ann Summers on

Oxford Street,' Umar explained. He slipped his arm round the waist of a pretty female constable called Wendy Saunders, who giggled appreciatively. 'But wait till you see the best bit.'

A much louder roar went up as a green-haired Asian girl in a WPC's uniform now appeared at the top of the stairs. The girl looked vaguely familiar but it took a moment for the inspector to place her.

Taking one of the Earth Angels from an officer in the crowd, the stripper licked the business end of it with gusto before rolling it across Lea's crotch.

Oh shit, thought Carlyle nervously.

'It's the entertainment,' Umar shouted in his ear. 'We hired her from Everton's.'

Not wishing to have to explain *this* when he got home, Carlyle quickly drained the last of his whiskey. 'I'll see you tomorrow,' he said hastily, as he began pushing his way towards the exit.

'What?' Umar frowned, but the inspector was already on his way. By the time he passed her, the girl had already shed her uniform and was down to an emerald green bra and G-string. Halfway down the stairs, another roar went up, suggesting that the underwear had now gone as well. Feeling hot and bothered, Carlyle fled into the night.

Adrian Gasparino looked at the blank screen on his MP3 player and sighed. How was he going to get the damn thing recharged? The music helped him get to sleep. Without it, he was in for a long night. Stuffing the machine into his coat pocket, Gasparino took a swig from his 700 ml bottle of

Tesco Value Gin, feeling it slip all the way down his throat and into his empty stomach. Keeping the bottle close to his lips, he let out a small sigh as he lay back, lifting his hips off the ground and pulling his sleeping bag up around his waist. This doorway would be his bed for the night and he was glad to have found it. Out of the persistent, niggling rain, it was relatively dry. No one had pissed in it recently, which was another plus. But the clincher was the vent in the corner supplying a welcome stream of warm air from the building inside.

All in all, it could only be described as a desirable spot in a chi-chi Central London location. Certainly, it was the best place he had found on his travels so far. It hadn't taken Gasparino long to realize that sleeping rough in the infantry was not the same as rough sleeping on the streets. This would be his third night on the street since leaving the hostel. On the first, he had sneaked into a car park on Shelton Street, near Covent Garden tube station. But he had been discovered sleeping underneath a Range Rover by a parking attendant, who'd kicked him out into the night at 4 a.m. The second night had been worse. Trying to claim a spot behind St Giles-in-the-Fields parish church, he had been attacked by a couple of junkies who had chased him off.

After days and nights of aimlessly trudging the streets, Gasparino felt weary to his very marrow. All he wanted was to be left alone and get something approximating a good night's sleep. In the morning, he would head down to the toilets at Charing Cross railway station and have a wash and a shave. Maybe then he could come up with some kind of idea about what he should be doing.

Gasparino looked vacantly at the bottle. It was four-fifths empty and his head was already swimming. 'No point in leaving the rest,' he mumbled to himself, tipping his head back and pouring the last of the gin down his neck.

Wiping his mouth with the back of his sleeve, he screwed the cap back onto the empty bottle, placing it in the side pocket of his rucksack, which was stuck behind his head as a pillow. Breathing through his mouth, Gasparino stared vacantly down the street. Despite the late hour, there were still plenty of people around, drunks and other revellers in no hurry to leave Central London and head back home to the suburbs. On the far side of the street, he watched a young woman, blind drunk, support herself against the back of a parked car. With her free hand, she hitched up her red skirt and pulled down her knickers, before squatting and aiming a stream of piss towards the tarmac. The pool of steaming urine made it a couple of inches away from the girl before the camber of the road sent it back towards her outsized platform shoes.

Behind her, a girlfriend leaned against another parked car, laughing drunkenly. 'You're getting it on yourself!'

'Piss off!' the squatting woman grunted as she did a little jig, trying to avoid stepping in her own wee.

Shifting in his sleeping bag, Gasparino caught the eye of the standing woman. She was wearing a thin, sleeveless dress that ended about half-an-inch below her crotch. A small bag hung from her left shoulder. She had no jacket and her legs were bare. The regulation over-sized shoes were strapped to her feet. Intoxicated as he was, Gasparino imagined he could see the goose bumps on her arms, even from fifteen feet away.

Glassy-eyed, the shivering girl stared right through him, as if he was invisible 'C'mon, Jen,' she shouted, 'let's get going.'

'Hold on!' the woman shrieked. 'I'm almost done.' Finally, she levered herself back into something approximating a standing position, pulling up her pants as she did so. Stepping over the lake she had just created, she wobbled towards her friend, who reached out with a supporting arm. 'Will we make the train?'

'Dunno.'

Gasparino watched the two of them stagger off down the road. *You don't know how lucky you are,* he thought groggily, *having somewhere to go, a bed to sleep in.* As they disappeared round a corner, he closed his eyes, knowing that, for him, sleep was unlikely to come.

After more than twenty years in the Duke of Lancaster's Regiment, serving in Saudi Arabia, Northern Ireland, Germany, Bosnia, Iraq and Afghanistan, it had taken barely a couple of weeks for his marriage to collapse and his life to unravel. Trying to ignore the pain in his leg, Adrian Gasparino picked up a grubby copy of a freesheet that had been discarded in the doorway. He checked the date on the front page. Maybe it was today; maybe it was yesterday. Thinking about it for a moment, he realized that, either way, his baby's due date was only a couple of days away.

If it actually was *his* baby.

'Hey! Mister!'

Gasparino looked up but said nothing.

'Got any money?' A tall skinny boy, wearing jeans and a red hoodie with the legend *ANIMAL* on the front, stepped towards him. He had a blank, acne-scarred face, with no obvious signs of intelligence behind his dead, dark eyes; the type of kid he'd last seen cowering in a compound in Helmand. Hovering behind him, Gasparino counted four others, all dressed in similar fashion, a posse of evil urchins.

'Gimme your cash,' the boy repeated, his scrunched-up mockney accent harsh and unforgiving.

Gasparino's hand reflexively slipped inside his sleeping bag. In his trouser pocket he had twenty-three pounds and seventy-six pence. Twice, earlier in the day, he had counted it, each time coming up with the same number. He had no idea how long he would have to make it last.

The boy took a swing at the end of Gasparino's sleeping bag with the toe of his Nike trainers. 'Are you stupid?'

The sound of bovine laughter came from the boy's mates.

'I don't have anything,' Gasparino protested. He tried to struggle out of his sleeping bag but a kick in the stomach sent him back down.

'Don't take the fucking piss,' the youth shouted. 'Give us your fucking booze money.'

Gasparino felt a spasm of anger in his chest. Why couldn't people just leave him alone? 'Fuck off, you little bastard!' he hissed. Pulling his arms out of the bag, he grabbed the kid's ankle and pulled his attacker towards him.

Unable to keep his balance, the boy fell on top of the ex-soldier, arms flailing. Blood pumping, Gasparino tried to get his hands round the kid's neck before he could escape. The urge to do some serious damage to the little bastard was overwhelming. He got one hand over his Adam's apple and squeezed. The kid let out a satisfying gurgling noise as his eyes rolled back in his head.

'You little shits!' Gasparino shouted, squeezing harder.

'You cheeky cunt!' someone shouted. Then they were all upon him, kicking, screaming and biting. He grabbed hold of an ear but couldn't get a grip. Then a face appeared in front of him and for a moment he thought it was Justine. Confusion spread through his brain as someone ripped his hand from the kid's throat, snapping a finger in two in the process.

'Bastard!' Again, he tried to struggle to his feet but two of them had him pinned down against his rucksack.

'Fucker!'

The last thing Adrian Gasparino remembered seeing before the lights went out was the dirty sole of a boot heading for his face.

'What the hell are you doing, representing Clive Martin?'

A dark look passed across Abigail Slater's face. 'Surely,' she glowered at her lover sitting opposite, '*I* have discretion – total discretion – when it comes to deciding on the clients that *I* choose to take on.'

'Well, yes,' Christian Holyrod stammered, 'but come on. On the one hand I'm trying to clean things up, and here you are, getting in the way.'

Slater placed her knife and fork carefully on her plate and looked slowly round the restaurant. For an evening early in the week, The Triangle was doing more than brisk business. There was not an empty table in sight and a growing crowd at the bar, waiting to be seated. You would hardly think they were in the middle of the worst recession since the Second World War. Then again, economic austerity was for the little people. The Chancellor of the Exchequer, one of Christian's more lame-brained colleagues, famously said, 'We're all in it together'; what he meant was, 'You're on your own, losers'. The little berk had last been seen on the slopes of some swish Swiss resort, enjoying a ten-grand skiing break, while his minions were busy trying to cut all the social services they could. Politicians, Slater thought contemptuously, they were such useless cretins. For a moment, she tried to remember why she was having a relationship with one. Nothing came to mind.

'What's so funny?' Christian asked, a sour look upon his face as he played with his glass of Vega Sicilia Unico 1996.

'Nothing.' Slater cut a large slice off her mound of beef tartare. Popping it into her mouth, she chewed lasciviously, licking her lips as she swallowed. The look on Christian's face signalled the rush of blood to his crotch, amusing her even more.

'He's a very interesting and articulate guy.' Slater washed down the steak with a mouthful of wine.

'Who – Martin?'

Slater nodded. 'He talks well about the grotesque sexualization of our society.' Slipping off one of her pumps, she inserted her foot between Holyrod's legs and began gently massaging his groin with her toes.

The Mayor's eyes widened. After a moment, his mouth opened slightly but no sound came out.

'The way he explains it,' Slater continued, feeling him stiffen under the arch of her foot, 'we're all in the sex industry, one way or another. Sex is used to sell everything – films, music, cars ... even Entomophagous Industries.'

'What do you mean?'

Slater put her cutlery back on the plate and pushed the half-finished meal away. 'Have you seen the latest corporate advertising?'

Holyrod, rapidly losing interest in the conversation, shook his head.

'There was a full-page ad for Entomophagous in the *Economist*, the *Journal* and the *Herald Tribune*. It was a picture of a naked woman,' Slater explained, 'or I should say "girl", she looked about fifteen at best, sitting on a horse in a field with a slogan that said something like "beauty and strength", something like that.'

Pulling her foot away from him, she slipped it back into her shoe. 'So don't come all high and mighty with me. And don't try and tell me who I should choose as my clients.'

Slater dropped her napkin on her plate and sprang to her feet. Leaning over the table, she

163

patted the Mayor on the cheek.

'You never know,' she smiled maliciously. 'Maybe if you go home, your wife will let you fuck her tonight.'

Not very likely, Holyrod mused, trying to recall the last time they'd had sex.

'Or,' Slater continued, 'maybe you could just wank off to one of your ads ... if you like that sort of thing.' Stepping away from the table, she headed off to get her coat.

Holyrod quickly pulled himself together as a hovering waitress approached the table.

'Was the meal all right, sir?'

'Fine, fine,' said Holyrod brusquely as he watched his mistress disappear into the night. Maybe he *would* go home and fuck his wife, just to spite her. 'Just get me the bill and a large glass of the twenty-year-old Pittyvaich.'

TWENTY

Carlyle wondered how long it might be before he could slink off and get a cup of coffee. He thought about the dozens of different cafés within a five-minute walk of the crime scene. As he went through the list, most of them were immediately ruled out on quality grounds. This was not the kind of morning when any old rubbish would do. He definitely was not in the mood for flavourless generic offerings doled out by some grumpy East European who hadn't yet realized she should have stayed at home, rather than running off to a city that even he, a resident here all his life, found dirty, expensive and unforgiving.

The working day had started as he was brushing his teeth. Standing naked in the bathroom, he was wondering whether his gut was expanding as the desk sergeant phoned and informed him of the homicide. An unidentified tramp had been kicked to death in a doorway at the back of the London Coliseum, home of the English National Opera, not much more than fifty yards from the police station at Charing Cross.

'Not so good for the crime statistics,' the sergeant reflected.

Not so good for the poor bugger who is dead, Carlyle replied silently, holding his mobile to his ear while he continued brushing his teeth.

'And just round the corner from where I'm standing,' the sergeant sighed. 'Doesn't look too clever, does it?'

Still looking in the mirror, sucking in his stomach, Carlyle told him, 'I'll be there in ten minutes or so.' Ending the call, he reached for the mouthwash.

Helen appeared behind him. Stepping out of her pyjama bottoms, she sat down on the toilet and began to pee. She gestured at the mobile as he set it down by the side of the bath. 'Work?'

Carlyle nodded as he gargled. Spitting the mouthwash into the sink, he took the T-shirt that had been warming on the radiator and put it on. 'Yeah. Dead tramp. Nice way to start the day.'

'Ah well,' she said, 'good luck.'

'Thanks.' He kissed her gently on the top of the

165

head. 'I'll tell you about it tonight.'

Umar Sligo turned up the collar of his raincoat and flashed a cheesy smile at the pretty blonde WPC standing by the police tape. He was sure he hadn't seen her before; if he had, he would have remembered. Umar prided himself on always remembering a pretty face. Tossing her head, the girl looked away. Umar didn't mind. Making a note of the number on her epaulette, he knew he would have her mobile number by the end of the day, no problem.

'Sergeant...'

Turning back to face his boss, Umar gestured at the Fulham FC baseball cap pulled down low, with the brim concealing most of John Carlyle's face. 'Nice hat, Inspector.'

Stepping out of the rain, Carlyle tugged the brim down even further and grunted. The downpour was getting heavier but in the enclosed space of the doorway there was no chance that the stink of death was going to be washed away any time soon.

It wasn't much of a crime scene, just a pair of battered Gola trainers sticking out from a heap of smelly clothes. If it wasn't for the congealed blood spreading along the grimy concrete, you would assume the guy – Carlyle assumed that the victim was a man – was just another sleeping dosser of the kind that were to be found sprinkled around Covent Garden at any time of the day or night.

Nameless people living in a different world on the same streets.

'Any ID?'

'Nah.' Umar shook his head. 'They took everything.'

'They?'

'The techies reckon four or five people were involved. Anyway, they cleaned him out, took whatever money and possessions he had. All he had left were his clothes and the sleeping bag.'

'Great.' Turning away from Umar, Carlyle watched the pathologist, a small bearded guy called Evan Milch whom he hadn't worked with much before, snap off his latex gloves and drop them into his bag. Closing the bag, he stretched and shook out his shoulders, catching Carlyle's eye as he did so.

'Nasty,' said the pathologist.

Carlyle nodded.

'We have just about finished here, I think.' Milch wiped his hands on his green corduroy jeans. 'I will let you have some initial thoughts by close of play.'

Someone kicked the poor bastard to death, Carlyle thought. *What's to know?* He smiled thinly. 'Thanks.'

'My pleasure.' Zipping up his padded green Barbour jacket, Milch gave a small bow and moved off the pavement, heading for the far side of the police tape and the peace of his mortuary.

As he watched him go, Carlyle stared vacantly at the corpse. For no particular reason, his mind alighted on a memory of Walter Poonoosamy, a local drunk known as 'Dog' on account of the fictitious pet he used to panhandle money from tourists. For a while, a few years back, Walter had been a local micro-celebrity, a regular fixture in the

167

waiting room of Charing Cross police station. Then he disappeared, his fate unknown. Or, rather, the *details* of his fate were unknown. But, for a while at least, Walter had a name, an identity of sorts.

This guy, Carlyle thought sadly, was probably just a corpse long before he had breathed his last.

'Fuck!' Looking down, Carlyle saw that he had stepped in the victim's blood. He took a step backwards, ignoring the disapproving looks of the two technicians still working on the crime scene. Standing in the rain, he wiped the toe of his shoe in a pool of murky water and looked across at his sergeant, standing vacantly in the gutter waiting for something to happen.

Umar caught him staring. He nodded again at the inspector's cap. 'Bad result for Fulham last night.'

Tell me something I don't know, Carlyle thought. Fourth defeat on the bounce, a shell-shocked manager and another wearisome relegation battle looming. 'We're not like United,' he said maliciously, 'with dodgy decisions from helpful referees every week.'

Umar shook his head. 'I'm a Citeh man,' he said, 'as you well know. I don't like United any more than anyone else.'

'These days that's probably worse,' Carlyle said morosely. Manchester City, for so long the poor relations of their local rivals, had been bought by some rich Arabs intent on buying their way to success. In football, where money was everything, even perennial losers like City could be transformed ... eventually.

Umar shrugged his shoulders. 'You're just jealous of our money,' he said almost wistfully in a soft Lancashire accent that had clearly been honed in some of the smarter parts of Cheshire.

'You can't buy class.'

'Yeah,' Umar agreed, puzzled by his boss's obvious hostility over such a trivial matter. 'Like your cap – very classy.'

Finally, Carlyle managed a grin. 'At least it keeps my head dry.'

Umar Sligo pulled himself up straight so that he could profit from his three-inch height advantage over his boss. 'A bit of rain never hurt anyone,' he said.

Thrusting his hands deep into the pockets of his North Face jacket, Carlyle pawed the ground restlessly. Breakfast was long overdue. 'Where you come from,' he said, 'I suppose it rains all the time.'

'Manchester's not that bad,' Umar said defensively.

'Yeah, right,' Carlyle nodded. 'Just be grateful that you've finally made it to civilization.'

Umar looked at him defiantly. 'Have you ever been there?'

Carlyle frowned as if the question was crazy. He lived and worked in London. Why would he ever want to venture into the provinces? Letting his gaze slip from his sergeant, he watched an ambulance appear from round the corner, its blue lights flashing, then pull up to the tape.

'We're done here,' he said. 'Let's go and get a drink.'

Sitting in a cramped booth at the back of the Monmouth Coffee House, just off Seven Dials in Covent Garden, Carlyle took off his cap and hung his jacket over the back of his chair. He could feel a headache coming on. A trio of baristas expertly worked the red Gaggia Deco machines lined up against the far wall, and while he waited, he read the notice hanging above them that explained the characteristics – *toasted almonds with smooth body and balanced fruity acidity* – of his espresso. *We currently use Fazenda do Serrado (Brasil) as the base of the espresso, adding Lo Mejor de Nariño (Colombia) for high notes and complexity and Finca Capetillo (Guatemala) for cocoa notes.*

Carlyle didn't know whether to be impressed or embarrassed. Sipping his drink, he scanned the room. At a nearby table, a hugely famous, jaw-droppingly gorgeous young actress was canoodling with a young pretty boy who looked even more feminine than she did. Carlyle was no stargazer – in Central London, celebrities, even proper celebrities, were ten a penny, but even so, he found it hard not to gawp.

Finishing his cappuccino, Umar noisily dropped his cup back on its saucer, bringing the inspector back to the present. 'Shall we get going?' he asked, bouncing around on his seat like a hyperactive five year old.

'Yeah,' said Carlyle. Making no move to get up, he gave his sergeant the onceover. They had been working together for a while now but Carlyle, usually a man quick to make a judgement on people, felt like he was still a long way off making a decision about Umar Sligo. Dark and clear-eyed, with a strong jawline, high cheekbones and a mane of pitch-black hair that was considerably longer than allowed for in the Met's regulations, Umar was a pretty boy too, and no mistake. Sitting in a charcoal, single-breasted Jil Sander suit, something that Carlyle could never have afforded on his inspector's salary, and with an aqua-blue Hugo Boss shirt, open at the neck, the young man looked more like a model than a policeman. Carlyle watched as the actress turned away from her boyfriend and blatantly gave Umar an appraising look. The stab of envy that Carlyle felt was sharp and lingering. What is it today, he wondered grumpily, with all these beautiful people? Glancing up, he caught sight of his reflection in the mirror that ran the length of the wall behind the bar. His hair was greyer than he remembered and his plebeian build, always slight, seemed to be shrinking as he hunched over his demitasse. To his own hypercritical eye, he looked at least ten years older than his actual age. *You're past your sell-by date,* he said to himself, *too old to be a foot soldier in the battle for law and order. You've been doing this job for far too long – you should have found something else to keep you busy by now.*

Umar had started reading a story on his Black-Berry Curve 8520 and was soon laughing out loud. 'Have you heard the latest about Gavin Swann?'

'His new contract?'

'Nah. That was sorted weeks ago. Two hundred grand a week *after* tax, apparently.' He turned the BlackBerry round in his hand, so that Carlyle could see the screen. It showed an image of a sleek white automobile. Gavin Swann was leaning out of the driver's window, signing autographs for a couple of young boys. In the background, a gaggle of middle-aged men in shell-suits looked on. 'The latest addition to his stable of high-end motors. A Bentley Continental. One of the most popular cars with Premier League footballers. More than a hundred grand's worth of style and grace.'

'Nice.' Carlyle failed to fake much interest. The truth was that he knew nothing about cars and cared even less. 'Bit of a cliché, though, isn't it?' he went on. *Footballer buys flash car.* Not very imaginative.'

'By and large,' Umar acknowledged, 'it is pretty much what you'd expect. English footballers tend to come either from the working class or from the underclass. Young men, lacking in both formal education and life skills, with a lot of disposable income ... they like their expensive toys. A lot of them have a problem when it comes to managing money.'

'He's a chav,' Carlyle sneered.

'Like all of us, Gavin Swann is a product of his environment. Until he signed as a professional footballer, no one in Swann's immediate family had worked for almost thirty years. He lived in a one-bedroom council house in Elephant and Castle until he bought a six-million-pound mansion in Surrey. He played for England before he had even qualified for a driving licence.'

'Part of a long tradition of lovable "bad boys" like George Best, Stan Bowles, Paul Gascoigne.'

'His is the kind of story you'd expect from this society.'

Carlyle let out a short, harsh laugh. 'You sound like you've been on one sociology course too many.'

'Nah.' Umar shook his head. 'But I read an interesting article about it in the *FT* at the weekend.'

The *FT*? What kind of bloody copper, Carlyle wondered, reads the *Financial Times*?

'They have a guy called Simon Kuper who writes lots of interesting stuff.'

Carlyle gave him a blank look.

'He co-wrote a book,' Umar continued, 'called *Why England Lose*.'

For a nanosecond, Carlyle rediscovered his Scottish roots. 'England lose because they are not very good,' he said.

'No, well, actually...'

Carlyle held up a hand. 'Let's not go there.' However shit England were on the football field, he knew only too well that Scotland were far worse.

With a sigh, Umar realized that he was wasting his time, trying to have an intelligent conversation with his boss about anything that was not directly related to work. It was clear that the inspector was two-dimensional – at best – and Umar wondered just how much he would learn from working at Charing Cross. Hopefully, his stay would be a short one.

'Okay,' he asked, looking up from the screen of his smartphone, 'what do you want me to do next?'

Carlyle finished his drink. 'Your call.' The boy had to start making his own decisions. Until he did that, the inspector wouldn't know if he was any good or not. Simpson hadn't explained why Umar – academic, matinée idol and rising star in the provincial police force – had upped sticks and come to London. A restless spirit? A dark secret? A hidden agenda? Or simply an understandable desire to play with the big boys? There were various possibilities. Not that Carlyle cared much one way or another. As a Londoner, he always assumed that anyone unfortunate enough to find themselves living in another part of the country would try and make it to the capital at the earliest opportunity, before life passed them by completely. As a policeman, he was not overburdened by curiosity. Anyway, whatever Umar's reasons for heading south, they were unlikely to have much bearing on how things worked out between the two of them at Charing Cross. The kid would either stick around or he wouldn't. Only time would tell. If they established a good partnership, terrific. If not, he would get someone else. That was one of the great things about London: there was always someone else. You were never missed for long. No one was indispensable. Ever. It was not a place for sentimentality.

Looking up, Carlyle saw the poster on the wall behind Umar's head. It was for one of the ENO's current shows called *A Dog's Heart*. Bored, he read the blurb: *…a new work by Russian composer Alexander Raskatov, based on a classic novella by one of the Soviet era's best-known writers, Mikhail Bulgakov. Banned for many years under Stalin's rule, Bulgakov's absurdist tale tells of a stray mongrel*

174

that becomes human after a Frankenstein-like organ transplant by his master. Carlyle had never been to an opera in his life, but at least this one sounded interesting. At the bottom of the poster was a quote lifted from a *Financial Times* review: *a total sensory extravaganza. Well, if it's good enough for the FT...* Carlyle thought sarkily.

Maybe he should ask Umar his opinion.

Maybe not.

Shocked by his willingness to contemplate trying something new, he made a mental note to ask his wife about it. He chuckled to himself. Was an opera about a Frankenstein dog a good choice for a date? Was there even such a thing as a date opera anyway? Helen would have to be the judge of that. The point was that it was up to him to make the effort to do something.

Umar finished typing some notes into his mobile device and looked up. 'I'll see if I can get a name, see what the uniforms come up with, knocking on doors, and chase up the pathologist's report.'

'Talk to the people at the halfway house on Parker Street and also the St Mungo's hostel on Endell Street. They might be able to tell you something useful.'

'Okay,' Umar nodded.

'Good.' Carlyle got to his feet. 'Get an estimated time of death and check the CCTV as well. I counted at least four different cameras that should have caught something.'

Umar grinned. 'That would make our life easier.'

'We'll see.' Carlyle let out a deep breath. Accidentally catching the eye of the actress, he looked away quickly, feeling like a berk. 'I'll see you later.'

Apparently oblivious to the star in his midst, Umar dropped the BlackBerry into his pocket. 'Where are you going?'

'Stuff to do,' said Carlyle, as he headed for the door. 'I'm off to see your predecessor.'

TWENTY-ONE

Was he imagining it, or did Roche look different? Scanning her face, Carlyle thought there was something missing. And then he saw it: the loss of sparkle in her eyes as she looked at him made him wonder if she could really recover from her tussles with Alain Costello.

Stepping forward, she greeted him with a limp handshake. 'Hello, Inspector.'

'Sergeant.'

She looked him up and down. 'Like the specs. They make you look ... different.'

'So I'm told.' Carlyle glanced down the suburban street. There was no sign of the two dozen or so police officers stationed within 100 yards of where they were standing. The neighbourhood looked deserted. 'Are you ready to go?'

'Just about.' Roche pointed to a large, unmarked van parked twenty yards down the road. 'My boss is in there,' she mumbled. 'I'd introduce you, but you wouldn't like her.'

'Fair enough.' Roche might have lost her edge but she still knew him well enough. There were already plenty of police officers the inspector didn't like; he didn't need to meet another one.

'The target address is the next street over,' Roche said. 'It's called Fortune Street – a top-floor flat. As far as we can tell, Costello is in there alone. We're going in, in around five minutes. Straight through the front door. There is no alternative exit.'

Third time lucky, Carlyle thought. *Don't fuck it up this time. If you have to shoot the bastard, that's fine by me.* 'Okay,' he said. 'I'll stay in the background.'

As if reading his thoughts, Roche lovingly patted the Glock on her hip. 'Are you armed?' she asked.

'No,' Carlyle said. 'Not really necessary, is it?'

Roche made a face that suggested his statement lacked a certain degree of wisdom.

'Anyway,' Carlyle continued, 'I am not an Authorized Firearms Officer. As it happens, I've never fired a gun in my life.'

'No? Maybe you should learn,' Roche replied as she turned and headed off down the street.

'Maybe I will,' Carlyle lied as he watched her disappear round the corner. There was no way on God's earth you would get him anywhere near an armed weapon. He knew that if he ever ended up with a gun in his hand, most likely the only person he would end up shooting would be himself. No, guns were definitely not on his agenda. He glanced at his watch; a couple of minutes to kick-off. After a moment's reflection, he began walking down the street at a brisk pace, heading in the opposite direction to Roche.

At the end of the street, Carlyle crossed the two-lane road and went and sat on a grubby red plastic bench in a bus shelter that offered him a clear view down the length of Fortune Street. Arms folded, he watched as the snatch party of half a dozen uniformed officers smashed down a door halfway down the street, about 150 yards from where he was sitting. Carlyle saw an old woman, tartan shopping bag in hand, shuffling along the far side of the street, oblivious to what was going on around her. Otherwise, the place was deserted. Three buses trundled down the road in convoy, not bothering to stop. By the time they had passed, the police had disappeared inside, leaving a lone constable to stand duty outside. Carlyle heard a couple of quiet thuds and some indistinguishable voices, which quickly disappeared beneath the relentless hum of the traffic.

Another bus passed. Carlyle watched as the scruffy figure of a young man slipped out of the front door of the house at the end of the street, nearest to the bus stop. Head bowed, he crossed the road while still playing on his games console. Stepping into the bus shelter, he looked up at the indicator board, which said the next bus was due in one minute.

Bloody good service here, Carlyle thought, as he watched the single-decker lumber into view. Standing on the kerb, he fished his Oyster Card out of his pocket. Slipping his computer game in his pocket, the other passenger reached out and signalled to the driver to stop. The bus came to a halt and Carlyle listened to the familiar hiss of pressurized air as the doors opened. Stepping behind the man, he gripped the back of his neck and smashed his face into the side of the bus. Looking up, he caught the gaze of a middle-aged black woman who quickly glanced away, obviously not wanting to get involved. When Carlyle realized that the dazed man wasn't going down, he grabbed the back of his jacket and hoisted him backwards towards the plastic bench. Taking his cue, the bus driver quickly closed the doors and moved off.

Carlyle's target tried to wriggle free. As he did so, the games console fell out of his pocket and onto the pavement.

'*Fils du pute!*'

Ignoring his attacker, the man reached down to pick it up, allowing Carlyle to give him a swift, gratuitous kick in the ribs. With a groan, the man went down on one knee. Pulling his hands behind his back, Carlyle clipped on a pair of handcuffs, relieving him of his console as he did so. 'Alain Costello,' he said in his most official-sounding voice, 'you are under arrest.'

Struggling upright, Costello spat against the Perspex of the bus shelter. With a mixture of annoyance and despair, he watched Carlyle place the console into his pocket. 'Give me back my PSP,' he whined.

'Shut the fuck up,' Carlyle snorted. Resisting the temptation to drop the bloody thing down a drain, he took Costello by the arm and frog-marched him back across the street and into the waiting arms of SO15.

Sandy Carroll chucked her handbag towards the

chair in the corner of the room and watched, mortified, as it hit the arm and fell onto the floor, emptying half its contents onto the carpet. Grinning, Gavin Swann bent down and picked up a packet of Durex Extra Safe.

'I see you've come prepared this time!'

Sandy blushed. 'Where's Kelly?'

Swann made a face. 'Dunno.' Undoing the white towel around his waist, he tossed it on the bed, inviting her to appreciate his nakedness.

Sandy felt a flutter of concern in her stomach. Kelly was supposed to be bringing the recording device that Frank Maxwell's PA had set them up with. 'I thought you wanted another threesome,' she said, keeping her gaze at eye-level.

Swann's grin grew even wider. 'We do.' He gestured towards the open bathroom door and Sandy realized for the first time that the shower was running.

'Who's in the...?'

Before she could finish the question, the water stopped. Through the door appeared a massive-looking guy, easily six five, drying his hair in a bath towel. This time, Sandy could not keep her gaze from heading south, past the guy's well defined abs towards a piece of equipment that, on first glance, was easily twice the size of Swann's.

'I don't–'

'This is Paul, our reserve goalie. Big boy, isn't he?'

Looking pleased with himself, Paul dropped his towel back onto the carpet, saying nothing.

Mesmerized and horrified in equal measure, Sandy watched as he started getting bigger.

'He's a shit goalie,' Swann joked, 'but he can screw for England.'

'Fuck off,' Paul laughed.

'I wanna go,' Sandy sobbed.

'Strip!' Swann commanded, pushing her onto the bed.

'No!' Sandy screamed. Bouncing back off the mattress, she got to her feet and made a grab for her bag. Dropping on one knee, she tried to scoop as much of the contents back inside as possible. Standing upright, Swann clasped her hair from behind, yanking her towards him. His hot breath on her cheek smelled of a mixture of beer and cheese and onion crisps. 'You bitches were going to sell me out to the papers.'

'No,' Sandy snivelled unconvincingly. Turning her head, she could see his face turning puce with rage, beads of sweat forming on his brow. Behind him, the goalie laughed nervously.

'Do you think I am stupid?' Swann roared, pulling her head back as far as it would go.

Sandy shook her head. Her eyes blurred with tears.

'Do you know how much I pay Frank every bloody year to keep me *out* of the papers? Do you think he's going to give all that up for a few extra quid?'

'Please...' The laughing behind her had been replaced by a series of animal grunts and Sandy was horrified when an arc of semen flew past her right shoulder and splattered across the LCD screen in front of her, hitting the Sky Sports News weather girl smack in the face.

Releasing her hair, Swann almost fell over

laughing. Blushing, Paul picked up the towel at his feet and wiped himself down.

Masturbating with one hand, Swann smiled maliciously at Sandy. 'He's just making sure he doesn't finish too quickly ... when it comes to the real thing.'

Regaining some of her composure, Sandy hoisted the bag over her shoulder and stepped towards Swann. Placing a hand on his chest, she pushed him firmly out of the way and headed for the door. 'You are a pair of sick bastards,' she shouted, hoping someone outside would hear her distress. 'Fucking perverts. You should fuck each other. I'm going.'

'I don't think so,' Swann growled.

Expecting him to grab her hair once again, Sandy flinched. But this time, he clutched her by the shoulder and spun her round, gesturing at his now fully erect penis. 'Suck me off,' he commanded.

Sandy started crying again. Massive, ripe tears rolled down her cheeks. The kind of tears she hadn't cried since she was eight and Santa failed to bring her the right kind of Barbie for Christmas. 'Piss off!' she cried.

Placing a meaty hand on the top of her head, Swann tried to push her down towards his groin. When she resisted, he took a step back, unleashing a vicious right upper cut that caught her flush under the chin, sending her collapsing to the floor.

Letting go of Costello's collar, Carlyle pushed him in the direction of the ashen-faced Roche.

'You looking for this guy?'

Roche raised her eyes to the darkening heavens but said nothing. Standing next to the sergeant, a po-faced woman made a show of looking Carlyle up and down.

'Who are you?' she asked snootily.

'This is Inspector Carlyle,' said Roche, snapping out of her torpor as she stepped between them. She gestured at her boss. 'Inspector, this is Chief Inspector Cass Wadham.'

Carlyle gave a curt nod. He already knew that Roche was right. Wadham was another paper-pushing copper destined to get up his nose; someone best left well alone.

'How did the prisoner get those marks on his face?' Wadham asked brusquely as Roche, taking possession of Costello, levered him into the back of a police car parked at the kerb.

'He hit me,' the Frenchman whined as he fell onto the back seat. 'And he stole my PSP.'

Good point, Carlyle thought. Pulling the console out of his pocket, he threw it underarm to Roche. Fumbling the catch, she watched in dismay as it fell into the gutter.

'Hey!' Costello protested as Roche bent down to retrieve it.

It would be a shame if it happened to get broken, Carlyle mused.

'I was asking...' Wadham interjected.

Carlyle shot her a sharp look. 'Just be grateful I recovered your man for you.' He gestured towards the car. 'Your track record when it comes to trying to arrest this guy is on the bad side of appalling.'

Making a sound like a deflating beach ball,

183

Wadham stepped forward. For a moment, Carlyle thought she was going to give him a slap. Then, thinking better of it, she turned on her heel and stalked off down the street.

Carlyle watched the exaggerated swing of her hips.

Roche followed his gaze. 'Are you checking out my boss's arse?'

'No way,' Carlyle frowned.

Laughing, Roche slammed the door shut on Costello. 'I told you that you wouldn't like her.'

'And you were right.' Carlyle thrust his fists into his pockets. 'How did you manage to lose the scumbag this time?'

Roche sighed. 'Through the attic. He scuttled up there when he heard us coming in, and was able to get all the way along to the end of the row. It was just as well you were waiting for him.'

'I was waiting for a bus,' Carlyle quipped. 'They seem to have a very good service round these parts.'

Roche stared at him uncomprehendingly.

'Look − just don't lose him again, eh?' Carlyle told her.

'I'll try not to.' Roche's gaze fell to the pavement. 'Thanks.'

'No problem.' Carlyle looked at his watch. 'I need to get going.'

'How are things back at Charing Cross?' Roche asked quietly.

'Fine.'

'Have you replaced me yet?'

Carlyle gave her his cheesiest grin. 'You're irreplaceable.'

She lifted her eyes to meet his gaze. 'I might want to come back.'

You made your bed... 'They've given me some-one.'

'Any good?'

'Too early to tell.'

'Well,' she said, 'keep me posted.'

'Of course.' Carlyle was already heading back down the street. 'See you later.'

TWENTY-TWO

Gazing vacantly out of the window, Carlyle sat on the 243 bus trundling back towards Central London, enjoying the luxury of an empty mind. His pleasant journey came to an end halfway down Clerkenwell Road when his mobile sprang into life. He looked at the screen. *Alex Miles.* Miles was the chief concierge at the Garden Hotel, round the corner from the police station. The inspector hesitated for a moment before answering.

'Alex,' he said tiredly. 'How are you?'

'Inspector?'

'Yeah. It's Carlyle here. What can I do for you?'

There was a long pause on the other end of the line.

Must be bad, Carlyle thought.

Finally, Miles cleared his throat. 'Well...'

Distracted by a pretty girl walking by, Carlyle tuned out of the conversation.

'Inspector?'

185

'Yes?'

'Were you listening to what I said?' Miles huffed.

'Yes, yes,' Carlyle snapped. 'Just sit tight. I'll have some uniforms there in five minutes. Do nothing until I get there.'

Ending the call, he quickly dialled the station and told Angie Middleton to have a team meet him at the hotel.

'Shall we go up?' Carlyle faced Alex Miles across the concierge's table, a mahogany Regency writing desk, largely hidden behind an oversized sofa in the left-hand corner of the hotel lobby. They had been joined by a bored-looking uniform, PC Tim Burgess. Burgess had been a constable for the best part of a decade now and Carlyle knew that, even if he stayed in the Met for another thirty years, a constable he would remain. Useless was not the word.

As Miles headed for the lifts, Carlyle nodded at his colleague. 'Stay here. I'll give you a shout if you need to come up.'

'Yes, sir,' said Burgess glumly.

Upstairs, he met Susan Phillips coming the other way. Working out of Holborn police station, Phillips had been a staff pathologist with the Met for more than twenty years now, and she and Carlyle had worked together many times.

'John!' she smiled, giving him a peck on the cheek.

'Susan,' he smiled in return, 'you got here quick.'

'Too quickly,' Phillips told him. 'I left some stuff in the car and need to nip back downstairs.' She gestured over her shoulder. 'But my colleague is in there. You can take a look.'

'What happened?'

Phillips glanced at Miles, who bowed his head and retreated a respectful distance.

'Simply speaking,' Phillips whispered, 'someone punched her lights out.' She added: 'Is it true the room was booked to Gavin Swann?'

Carlyle sighed. 'So I'm told.'

Phillips shook her head. 'What a bloody mess.' She patted Carlyle on the shoulder. 'Good luck.'

'Thanks,' said Carlyle, heading unhappily towards the door.

Less than twenty minutes later, Alex Miles stuck his head round the room door. He looked stressed. 'Inspector! There are half-a-dozen journalists downstairs in the lobby already.' He made it sound like this was somehow the inspector's fault.

'Not that surprising, is it?' Carlyle affected an air of insouciance. Inwardly, however, his heart sank. The fact was that he shouldn't have touched this case with a bargepole. But no, he'd had to play the big 'I am' and wade right in. As a result, he'd fucked himself good and proper. He turned grimly to the concierge. 'Try to keep them downstairs,' he instructed.

Well aware of the drill, Miles nodded and quickly disappeared. Carlyle turned to Phillips. 'How much longer do you need?'

Standing over the crumpled body, the pathologist allowed herself a stretch. 'An hour, maybe. No more than that.'

'Okay.' Studiously ignoring the victim, Carlyle stared out of the window. The view wasn't much

– just a brick wall – but it was better than looking at another body. He didn't need to look at the poor girl's face to know what had happened, broadly speaking. And pulling out his mobile, Carlyle dialled the number of Carole Simpson.

The Commander picked up on the second ring, catching him by surprise. 'Yes?' she asked brusquely. 'What can I do for you, John?'

'We need to call a press conference for an hour's time...'

There was a pause while he listened to the negative vibes coming over the airwaves. Then, taking a deep breath, he explained what he wanted, and why. 'I need to get the press away from the crime scene and into the station.'

'And what am I supposed to tell them?'

'Just the bare minimum; enough to be going on with.'

There was another pause, less hostile this time. 'I'll see what I can do,' she said finally, ending the call.

Phillips watched him put away the phone. 'Playing the media game, eh?'

'Do I have a choice?' Carlyle stepped towards the door. 'We'll get the reporters out of here and you can take the body back to the lab.'

Phillips nodded. 'Okay – thanks. I'll let you have more detail later. But I would say that Mr Swann should be helping you with our enquiries.'

'Yes, indeed,' Carlyle said wearily. 'I wonder where the stupid little scrote has run off to.'

Thinking through his 'to do' list, Carlyle headed for the lifts. When he reached the hotel lobby, he was pleased to see that it was now clear of journalists who had, presumably, taken the bait of Simpson's press conference. Heading for the exit, he felt his stomach rumble. Remembering that there was a Caffè Nero two doors down, he decided that a latte and a panini were in order before he returned to the station.

He was less than ten feet from the street when he felt a hand on his shoulder.

'Inspector,' said Alex Miles in a low voice. Clearly embarrassed to be consorting with a policeman, the concierge scanned the room anxiously.

Reluctantly stopping, Carlyle half-turned and looked around for himself. Apart from a few tourists milling aimlessly about, the place was empty. No one was interested in their conversation.

'How's it going?' the concierge asked.

'I need to get on,' Carlyle said brusquely.

'There is someone,' Miles coughed, 'whom you need to see.'

Carlyle gave him a *convince me* look.

'Trust me, you *do* want to see this guy.' Miles gestured towards the lift. 'He's in the Light Bar.'

Carlyle thought about it for a second. 'Are you serving food at the moment?'

Miles glanced at his watch. 'Yes.'

'Let's go then,' said Carlyle, heading back the way he had come.

Bathed in a pale violet light, the bar was completely empty, apart from a large man sitting in a booth at the back. Letting Miles lead the way, Carlyle checked out the succession of enormous

189

black-and-white close-up photographs of various celebrities that hung on the walls. Some – Neneh Cherry, Vanessa Paradis, Lenny Kravitz – he recognized, but the majority he did not, which pleased him considerably. As they approached the table, Miles nodded nervously at the man, who was busy tucking into a beef sandwich and a side order of chips.

'This is the officer in charge of the investigation,' the concierge announced *sotto voce*.

Inspired by the food, Carlyle pulled up a chair and sat down.

'Inspector Carlyle,' he said, extending a hand. 'I work out of Charing Cross, just round the corner.'

The man swallowed a mouthful of chips and took a couple of gulps from a bottle of Singha beer. Placing the bottle on the table, he wiped his oversized mitts on a napkin and then finally shook hands. 'Clifford Blitz, pleased to meet you.' Carlyle noted the indistinct provincial accent; impossible to place, he knew it would be from somewhere he had never heard of.

'Mr Blitz,' Miles interjected quickly, pulling up a chair for himself, 'is Gavin Swann's agent.'

Is he now? Carlyle thought. His phone started up but he ignored it.

Blitz handed over a business card, which Carlyle dropped in his pocket. 'Thanks.'

Blitz nodded graciously.

Carlyle turned his gaze to the concierge. 'Alex,' he said pleasantly, 'I need something to eat as a matter of some urgency.' He gestured at Blitz's half-empty plate. 'The same as Clifford's having would be great.'

Miles shot him a dirty look. 'Including the beer?'

Especially the beer, Carlyle thought. 'Yes, please.'

'And I'll have another,' Blitz grunted, finishing off the last of his chips.

'But,' Miles started to whine, 'I thought you weren't allowed to drink on duty?'

'That's a myth,' Carlyle lied as he looked the concierge straight in the eye. 'Some sustenance would be gratefully appreciated while I have a *private* conversation with Mr Blitz.'

Miles reluctantly got to his feet. 'Of course.'

'Thank you.' Carlyle watched the concierge slink off before turning back to the agent. 'Now,' he said evenly, 'where is your client?'

Holding up a hand, Blitz drained the last of the beer from his bottle. 'First things first,' he said, placing the empty bottle on the table. 'What's the deal? I need to make sure my guy will be looked after.'

'I don't know what happened yet,' Carlyle told him.

Blitz sat back in his chair as a waiter appeared with their beers. 'I can fill all that in for you.'

I'm sure you can, Carlyle thought. He nodded to the waiter. 'Thanks.'

'What have you got so far?'

'That's a very cheeky question,' Carlyle said, chugging on his beer. It tasted good going down his neck, but in his empty stomach it felt cold and unsettling.

Blitz lifted his fresh beer bottle to his mouth. 'I'm a cheeky guy,' he grinned. Watching him sink half the beer, Carlyle pegged him at around five feet ten, well dressed in an expensive-looking

191

navy suit and a white shirt, open at the neck. Maybe in his late forties, he was hard to age, with few lines around his eyes and remarkably little grey in his short brown hair. He wore a goatee, which, Carlyle thought, gave him a rather dissolute look, as did his overly full midriff.

Carlyle was delighted to see his sandwich arrive. He added some ketchup and took a hearty bite, then another. Blitz watched him as he swallowed.

'Good?'

Carlyle nodded. 'Not at all bad.' He took another sip of his beer and sighed. His phone started ringing again. Again, he ignored it.

'A sandwich is just a sandwich though, isn't it?' Blitz said, lifting the bottle back to his lips.

'A great invention.' Carlyle shoved the rest of the bread into his mouth and swallowed without chewing. 'You can't go wrong.'

Blitz signalled to the barman for another beer. 'Want one?'

Carlyle shook his head. Turning in his seat, he shouted over, 'I'll have an espresso.'

'So,' said Blitz, 'you were telling me about your investigation...'

'No. I was waiting for you to answer my question,' Carlyle said.

Sitting forward, Blitz leaned over the table and lowered his voice. 'Inspector,' he said, 'you have a young girl's body upstairs and a media circus on your doorstep.'

'That, Mr Blitz, is all part and parcel of the job.'

A waiter reappeared with the drinks. Blitz let him clear the table. 'I can sort this out for you,' was all he said.

'That's very kind of you.'

The waiter left.

'With the one condition...'

Here we go, Carlyle thought, downing his coffee in three quick gulps.

'That my client is properly looked after.'

This is not some fucking contract negotiation, Carlyle objected silently. He placed his demitasse on the saucer and looked Blitz squarely in the eye. 'Did he do it?'

Blitz didn't blink. 'No,' he said evenly, 'of course not.'

'There's no problem then. Tart battered by nobody. End of story.'

Blitz sighed. 'You don't know, do you?'

Obviously not. 'What are we talking about?' Carlyle asked, trying to sound nonchalant. 'Known unknowns or unknown unknowns?'

'Fucking coppers.' Blitz tutted. 'The dead girl – don't you realize who she is?'

'Was.'

'Whatever,' Blitz snorted. 'Don't you know who she *was?*'

TWENTY-THREE

Sitting in the back of a black cab, Carlyle looked morosely at the line of traffic crawling up Tottenham Court Road. The taxi meter had already ticked up to £8.60 while covering a distance that he could easily have walked in less than two

193

minutes. The taxi driver, happily listening to the usual procession of morons on a TalkSport radio call-in show, whistled to himself, secure in the knowledge that he was on for a bumper fare.

Carlyle shifted somewhat uncomfortably in his seat. His best guess was that he had something in the region of £3.50 on his person. Presumably Clifford Blitz, who'd already coughed up for their snack in the Light Bar, would be solvent enough to pay. *After all,* the inspector thought, *he can always write it off against his tax bill.*

Blitz ended a phone call and opened the window on his side of the cab a couple of inches.

'Where are we going?' Carlyle asked.

'A safe house,' Blitz said. He pulled a Romeo y Julieta Churchill out of the inside pocket of his jacket and stuck it in his mouth.

The driver eyed him warily in the mirror and pushed the button on the intercom. 'Sorry, sir, no smoking in the cab.'

'Don't worry,' Blitz told him. 'I won't light it until I get out.'

'Why do you have a safe house?' Carlyle asked.

'It's a place that I use to stash clients in when they're in trouble. Everyone thinks they're off in rehab in the countryside or have done a runner to the Seychelles, or wherever, when in reality they're here, hiding right under the noses of the news-papers.' He gave Carlyle a stern look. 'This is all confidential.'

The cab edged forwards another ten yards.

The meter now read £10.20.

Carlyle gazed aimlessly out of the window. 'Of course.'

'You should really be wearing a blindfold.'

'We have a deal. I keep my deals.'

Blitz clamped the cigar more firmly between his teeth. 'We'll see.'

'Yes, we will,' Carlyle replied. 'My view is that you give someone the benefit of the doubt to start with. If people don't live up to their word, that's it.'

Blitz grunted something that could have been agreement or disdain.

'You let me speak to Gavin Swann and–'

'He won't be arrested,' Blitz interjected.

Carlyle nodded. 'Nor will he be taken back to the station for further questioning. The conversation will not be a formal interview, nor will it go into the official police report at this time.'

Unclamping his jaw, Blitz pulled out the cigar and waved it at Carlyle. 'And you won't say anything to the papers!'

'I don't deal with journalists,' Carlyle said firmly.

'Yeah, right,' said Blitz, with feeling, as he stuck the Romeo y Julieta back between his teeth.

'I will carefully pursue the various lines of enquiry that need to be checked out, and when–'

'If.'

Carlyle smiled. 'If I need to speak to Mr Swann a second time, I will come through you.'

'Good.'

Finally, the traffic eased and they accelerated across the Euston Road, heading towards Camden.

'Thank God for that,' Blitz sighed. 'It should take about ten minutes from here.'

Carlyle felt his phone go off. No number was displayed but he had a sixth sense that it was

Simpson and slipped the phone back into his jacket.

'Hiding from the boss?' Blitz grinned.

Carlyle shook his head. 'How long have you known Swann?'

'Gavin? Donkey's years. I first saw him playing on Hackney Marshes when he was eight. The little bugger was brilliant – scored six goals in a single game. It was obvious he was going to be a top player.'

Carlyle knew a well-rehearsed spiel when he heard one but he nodded amiably.

'I signed him on the spot,' Blitz continued. 'Since then, I've been taken to court three times, been banned by those numpties at the Football Association twice, *and* fined a total of a million and a half quid.'

'Blimey!' said Carlyle, turning up the fake empathy as high as it would go

'I've lost count of the number of times I've been sent bullets through the post,' Blitz said smugly. 'One time I was actually shot at but, through it all, I've still held on to my client.'

'You must have made a mint.'

'I've done all right,' Blitz reflected. 'I remember one meeting at a hotel at Heathrow. There was a Gola holdall with two million quid inside. It was sitting on the bed, next to a piece of paper and a pen. The bit of paper had just been torn from a lined notebook. On it was three lines of hand-written scrawl. It was supposed to be a contract with me signing over Gavin to this other agent, a twat called Marcus Angelides. Angelides was clearly scared shitless. I don't know what he thought I would do to him. He was there with two Belgian cage fighters as muscle. He nodded at the bit of paper and said, "Sign it, take your money and fuck off".' He shook his head, smiling at the memory. 'It was all in the papers.'

Knowing better than to spoil the moment, Carlyle waited. Reaching Camden tube, the cab took a left, heading towards Regent's Park.

The meter now read £25.

'So I looked him in the eye,' said Blitz, as they turned into Gloucester Avenue, 'and said "Marcus, you know I'm not going to sign that; don't be so fucking stupid." I knew that Gavin was going to be worth a hell of a lot more than that over the next ten years. I accepted that I might have to take a shoeing there and then but it would be worth it – as long as they didn't actually kill me.' Leaning forward, he rapped a knuckle on the glass window behind the driver's head. 'Anywhere here's good – thanks, mate.'

Carlyle watched relieved as Blitz took out his wallet and removed a pair of crisp £20 notes to pay the fare.

'How did you know that they wouldn't kill you?' he asked as the driver pulled up at the kerb.

'I didn't,' Blitz shrugged. 'But I had to take a punt, didn't I? In the end, I didn't even get thumped.'

'So those weren't the guys who shot at you, then,' Carlyle asked, amused.

'Nah. That was someone else. This time round, with the cash in the bag, it was just a lot of swearing and posturing. But that's what you have to expect in this game.' The driver stopped the meter at £27.80 and slid open the glass partition. Blitz slipped through the cash. 'Thanks mate,' he said cheerily. 'Keep the change but give me a couple of blank receipts.'

'I thought she was just some slapper.' Slumped in a chair at the kitchen table, Gavin Swann looked down into his mug of tea. He was wearing jeans and a blue T-shirt with the legend *BENCH* emblazoned across the chest in white lettering. On his chin was a couple of days' stubble, but he looked alert and relaxed. 'Kelly brought her.'

Carlyle noticed the slightest grimace from Blitz. 'Kelly?'

'Kelly Kellaway,' Swann explained, oblivious to his agent's annoyance. 'I'd hooked up with her a few times before she brought Sandy.'

'I'll give you her number,' Blitz said, keen to move the conversation on. He was leaning against the sink, a tumbler of Grey Goose vodka in his hand, his half-smoked Romeo y Julieta smouldering in an ashtray nearby. Carlyle turned his attention back to Swann.

'So you didn't know that Sandy Carroll was the daughter of Dino Mottram?

Swann shook his head.

'She was Dino's step-daughter,' Blitz corrected him. 'From his first marriage. He gets through them at a steady rate. The last one was number three, I think. I hear he's on the lookout for number four.'

Good luck, Commander Simpson, Carlyle thought. Increasingly, he was struggling to understand why his boss was going out with the old rogue. Then again, her track record with men was uniformly bad, so why not?

'Dino is a great guy,' Blitz said, 'but why he feels he has to marry every bird that he ever shags is beyond me.'

'Never heard of him. Who is he?' asked Swann.

'Dino is the bloke who owns the football club you play for,' Blitz told him gently.

'The old bloke?'

'Yeah.'

Swann frowned. 'I thought that Ricky owned the club.'

Blitz sighed. 'He's the Chief Executive.'

Carlyle drummed his fingers on the table. 'Getting back to the matter in hand...'

'It was Paul,' Swann bleated.

Carlyle looked at Blitz. 'Who's Paul?'

'Paul Groom. He's a reserve goalkeeper – third or fourth choice. Played in the first team just the once, for a grand total of ten minutes. Been out on loan at Gillingham earlier this season.'

Poor bastard, Carlyle thought.

Finishing his vodka, Blitz stepped over to the fridge to retrieve the bottle. 'Not a client of mine, in case you're wondering.'

Carlyle looked at Swann. 'What was he doing in your hotel room?'

Swann gave the question some thought. 'Sometimes,' he said finally, 'we hang out together.'

Carlyle grinned. 'And you like to share the ladies?'

Swann shrugged, as if he didn't understand the point that the inspector was trying to make.

'You shouldn't read anything into it,' Blitz said.

'Team-mates like to hang out together. Groupies get handed round. It happens all the time.'

'Groupies?' Carlyle frowned. 'I thought she was a hooker.'

Swann gave the impression of serious thought. 'She wasn't on the game.'

'She just put herself about,' Blitz explained. 'They tend to call them "sport fuckers" these days.'

Charming. 'But she took money?' Carlyle asked.

Swann thought about it some more. 'Yeah, well, she would have done, I suppose.'

'You suppose?'

Swann looked at the inspector earnestly. 'Well, we didn't get that far, did we?'

The cretin was beginning to wear him out. Carlyle took a deep breath. 'Why do you even have to pay for it, anyway?'

'Kids today,' Blitz laughed. 'They're not like us, Inspector. They're all watching porn on the internet by the time they're five and fucking around by thirteen.'

Carlyle thought of Alice and shuddered.

'It's a completely different game from when we were kids. None of this sticking your hand down a girl's bra and maybe up her skirt if you were really lucky. Now it's all gang bangs and aping the shit they see online. If you don't scream the place down, you're not doing it right. So a girl you've just met lets you have sex with her and you hand over a bit of cash at the end of it, so what? It's the same for all of them, not just celebs like Gavin.'

'We are all prostitutes,' Carlyle mused.

Swann looked at him blankly.

'The Sex Pistols.' The inspector could hear 'Anarchy in the UK' filling his head.

Swann made a face.

'Sid Vicious ... Johnny Rotten?' Carlyle tried.

Still no sign of any recognition.

'John *Lydon*.'

'Who?'

Jesus Christ! The kid was a black hole of stupidity.

'You're wasting your time,' Blitz chuckled.

'Looks like it,' Carlyle sighed. He said to Swann: 'What kind of music do you listen to?'

'Dunno,' Swann mumbled, before reeling off three or four names that Carlyle had never heard of.

Now it was the inspector's turn to look blank.

'You need to get some of your younger colleagues to fill you in on the ways of the modern world, I think,' said Blitz.

'We're not just talking about changes in musical tastes here,' Carlyle replied.

'That's what I just said,' Blitz smiled. 'You've got to realize that there's no stigma attached to anything.'

Carlyle shot him a look. 'Even murder?'

'Okay.' Blitz held up a hand. 'There's no stigma attached to almost anything. Short of something like murder, there's not much that can't be squared away when you're earning millions.'

That's why you're so fucking scared of this, Carlyle thought. *It's one of the few things that could derail the gravy train.* 'I suppose not,' he said ruefully. 'Okay, moving on, what happened when Sandy Carroll was in the room? How come she got killed?'

As Swann raised his gaze, his eyebrows knitted together, giving him a rather constipated look. 'Paul wanted to have sex with the girl. She didn't want to and he went mad, kicking her and hitting her.'

How very convenient. 'Why didn't you stop him?' Carlyle asked evenly.

Swann looked over to his agent. Refilling his glass, Blitz gave him the slightest of nods.

'I tried,' Swann continued, 'but he elbowed me in the face and I fell down.'

Now Carlyle went for a slightly doubtful look. The boy's face did not have a mark on it.

'He's a big lad,' Swann explained. 'Anyway, as I got up, he caught her smack in the face with a right hook and she just kinda ... collapsed.'

'Why did you run away?'

'He called me,' said Blitz, putting the vodka back in the fridge, 'and I told him to come here.'

Carlyle gazed out of the kitchen window at a garden that had to be at least seventy-five feet long. In Primrose bloody Hill! God knows how many millions this place must have cost. He watched Blitz tuck away another slug of booze. 'Leaving the scene of a crime is a serious offence.'

'We have a deal,' Blitz said firmly.

'We do,' Carlyle conceded, 'so we'll park that. What I need to know is: where can I find Mr Groom?'

TWENTY-FOUR

Ambling back towards Camden Town tube station, Carlyle stopped in front of an estate agent's office while he sent Umar an email, asking him to track down Ms Kellaway. After hitting Send, he lingered in front of the window, scanning the properties on view and eventually caught sight of one that looked similar to Blitz's place.

'Six point five million.' Carlyle let out a low whistle. 'Fuck me sideways.' His phone went off. Lost in a sea of envy, he answered it without thinking.

'Carlyle.'

'Where the hell have you been, Inspector?'

Simpson sounded extremely pissed off. It always amused him when she was like this and he had to make an effort not to laugh.

'I...'

'And why haven't you been answering your phone?'

'Well...' struggling to get his story straight, he thought about ending the call.

'I had to do *your* press conference on my own.'

Oops.

'With no idea what I was supposed to be saying.'

Carlyle remembered the days when Simpson, still climbing up the greasy pole, loved nothing better than a good presser. Back in the day, when she was one of the pushiest bastards around, she couldn't wait to get her face on the telly. 'Did you get a good turnout?'

'What?'

'Nothing, nothing.' He took a deep breath. 'Look, things are moving on quickly. We should talk face-to-face but there are a couple of things I need to do first.'

'For fuck's sake, John.'

Carlyle pulled the phone from his ear in shock. Simpson was usually sparing in her use of the f-word; he really must be pushing his luck. Returning the phone to his ear, he tried for what he hoped was a conciliatory voice. 'We may be able to make an arrest.'

There was a pause on the line. 'Get on with it then,' she said impatiently, 'and then come straight to my office.'

'Of course.' Ending the call, he pulled up his sergeant's number.

Umar answered on the third ring.

'Simpson's on the warpath,' he sniggered.

'Don't worry about that,' Carlyle said sharply, giving him the address. 'That's the training ground for Swann's club. Take a couple of uniforms. Go and pick up a guy called Paul Groom. Gavin Swann says he killed that hooker in the Garden Hotel.'

'Gavin Swann?' Umar cackled. 'This is getting tasty!'

'Bring him back to Charing Cross. I'll be there in a couple of hours.'

'Hold on, hold on, give me that address again.'

Sighing, Carlyle repeated the details.

'Okay. Got it. On my way.'

'Keep me posted.' Ending the call, the inspector spent another couple of minutes looking in the estate agent's window for a property that he could conceivably afford. Finding nothing, he shrugged and continued on his way to the underground.

With no intention of going to see Simpson, Carlyle sat on a Northern Line train as it trundled south and wondered just what he was going to do next. Getting out at Leicester Square, his dilemma was solved by a call from Dominic Silver.

'We need to chat.'

Standing on the Charing Cross Road, Carlyle glared at an Italian tourist who walked into him while reading his A–Z. 'Okay.'

'Are you busy?'

'Yes,' Carlyle lied. 'But I can always make time for you.' He told Dom where he was.

'Okay,' Dom said cheerily. 'Why don't we go and get some culture? Take the Northern Line up to Euston and we'll meet at the Wellcome Collection.'

'Humankind cannot bear very much reality.'

And I cannot bear very much bullshit, Carlyle thought. Condemned to live in a wasteland of soundbites, jargon and empty words, he offered the most grudging of smiles. 'What is that? The wit and wisdom of Dominic Silver?'

'T. S. Eliot, actually.' They were at the exhibition called 'High Society: Mind-Altering Drugs in History and Culture'. Dom stepped in front of a poster for 'Hall's Coca Wine – The Elixir of Life' and looked it up and down. A middle-class Victorian woman in a yellow cape and dress gazed into space, blissed out, clearly doped up to the eyeballs.

'Whatever,' Carlyle scowled, adopting the tone he used with Alice when she was pissing him off. Vague memories of double periods of English Lit at school flitted through his mind. Did they still teach poetry? He sincerely hoped not. What was it that Sherlock Holmes had said? 'I crave for mental exultation.' Something like that.

Carlyle leaned forward to read the caption next to the black-and-white drawing he'd been staring at vacantly for the last few moments. Struggling to get the text in focus, he stuck his hand inside his jacket pocket.

'Shit!'

'What's wrong?'

'Nothing,' said Carlyle, cursing under his breath as he tried to remember where he had left his specs. The thought of three hundred quid being casually misplaced filled him with mortal terror but, try as he might, he couldn't recall where he'd last seen them. Unable to do anything about it, he took a step closer to the picture and stuck his nose right in front of the description: *A busy drying room in the opium factory in Patna, India, After W S. Sherwill, lithograph, c. 1850.* It looked like a multi-storey car park with no cars in it. A handful of workers were placing what looked like row after row of footballs on the floor. *The print shows one of the stages in the processing of opium at the factory in Patna, the centre of the British East India Company's opium plantations in Bengal. The raw opium was formed into a ball about 3½ lb in weight and wrapped in poppy petals to protect it from damage. The balls were then dried on shelves and boxed into chests each containing 25−40 balls before shipping to China and Europe.*

Dom appeared at his side. 'They could make the text a bit bigger,' he said. 'I've left my reading glasses at home.'

Grunting in sympathy, Carlyle eased himself back into a standing position. He tapped Dom on the arm. 'I always said you were a man out of time.'

Guessing what was coming, Silver indulged his friend. 'Go on.'

Carlyle pointed at the print. 'A hundred and fifty years ago, you could have been a respectable businessman.'

Dom grinned. 'I *am* a respectable businessman.'

'Yeah, right.' Carlyle felt his stomach grumble. 'There's a café back at the entrance. I could do with something to eat.'

'Me too. Let's go.'

After a sandwich, Carlyle was feeling just a little bit less grumpy. Dom sipped his green tea and graciously acknowledged his friend's belated willingness to resume polite discourse.

'Not bad here, is it?' They'd chosen a table in the corner by the window, well away from other people and from the browsers in the adjacent bookshop.

Carlyle made the effort to agree. 'Very interesting.'

'And this exhibition,' Dom grinned, 'well, it could have been put on especially for me.'

'I suppose so.' It was true enough. The show looked at the use of drugs through the ages, from the Ancient Egyptians through to the British Empire. It was a reminder that prohibition was not always the status quo. Carlyle looked at the blurb on a flyer for the exhibition which had been left on their table: it informed him that alcohol, coffee and tobacco had all been illegal in the past. And the use of psychoactive drugs dated back millennia.

'I love coming to this museum,' Dominic said. 'It's probably my favourite in the whole of London; a haven for the incurably curious.'

On autopilot, Carlyle lifted the demitasse to his mouth even though it was empty. 'Quite.'

'Sir Henry Wellcome was a fascinating guy. The son of an itinerant preacher, he helped create one of the first multinational pharmaceutical companies, funded medical research and was a great collector. He was a great philanthropist too.'

'You sound jealous.'

'I am,' Dom shrugged, 'I don't mind admitting it. It's an amazing story.'

'Yes, indeed,' said Carlyle. In his book, amazing stories were ten a penny, but he didn't want to rain on Dom's parade. His friend had a point and Carlyle felt a bit of a philistine. The Wellcome Collection, hidden behind an imposing façade of what looked like an office building, stood on the six-lane, smog-choked Euston Road, opposite the eponymous station. It was maybe ten minutes' walk from his home in Covent Garden and Carlyle was loath to admit to Dom that this was his first-ever visit. He was even more loath to admit that he was quite chuffed at being introduced to such a gem on his doorstep. He would have to bring Helen and Alice

'So,' he said, placing his cup back in its saucer, 'what did you want to talk to me about?'

'The Samurai,' Dom beamed.

'The Samurai?'

Dom explained about Eli Wallach and Tuco, and *The Good, the Bad and the Ugly,* and Forest Whitaker, in *Ghost Dog: The Way of the Samurai* and 'the Samurai'.

Carlyle was puzzled. 'So what's his real fucking name?' he asked quietly.

'No idea,' Dom replied. 'I suppose he doesn't really need one.' Then he went on to explain about Alain Costello.

Carlyle poked a bony index finger in the direction of his friend. 'You've got yourself into a really dodgy situation here.'

Dom ran a hand round the neck of his black T-shirt. It had a drawing of a guitar amplifier underneath the legend *SAL'S TUBE AMP REPAIR.* 'That's what Eva says.'

'Well, guess what?' Carlyle growled. 'She's right. This kid is going to jail for a long, long time. I hear that it's going to be a fast-track trial. If I were him, I would just plead guilty and try to get the best deal I could.'

'Tuco isn't going to like that,' Dom mused. 'He wants his boy back in France.'

'What can I say?' Carlyle shrugged. 'Life is a bummer, get used to it.'

Dom stared morosely into his tea cup.

'There's nothing I can do to help you on this

one, Dominic,' Carlyle added quietly.

'I know.'

'And even if I could, I wouldn't.'

Spreading his hands in supplication, Silver smiled weakly. 'Fair enough.'

'This is too far over the line, even for me. There is a point where even pragmatism can be taken too far.'

Dom looked up, grinning despite himself. 'And we've found it.'

'Yes, we have,' said Carlyle, exhaling deeply. 'What are you playing at?'

'The thing is, there are more opportunities than ever. After this Royal Oak thing, there's a lot of unmet demand out there.'

'Operation Eagle?' Carlyle asked. The Met's PR machine had been busy talking up the arrest of fifty-odd criminals accused of conspiracy to supply cocaine, money laundering and firearms offences, by forces under the command of the Special Intelligence Section (SIS). Their operation had been based out of Royal Oak Taxis, a black-cab repair garage under the Westway, the elevated motorway leading out of West London. Millions of pounds of drugs, smuggled across the Channel and up to London through Kent, moved through the specially fortified garage every month, with the cash being laundered through a nearby foreign exchange for a five per cent commission.

'Yeah,' Dom nodded.

'Good result.'

Dom raised his eyebrows. 'It's all very well crowing that you've smashed a major Class-A supply network. How long do you think it will be until the next lot move in?'

'Dunno. Six months?'

'Six weeks, tops,' Dom informed him. 'The investigation has taken years. Cost millions. What's the point? Everyone worked together well, ran professional operations, with next to no violence. The idea that you have dealt a huge blow to the UK Class-A drug industry is bollocks. It's just basic capitalism – you can't buck the market.'

Carlyle wasn't in the mood for one of Dom's rants on the stupidity of drugs policy. He might well be right – but so what? Nothing was going to change any time soon. 'Look,' he said, 'think of it as just another wake-up call. The SIS guys have got time on their hands now. Stick your head back above the parapet and they may come after you.'

Dom looked at him suspiciously. 'You gonna give them a tip-off?'

'Maybe I should,' Carlyle replied, holding his gaze.

For a moment, they sat there in exasperated silence, both of them knowing that would never happen.

'You've always played it so well,' Carlyle said finally, keeping his voice low, 'for a criminal.'

'Thank you,' Dom said tartly.

'You know what I mean. You had actually managed to quit while you were ahead and now you've put yourself in the firing line again.'

Dom shot him an angry look. 'You know what?' he hissed, tapping the table with his index finger. 'I was getting bored. Everything was too easy. There was no one to compete against.'

Carlyle frowned. 'Who were you competing against?'

Genuinely annoyed by the question, Dom slumped back in his chair. 'Everyone ... anyone.'

'It doesn't matter what you do, Dominic. You are always on borrowed time.' Carlyle wagged an admonishing finger across the table. 'There's always someone younger, prettier, richer, more driven.'

'Yeah, yeah, yeah.'

'Or in your case,' Carlyle said grimly, 'more ruthless, more willing to screw you over.'

Taking his time, Dom looked his friend up and down. 'So, who do *you* compete against?'

Carlyle was puzzled. 'No one.'

Looking genuinely angry, Dom snapped, 'That's bullshit. Don't pretend to be so bloody soft.'

'Seriously, who would I compete against? Only myself, really.'

Dom let out a bitter laugh. 'You're gonna make me puke.'

'C'mon,' Carlyle grinned, trying to take the edge off the conversation, 'who would I compete against? Nobody in the Met. All of my peers–' he nodded at Dom – 'including you, have moved up or moved out. Why should I measure myself against them?'

Dom grunted but said nothing.

'If I did,' Carlyle went on, lowering his voice, 'I could only conclude that I was fucked. Look – my card was marked by the Met a long, long time ago, and there's nothing I can do about it. I can do a decent job, but it's still just a job; if I think of it as anything more than that, then I'm a real

212

mug, aren't I?'

'You should have come and worked for me when you had the chance,' Dom said quietly. 'You'd have made a packet.'

Carlyle lowered his gaze to the table. Back in the 1980s, not long after leaving the police force, Dom had offered him a job. Carlyle didn't say yes; he didn't say no either, he just let it slide. The whole thing had been a non-starter. Instinctively, Carlyle knew that, while he could live with Dom being on the wrong side of the law, it was not a move he could ever make himself. Not if he wanted to sleep at night.

'That was a long time ago. And we both knew I wasn't up for it.' He looked up. 'Anyway, we'd have probably both ended up in jail.'

'Maybe.' Dom laughed, easing the tension.

'I don't compete against you,' Carlyle went on, 'and I don't compete against anyone in the Met. It's the only sensible way.'

Dom's eyes narrowed. 'But you compete against yourself.'

'Yeah.' Carlyle was worried that he really was beginning to sound like a total plonker. 'I want to be a good husband and a good father.'

'Who doesn't?'

'Well,' said Carlyle gently, 'that's another reason for not putting yourself into the middle of this mess.'

Dom grimaced. 'Too late for that now.'

TWENTY-FIVE

When Carlyle finally returned to the station, Angie Middleton was waiting for him behind the front desk.

'Why haven't you gone to Paddington Green?' she demanded.

Carlyle gave her what he hoped was a confused look.

'Commander Simpson wants to speak to you,' Angie boomed, *'urgently.'*

'Okay.'

'In her office.'

As he headed down the corridor, Middleton shouted after him, 'There's good news as well!'

'Oh?' Carlyle turned, but made no effort to move back to the desk.

'The Everton's guy,' Angie explained. 'Clive Martin. He's dropped his complaint.'

'That's not much of a shock,' Carlyle shrugged, 'given that he didn't have a bloody leg to stand on, but welcome news nonetheless.'

'And,' Angie's face broke into a toothy smile, 'there's a message from Christina O'Brien. She says she'll be working from ten if you want to pop round to Everton's for your private dance.'

'What?' Carlyle scowled. 'I thought she was being deported.'

'Those charges have been dropped too. Martin's brief came round earlier and we had to release her.'

That damn lawyer, Abigail Slater. 'But she assaulted a police officer,' Carlyle protested.

Amused by his annoyance, Middleton chewed the end of her biro. 'PC Lea's very happy about it. Everyone's been taking the mickey out of him something rotten.'

'What the fuck's that got to do with anything?'

'I'm just saying...' Middleton began doodling on the pad in front of her. 'The word is,' looking past Carlyle, she lowered her voice, 'that she was allowed to skate in exchange for Martin going away.'

Carlyle made a disgusted noise and turned back towards the stairs.

'So,' Middleton called after him, 'are you going to get your dance?'

Walking away, Carlyle grinned and blushed at the same time.

'Well?'

'Maybe,' he said, over his shoulder, 'but only if she brings her Earth Angel.'

'Triste?'

Tuco grunted. The smell of her sex permeated his nostrils, filling his heart with lust, but his dick was so soft he couldn't even get it inside her. It offended his sense of self but maybe it was time to get some help.

Monica smiled sadly. *'Triste comme un jour sans pain...'* Taking his shrivelled member between her fingers, Monica began massaging it gently. Tuco watched in horror as it shrank even further. He tried to remember when exactly she had graduated from whore to mistress. After they had returned from Marseille, Monica had just moved in. He hadn't suggested it, it had just happened. He felt old – too old to run his own household; too old to fuck.

Giving up, Monica idly scratched her left breast. *'Alain tu as comme ça.'*

Tuco knew she was right. The situation with the boy was driving him mad. He needed to do something about it. Getting to his feet, he looked around for a pair of boxer shorts to cover his microscopic nakedness. *'J'ai besoin d'être seul. Je vais regarder un film.'*

'I've got some dope...'

Standing at the gates of City School for Girls, Alice pulled her bag over her shoulder. 'I told you,' she said firmly, 'I've given up.'

'But that was days ago,' Olivia objected. 'Weeks. This is good stuff; even my mother liked it.'

'You get blasted with your mum?'

Olivia frowned. 'It was strictly a one-off. It gave her something to write about for her next column. Anyway, do you want some?'

Ignoring the offer, Alice wearily took the first step on the long march home. 'I've had it for today. Two hours with Sherwood is a killer.'

'Yeah.' Olivia nodded. Everyone agreed that Mr Sherwood's French lessons were one of the most effective forms of torture that the Headmaster had ever managed to inflict on his pupils.

'Are you Alice Carlyle?'

Looking up, the girls were confronted by a tall young man in his early twenties, dressed in trainers, jeans and a brown leather jacket. His long dark hair reached his shoulders and he had a couple of days' worth of stubble on his chin. Although it was a dreary, grey day, he wore a pair of Ray-Ban Aviators.

Olivia let out a low whistle. 'Whoa! Who're *you?*'

Ignoring the panting girl beside her, the boy gestured at Alice. 'Are you?'

Dropping her bag at her feet, Alice nodded. 'Yes.'

The guy pulled a small padded envelope from his back pocket and thrust it towards her. 'Give this to your father.'

'Okay.' Taking the packet, she watched as he turned on his heel and headed off in the direction of Moorgate.

'What a hunk,' Olivia gushed. 'Do you know him?'

'Never seen him before in my life.'

Olivia snatched the packet from her hand and gave it a shake. 'What is it?'

'How the bloody hell should I know?' Alice scowled.

'Are you going to open it?'

Taking it back, Alice turned the envelope over in her hand. No name or address had been written on the outside and it was sealed with sellotape at both ends so there was no way she could get into it without her father knowing.

Olivia prodded her gently on the shoulder. 'Go on!'

'Nah.' Alice opened her bag and dropped it inside. 'I'd better just give it to my dad.' Deciding she would walk home through Smithfield, she hoisted the bag on to her shoulder for a second time. 'I'll see you tomorrow.'

Carlyle bought a juice and a cheese sandwich from the station canteen and headed back upstairs. Relieved to find his spectacles sitting just where he'd left them on his desk, he slipped into his chair and swung his feet onto the desk. Polishing off the sandwich in about ten seconds, he looked around for something else to eat. On Umar's desk, he spotted a king-size Mars Bar. After a moment's contemplation, he reached over and swiped it. Tearing open the wrapper, he took a happy bite while reading a story in the evening paper about an undercover copper who had gone native. PC Marcus Bingle had been a tattooed, ponytailed eco-warrior. Operating as a green campaigner, he had been shagging his way through the ranks of the ideologically unwashed for years while diligently reporting to his case officer along the way. But 'police sources' were now claiming that Bingle had gone native. It was a classic bit of attempted damage limitation when a £2 million trial of environmental activists collapsed, allegedly after Bingle offered to give evidence on their behalf.

'Bloody idiot,' Carlyle harrumphed. Shoving the last of the Mars Bar into his mouth, he watched his mobile vibrating across the desk. Chewing rapidly, he picked it up.

'Yeah?' he said indistinctly.

'Inspector?'

Carlyle swallowed quickly. 'Yes, Umar.' With his free hand, he guiltily scrunched up the empty Mars wrapper and threw it in the direction of a nearby bin, missing by a good foot.

'I'm at the training ground.'

'Good. Have you got the goalie?'

'No.'

Carlyle felt his sugar-rush tail off dramatically. 'Where is he then?'

'He's gone to Middlesbrough,' said Umar apologetically.

Don't make me ask, Carlyle thought.

After an extended pause, Umar realized that he owed his boss an explanation. 'The team had an injury crisis, apparently. Groom is supposed to be on the bench for tonight's game.'

'What game?' Carlyle drew the line at paying attention to anything that didn't directly involve his own club, Fulham. How could he have gotten involved in such a messed-up series of investigations? Getting to his feet he began pacing between desks like a caged baboon with a mental disorder.

Umar mentioned some minor cup competition.

'For fuck's sake,' the inspector grumbled, 'a fucking meaningless game in an empty fucking stadium in a pointless fucking competition. And he's still on the fucking bench. This guy must be really useless.'

'What should I do?'

'Are you joking?' Carlyle shouted at the handset. 'This is a murder investigation. Go and get the fucker.'

Umar groaned. 'In Middlesbrough?'

'Yes, in fucking Middlesbrough,' Carlyle said maliciously. 'I hear it's lovely this time of year.'

'He'll be back tomorrow,' Umar protested. 'It'll take me five or six hours to get there.'

'Just fucking get on with it,' Carlyle snarled.

'And, by the way, thanks for the Mars Bar.'

'What–'

Before his sergeant could complain any further, Carlyle ended the call. Still hungry, he stalked off in search of more food.

On the way back down to the canteen, his phone rang again.

'Yes?'

'On the other thing,' Umar said, clearly irritated at being cut off.

'What other thing?'

'The tramp who was kicked to death round the back of the ENO.'

'Yes, yes,' said Carlyle brusquely. 'What have you got?'

'I spoke to Milch. He was cagey about saying too much at this stage, but he thinks it will be difficult to work out which blow actually killed him. We have CCTV pictures showing four hoodies laying into the poor bastard, but it will be hard to prove that one of them landed the fatal blow.'

'Bloody pathologists,' Carlyle grunted. 'Do we have an ID for the stiff yet?'

'Not yet.'

'For fuck's sake!'

'We have uniforms going round the hostels and speaking to the local dossers,' Umar explained patiently. 'And I've got a couple of CSOs going through Missing Person reports.'

'Good luck.'

Umar paused for effect. 'However, what we do have is some DNA.'

'Do we, indeed?' Carlyle felt his mood improve.

'The security pictures show one of the little

bastards gobbing at the victim. He missed, leaving us a nice little present on the wall.'

That's the great thing about scumbags, Carlyle smiled to himself. *They tend to be very good at messing up.* 'Have we got a match?'

'It's going through the database now,' Umar replied. 'We'll have the results tomorrow.'

'Excellent,' said Carlyle cheerily. Reaching the basement, he made an executive decision to treat himself to a mushroom omelette with chips and beans. 'Something for you to look forward to when you get back from Middlesbrough.'

Silence.

He looked down at the phone. The signal had gone and he had lost the call. 'Ah well,' he mumbled to himself, 'onwards and upwards.'

TWENTY-SIX

Lying on a king-sized bed in the penthouse suite on the fifth floor of the Dukes Hotel in St James's, Christian Holyrod gazed morosely at Abigail Slater. Also naked, she was standing at the end of the bed, bent over her black leather shoulder bag.

Holyrod's eyes narrowed. *Her arse is getting fatter,* he thought. That wasn't necessarily a deal-breaker but, in the Mayor's book, it was always better to err well on the skinny side of voluptuous. His wife could pile on the pounds; he expected considerably more restraint from his mistress. Taking a mouthful of whisky, his thoughts turned to his new PA in City Hall. Clara Hay, the third of his three assistants, had joined the Holyrod express a few months earlier. Twenty-four, she had a Double First in something or other from Cambridge and, rather annoyingly, a television presenter boyfriend who fronted something totally unwatchable on the BBC. Clara was slim, blonde – and smoking hot. Holyrod had a vision of her shimmying through the office in her slit leather mini-skirt and smiled happily.

'Are you checking out my arse?' Abigail said archly as she approached the bed.

'Have you been going to your personal trainer?' he asked before he could think better of it.

She gave him a quizzical look. 'Not for a while. Been too busy. Why?'

'Er, I just thought I might give her a go myself.'

They both appreciated the feebleness of the lie. The woman who organized Slater's training sessions only took on female clients. To Holyrod's relief, however, Abigail let it slide. Then he noticed the over-sized albino carrot in her hand. All evidence of life down below disappeared. He felt a sinking feeling in his stomach as he drained the last of the scotch from his glass. 'What the hell is that?' he asked.

'It was a present from a grateful client, Christina O'Brien.'

The Mayor gave her a blank look.

'One of Clive Martin's girls,' Slater explained. 'Works at Everton's. She was the one who assaulted the policeman during the raid there. Clive agreed to drop his claim, by the way.'

'Which he would have lost anyway,' Holyrod

222

pointed out, refilling his glass almost to the brim.

'*If* I agreed to sleep with him.'

'What?' Holyrod squawked, spilling some of his drink onto the carpet.

'The dirty old goat wanted a shag,' Abigail snorted. 'Of course, I told him to get stuffed. We agreed on a compromise. I promised to get the charges dropped against Christina so that she could get back to work. Apparently she is Everton's biggest earner by some margin.'

Christina O'Brien... Holyrod remembered the footage from the police raid that hadn't made it onto his website and his reluctant penis began to stiffen just a little. *Make a note of the name,* he told himself. Everton's might be worth a visit once he had stood down as Mayor. 'How did you manage that?'

Leaning across the bed, Slater kissed him on the forehead. 'That's on a need to know basis, and you, Mr Mayor, do not need to know.'

Holyrod pushed himself up on his elbows, wondering whether he might order them a little something from room service. He wasn't sure he could summon up the energy to go to a restaurant and, anyway, the menu at Dukes was really quite good. The grilled sardines on sourdough toast was one of his favourites. He was about to reach for the phone, when he saw that Abigail was fumbling with the albino carrot again. The thing seemed to have some kind of belt attached to one end. Concentrating, she pulled it around her waist and adjusted the straps.

'What are you doing?' he asked nervously.

Ignoring him, she removed a small tub of

223

Vaseline from her bag. Twisting off the lid, she began smearing it along the length of her new appendage.

'Abigail!'

'Roll over,' she commanded gruffly. 'Let's try something new...'

'Where's your mother?'

Alice gave her father a peck on the cheek. 'She's got a planning meeting tonight for the Liberia trip.'

'Okay.' Carlyle had forgotten all about Liberia. 'What do you think about it?'

'I think it's a great idea,' Alice said cheerily. As she stepped back, he realized she was still wearing his Clash T-shirt. Hopefully, it had been washed in the interim. 'Mum says you might come too.'

'We'll see how work is shaping up,' Carlyle said warily. 'Have you eaten?'

'Yeah. I was just about to start my homework.'

'What is it?'

'Maths and French.' Two of her better subjects. Carlyle nodded. 'Good.'

'It shouldn't take long.'

'Okay, I'll sort myself out with something to eat.'

Carlyle was just pouring some olive oil onto a plate of penne, when Alice reappeared in the kitchen doorway.

'I forgot,' she said, putting a small packet onto the kitchen top next to the plate. 'Someone asked me to give you this.'

Carlyle looked at the envelope and frowned. 'What?'

'When I was coming out of school this afternoon,' Alice explained, 'a guy handed it to me and asked me to give it to you.'

Carlyle's mind went off in a dozen different directions, none of them good. 'Is that all he said?'

'Yeah. He asked me if I was Alice Carlyle and then he gave me your package.'

'He didn't say anything else?' Carlyle asked, careful to keep any edge from his voice.

'Dad,' she complained, 'if he'd said anything else, I'd have told you.'

'Okay, okay.' Leaving the packet where it was, Carlyle opened a drawer and pulled out a fork. Picking up his plate, he headed for the living room. 'What did this guy look like?'

'Aren't you going to open it?'

'Later,' Carlyle said, spearing a couple of tubes of pasta and popping them into his mouth. 'What was he like?'

Alice blushed slightly. 'He was a young guy, quite cute.'

Carlyle nodded. 'What did he look like?'

'I dunno, just cute.'

Stepping into the living room, Carlyle grabbed the remote and switched on the TV.

Alice stood in the doorway, leaning against the frame. 'Do you know him?'

'Sounds like one of my snitches,' Carlyle lied.

'Ooh,' Alice squealed. 'An undercover operation!'

'Something like that.' Flicking through the channels, he opted for Sky Sports News. Sitting down on the sofa, he said to his daughter, 'Thanks for bringing it to me. Now go and finish

225

your homework.'

Umar Sligo stood in the away dressing room wondering why Paul Groom needed to have a shower. The goalie had just sat on the bench for the last 120 minutes plus penalties, watching glumly as his team had gone down to a predictable but embarrassing defeat in front of a four-fifths empty Riverside Stadium. Despite that, the only person who seemed in any way pissed off was Umar himself. The players and coaches were going mechanically about their business. Everyone just wanted to get back on the motorway and head for home. Umar could relate to that. Glancing at his watch, he realized that it would probably be about 4 a.m. before they made it back to London.

The team manager, a former England international rumoured to have a serious coke habit and an underage mistress, glared at the sergeant. When Umar had taken him aside and explained why he was there, the manager's only response had been: 'You plod, you pick your moments, don't you?' After a few minutes pacing the room like a demented hamster, he had skulked off to do his post-match press conference and answered the inevitable questions about his future or, more accurately, lack of one.

'Twat!' one of the players hissed after the boss as the door shut behind him.

'Yeah,' another laughed, 'surely they've got to sack the bastard now.'

Keeping his gaze on the floor, Umar tried not to be too obvious in his eavesdropping.

Finally, Groom appeared from the showers.

Umar recognized him from his picture on the club website. Naked, he was drying off his hair with a towel, which only served to draw the sergeant's attention to the goalkeeper's most celebrated asset. And, sweet Jesus, it was most certainly worthy of celebration. He cleared his throat but kept his voice low. 'Paul Groom?'

The keeper eyed Umar with dull resentment. 'Yeah?' He began drying his genitals with the towel.

'I'm...'

'I know who you are,' Groom said sullenly. He nodded at the door. 'Give me five minutes to get dressed and I'll meet you outside.'

The civilians who worked the scanning machine in the post room at Charing Cross police station had long since gone home. Scratching his head, Carlyle tried to convince himself that it couldn't be that difficult to use. Basically, it looked like a smaller version of the X-ray machines at airports. On the side of the tunnel was the legend: *Threat Protection Systems: Next Generation X-Ray Screening Solutions*.

Sounds good, Carlyle thought. *Now all I've got to do is work out how to switch the bloody thing on.*

'Inspector?'

Looking up, Carlyle saw a mixture of amusement and concern on Angie Middleton's face.

'Hi.'

'What are you doing?' the sergeant asked. 'I thought you'd gone home.'

'I came back. You're on late tonight.'

'My replacement called in sick. I had to pull a

227

double shift.' Middleton carefully took a bar of milk chocolate from her shirt pocket and placed it on the top of the machine. 'I was just on my way back from the canteen.'

The inspector said, 'I don't suppose you know where the "on" switch is, by any chance?'

Middleton crossed her arms over her more than ample bosom. 'Only properly qualified personnel are supposed to operate this machine.'

'I know.'

'And everything that goes through it needs to be logged.'

'Of course.' Carlyle gestured at the packet that he had carefully placed in the middle of the conveyor belt. 'But I just need to look at something quickly.'

Sighing, Middleton stepped round the back of the machine and flicked a switch. 'Come here.'

Carlyle did as he was told.

'See?'

'Mm.'

At the back of the machine was a monitor next to a control panel with four buttons. Middleton switched on the monitor and an image of inside the machine appeared on the screen. 'It's very simple,' she explained, running her finger down the buttons. 'Start. Stop. Backwards. Magnify.'

'Okay,' Carlyle nodded. 'I'm sure I'll be fine from here. Thanks, Angie.'

Angie gave him a weary shake of the head. 'I'll be at the desk if you need any more help. Remember to switch everything off when you go.'

'I will,' Carlyle smiled. 'Thanks again.'

Retrieving her chocolate bar, she headed for

the door. Once she had gone, the inspector quickly pressed the start button and listened to the machine rumble into action.

By the time Carlyle made it home for the second time that evening, the flat was dark and silent. After brushing his teeth, he had a piss before undressing in the bathroom. Tiptoeing naked into the bedroom, he slipped under the duvet.

Rolling into the middle of the bed, Helen pulled him towards her. 'So what was in the envelope?' she asked sleepily.

'I don't know,' he whispered. 'Anything like that has to go through the scanner at work. The scanner guys knock off at six, so I logged it in and they'll check in the morning.' He had composed the lie on the way home; it sounded good enough.

Helen slipped a hand between his legs and he felt a pleasing tingle in his crotch. 'Couldn't it have waited until the morning, then?' she asked, sounding rather more awake now.

Her hand slid away from him and Carlyle pulled it gently back. 'I won't be at the station first thing,' he murmured, 'so my sergeant can get on with it.' He wondered how Umar was doing on the road back to London and stifled a chuckle.

'What's so funny?' This time when Helen removed her hand, she did not let him guide it back.

'My poor bastard of a sergeant had to go up to Middlesbrough tonight to track down a suspect.'

'Look, John,' said Helen, clearly not interested in the fate of Umar Sligo, 'I don't like Alice being accosted outside the school. Who is this informer anyway?'

229

'Eh?'

'Alice said it was a snitch.'

'Yeah. He thought he was using his initiative. I'll speak to him. It won't happen again.'

'If he's someone you know,' Helen persisted, 'why do you have to go through such a performance?'

'He thought he was being helpful.' It was time to change the subject. 'How was your meeting?' he asked.

'Good. We've got the confirmed dates for the Liberia trip.'

'That's great.'

Turning to face him, Helen looked her husband in the eye, the way she did when she wanted to steamroller him on something. 'It's been moved forward.' She mentioned some dates.

Frowning, Carlyle thought it through. 'You're going next week then?'

'Alice really wants you to come.'

'Shouldn't she be in school?'

'I spoke to the Headmaster. He's happy for me to take her out of school for such an educational trip.'

'For two weeks?'

'It takes forever to get around,' Helen explained. 'It's not just like jumping in a car and zooming up the M1.'

'No, no, of course not.' He knew better than to get into an argument with his wife on the subject of Third World countries.

'You must have plenty of leave you can take.'

'Mm.'

'Come on, you never use it all up.'

'It's not as easy as that, as you well know. Maybe I could come for the second week. Let me talk to Simpson.'

'Okay.' Turning away from him, Helen signalled the end of the conversation. Within a few moments, she was snoring gently. Lying in the darkness, Carlyle stared at the ceiling, coming to terms with the impending trip.

TWENTY-SEVEN

A bored-looking Paul Groom sat behind a desk in the interview room, flanked by two men in suits. Both of the suits, dwarfed by the young goalkeeper, looked old and shrunken. Carlyle recognized the one on his left, an ambulance-chasing lawyer called Kenneth Moynahan, but the other, he had never seen before. Better dressed than either Groom or Moynahan, the third man ignored the inspector's entrance as he tapped away ostentatiously on his iPad.

Carlyle nodded at Moynahan and glared at Groom, who made a half-hearted attempt to hold his eye, giving up almost immediately.

'Who are you?' Carlyle asked the man with the iPad.

The man finished what he was typing and put the tablet down on the desk. He then offered the inspector a limp hand. 'Wayne Devine, pleased to meet you.'

Ignoring the man's hand, Carlyle glanced at

Moynahan but the lawyer's expression was giving nothing away.

'And what are you doing here, Mr Devine?'

Devine grinned as if that should be obvious. 'I'm Mr Groom's agent.'

Moynahan began doodling frantically on a notepad on the desk in front of him. He looked as if he was trying hard not to smile.

Getting ready to work himself up into a state of aggravated annoyance, Carlyle planted his hands on his hips. 'Excuse me?'

Slipping a business card across the table, Devine sat back in his chair. Looking Carlyle up and down, he decided that he would have to take things slowly with the stupid plod. 'I represent–'

'What the fuck are you doing here?' Whoever gave the agent access to the interview room was gonna be in big trouble, once Carlyle got hold of them. He glanced down at the card. At the top, in bold red lettering, it bore the legend *DF&K Associates*.

Unable to keep the smirk from his face any longer, Moynahan ducked under the desk, on the pretence of getting something from his case. Groom was still staring into space, giving no indication that he was following the conversation at all.

'Mr...' Carlyle stole another quick look at the card: 'Devine.' He gestured around the interview room. 'In here, Mr Groom is *Mr Moynahan's* client. We are here in relation to a very serious investigation.'

The agent sighed. 'I am well aware of the situation, Inspector. What you have to understand is–'

'What *you* have to understand,' Carlyle hissed, leaning across the table and jabbing an angry index finger in front of the agent's face, 'is that if you don't get your arse out of this fucking room right now, I will have you charged with both accessory to murder and obstruction of justice.'

'But–'

'You have precisely thirty seconds to get out of this room and out of this building.'

Devine looked past his client towards Moynahan.

'I think,' said the lawyer quietly, 'the inspector has made his position quite clear.'

'Very well,' said Devine evenly. Getting to his feet, he addressed Groom directly. 'Remember, Paul, just sit tight. Say nothing until I get back to you.' Nodding at Moynahan, he picked up his iPad and stalked out.

'What the fuck are you playing at?' Carlyle asked the lawyer as the door closed and the agent disappeared down the corridor.

Moynahan was neither apologetic nor insightful. 'Nothing to do with me.'

Rubbing his neck, Carlyle wondered quite where they should go from here. His dilemma was solved by the appearance of Umar with a large mug of steaming tea in his hand. Putting the mug on the table, he pulled up a chair and sat down next to the inspector. Unshaven, with dark rings under his eyes, his dishevelled appearance immediately made Carlyle feel better.

'Tough night?'

Umar nodded as he sucked up some of the tea from his mug. 'I got two hours' sleep.' He waved his mug in the direction of Groom. 'You could at least have played at home, couldn't you?'

For the first time, the vaguest flicker of an expression crossed Groom's face.

'And you got beat,' Umar added gratuitously.

The goalie shrugged. 'Shit happens.'

It speaks, thought Carlyle.

'Shall we get started?' Moynahan asked.

'My sergeant will conduct the interview,' Carlyle said, standing up. He grinned at Groom. 'Feel free to confess, given that we know you did it. Save everyone a lot of time.'

Without waiting for any response, he headed back upstairs.

Back at his desk, Carlyle decided he needed a break from the station. Grabbing his jacket, he headed back downstairs and nipped across Agar Street, heading towards the piazza. Outside the Box Café on Henrietta Street, he caught the eye of Myron Sabo and signalled that he wanted a green tea. Remaining on the pavement, he pulled out his private pay-as-you-go Nokia from one pocket, and Clifford Blitz's business card from another. With some difficulty, he laboriously typed in Clifford Blitz's number and hit Call.

To his surprise, Gavin Swann's agent picked up almost before he had time to lift the handset to his ear.

'Blitz.'

'It's John Carlyle from—'

'Inspector,' said Blitz, all business, 'how are things going with Mr Groom?'

'The investigation is proceeding,' Carlyle said

stiffly, 'but that's not why I'm ringing.'

'Let me guess,' Blitz sighed, 'you would like some tickets for a game and–'

'No, *no*,' Carlyle interrupted. 'I wanted to ask you about something you said when we last spoke.'

'Hold on.'

Down the line, Carlyle could hear Blitz bark a series of instructions to a hapless minion. Among the words that were clearly distinguishable were 'Laurent Perrier' and 'blow'. Overlooking that, the inspector waited patiently for the agent to come back on the line.

'Fire away.'

'When we were talking last time,' Carlyle said cautiously, 'you said that you had received bullets in the post.'

'Yeah,' Blitz replied. 'It's happened a few times, always the same carry-on: some lame-brain with the imagination of a pea wants to threaten you. Thinks that all they have to do is pop a little something in the post.' He paused to shout a few more instructions to his assistant before coming back on the line. 'Why do you ask? Is someone trying to put the frighteners on you?' He let out a loud gaffaw.

'No, no,' Carlyle lied, thinking about the three cartridges in the still-unopened envelope that was locked in a drawer in his desk. 'It's just something that's come up in another investigation; nothing to do with Gavin Swann.'

'Oh.' If Blitz was curious, he kept it well hidden. 'I gotta go, Inspector. All I can say is that you don't have to worry about the kind of people who do this sort of thing. In my experience, it's always bullshit. They never have the balls to follow through.'

'No?' Carlyle asked, wanting to be convinced.

'It's strictly for tosspots whose balls haven't dropped. Real criminals don't make threats,' Blitz sniggered, 'as I'm sure you know.'

'Yes,' said Carlyle, not sure that he knew at all.

'Put it this way,' Blitz said. 'If it was me, and I was really pissed off, I wouldn't send you a bullet, I'd blow your fucking head off.'

'About Mr Swann,' Carlyle started, but Blitz had already hung up. Through the window, Myron held up a mug, to show Carlyle that his drink was ready. Nodding, the inspector gestured for him to put it on the table next to where he was standing. Staying outside, he called another number.

Silver answered on the third ring. 'I was wondering when you were going to get in touch. What's happening?'

'Nothing good.' Carlyle quickly brought him up to speed with a brief run-through of selected recent events.

When he finished, there was a pause.

Finally, Dom spoke. 'No lecture this time?'

'No.'

'Good, because I'm getting more than enough of that at home.'

Carlyle kept his mouth clamped firmly shut.

'Where are you now?'

'The piazza.'

'Okay.' Dom gave him the address of a bar in Soho. 'Meet me there in fifteen minutes.'

'Make it half an hour.' Ending the call, the

inspector went into the café, nabbing a copy of the *Metro* that one of the other customers had left behind. Unfolding the paper, he turned, as was his wont, to the back page, which was dominated by a picture of Gavin Swann hobbling out of a game after being injured. The story was based around a quote from his manager saying that he hoped to have his star striker back playing within the next couple of weeks.

'*The boy should be back in training on Monday,*' the manager said, '*and we'll take it from there. Obviously, he will have to work on his match fitness levels but he's been living like a monk since the injury and I know that he's in great shape. I want to get Gavin back on the pitch as soon as possible, certainly before the end of the month.*'

A horrible thought popped into Carlyle's head: Swann's return should be just in time for the game against Fulham. That was the last thing that his struggling team needed. *Maybe I should arrest the little sod*, he thought, *put his recovery back a bit. After all, we can do with all the help we can get.*

For a moment, he gave the idea some serious consideration. Then his eye caught the teaser at the bottom of the story: *KEEPER QUES-TIONED OVER HOTEL DEATH, P. 6.*

It was beyond a miracle that Swann's name had, so far, been kept away from the case. Whether you loathed them or detested them, British journalists were normally relentless in their pursuit of stories like this. Tabloid hacks in particular had shown time and time again that they were far better at tracking down both people and information than the police themselves. And the inspector had absolutely no doubt whatsoever that every paper on the news-stand would have been called by someone at Charing Cross wanting to sell them some gossip about Swann's alleged involvement.

The only explanation Carlyle could come up with was that Clifford Blitz was one hell of an operator. Doubtless, he was trading favours and making threats like they were going out of fashion to protect Swann, helped by the fact that an army of £1,000-an-hour lawyers would be trying to bludgeon every hack in town into submission. The inspector felt a grudging admiration for Blitz; very few people were able to play this kind of game with any measure of success. It was almost impossible to beat the press at their own game.

Flicking through the paper, he came to the story on page six just as Myron appeared at the next table and began clearing it away. He was staring at the inspector.

'What?' Carlyle snapped.

'You've got glasses.' Myron wiped his hands on a tea towel with a picture of Buckingham Palace on it that was hanging over his shoulder. 'Makes you look ... different.' Without waiting for a reply, he retreated behind the counter to take payment from a customer waiting by the till.

Shit, Carlyle thought, *I don't even remember that I'm wearing the bloody things now. Surely a sign that I'm getting more decrepit in both mind and body.* A pang of self-pity was quickly replaced by the realization that there was sod all he could do about it.

TWENTY-EIGHT

Zatoichi was situated at the northern end of Beak Street. As he walked in, a creature in a black vest with orange hair scowled at him from behind the bar. On balance, Carlyle decided that it was probably female.

With a sigh, she gestured across the empty room. 'We're closed.' To his plebeian ear, the accent sounded South African, or maybe Australian.

He took another couple of steps towards the bar. 'I'm here to see Mr Silver.'

If mention of the boss's name had any effect, it didn't show. 'Are you the cop?'

Carlyle felt anger flare in his chest. *For fuck's sake, Dominic, why not tell everyone who I am?* He nodded.

The girl gestured to a set of stairs at the end of the bar. 'He's in the office, second floor.'

Jogging up the stairs, Carlyle found himself seriously winded by the time he reached the blue door marked PRIVATE: STAFF ONLY. As he walked into the room, Dominic Silver looked up from behind his desk and grinned.

'Nice specs,' he noted, pushing his own, rimless frames further up his nose. He was wearing an ancient Kurt Cobain T-shirt, which made him look like a fifty-year-old student.

'I know, I know,' said Carlyle grumpily. 'They make me look "different".'

'They make you look old.'

Gesturing over his shoulder, Carlyle quickly changed the subject. 'Where did you get Lisbeth Salander?' he asked, giving a name-check to Stieg Larsson's anti-heroine.

'Michela?' Dom laughed. 'She might be borderline autistic, but I don't think she's very good with computers or guns.'

'You don't do customer service then?' Parking himself in the low leather chair in front of the desk, Carlyle looked round the office. The bar, in various incarnations, had been part of Dom's portfolio of businesses for many years now and the inspector had been here several times before. The room had, however, been redecorated since his last visit, in a bright, minimalist style. To Carlyle's untrained eye, the furniture looked like it came from IKEA but he knew that it was more likely to have been purchased at some top-end West End retailer like Heal's or the Avram store. To his left, a large window gave a view down Regent Street towards Piccadilly Circus; on the opposite wall, above a tattered brown leather sofa, hung a massive screen print of *The Island,* one of Stephen Walter's series of idiosyncratic maps of London, full of humour and autobiographical detail. Carlyle wasn't a great one for art, but he knew that he could find infinite pleasure exploring Walter's work, in the unlikely event that he could ever afford to put one on *his* wall. He searched unsuccessfully for Charing Cross, somewhere in the centre of the dense forest of detail. This was one time when his spectacles wouldn't help; the piece could only be properly viewed with the aid of the large Silverline magnifying glass sitting on the corner of Dom's desk.

'The customers love her,' said Dom, bringing Carlyle back to more mundane matters. 'Michela's a great girl. You work in here, you have to be a bit robust, otherwise you wouldn't last a single shift. Michela's been here almost two years now.' Both of them knew that was the best part of a lifetime in the transitory world of Soho. He gestured at an empty plastic drinks container on his desk. 'Want a juice?'

Carlyle felt vaguely tempted. 'What is it today?'

'It's an Organic Eggnog Super Smoothie.'

Carlyle made a face.

'It's from the juice bar next door,' Silver told him. 'It really is good stuff. I can get Michela to nip round and get you one.'

'It's okay.' Carlyle held up a hand. 'I'm fine.'

'Okay.' Sitting forward in his chair, Dom started drumming his fingers on the table. For a moment, Carlyle wondered if he might be partaking of his own product.

Then: 'The matter in hand.'

'Yes?' Carlyle replied.

Dom stopped drumming as quickly as he had started. 'I've got a plan,' he said, picking up a Mont Blanc fountain pen from the desk.

Oh, have you? Let's hear it then.

Silver unscrewed the cap and scribbled something down on the A5 pad on the desk in front of him. Tearing off the top sheet, he waved it in front of Carlyle, like a doctor bestowing a prescription.

Carlyle leaned over and accepted the offering. Sitting back down, he looked at the address Dom had given him. 'Docklands?'

Dom nodded. 'It's a small office block. Get your people to check it out; top floor.'

'My people?'

'Someone you can trust.'

'That narrows it down,' Carlyle snorted.

Dom put the cap back on the pen and tossed it onto the table. 'Someone who is reliable; who cannot be directly connected to you by an outsider.'

'Mm.'

'No one from Charing Cross.'

'Okay.' Carlyle started going through a list of possible colleagues in his head. 'What will they find when they get there?'

'The place is currently being squatted by a bunch of students complaining about "locals" being priced out of the neighbourhood.'

'Great.' Carlyle could already imagine the pitched battle when the police went in.

Dom smiled weakly. 'Free security. What they don't know is that in the ceiling there is stashed some 40 kilos of coke. Not great stuff, but reasonably pure.'

'Not yours, presumably.'

Dom sat back in his chair and brought his hands together, the tips of his fingers touching as he adopted a pose of earnest contemplation. 'It's supposed to be a joint venture but ultimately, the stuff belongs to the Samurai.'

'Your business partner.'

'My soon-to-be ex-business partner.' Dom held up his hands in surrender. 'I have already admitted my mistake in getting into bed with Tuco Martinez, so I think it is time we should all move on.'

Carlyle nodded graciously.

'If Tuco loses this load,' Dom continued, 'it will seriously bugger up his operations. Throw in his problems with his moronic son and I think he'll have to abandon his plans to expand in the UK.'

'You think?' Carlyle had intended to raise the issue of the three bullets in the envelope that had been handed to Alice, but now he decided to leave it. If they could run Tuco out of town, it would be problem solved.

Dom thought about it for a moment. 'Yeah. Alain Costello will get sent down for a good stretch but will probably get transferred back to a French prison fairly quickly...'

'I suppose so,' Carlyle agreed.

'And the vacuum created by the Special Intelligence Section and their Operation Eagle will make London a complicated place to operate in for a while, especially if you are struggling for product.'

'How are people dealing with the market disruption?' Carlyle asked casually.

'As I said, it will be filled soon enough,' Dom replied, 'but inevitably there will be some blood spilled along the way.'

Carlyle shot him a questioning look.

'You don't need to know.'

'Okay.' Carefully folding the sheet of paper into quarters, Carlyle got to his feet.

'What did you want to talk about?' Dom asked.

'It can wait.' Carlyle waved the square of paper at Dom before putting it in his trouser pocket. 'Let's sort this out first.'

Dom nodded. 'They need to move today.'

'Understood,' Carlyle said briskly, heading for

243

the door.

Carlyle had been sitting in the Vida Sana juice bar on Glasshouse Street, just round the corner from Silver's office, for more than half an hour, still trying to decide what best to do with Dom's tip-off, but without coming to any conclusion. Looking out of the window, he watched a pretty, hippy-looking girl and her grungy boyfriend stroll past. Deep in animated conversation, the boy took a long drag on a monster joint, holding in the smoke as he handed it to the girl. Apropos of nothing, The Clash popped into Carlyle's head and started up a spirited rendition of 'Julie's Been Working for the Drugs Squad'. Smiling, Carlyle tossed his empty beaker of Cactus Detox (Organic cactus, pineapple, lime, banana, pineapple juice and 98 per cent fat-free probiotic yoghurt) into a nearby trash can.

'Brilliant,' he mumbled to himself. 'Problem sorted.'

Turning into Agar Street, Carlyle skipped up the steps of the station. He had barely reached the top when he was accosted by his sergeant.

'He's confessed!' Umar cried. Carlyle made a point of looking theatrically towards the unsettled grey heavens.

'Groom,' Umar added, lowering his voice to a whisper. 'He signed a written confession a couple of hours ago.'

You could have called me, Carlyle thought angrily.

'I tried calling you,' Umar continued. 'Did you not get my message?'

Carlyle grunted. Doubtless the voicemail would turn up in a couple of days. 'Presumably he acted on the advice of his sodding agent.'

'What?'

'Nothing.'

Umar gave him a funny look. 'Anyway, he admitted he tried to force the girl into having sex with him and says he lost his temper when she refused. Things got a bit out of hand.'

'Didn't they just,' said Carlyle, distinctly unconvinced.

'According to Groom's version of events,' said Umar, picking up on his boss's sceptical tone, 'Swann tried to stop him, there was a fight and Sandy Carroll got accidentally smacked in the face.'

Trying not to get too angry, Carlyle said, 'Do we have any forensic evidence?'

Umar shook his head. 'Nothing we can use, apparently.'

Fuck. Two men, one body, how fucking hard could it be? Surely they could give him something? 'I'll call Susan Phillips.'

'I've read through her preliminary report,' Umar protested.

'I'll call her anyway. Groom, where is he now?'

'They've moved him to Belmarsh.'

'That's just great,' Carlyle complained. If he wanted to quiz the prisoner himself, a trip to Belmarsh, in the arse end of Greenwich, would take the best part of a day. Parking Groom in Brixton or Wormwood Scrubs or, indeed, just about any of London's other jails, would have made his life a lot easier.

Umar shrugged. 'Not my call, boss.'

'Yeah, yeah,' Carlyle sighed.

'I'm off to get some kip,' Umar mumbled. 'I'll be back later.'

'Let's speak later, then.' Carlyle patted him on the arm. 'And well done.' He coughed to try and mask the obvious lack of conviction in his voice. 'You've done a good job on this one.'

Umar nodded. 'Thanks.' Zipping up his jacket, he jogged down the steps.

TWENTY-NINE

Carlyle stood at the door of the station and watched Umar walk down the street until he reached the Strand and disappeared amongst the crowd. Pulling out his mobile, Carlyle called Susan Phillips' work number. Tapping his foot impatiently against the edge of the top step, he listened to it ring for what seemed like an eternity before her voicemail message finally kicked in.

'Susan,' he jumped in too quickly and was silenced by the beep. 'Fuck ... Susan, it's John Carlyle. Give me a call.'

Heading inside, Carlyle tried to convince himself that he wasn't really bothered by the lack of forensic evidence in the Sandy Carroll case. After all, he had never been the kind of copper who relied on the test tube and tweezer brigade to bail him out. Indeed, the fact that forensics remained so fashionable made him uncomfortable. He had a lot of time for diligent and expert colleagues like Susan Phillips and also for the Met's Scientific Support Unit, which co-ordinated crime scene activities. But popular expectations of forensic science, especially crime scene investigation and DNA testing, were way too high. This put everyone under huge pressure to solve everything in the blink of an eye.

The word *'forensic'*, Carlyle was never slow to point out, came from the Latin *forensis*, meaning *before the forum*. Basically, back in Roman times, accuser and accused would make their case to the authorities. Whoever gave the best pitch would win and the facts rarely got a chance to speak for themselves.

The truth was that some cases just didn't get solved. Those that did were usually down to the basics – luck, confession, betrayal or, Carlyle's own personal favourite, simple basic incompetence on the part of the criminal. Covering up a crime that was bad enough for anyone to bother to investigate seriously was a very difficult task. It required determination, stamina and considerable attention to detail. Most people didn't think that far in advance. Or they couldn't be bothered with the hard work required. The police, on the other hand, did it for a living. Carlyle knew who his money was on.

He also knew that, out of eight million people, London managed less than a hundred and thirty murders in the previous year. As always, more than half of those were domestics – when the victim usually knew the killer – so you always knew where to look first.

Then there was the fact that around 90 per cent of murderers are men.

In any given year, the murder clean-up rate was 90 per cent plus, often as high as 97 or 98 per cent; you either find them, or they come to you.

Those were good odds, statistics that gave Carlyle a great sense of wellbeing. It told him that he lived in a very safe city. Of course, some places in London were safer than others. And some people were safer than others. But most people – by a very, very big majority – had nothing whatsoever to worry about.

Sadly for Sandy Carroll, she wasn't most people.

The inspector had never been a *'let's do it for the victim'* kind of guy. The victim was dead, what did he or she care? Do it for the family? Maybe, but in Carlyle's experience, the family sometimes cared, sometimes didn't. No, his primary motivation was catching the perpetrators. He just hated the thought of the bastards getting away with it. Maybe Paul Groom landed the fatal blow on Carroll's jaw, maybe not, but there were two men involved, and in his book, they were both responsible. It was Gavin Swann, with his poisonous mix of money, arrogance and stupidity that had put them all in that room, and it was Swann who thought his money could buy him a free pass.

The thought really pissed Carlyle off. It bounced around his brain like a migraine while he told himself that, one way or another, he would nail the stupid little fucker.

As he climbed the stairs to the third floor, he called Phillips again on her mobile. The call went to voicemail and he hesitated before deciding not to leave another message. Arriving at his desk, he tried to work out what to do next, but his mind was blank. Switching on his PC, he remembered that a call to Simpson was long overdue, even by his standards. The thought of having to talk to the Commander filled him with something approaching physical pain. Picking up the handset on his desk, he began dialling the number for Simpson's office in Paddington Green before changing his mind and calling her mobile instead. Holding his breath for a moment, he punched the air when the call went to voicemail.

'Result!' A passing WPC gave him a funny look. After the beep, he left a desultory message and promised to call back later. Hanging up, he headed for the canteen, just in case Simpson called straight back.

Twenty minutes and a double espresso later, he was back at his desk, sifting through his emails. The Police Federation had sent him a draft letter to send to his MP complaining about attempts to reduce police pensions. 'Good luck with that,' Carlyle mumbled to himself as he deleted it.

Next up was a children's ticket offer from Fulham FC. Carlyle was tempted but he knew that trying to convince Alice to go to a football match with him was a lost cause. Her mother's virulent hostility towards the sport had infected their daughter at an early age and she had always refused his attempts to drag her along to Craven Cottage. Sadly, that too went into the cyber bin. Moving on to the BBC website, he checked out upcoming fixtures. Carlyle knew that if he didn't start going to more games, Helen would start to complain about the cost of his season ticket.

According to the BBC, there were six games being played that evening. Sadly, Fulham were playing in Manchester, which was pretty much another guaranteed defeat. Glancing down the list, he noted two other games in London.

'Interesting...' As the germ of an idea formed in his head, a call came in on his mobile. Seeing Simpson's number on the screen, he ignored it and went back to cleaning out his inbox.

Five minutes later, Angie Middleton puffed up the stairs and staggered in his direction. Reaching his desk, she took a moment to catch her breath. 'Simpson's looking for you ... again,' she wheezed.

Don't have a heart attack, Carlyle thought. 'I'll get back to her straight away,' he lied.

Middleton looked doubtful. 'She's not very happy.'

'She never is,' Carlyle grunted.

'We seem to be having this conversation a lot recently.'

'Yeah, like a couple of losers in a Samuel Beckett play.'

'Eh?'

'Never mind.' Switching off his computer, Carlyle got to his feet.

'So, are you going to call her?'

'Angie,' Carlyle said patiently, 'I can walk and talk at the same time.'

Middleton looked doubtful.

'I need to check something out,' Carlyle improvised. 'I'll call her on the way.' Then, seeing her expression, he grinned, crossing his heart with his index finger. 'I promise.'

Susan Phillips gestured with her fork for Carlyle to sit down in the empty chair on the opposite side of the table.

'Nice of you to come and see me,' she smiled, spearing a tomato and popping it into her mouth.

The owner of Tutti's café on Lambs Conduit Street, up the road from Holborn police station, gave him an enquiring look. Having had more than enough coffee already, Carlyle ordered a green tea.

Phillips picked through the remains of her salad before letting the fork fall on the plate. 'Don't you want anything to eat?' She lifted a small glass bottle of peach and mango juice to her lips and took a swig.

Carlyle shook his head. 'I just thought I'd try and catch you before I head home.'

Phillips nodded. 'How are the family?'

'Good,' Carlyle replied enthusiastically. 'All good. You?' He wasn't sure what Phillips' domestic arrangements were but he wanted to show willing.

'Good,' Phillips parroted.

His reserves of small talk exhausted, Carlyle turned to the matter in hand. 'About Sandy Carroll...'

'Didn't you read my report?'

'Haven't had a chance yet.'

The café-owner came with Carlyle's tea. Sweeping up Phillips' plate, he retreated behind the counter. Shaking her head, the pathologist glanced at her watch. 'Look, I've got to go in five minutes.'

'Just give me the highlights.'

She gave him a sly smile. 'Well, one of them killed her, but we can't be sure which one. We have nothing which corroborates Groom's story and, of course, we haven't been able to process Swann – yet.'

Ignoring the barb, Carlyle took a sip of his tea. 'What are the odds?'

Phillips finished her juice. 'Based on what we know?' She screwed the cap back on to the empty bottle. 'Fifty-fifty. Assuming it wasn't a joint effort, of course.'

'So we have nothing.'

Phillips pulled a small red leather notebook from her bag. 'That's the way it goes. We might have had more if I could have seen Mr Swann?'

Okay, okay, Carlyle thought, *give it a rest.*

'But, anyway,' she said, taking a crisp twenty-pound note from her purse, 'I hear that you, or rather your dishy new sergeant, have already got a confession.'

Fucking Umar. Carlyle raised his eyes to the heavens. 'Good news travels fast.'

'It sure does,' Phillips agreed. 'That's because there's so little of it about.' Getting to her feet, she walked over to the counter and paid for her lunch and for Carlyle's tea.

'Thanks.'

'My pleasure,' said Phillips, putting away her change. Leaving the café, they walked to the corner of Theobald's Road. 'Surely,' said Phillips, 'the confession solves your problem?'

Carlyle sighed. 'It depends what you think the problem is.'

'You don't reckon Groom did it?' Phillips asked, dangling a toe over the edge of the kerb.

Carlyle smiled mirthlessly. 'I think it's fifty-fifty.'

Alex Miles ushered Kelly Kellaway towards the table at the back of the Light Bar occupied by Clifford Blitz. Recognizing Gavin Swann's agent, Kelly gave her best smile as she dropped her designer leather hobo bag on the floor and slipped off her Juicy Couture faux fur jacket, draping it over the back of a chair.

'Sit.' Blitz nodded at the chair.

'Thank you,' said Kelly, primly lowering her rump into the seat.

Blitz glowered at the concierge. 'Leave us.' Kelly tried and failed to suppress a smirk.

'If you need anything...' Miles said, the exasperation clear in his voice.

'Sure, sure.' Blitz waved him away with a dismissive hand. 'For now, what I need is to be able to have a private conversation with the young lady here.' Kelly's smirk got wider. Tut-tutting to himself, Miles trotted off.

Turning to the girl, Blitz looked her up and down. With her hair pulled back into a ponytail, she was wearing minimal make-up, making her look even younger than her twenty-two years. He spent several moments contemplating her décolletage – a black bra clearly visible beneath her expensive silk blouse – before dragging his gaze back up to eye-level. Not a bad-looking girl, if you liked that kind of thing. Definitely pretty. Her face, however, was disfigured by a blandness that suggested laziness and a lack of imagination.

253

Kelly caught him looking at her chest. That was the great thing about men, they were all the same, totally predictable. Emboldened, she grabbed the litre bottle of Evian on the table and filled one of the two glasses that had been left beside it. She pointed the bottle at Blitz. 'Want some?'

The agent shook his head.

Kelly took a mouthful of water. 'So,' she said, as casually as she could manage, 'what happened to Sandy?'

Sighing, Clifford Blitz reached into his jacket pocket and pulled out a cheque. A fucking cheque! It had taken his PA three bloody hours to find the company cheque book. Clifford – proud owner of eight different credit cards – couldn't even remember the last time he had written one. He vaguely recalled seeing something on television that said they were going to be phased out. He dropped it on the table. 'Here.'

Kelly scooped it up quickly, her tongue running along her upper lip as she read and re-read what it said. Finally, she looked up at Blitz. 'A hundred grand?'

Blitz nodded. He wasn't sure of the wisdom of giving her a cheque but it was too much cash to carry around. 'Take it,' he said quietly.

Kelly folded the cheque, then unfolded it again.

Blitz leaned across the table. 'Take it,' he repeated. 'Put it in the bank and fuck off back to the provinces. Get a husband who works for the council or something. Have some kids. Just fuck off.'

Kelly took another look at the cheque. 'A measly hundred grand,' she hissed, her pseudo-Sloane Square accent washed away in a wave of estuary English, 'is fuck all. Get real.'

Blitz glanced round the largely empty bar to check that no one was paying them any attention. Leaning closer, he opened his jacket just enough for the girl to be able to get a glimpse of the handle of the Smith & Wesson .45 in his inside pocket. The gun was a replica he'd bought from a model shop in Holborn but it was realistic enough. 'It's either a hundred k,' he said grimly, 'or a bullet in the face.'

'You wouldn't...' She tried to sound defiant, but her bottom lip had started to quiver and he could see the fear in her eyes. He slipped a hand under the table and ran it along her leg, squeezing her thigh tightly when she tried to smack it away. Tears appeared in her eyes.

'Try me.'

After a moment's reflection, Kelly refolded the cheque and dropped it in her bag. 'You wouldn't be doing this,' she complained, 'if Gavin wasn't guilty.' Finally removing his hand from her leg, she thrust her chest out defiantly. 'How did you get that idiot Paul Groom to take the blame?'

Getting to his feet, Blitz reached across the table and grabbed the collar of her blouse. 'One more word...' He pulled her close, letting her feel his breath on her face. 'One more word out of you and you know what will happen. Don't try and get fucking clever with me.' Biting her lip, Kelly tried to free herself but he hoisted her even closer. He could smell the mix of her body odour and perfume. 'You will never say anything about this to anyone.'

She nodded, and this time he let her go.

'What if someone asks about the cash?' she queried shakily, straightening her blouse.

Blitz shook his head. 'They won't.'

'But if they do?' she persisted.

'Just send them to me,' Blitz sighed. 'I'll explain it was a pay-off for a story that never happened. If you stay out of London, no one will care,' he added. 'I don't want to hear that you're round and about here ever again.'

'Don't worry,' Kelly said huffily. Getting to her feet, she took her jacket from the back of the chair. 'I'm going. Who needs London anyway? They have footballers in Manchester, you know.'

As she bent over to pick up her bag, Blitz eyed her rear, displayed to good effect in a pair of Moschino jeans. He fingered the room-card key in his pocket.

'Hey, Kelly.'

Hoisting the bag over her shoulder, she straightened up. 'What?' she scowled.

'I suppose a quick blow job is out of the question?'

THIRTY

Alison Roche glanced at her watch. She was a third of the way through her session with Wolf, and the psychiatrist had yet to say a single word. That was fine by her but, after more than fifteen minutes of silence, she was beginning to worry that something might be wrong with the doctor.

'Just your bloody luck,' she mumbled to herself. 'They send you to see a shrink and he starts losing his own bloody marbles!'

'Huh?' Wolf brought his gaze down from the ceiling as if he was recognizing her presence in his office for the first time. Today he was wearing a shapeless grey Nike sweatshirt. His hair had been cut short, making him look about ten years older, and his blue eyes seemed paler than Roche remembered. His wedding band lay on the desk, next to Roche's file. 'I'm sorry ... Sergeant,' he said softly. 'I missed that.'

'Don't worry,' Roche replied, 'it was nothing.' Shifting her position in the armchair, she looked around the room; as far as she could tell, it was still littered with the same family photos and books. The only change was that the framed poster for *The Wild Bunch* had been removed and replaced by one for *Alien*.

'You've changed the poster?' Roche pointed at the wall.

'Yes,' Wolf nodded.

Roche waited for him to say something else, anything else, but he lapsed back into silence. *This is beginning to creep me out,* she thought. 'Shall we get started?'

Wolf frowned.

'With the session.'

'Yes, yes.' Wolf opened the notebook on his desk and chose a pencil from the selection that was held in a mug that bore the legend *Keep Calm and Carry On*. After scribbling something on the pad he looked up and gave Roche a weak smile. 'Now,' he asked, his voice barely more than a whisper, 'where shall we start?'

'Fucking hell, Carlyle, you never could sing, could you?' Sitting on a bench in Soho Square, Inspector Julie Crisp laughed indulgently. All he had to do was hum the first few bars of the chorus and she knew who it was. Julie had never really liked The Clash – she was more into Siouxsie and the Banshees and The Cure – and Carlyle had put her off them for life. His tuneless singing still made her smile, though.

She wondered why he had rung her out of the blue earlier and insisted they meet immediately. Thinking it through in her head, she realized that it must be more than ten years since they last worked together – on Operation Monkey, targeting heroin dealers operating out of Chinatown. Since then, she couldn't recall them ever having spoken. That was Carlyle, though; you only ever heard from him when he wanted something.

Abruptly ending his rendition of the chorus of 'Julie's Been Working for the Drugs Squad', Carlyle shrugged apologetically. 'Can't be good at everything, can I?'

'Mm,' Crisp said doubtfully, 'and I don't really work for the Drugs Squad these days, either.'

'No?' Carlyle's heart sank. 'Last I heard, you were working on that case in Stoke Newington.'

'The Turkish gangs? That had to be at least five years ago.'

'Christ! I suppose so.'

'I just got burned out,' Crisp explained. 'You know what it's like, especially with SOCA on your shoulder. Politics, bureaucracy ... you wind up forgetting that you're a copper.'

Carlyle nodded. The boys in the Serious Organized Crime Agency were indeed hard work. He made the most sympathetic-sounding noise he could manage. Crisp might not be the best person to receive Dom's tip-off about the Docklands drugs, but she would have to do; there was no way he was going through formal channels on this one and there was no time to try and hand-pick anyone else.

'And with three kids ... well, frankly, it's hard to know which way is up most of the time.'

'Three kids?' The Crisp he remembered had been a bit of a party girl, famous when they worked together in Bethnal Green in the late 1990s for always having a selection of condoms in her pocket. Looking at her now, the impression was more middle-aged cop than yummy mummy. Then again, the children would explain the dark rings under her eyes and the tired expression on her face.

'Yeah.' She gave an embarrassed smile. 'Eight, six and eighteen months.'

Christ, Carlyle thought, *I hope you didn't marry a copper.* 'Anyway,' he said, moving on before she could pull out any pictures, 'what I wanted to talk to you about is...'

You're a bloody mug, you are, WPC Heather Wilson said to herself. Trying to ignore the taste of the disgusting tea that she had been given, she gazed out of the window of the homeless men's hostel in Limehouse and across the Thames. It was her day off and Heather should have been enjoying a trip to Westfield with her mum. She thought about the lovely French Connection dress she'd had her eye on for ages and sighed. She should never have let that cute new sergeant sweettalk her into schlepping round some of the scummiest hostels in London, trying to find someone who knew that dead tramp, even if he had intimated that he might take her on a date. The more Heather thought about it, the less sure she was that he had actually promised to do so. She felt a knot of frustration in her stomach; he was *very* cute.

'I've met this guy...'

Startled, Wilson turned around, knocking her tea all over the table. She jumped up quickly before it ended up on her jeans.

'Sorry,' said the young woman who had appeared behind her, 'that was my fault. Give me a minute; I'll get some tissues.' Before Heather could reply, the woman scuttled off in the direction she had come from. It was only when she had disappeared into the toilets that the WPC realized what she had said.

'Are you sure you don't want another cup of tea?' Susie McCarthy asked as she cleared up the mess that Heather Wilson had made with the last one.

'No,' said Heather, shuddering inwardly. 'I'm fine, thanks.' Checking that the chair was dry, she sat down. 'You were saying – about the picture?'

'Oh, yes.' Piling the damp tissue-paper on the far side of the table, Susie tapped on the photograph of Adrian Gasparino's lifeless face with the index finger of her right hand. Wilson noticed that the nail had been bitten all the way down to the quick.

'He was here. Didn't stay for long; just upped and left one day.' She looked a bit sad. 'We were sitting here having a conversation, just like now, and he suddenly got his bag and left. Not that uncommon, really. Was he the guy killed near Trafalgar Square?'

'Yes.'

'I read about it in the papers. What a shame. Some people are horrible.'

'Yes, they are.'

'Really horrible.'

You're supposed to be a social worker, Heather thought grimly, *get used to it.* However, she smiled sympathetically. 'Do you have his details?'

Susie waved at a young man walking past. 'Yeah. We'll have the information he gave us when he arrived.' Pushing the chair back, she got to her feet. 'It'll be in the office. I'll go and get you a copy.'

'Thank you,' Wilson said politely. Pulling her mobile from the pocket of her jacket, she began searching for Umar's number. 'Dinner's on you,' she smiled to herself, 'and it's gonna be expensive.' Her smile broadened as she realized that she knew exactly the dress for the occasion.

THIRTY-ONE

Standing ramrod straight, the old fella waiting by the door to the Uzmanov Suite reminded the inspector of his neighbour in Covent Garden, Harry Ripley. Wearing a dark navy blazer and a white shirt, he had what Carlyle presumed was the official club tie pulled firmly up to his throat in a half-Windsor knot. The inspector nodded at him pleasantly as he headed inside.

But the doorman stepped nimbly into his path. 'I'm sorry, sir, you cannot go in.'

'What?' Carlyle said irritably. He noticed the man had a name-tag on his lapel: *Edward Hopkins.*

'I'm afraid you have not followed the dress code.' Wrinkling his nose, Hopkins gestured at the inspector's dishevelled appearance. 'A jacket and tie are required – and jeans are strictly not allowed.'

What is this, Carlyle wondered, the Royal Opera House or a bloody football ground? Sighing loudly, he pulled his warrant card from the pocket of his coat. 'Police.'

Hopkins gave the ID the briefest of glances. 'I'm sorry, sir. Rules are rules.'

Gritting his teeth, Carlyle told himself to take a deep breath and wait for the temptation to arrest the annoying old bugger to subside. Apart from anything else, it wasn't worth the paperwork. *Be calm,* he told himself. 'Mr Hopkins,' he said quietly, 'I am here on official business – not so I can eat your prawn sandwiches and watch your shitty football team get beaten.'

Standing his ground, Hopkins bristled but did not rise to the bait.

'You are obstructing me in the conduct of my duties,' Carlyle told him.

'There are rules,' Hopkins smiled widely as he nodded a couple of properly attired gentlemen into the room, 'and everyone else here has complied with them.'

Fuck the paperwork, Carlyle thought, *I'm gonna arrest you anyway*. 'This is your last fucking chance,' he hissed.

Hopkins's smile grew wider. 'Swearing is also not allowed.'

'Right, sunshine.' As Carlyle reached for his handcuffs, he felt a hand on his shoulder.

'John, what are you doing here?' Flustered, he turned to see Commander Carole Simpson standing behind him. She was wearing a quilted duvet coat that reached down almost to her ankles, with a club crest over the right breast.

'Nice coat,' he complimented her, happy to be able to ignore the doorman.

'It gets very cold sitting watching,' she explained, 'especially for these night games. I can't believe that Dino forces me to come along. The least he can do is make sure I'm warm.'

'I was after a word with him,' Carlyle told her, 'but Jobsworth, here wouldn't let me in.'

'Dress code,' Hopkins said stiffly.

'Don't worry, Mr Hopkins,' Simpson laughed. 'The inspector lowers the tone wherever he goes.'

'But...' the doorman complained.

'You can make an exception just this once,' Simpson said politely but firmly. 'I will take full responsibility.' Signalling that the conversation was at an end, she took Carlyle by the arm and ushered him past the fuming doorman.

'What a dick!'

'Edward is a bit of a stickler for standards. He's been here more than thirty years. You just have to get used to it.'

Let it go, Carlyle told himself. 'Thank you,' he

263

said gracelessly.

Steering him towards the bar, Simpson chuckled. 'How else am I going to get my most troublesome inspector to talk to me?'

'I've been trying to get hold of you,' Carlyle protested.

'Yeah, right.' Catching the eye of the girl behind the bar, Simpson ordered a large glass of Chardonnay. Carlyle wistfully eyed the bottles of spirits lined up at the back. Nestling in the middle was his favourite tipple, Jameson's. A nice whiskey would hit the spot right now but with his boss standing beside him, it made sense to abstain. With a heavy sigh, he asked for an orange juice.

Simpson lifted the glass to her lips. 'You know,' she said, 'I don't recall seeing any reports on your progress.'

Carlyle took his glass from the bartender. 'Umar Sligo ... he's taking his time to get up to speed. I will have a word.'

Simpson looked at him doubtfully. 'So,' she asked, 'what progress *are* you making?'

Carlyle scanned the room.

'Don't worry,' Simpson chided him. 'Dino will be here soon, Inspector, and you'll be able to pursue whatever agenda you've got going. In the meantime, I would appreciate a catch-up.'

'Of course.' Without articulating his suspicions, Carlyle explained where they were with the Sandy Carroll case and then gave the Commander an update on the second killing – the 'tramp', now known as a former soldier called Adrian Gasparino.

Well aware that she only ever got part of the

story from Carlyle, Simpson nodded politely. If she was either happy or unhappy with his reported progress, she didn't let it show. Finishing her wine, she handed the empty glass back to the girl behind the bar and asked for a refill. 'You know that you shouldn't be covering both of these cases at once.'

Carlyle found himself distracted by a pair of pretty blondes who were laughing and joking with a couple of much older men. 'One is almost sorted.'

'*Almost?*' Simpson queried. 'You have a confession?'

'It's sorted,' Carlyle said stiffly.

Simpson took possession of a new glass of Chardonnay. 'Good,' she said. 'Dino wants the whole thing dealt with quickly and cleanly.'

'Cleanly?'

'He's very upset.'

Carlyle gazed morosely into his orange juice. 'I'm sure he is.'

'Excuse me, sir.'

Carlyle looked round to see Edward Hopkins standing at his shoulder.

'I brought this for you to wear,' the doorman said, thrusting a grubby green tartan tie towards the inspector. MacLeod tartan, Carlyle guessed. He looked at the thing in horror, his disgust deepening when he realized it was a fake with an elastic neckband that you slipped over your head.

Simpson quickly lifted her wine glass to her mouth to hide a giggle.

'As you can see,' said Carlyle, tugging at the fabric of his Fred Perry polo, 'I'm not wearing a proper shirt.'

'You can still wear it,' Hopkins insisted, trying to pull the elastic over the inspector's head.

Simpson made a noise as if she were choking on her drink. She was laughing so hard there were tears in her eyes.

Carlyle pushed the doorman roughly away. 'If you don't fuck off – right now,' he murmured, 'I will have you arrested and in a cell before kick-off.'

Hesitating, the elderly doorman weighed up his options. After a brief moment, he threw the tie at Carlyle in one final act of defiance before stalking off. Letting the thing fall to the floor, Carlyle kicked it under a nearby table.

Struggling to regain her composure, Simpson dabbed at her eyes with the napkin. 'Oh, John...'

'How could I wear that?' he huffed. 'It's not my clan colours.'

'I think we'll have to take another look at your anger-management training.'

'What do you mean?' he said irritably. 'I'm still seeing that bloody shrink.'

'Dr Wolf.'

'Yes, indeed.' Giving up on the wretched orange juice, he placed his glass back on the bar. 'In fact, I'm due to be seeing him again next week.'

'Doesn't seem to be doing much good,' Simpson observed, still laughing.

'I'm sure it's doing the doctor the power of good,' Carlyle shot back. 'He's seeing so many bloody coppers that he must be raking it in from the Met.' Looking up, he saw Dino Mottram enter the room and head towards them. Mottram had Christian Holyrod in tow. Arm-in-arm with the

Mayor was Abigail Slater who, to Carlyle's amazement, was wearing a replica team shirt under her very expensive-looking brown leather jacket.

Simpson's expression darkened at the sight of Slater.

'Nice ensemble,' Carlyle quipped.

'Dino told me that Holyrod likes to shag her while she's wearing the shirt.'

I can see where he's coming from, Carlyle thought. He straightened his face. 'Doesn't seem the type, does he?'

Simpson lowered her voice as the trio approached. 'That's the thing,' she said. 'What people get up to behind closed doors never ceases to amaze me.'

'Prurience is a wonderful thing,' Carlyle grinned. 'He's certainly not shy about prancing around town with his fancy woman. Doesn't he ever go out anywhere with his wife?'

'From what I hear, she's too busy shagging her Close Protection Officer,' Simpson replied. 'By all accounts, SO1 has put the smile back on her face after quite a considerable drought.'

Carlyle blew out a breath. 'Those guys really are on a roll.' Scotland Yard's Protection Command had been embroiled in a series of high-profile cases where officers had been found to be 'identifying' too closely with the principals that they were detailed to guard. 'Who is the officer?'

Simpson mentioned a name that meant nothing to Carlyle.

'He's got quite a reputation,' the Commander smirked, 'amongst those in the know. As big as a baby's arm, apparently.'

Carlyle coughed uncomfortably. 'Naughty boy.'

'It happens,' Simpson shrugged. 'He has to hope it doesn't get in the papers or he'll be re-assigned to traffic duty in somewhere like Middlesbrough.' Putting down her wine glass, she stepped forward and kissed Dino on the cheek.

After kissing her back, Mottram nodded at Carlyle. 'It would help if you tried not to annoy the staff,' he said, by way of introduction.

'That's Inspector Carlyle in a single word,' Holyrod laughed nastily. 'Annoying.'

'Nice to see you again, Mr Mayor.' Carlyle flashed his most insincere smile.

Neither man offered a handshake.

'I was wondering,' Carlyle grinned innocently. 'How is your wife? No one ever seems to see her these days.' Glaring at the impudent policeman, Holyrod clamped his jaw tight shut. Carlyle felt Simpson's boot kick him right on the ankle. Refusing to wince, he pushed his smile as far across his face as it would go. 'I hear that SO1 are doing a *great* job taking care of her.' Eyes blazing, Holyrod looked like he wanted to throttle him, but still the Mayor kept his counsel.

Resisting the temptation to wring Carlyle's neck, Simpson put a restraining hand on his arm. 'John,' she said, her voice infinitely weary, like a disappointed teacher with a terminally wayward pupil, 'I thought that you wanted to speak to Dino?'

'That's correct,' Carlyle nodded, still eyeballing Holyrod.

'Now is not the time,' Dino grumbled. 'The game is starting soon; there's not that long till kick-off.'

'Dino,' Simpson commanded, 'I suggest you give the inspector ten minutes, in your office.'

THIRTY-TWO

Deep in the bowels of the stadium, Carlyle glanced around Dino's surprisingly small and rather cramped office. Bizarrely, the walls were crammed with framed photographs of cricketers, rugby players and golfers, with not a footballer in sight.

Gratifyingly, Dino made a beeline for the booze. 'Drink?'

'Yes, please.' Carlyle scanned the bottles on top of the sideboard, which stood by the far wall. In the absence of any whiskey, he went for a glass of twelve-year-old Glenkinchie, known as 'the Edinburgh Malt'.

'You are very good at annoying people,' Dino said gruffly, as he poured the inspector a less than generous measure.

'It's good to have a talent at something,' Carlyle said. Taking the glass, he took a sniff and then a sip. Very nice. Very nice indeed. Shame his glass was almost empty already. He watched in dismay as Dino poured himself a much larger measure before slumping into a nearby leather sofa.

'What do you want?'

'I am very sorry about what happened to your step-daughter.' Ignoring the armchair beside him, the inspector stayed on his feet.

Dino stuck his face as far into the glass as possible, sucking out the whisky with a loud slurp. 'Bah!'

Finishing his drink, Carlyle placed the empty glass on the sideboard, resisting the temptation to pour himself another. 'Car– Commander Simpson said you were very upset about it.'

'Carole is just trying to make me seem nicer than I am.' Dino threw the rest of the whisky down his throat. 'The reality was I couldn't stand her. Sandy was always a greedy little pain in the arse. To tell you the truth, I'm not surprised that something like this happened to her.'

Enjoying the warmth of the whisky in his gut, Carlyle rocked gently on the balls of his feet. 'No one deserves what happened in that hotel room.'

'No, no. Of course not.' Dino pushed himself off the sofa. 'All I'm saying is that it was very predictable – just like the girl herself.' Stepping in front of Carlyle, he looked him in the eye. 'Anyway, you got the lout who did it, so justice has been done.'

'Quite.' Carlyle took a step backwards.

'I'm just glad that Gavin Swann is okay.'

Only with the utmost effort did Carlyle manage to avoid doing a double-take in disbelief.

'We've spent months getting him fit enough to play,' Dino mused. 'Paying his bloody wages every week while he gets up to all sorts. With luck, he should be back next week. We need this like a hole in the head. The little bastard just can't keep it in his trousers.'

'Amongst other things,' Carlyle mumbled

Dino glanced at his watch. 'Time's up.' Before

270

Carlyle could utter a protest, he had reached the door. 'Hope you enjoy the game,' he said, before disappearing into the corridor.

Fuck the football, Carlyle thought, reaching for the Glenkinchie.

After enjoying a generous amount of Dino's fine malt, Carlyle encountered some difficulty in finding his way out. He was just about to enlist the aid of a steward, when he felt a hand on his arm.

'Inspector Carlyle! How're you doing?'

Trying not to sway, Carlyle turned to see a fresh-faced man with thinning blond hair and the general air of an ageing roué. *I know you,* he thought rather groggily, *but who the hell are you?* 'Hi.'

Shaking his hand, the man smiled. 'It's been a while,' he said.

'Yes, I suppose it has.'

The man finally picked up on Carlyle's confusion. 'Eddie Fitzsimmons.'

'Eddie! Yes, yes, yes,' Carlyle scratched his head, trying to clear it a bit. Eddie Fitzsimmons, the poor man's Gavin Swann fifteen years ago; famous for taking three hookers and a bag of coke on an open-topped-bus celebration after he won the FA Cup single-handed with two goals in the final. Slightly less famous for beating up his then wife, a former Miss Bournemouth or Brighton or something, and being arrested by one John Carlyle. 'What are you doing here? You never played for either of these clubs.'

'I'm working for radio.' Eddie pointed at a door down the corridor with PRESS stencilled above it in red paint. 'I do the summaries.'

'Nice job.'

'Nah.' Eddie yawned. 'It's boring as shit. The games are crap these days and the players are like robots.'

It was a familiar refrain; the kind of thing you heard in the media all the time.

'It's not like the old days,' Eddie droned on.

'Never is.'

'There's no fun in the game any more.'

Fun, Carlyle thought, *as in getting banned from playing for England for a year, after punching the manager.*

Or getting relegated twice on the bounce.

Or getting sent off before a game had even started for urinating on an opponent in the tunnel.

Selected highlights from the Eddie Fitzsimmons canon.

'Not like in my day.'

That was the great thing about never having been 'somebody'; you never had to worry about being a has-been. Carlyle smiled indulgently. 'Why do you do it then?'

'Need the money,' Eddie shrugged. 'Mrs F took me to the cleaners.'

Good for her.

'I'm living in a one-bed flat-in Kensal Green with the girlfriend and there's not room to swing a cat.'

Aw.

Eddie glanced at his watch. 'I've gotta go in a minute. You watching the game?'

'This lot?' Carlyle belched. 'You'd have to pay me.'

'Sooo,' a little lightbulb started glowing weakly above Eddie's head, 'you're here on business?'

Carlyle sighed. Anything that was said to Eddie would doubtless be round the press box before the first foul of the game; he had to stay schtum.

Something behind Carlyle caught Fitzsimmons' eye. 'If you're sniffing around Dino Mottram, this is your man.' Stepping away from Carlyle, he intercepted a tall Asian guy in a navy suit and white shirt, open at the neck, who was heading for the press box.

'Baz?'

With a curt nod, the guy tried to sidestep Eddie and reach the press room. However, Eddie still had some of the old magic in his feet and wasn't caught out by the feint.

A full-throated roar went up outside. On a monitor bolted to the wall, Carlyle saw the two teams take to the pitch.

'Kick-off,' the guy protested. Round his neck was a press pass with a passport photo of his mug and the legend *Baseer Yazdani, Honeymann*.

'What are you worrying about?' Eddie laughed. 'It's not like you have to file a match report. Anyway, with this lot there won't be much worth writing about!'

'Eddie!'

'You want to talk to this guy,' Eddie said, gesturing at Carlyle. 'He's a cop investigating Dino. You two should have a lot to talk about.'

Fuck, Eddie, Carlyle groaned to himself. *Tell everybody my business, why don't you?*

From outside came another roar. This time it really was kick-off.

'Shit!' Eddie turned and bolted for the door. The Honeymann hack started after him, then hesitated. Turning, he offered a hand to Carlyle, without quite managing to smile. 'Baseer Yazdani, Honeymann Newswire Services.'

'So I can see,' Carlyle frowned, shaking his hand. The men exchanged cards.

'Why aren't you investigating Gavin Swann?' Baseer asked.

Carlyle waved the guy's business card in the air. 'What's a reporter from Chicago doing at a football game?'

Baseer stroked the stubble on his chin. He was a good-looking guy – a poor man's Umar Sligo, if you will – but with the air of someone who hadn't slept for a week. 'I cover leisure industries.'

Carlyle nodded sadly. Sport was now big business and his enjoyment of the game was dying, day-by-day, as a result.

'I have been working on a special investigation into the sports interests of Dino Mottram and Entomophagous Industries.'

'Why?' Carlyle asked a bit too eagerly.

'The rumour is,' Baseer said, effortlessly returning to his own agenda, 'that Gavin Swann was in the hotel room when that girl was killed.'

'No one has written that.'

'That's hardly a surprise,' Baseer scoffed, 'given that Clifford Blitz got a super injunction within twelve hours of the body being found.'

How on earth had that one passed him by? A flash of intense frustration shot through the inspector's core, passing in an instant. *Then again,* he thought, *keeping the press out of it – if you can –*

is never a bad thing.

'What you've got to appreciate,' Baseer continued, 'is that you can't hide behind the courts forever. The injunction will get lifted in the end.'

'Or someone will run the story anyway,' Carlyle said wryly. 'Sooner or later.'

Baseer gave a small nod. 'Quite.'

'Not you, though.' Carlyle knew that Honeymann, being American-owned, had far more rigorous editorial checks and balances than most of its British media rivals. That meant Baseer had to reach much higher standards of accuracy than his rivals. It also meant that he was someone that the inspector could probably do business with.

'No.'

'Look,' Carlyle said, 'there's not a lot I can tell you at the moment but let's keep talking. If I can give you a heads-up on anything, I will.' An empty but friendly promise.

Baseer smiled. 'Okay.'

'You can call me at any time, but I can never be quoted.'

'That's fine.'

'And you can never write anything that can be traced back to me. No fingerprints.'

Baseer nodded and they shook again.

'One final thing,' the journalist said as Carlyle moved away.

'Yeah?'

'The other rumour that I don't expect you to comment on is that Swann is paying Paul Groom to take the fall for Sandy Carroll's death.'

Carlyle stopped and turned to face the journalist. 'Good luck getting that past your editor,' he said pleasantly.

'The gossip is that Groom's agent agreed a deal so that Groom gets a million pounds for every year he has to spend in prison.'

Carlyle resumed walking towards the stairs. 'Nice work if you can get it,' he commented drily. 'I'll be in touch.'

Shivering under his official team blanket – a bargain £29.99 in the club shop – Christian Holyrod gazed sullenly at the electronic scoreboard in the far corner of the ground. There were still more than ten minutes to go to half-time and the prospect of a nice double measure of Highland Park that would ease the pain of watching this rubbish. The crowd groaned as another simple ten-yard pass went astray. At least Abigail, sitting to his left in her replica shirt, seemed to be reasonably enthralled by it all. He was amazed by the way his girlfriend could develop new passions at the drop of a hat. He was fairly sure that Abigail had never been to a football match in her life before he had taken up this job. Now she behaved as if she'd been a season-ticket holder in the main stand for thirty years. The Mayor couldn't work out if it was really quite impressive or just rather sad.

Just then, the referee called a foul against the home side, much to the anguish of the crowd. Abigail promptly gave the official the kind of gesture usually seen from the cheaper seats.

Sitting to the Mayor's right, Dino pointed at a block of empty seats in the opposite stand. 'I reckon we are about ten thousand down on capacity tonight.'

'Mm.' Holyrod scanned the ground; there were clumps of empty seats at regular intervals all the way round.

'The locals aren't happy,' Dino grumbled, 'and they're starting to vote with their feet.'

'Isn't this about the time when you're supposed to sack the manager?' Holyrod asked, drawing on his non-existent knowledge of the football business.

'If only we could,' Dino replied. 'It would cost north of ten mill to get rid of the son of a bitch and all his support staff. That's ten million more than we can afford.'

'Jesus.'

'I know.' Dino pulled his scarf tighter around his neck. 'We just have to hope that Swann comes back all guns blazing. A couple of good results and the fans will be happy again.'

'*Referee!*' Slater and thirty thousand others rose in unison to protest at an unpunished assault in the centre circle.

Dino elbowed Holyrod. 'At least Abigail is getting into the spirit of things.' He allowed himself the smallest of leers. 'And that shirt looks very good on her.'

For the first time in the evening, the Mayor allowed himself a smile. 'It does, doesn't it?'

'Does she wear it in the bedroom?'

Holyrod glanced at the scoreboard. Five minutes and he would be at the bar. 'Amongst other things.'

'You are a very lucky man,' Dino congratulated him.

'You know what? It can be very exhausting.'

'Ah.' Dino gave him a knowing wink. 'I have just the thing to help you with that.' Not waiting for the half-time whistle, he struggled out of his seat. 'In the meantime, let's go and get a bloody drink.'

THIRTY-THREE

'I haven't been able to track down Kelly Kellaway.' Umar looked almost sheepish.

Kelly Kellaway? Carlyle had forgotten all about her. 'Why the fuck not?' he barked.

'Well,' Umar said stiffly, 'for a start, that number you gave me doesn't work.'

Carlyle's face crumpled in annoyance. 'Go back and hassle Blitz then. She can't have disappeared into thin air. What about her family?'

'I spoke to her parents. They haven't seen her in two years, apparently.'

'ATM records? Mobile records?' Carlyle threw his hands up in the air. He knew that Umar didn't have the time or resources to do what he was asking any time soon, but he didn't feel like being reasonable about it. 'What do they tell us?'

Umar stuck his hands into his trouser pockets. 'I haven't been able t–'

'For fuck's sake!' Carlyle exploded. 'Just fucking find her!'

'Did you get anything from Dino Mottram?'

Good question. The inspector had been too focused on the malt whisky in Dino's office to remember why he'd been there in the first place. 'Nah,' he said guiltily, forcing his anger to dissipate. 'He wasn't any help at all.'

'Did you stay for the game?'

'I wouldn't waste my time watching those berks.'

'Nil-nil,' Umar mused. 'Sounds like it was a good game to miss.'

'Yeah.' Carlyle looked at his watch. 'I haven't got much time. What are we doing here?' He looked around the New Belvedere hostel, in Limehouse, East London, unimpressed.

'We're seeing Dr Ian Bell. CEO of Veterans United.'

'Uhuh.' Carlyle suspected that this would be a waste of time. In his experience, anyone who called themselves 'Chief Executive Officer' of anything was not likely to have much of interest or relevance to say.

'He's also Visiting Senior Research Fellow in the Department of War Studies at King's College,' Umar added. 'He has a PhD in the causes of homelessness among veterans and wrote a book that came out last year on the war in Afghanistan.'

Over-achieving bastard, Carlyle thought.

'It's a good read,' the sergeant said. 'I can lend you a copy if you want.'

'Thanks,' Carlyle mumbled, with no enthusiasm whatsoever.

'It's very kind of you to say so.' A small, smiling man dressed in grey jacket over a button-down blue shirt, open at the neck, and a pair of freshly pressed jeans, appeared at Umar's shoulder and shook the sergeant's hand. 'You must be Inspector Carlyle.'

'I'm Sergeant Sligo,' Umar grinned.

'I'm Carlyle,' the inspector interjected abruptly, offering his hand.

'Ah, my apologies, gentlemen.' Bell gestured at some chairs clustered around a low coffee table in the corner of his office. 'Please, take a seat.'

'So,' said Carlyle when they were all seated, 'it looks like you've got a lot on your plate here.'

The smile that had seemed permanently plastered on to Bell's face faded somewhat. 'Well,' he said, 'we do a very important job, even if I say so myself. Veterans United has a uniquely holistic approach when it comes to trying to deal with the serious problems that ex-military personnel face in modern Britain. At the most practical level, it's about homelessness prevention; we provided more than thirty-five thousand nights of accommodation last year. At the moment, we provide a home to around a hundred and fifty-two veterans here at the hostel. We don't judge people. What we do is help them deal with the complexities of the welfare system and other aspects of state bureaucracy including, fairly regularly, the police.'

Carlyle shrugged. 'If you have any problems in the future, please call Sergeant Sligo. He will be delighted to try and help you.' Catching the grimace that flashed across Umar's face, he added, 'Any time of the day or night.'

'Thank you.' Bell bowed slightly. 'We also do our own original research, looking into the effects of military service on the health and well-being of personnel when they leave the military and take up civilian careers.'

'Or not,' Carlyle interrupted.

'Or not.' Bell's smile faded even further. 'Civilian careers are hard enough to find at the moment, even for civilians.'

'Adrian Gasparino,' said Carlyle, 'seems to have fallen through the net very quickly.'

'It doesn't take long,' said Umar.

Carlyle glared at him to shut up. He didn't schlep all the way out to Limehouse to listen to the thoughts of his bloody sergeant.

'Soldiers, sailors, airmen and -women are the same as everyone else,' Bell went on. 'They fall victim to homelessness for various prosaic reasons ranging from psychological disorders to alcohol and drug abuse or family breakdown. Once you are on the street, however, for whatever reason, it is hard to get back to something approximating what we might think of as a "normal" life.'

'Very true,' Umar nodded.

'Aside from the cold and hunger,' Bell continued, 'violence is commonplace. Those on the streets are either prey or predators.'

Spare me the homilies, the inspector thought wearily.

'We are no longer honouring the military covenant,' Umar said solemnly.

The what? Carlyle struggled to ignore an overwhelming desire to give his man a firm slap.

Sensing the inspector's confusion, Bell told him how, in the nineteenth century, the government had pledged to support and provide care for all service personnel in return for the sacrifices they made for their country.

'There are many,' Umar chipped in, 'amongst the media, senior military figures and politicians,

281

who feel that the Ministry of Defence has abandoned these people.'

'Yes,' Bell nodded. 'Recently, Edgar Carlton himself spoke out about the covenant in the House of Commons, stating that it was an unbreakable common bond of identity, loyalty and responsibility, which has sustained the Army throughout its history.'

That doesn't stop him from doing fuck all about repairing it, Carlyle reflected. His mobile started buzzing in his pocket. Pulling it out, he checked that it wasn't his wife before rejecting the call. The screen told him that he had six missed calls. Shrugging, he dropped the phone back into his pocket.

'The outlook is bleak,' Bell sighed. 'Poverty is on the rise, which means more homelessness, which means more homeless veterans. The government *must* act. No veteran in our country should be forgotten or lost.'

'Adrian Gasparino was forgotten,' Carlyle said flatly. 'What can you tell us about him?'

Bell reached inside his jacket and pulled out a single sheet of white A4 paper. Unfolding it, he handed it over to Carlyle. 'Here.'

'Thanks.' Squinting at the paper, Carlyle realized that he wasn't wearing his spectacles. Fortunately, he was quickly able to locate them in the breast pocket of his jacket. Slipping them on, he glanced down the list. Gasparino's military history was typed out in chronological order, along with his age, home address and National Insurance number; it even had the registration number of his car, a ten-year-old Nissan. Scribbled at the bottom were details of his next of kin, along with the names of his commanding officers and a couple of comrades.

Nothing, however, that would give any insight into who killed him, or why.

Carlyle nodded at Bell. 'Thank you for this.' He passed the sheet to Umar before getting to his feet. 'If there's anything else that comes to mind that might be of use, please let my sergeant know.'

'Of course,' said Bell, also getting to his feet. The two men shook hands. 'Good luck with your investigation, Inspector.'

'I'm sure we'll sort it out.' Carlyle smiled grimly. 'But you can be sure that there won't be any happy ending.'

'No.' Bell stared at his shoes. 'Quite.'

Carlyle gestured at the sheet of paper in Umar's hand. 'If you speak to some of the people on there, I will catch up with you later.'

'Yes, sir,' said Umar, slowly getting up.

Bell gestured to the door. 'Let me see you out.'

THIRTY-FOUR

Feeling rather glum, Carlyle sat between Helen and Alice in Terminal 4 at Heathrow, waiting for the Royal Air Maroc flight to Casablanca to be called. His wife and daughter were going on the cheapest tickets available, which meant a 24-hour stop-off in Morocco before boarding a flight to Monrovia Roberts International Airport the next day. Not a happy flier, the inspector was already worrying about making the journey himself in a week from now.

He shifted in his seat, unable to shake the sickly feeling in his stomach. This trip hadn't seemed the greatest of ideas at the outset, and now that they were actually about to depart, it seemed a whole lot worse. He felt bad about not going with them. It dawned on him that this would be the first time ever that he had been away from his daughter for more than a couple of nights; and even then she had only been in bloody Brighton with her grandma. Part of this whole thing was, he knew, about Alice growing up, which was important but still kind of sad.

'You'll let me know when you get there?'

'Yes,' said Helen, the exasperation clear in her voice. She didn't look up from her copy of the *West Africa Travel Guide*. 'You've asked me that a dozen times already. Of course I'll text you when we arrive.'

Alice flicked through a pile of newspaper articles that she had printed off the internet. In the margins, she had scribbled copious notes in a surprisingly neat hand.

Carlyle got out of his seat and kissed her on the head. 'You've done a lot of research on this.'

'I've got to do a report for the class at school,' Alice explained, waving him away. 'That was the deal when the Headmaster allowed me to come.'

'Good idea.'

Alice tapped the papers on her lap with her index finger. 'Basically, I've done it already, downloading stuff from the net. I'll add in some local colour when I get back.'

'Isn't that cheating?'

Now it was Alice's turn to frown. 'Cheating what?'

Good point, Carlyle mused.

'After all,' she said primly, 'I've got to put the trip into some kind of context.'

'Er, I suppose so.'

'Did you know,' she said cheerily, 'that around a quarter of a million people were killed in Liberia's civil war?'

Carlyle's stomach took another lurch downwards.

'Thousands more fled the fighting. The war left the country ruined.'

'Which is why Avalon is there in the first place,' Helen pointed out tartly. 'This *is* what I do for a living, after all.'

'There are weapons all over the place, but no mains electricity and running water,' Alice went on. 'Corruption is rife and unemployment and illiteracy are endemic. Life expectancy is just fifty-nine for men and sixty-one for women.'

'Sounds like Tower Hamlets.' Carlyle's feeble attempt at humour got him a dirty look from his wife.

'The United Nations,' Alice continued, reading from her notes, 'has fifteen thousand soldiers there for its peacekeeping operation.'

'Thank God for that.' Carlyle seriously wondered if he should grab their passports and leg it back into the city.

'People there speak English and twenty-nine African languages belonging to the ... Mande,

Kwa or Mel linguistic groups.'

'Is George Weah still around?' Carlyle asked. He knew that the former AC Milan star came from Liberia and had run for President a few years earlier. *That really is the definition of a fucked country,* he thought to himself, *when your best hope is a former footballer.*

Alice consulted her notes. 'He's the leader of the opposition. The President is a woman called Ellen Johnson-Sirleaf, known as the "Iron Lady".'

Where've I heard that before? Carlyle wondered.

Helen elbowed him in the ribs. 'Time to go.'

Carlyle looked up at the screen above his head. Flight 801 would be boarding in just over forty-five minutes. With a heavy heart, he walked them to Passport Control.

Heading back to the tube, he got a call.

'Yes?'

'John, it's Julie Crisp.' The inspector sounded more than pissed off.

Shit, he'd forgotten all about the Docklands drugs bust.

'Why haven't you returned any of my calls?'

'What calls?' Carlyle said guiltily, knowing that his track record in this area was far from the best.

Crisp let out an exasperated sigh. 'I've been trying to get hold of you for the last four days. There were no fucking drugs in that house you sent us to.'

'Ah.'

'All we got were a couple of joints that some of the squatters were smoking at the time, and half a gram of speed. Not a lot for a police operation

286

that cost the thick end of ten grand in overtime.'

'No.'

'So what am I going to tell my boss?' Crisp demanded

Carlyle thought about it for a moment. 'It was a solid tip,' was all he could think of to say.

'Fuck!'

'I'm sorry, Julie. I didn't mean to drop you in it.'

'I know, I know,' she said, calming down a little. 'There was evidence that stuff had been stored in the attic, but the place had been cleaned out before we got there.'

A thought danced across Carlyle's brain. 'Let me talk to my source,' he said, 'and see what he has to say for himself.'

'Okay. But I could really do with something to help me out of this hole.'

Carlyle adopted his most reassuring tone. 'Leave it with me. I'll get back to you asap.' Ending the call, he jumped onto a downward escalator and descended into the bowels of the underground network.

'Hi, Harry. How's it going?'

'Fine. You?' Sticking his copy of the *Daily Telegraph* under his arm, Harry Ripley held open the front door of Winter Garden House to let Luke Patten step inside. Short, bald and chronically overweight, Luke had joined the Royal Mail around the time that Harry had left it. Working out of the Mount Pleasant sorting office near King's Cross, he had been delivering the post to this part of Covent Garden for more than fifteen years. He waved the fat packet of letters that he held in his left hand. 'Got a lot this morning,' he said, slipping off the red rubber band that had been holding them together. 'Don't think I've got anything for you, though.' Letting the elastic band fall to the entrance-hall floor, he walked on.

Harry grunted. Letting the door swing shut, he bent down and picked up the rubber band before slowly straightening himself up and shuffling towards the lift, scowling at the back of the post-man's head. As far as Harry was concerned, Patten typified the way that the postal service had gone downhill. The pensioner was always collecting other people's post that had been incorrectly put through his letterbox. Muttering under his breath, he would take it to a different flat in the building or even to a completely different address down the street. It vexed him sorely that there was no pride in the job any more; no one cared. They just wanted to get through their round as quickly as possible and bugger off home.

With his free hand, Patten flipped open his oversized satchel and pulled out an A4-sized jiffy bag. 'I've got this packet for Carlyle,' he said. 'Is anyone in, do you know? I don't want to schlep all that way up there for nothing.'

Harry pressed the button for the lift, which slowly began making its way down from the third floor. He knew that the wife and daughter had gone on holiday but that wasn't the kind of information you just shared around casually. 'I don't think so,' he said, gesturing at the parcel. 'If it's too big to go through the letterbox, just leave it by the front door.'

'Needs a signature.' Patten rubbed his nose. 'Must be important. Don't want to leave it lying around.'

'What is it?'

'No idea.'

Harry sighed. 'Give it here then.' The lift arrived and he held his foot in the door as he signed for the packet.

'There you go,' said Patten. 'Ta, mate.' After handing over the package, he headed for the stairs.

'Don't you want a ride up?' Harry asked, stepping inside.

'Nah.' Patten shook his head cheerily. 'My wife's got me on this new exercise regime. It's a killer.'

'About bloody time,' Harry grumbled under his breath as the doors closed.

Back at the station, Carlyle was staring into space when Angie Middleton appeared behind his desk and put a hand on his shoulder. Leaning back in his chair, he looked up at her. 'What is it?'

'There's been a small explosion on Macklin Street. In your building.'

Carlyle almost fell out of his chair before leaping to his feet and grabbing his jacket. Then he remembered that Helen and Alice should be in Monrovia by now and his panic subsided a little. 'A bomb?'

'Looks like it,' Middleton nodded. 'One fatality, apparently. The Explosive Ordnance Disposal Unit is already there.'

'Okay,' he said, heading swiftly for the exit. 'If you get anything else, let me know.'

The building had been emptied and the road sealed off. Carlyle slipped under the tape and showed his ID to a succession of uniforms until he reached Winter Garden House. As he stepped inside, his mobile signalled that he'd received a text. He was pleased to see that it was a message from Helen: *Arrived safely. Amazing place. H+A xx.* Smiling with relief, he typed out a short reply and hit Send.

'Who are you?'

Carlyle looked up from the screen of the phone and recognized the scowling face of the young EOD inspector from the time that he now referred to as 'the Amazon false alarm'. The officer didn't, however, remember him, which was probably a good thing. Carlyle flashed his warrant card for the fifth time in as many minutes. 'I live in the building,' he told him. 'What happened?'

'A device detonated in the lift,' the EOD guy grudgingly explained, 'just as it was reaching the eighth floor.' Carlyle belatedly noticed the name stencilled on to the officer's navy jumpsuit in small white letters: *Gravesen*. 'The guy carrying it must have had it stuck under his arm; the whole thing came clean off at the shoulder.'

Carlyle thought back to the recent case of the Moscow suicide bomber who was killed in her flat after a spam text message from her mobile phone company triggered the device early. 'Was it the bomber?' he asked hopefully.

'Nah,' Gravesen grinned, 'not unless they're using pensioners now.'

Oh fuck. Carlyle's heart sank 'Have you identified the victim?'

'Not yet.'

'Let me take a look,' said Carlyle. 'I might be able to tell you who he is.'

The lift doors were open, but only the top three feet of the lift protruded above the edge of the eighth-floor landing. Squatting down, Carlyle peered inside.

'Don't get too close,' one of the technicians admonished him. 'We haven't started processing the scene yet.'

'Okay.' Carlyle edged back a centimetre or so. He gazed down at Harry Ripley's body, slumped in the far corner of the blackened elevator. From the way he had fallen, it wasn't clear that Harry had lost an arm, but the dark mess on the floor indicated a large amount of blood loss. Incinerated debris littered the lift floor around him.

'He signed for a package from the postman,' Gravesen informed Carlyle. 'We found him on the sixth floor. He's a lucky sod; using the stairs because he was on a health kick. Mind you, the exertion damn near killed him as well.'

Turning awkwardly on the balls of his feet, Carlyle gestured inside the lift. 'How did he die?'

'Take your pick,' Gravesen replied, 'but the explosion probably gave him a heart attack.'

'Heart-attack Harry.' Carlyle cleared his throat. He didn't know whether to laugh or cry.

'What?' Gravesen asked.

'Nothing. His name is Harry Ripley. He lives – *lived* in number twenty.'

'Why would anyone want to blow him up?'

Carlyle shook his head. 'They wouldn't.'

A young female officer appeared at Gravesen's

side. She whispered something in his ear and they stepped away from Carlyle, moving five yards down the hall. Carlyle tried not to look too interested as she handed over a piece of A5 paper. Gravesen made a show of reading it carefully before stepping back to Carlyle.

'Looks like you're right,' he said.

'What do you mean?' Carlyle asked, irritated that he was having to drag the information out of the EOD.

'No one was trying to blow up Mr Ripley,' Gravesen said. 'The parcel was addressed to you.'

THIRTY-FIVE

Upstairs, he tried to call Helen on her mobile but couldn't get through. Pottering around the cold, empty flat, Carlyle checked and re-checked his passport and his travel documents, before making himself a cup of green tea. Not knowing what to do with himself, he called Umar to see how the Gasparino investigation was going. But when his sergeant's mobile went to voicemail, he felt too lethargic to even leave a message. Finishing his tea, he put his empty mug in the sink and looked out of the window, thinking about what he should be doing next. Harry was gone; now he had to look after his family.

But how exactly?

For a long while, the inspector simply stared out of the window at the sullen sky, letting his thoughts slowly come into focus. When he finally came to a conclusion, he grabbed his jacket and headed back out of the door.

It was his first time and, clearly, he hadn't done it right. Christian Holyrod looked down at the massive erection threatening to burst out of his trousers and winced. Had he done too much? Had he taken it too early? One thing was for certain: the Viagra Professional that Dino had given him had done the job all right; to the extent that he dared not get up from behind his desk for fear of provoking much hilarity amongst the underlings and perhaps also a sexual harassment suit.

The Mayor glanced at his expensive watch and groaned – he wasn't supposed to see Abigail for another three hours. How could he subdue his ridiculous boner? He wondered if a quick hand job might relieve the situation; maybe he should call Dino and ask.

'You realize what time it is?' Clara Hay, his hot new assistant, stuck her head round the door of his office.

Go away, woman! Holyrod pulled his chair in as far as he could, lest she catch a glimpse of his problem. 'I do,' he nodded, trying to smile.

'Are you okay?' Clara stepped into the room and, despite everything, he was compelled to gaze into the possibilities that lay beneath her ruffle blouse.

'I'm fine.'

Standing in front of the desk, hands on hips, she gave him a funny look. 'We have to get going.'

'Mm.' He caught a whiff of her perfume –

Blossom Bomb – mixed with just the merest hint of perspiration.

'The reception for the Women's Institute,' Clara persisted. She waved the papers she had been holding in front of his nose. 'You're giving a speech on City Hall's commitment to sexual equality in the twenty-first century. It's called *Smashing the Glass Ceiling for Good.*'

'I can't,' Holyrod moaned. Then a thought crept very slowly across his addled brain. He gestured at the speech. 'Is it any good?'

'Very,' Clara beamed, 'I wrote it myself. We are a best practice thought leader, striving for three hundred and sixty-degree transparency and continuous improvement.'

'Good, good,' the Mayor nodded, not having the remotest clue what she was talking about. 'In that case, I want *you* to give the speech.' He smiled slyly. 'It will be a definitive *proof point* of our good intentions.'

'But–'

'Yes,' Holyrod continued, on a roll now, 'you are a role model for those who want to smash the, er, glass ceiling and ensure that London is a beacon in the ongoing fight for gender equality.' It was amazing how easy it was to churn out this verbiage once you got started. He gestured at the door. 'Send my apologies to the ladies for being unable to make it. And tell the girls outside that I am not to be disturbed. I need to get on with some very pressing work.'

Undecided, Clara stood for a moment before turning and heading out of the room. As the door clicked behind her, Holyrod pushed his chair back from the desk and unbuttoned his trousers. Opening the bottom drawer of his desk, he pulled out a well-thumbed copy of *Readers Wives* and gave it an appreciative sniff. Now it really was time to deal with the matter in hand.

Behind the bar at Zatoichi, Michela was in good form. She was still in the black vest Carlyle remembered from last time, but her orange hair was now platinum blonde. Chatting up a couple of awestruck boys while pouring bourbon into outsized shot glasses, she seemed in her element. As he headed for the stairs, Carlyle tried unsuccessfully to catch her eye. He fancied a drink; hell, he fancied several drinks, but doubtless he could get them upstairs.

When the inspector burst into his office, Dom tried to look surprised, failing miserably. Lounging on the sofa under the screen print of *The Island* was Gideon Spanner. Carlyle nodded at Gideon and threw himself into the armchair between the two men.

'We've got a few things to talk about.'

'Want a drink?'

Carlyle nodded. 'Maybe you could see if Lisbeth Salander could bring up a bottle of Jameson's.'

'He means Michela,' Dom explained.

Gideon almost laughed. 'I see her more as Charly Baltimore.' Sliding off the sofa, he headed for the door.

Carlyle was so shocked by Gideon's reaction – the man rarely spoke and he certainly never smiled – that it took him a moment to recall Charly

Baltimore, the CIA assassin played by Geena Davis in *The Long Kiss Goodnight*. As it happened, it was one of his favourite films. He remembered that he had the DVD at home and, with Helen and Alice away, there was no one to stop him from watching it. He looked at Dom. 'We could do with Charly Baltimore now. Or,' he laughed humourlessly, remembering Samuel L. Jackson's useless sidekick, 'even Mitch fucking Henessey.'

'Bad day?'

Carlyle talked him through the bomb problem. The drugs problem could wait until after he'd had a drink.

'Tuco?' Dom asked.

'The so-called Samurai.' Carlyle made a face. 'Who else could it be?'

'I dunno.' Dom decided to make a joke of it. 'The possibilities are endless. You have always been quite good at pissing people off.'

'Ha fucking ha.'

Gideon reappeared with the whiskey, three shot glasses and three open bottles of Peroni Red. Placing them all on the desk, he helped himself to a Peroni and repaired to the sofa. Ignoring the beer, Carlyle reached over, poured himself a double and took a mouthful. Immediately, he felt a little better.

Dom took one of the beers. 'Cheers.'

'By the way,' Carlyle asked, 'what did you do with Tuco's coke?'

Dom took a long drag on his beer. 'Your people got there too late.'

You fucking nicked it, is what you mean, Carlyle thought. 'I gave them the tip-off; I need to be able to deliver something to justify the cost of the operation.'

All Dom gave him was a non-committal shrug.

Carlyle changed tack. 'So what are you going to do about Tuco now?'

A look of annoyance flashed across Silver's face. 'Just leave him to me.'

'How can I do that?' Carlyle shot back. 'He blew up a fucking pensioner with a bomb meant for me. EOD are all over it.'

'Explosive Ordnance Disposal?' Dom glanced at Gideon. 'What did you tell them?'

Carlyle drained his glass. 'I haven't spoken to them yet.' With some reluctance, he put the empty glass back on the table and sat back in his chair, resisting the siren call of the whiskey bottle.

'Good,' Dom nodded. 'Keep it simple. Don't speculate. Wait and see how the investigation progresses.'

'For fuck's sake, Dom.'

'Just leave Tuco to me,' Silver repeated firmly.

'Okay,' Carlyle sighed.

'Thank you.' Dom finished his beer and started on a second one. 'Now,' he said briskly, as if he was moving quickly through the agenda at some boring business meeting, 'Gideon has something he wants to ask you about.'

Gideon? Carlyle frowned, turning in his seat to eye the henchman. 'Fire away.'

Avoiding eye-contact, Gideon bounced his beer bottle on his knee. 'Adrian Gasparino.'

Carlyle's frown deepened. 'What about him?'

'He served with my brother in Afghanistan.'

'Okay...' Carlyle looked at Dom.

Silver shrugged. 'It's a small world.'

Sometimes too small for my liking, Carlyle thought.

Gideon fixed him with a blank stare. 'They were good mates. Adrian was with Spencer when he died.'

Way too fucking small.

'I want to know who killed him.'

Reaching for the Jameson's, Carlyle knew better than to ask why.

THIRTY-SIX

Enveloped in the warm embrace of Dom's whiskey, Carlyle picked up his own bottle of Jameson's from Gerry's Wines & Spirits on Old Compton Street on his way back to the flat. Crossing Shaftesbury Avenue, he tried Helen's mobile but was unable to get through. Then he tried calling Umar. The call went to voicemail. Picking his way through the late-evening crowds, Carlyle left a curt message telling his sergeant to call him back.

Turning into Macklin Street, he grimaced at the strong smell of cooked meat coming from the kebab shop as he approached the entrance to Winter Garden House. Inside, unable to take the lift, he slowly slogged his way up the stairs, pausing on the eighth-floor landing to survey the deserted crime scene. The last remains of Harry Ripley had been removed and a sheet of opaque plastic stood across the open doors of the ruined lift. The unhappy realization dawned on the inspector that it would probably be weeks, if not months, before the lift was working again. With a heavy sigh, he continued upwards.

Outside the flat, Carlyle fumbled in his jacket pockets for his key. It was only when he went to place it in the lock that he realized that the door was already open. Taking a firm grip of the neck of the whiskey bottle in his right hand, he pushed the door slightly ajar with his left. Listening intently, he thought that he could make out noises coming from inside. Bemused, he opened the door just enough for him to step inside.

Standing in the hallway, he listened carefully for five, six, seven seconds. The sounds were coming from the living room. Animal grunts, followed by extended female moans that were obviously fake. His head felt thick and he couldn't make sense of what he was hearing; it sounded like someone was watching a porn movie on his TV. Carlyle tiptoed down the hall and stepped into the doorway, bottle raised to shoulder level.

'What the fuck?'

The television was turned off. Instead, he was confronted with small, white-haired man, who looked like he was no stranger to a tanning bed, grappling with a voluptuous black woman who was bent over Carlyle's sofa.

Both of them were completely naked. How, in the name of God, he wondered, was he going to explain this to Helen?

Acknowledging the inspector's arrival with a grin, the man slapped the woman hard on her right buttock and upped his tempo.

'What the hell is going on here?' Carlyle asked,

somewhat redundantly.

'Viagra,' the man panted. 'Good stuff, no?' His face was going a deeper shade of orange by the second and his brow was bathed in sweat. 'The only problem is when you want to stop.'

'Tuco,' the woman said tiredly, 'enough!' She stood up and thrust her pelvis backwards, sending her diminutive lover into space with such force that he almost fell over the coffee table.

Carlyle felt his jaw drop at the sight. Then he recalled what the woman had said. 'Tuco?' He frowned. 'You're...'

'That's right,' the man smiled.

From down the hall, Carlyle heard the sound of the toilet being flushed. Out of the bathroom came a much younger man. Realising that the master of the household had returned, he casually pointed a pistol at Carlyle's head.

'Take a seat, Inspector.' Tuco Martinez picked up a pair of trousers from the floor and pulled them on.

After what he'd seen, Carlyle decided to sit in one of the armchairs. Placing the bottle of Jameson's on the floor beside him, he watched as the woman picked up a pile of clothes from beside the sofa and headed for the door.

Rico followed his gaze. 'Quite a woman, my Monica, don't you think?'

Carlyle tried to regain his composure. 'Why were you having sexual intercourse in my home?'

'These things happen.' Tuco tugged a powder-blue sweater over his head. 'I took the pill and was ready to go.'

'Mm.' Carlyle wanted to be outraged at the intrusion but, somehow, couldn't quite manage it.

'*C'est génial.* It's really something.' Tuco ran a hand through his hair. 'Have you ever tried this stuff?'

Carlyle shook his head.

Taco looked him up and down. 'Everyone is using it these days.'

'I don't need it,' Carlyle mumbled, somewhat defensively. Why the hell was he having this conversation?

'People use it whether they *need* it or not,' Tuco informed him. 'It's like a...' he groped for the word, 'a *social* thing. Very common. You should give it a go. Maybe I could send you some samples.'

'I don't need it,' the inspector repeated.

Tuco gave him a thoughtful glance. 'Well, a man like yourself, at your stage of life, I suppose that you are not quite there yet.'

'No.'

'But soon...' Tuco smiled sadly. 'It's embarrassing to have to use it, but trust me – it works. The only problem is that you can't exactly switch it on and off quite as easily as you might want.' He patted his trousers, which were still showing a massive bulge. 'This thing will last for hours and hours.'

'You're called the Samurai,' Carlyle said, trying to move the conversation on.

Tuco smiled. 'Dominic Silver told you about that?' Then his face darkened. 'I see that you two have been busy conspiring against me.'

'Hardly,' Carlyle snorted. He gestured at the young guy, who was now leaning against the door with the gun dangling at his side. 'I presume he's the guy who was at my daughter's school.'

Tuco nodded.

'Who is he?'

'Just a footsoldier. Not on your records. Never will be. Not someone you have to worry about.'

'What do you want?'

Tuco slipped into a pair of black Gucci loafers. 'Inspector,' he said, 'you know me well enough by now. You have even seen me naked.'

'You don't want to fuck me, too?' Despite the circumstances, Carlyle's grin was genuine enough.

'No,' Tuco laughed. 'You are not my type. What I am saying is that we are both intelligent men.'

Carlyle did not demur.

'So let's not pretend you don't know what I want.'

'I can't do anything about Alain Costello,' Carlyle said. 'Your son is in the system. His trial is being fast-tracked on the grounds that the outcome is inevitable.'

Tuco looked at him expressionlessly. He said, 'You don't seem to understand.'

'Understand what?'

'I will get what I want,' Tuco said slowly, 'or I will kill you and your family.'

Monrovia, here I come, thought Carlyle, smiling to himself.

'What's so funny?' Tuco demanded.

'Nothing,' said Carlyle, holding up a hand. 'I understand what you're saying. After all, you've already tried twice.'

'I'm glad you noticed.' Tuco beamed at him as

the woman reappeared from the bathroom. She was wearing a pair of jeans and a grey silk blouse, and it struck Carlyle that she seemed far less attractive with her clothes on.

'Tuco, *où sont mes chaussures?*' Without waiting for an answer, the woman fell to her knees and began looking under the furniture.

Tuco Martinez kept his gaze on the inspector. 'You have one more chance,' he said. 'I want my boy and I want my drugs. I know that you and Silver stole them.'

'Not so.' Carlyle shook his head and tried to look surprised. 'I don't work with Dominic Silver.'

'*Voilà!*' The woman squawked, pulling a pair of studded ankle boots out from under Carlyle's chair.

'Wait outside!' Tuco demanded, looking exasperated. He turned back to Carlyle. 'Silver told me you were a corrupt cop. He said he'd had you in his pocket for years.'

Bollocks, thought Carlyle. 'That's nonsense.'

'Then why have you let him operate freely all these years?'

Carlyle said nothing.

'Don't worry,' Tuco grinned, 'I will deal with him. Think of it as my present to you.' He signalled to the minion who pulled an envelope out of the back pocket of his jeans and tossed it on the coffee table.

Tuco gestured at the table. 'Passport, cash and travel documents. Give them to Alain when you get him out. Leave the rest to me.'

Carlyle looked at the packet then at Tuco.

'This is your last chance,' said the Samurai. 'Or,

next time, I will kill you and your family.'

When the door slammed shut, Carlyle sat listening to the slight buzzing noise in his head. A few moments later, he got up and stepped into the kitchen. After washing his face and drying it with a tea towel, he took a small Tesco bag from under the sink. Returning to the living room, he placed Tuco's packet in the plastic bag, careful not to get his fingerprints on the envelope. After some further thought, he stuffed the bag under a pile of magazines next to the sofa, happy to hide it in plain sight, given that it wouldn't be there for long.

It took him a couple more minutes to find his private, pay-as-you-go mobile and ring Dom's number. Cursing, he ended the call as it went to voicemail.

Grabbing a directory from the hall, he was surprised to find a listing for Zatoichi and even more surprised when he dialled the number and it worked.

'C'mon!' he hissed, slumping back into his armchair.

The number rang for what seemed like an eternity before someone picked up.

'Yeah?'

He recognized the accent immediately. 'Lisbeth...'

'What?'

Oh God. What was the bloody girl's name? He'd forgotten. 'It's Carlyle – the cop – I need to speak to Dom – no, Gideon.'

There was a pause.

'They're not in the bar,' she said.

'Then put me through to the office,' Carlyle demanded. 'It's fucking urgent.'

'What am I,' the girl growled, 'your bloody personal slave or something?' There was the sound of the phone being dropped on the bar and Carlyle's handset was filled with the sound of background chatter. After another eternity, someone picked up again.

'What's so important?' Gideon asked by way of introduction.

Carlyle spoke clearly and slowly. 'I've just had a visit from the Samurai. He's coming to see you next.'

Without another word, Gideon ended the call.

Time for a new phone, Carlyle decided. Struggling to his feet, he removed the battery from the back of the mobile, pulled out the sim card and went in search of a pair of scissors.

He was just about to head for bed when the front-door buzzer sounded.

'What now?' Carlyle said grumpily as he padded down the hall. Opening the front door, he found Umar grinning in the walkway outside.

'What are you so cheery about?' Carlyle asked, turning and heading back to the living room.

Following on behind him, Umar nodded at the bottle of whiskey, which was still standing on the floor. 'Having a bit of a session, are we?'

'Haven't even broken the seal,' Carlyle pointed out. 'Want some?'

'Nah.' Umar shook his head. 'I could do with a cup of tea, though.'

Slumping back into the armchair, Carlyle

wearily wafted a hand in the direction of the kitchen. 'Help yourself – and make me a green tea while you're at it.'

Umar reappeared with two mugs of freshly made tea. Handing one to Carlyle, he took a grateful sip from the other. 'Why have you got a cut-up sim card in the sink?' he asked, taking a seat on the sofa.

Fuck. 'Er, it was Alice's,' Carlyle lied. 'She ran up a ridiculous bill on her phone, so I cut it up.'

'Tough love,' Umar noted.

'Quite. How did you get on in the sticks?'

'Oh, a complete waste of time. Spoke to some snotty pen-pusher in uniform who told me absolutely nothing that wasn't on Dr Bell's piece of paper.'

Carlyle let out a long breath. Events had overtaken Adrian Gasparino. Now he had more pressing things to worry about than the hapless soldier. 'Did you see his missus?'

'Yeah.' Umar blew on his tea. 'Their kid was born four days ago. She had just returned home. In a bit of a daze.'

Carlyle surprised himself by dredging a scintilla of empathy from somewhere. 'You would be.'

'She says she never even saw Adrian when he got back from Afghanistan.'

'So, all in all, it was a complete waste of time, then?' Carlyle could feel his eyelids drooping. He wanted to crawl into bed and sleep for at least ten hours.

Umar beamed. 'Luckily for you, though, I can multi-task.'

A pained expression settled on Carlyle's face. *I want to go to sleep,* he thought. *Why don't you go home?* 'Eh?'

'Milch came up with a DNA sample that I was able to match to Clive Martin.' Umar sat back on the sofa, waiting for the applause to start.

Placing his mug on the coffee table, Carlyle slowly processed that piece of information. 'The strip-club guy? Abigail Slater's client?'

'Yes, indeed,' Umar smiled. 'Mr Everton's, no less.'

Can I please go to bed now? Carlyle wondered. His brain, however, kept ticking over. 'How come we have his DNA in the database?'

'He was done for driving while banned – and being three times over the legal limit – ten years ago. One of the people who kicked Gasparino to death was a close family member. I'm guessing a grandson.'

'Result,' Carlyle nodded. 'Well done.'

Umar looked at his watch. 'We could head round to Everton's now, if you want.'

You've got to be fucking kidding. Carlyle shook his head. 'Nah. Bring the offending toe-rag in and work out the details. You'll have the case closed by tomorrow night.'

'Okay.'

'And say thanks to Milch for me.' Carlyle got to his feet and gestured towards the hall. 'Now, if you don't mind, it's my bedtime. I need to get my beauty sleep.'

THIRTY-SEVEN

Placing his beer bottle on the bar, Dominic Silver scanned the story in the *Standard* – *Gavin Swann: MY KISS 'N' TELL SHAME* – and muttered to himself, 'Bloody footballers, they should be outlawed.'

Gideon Spanner appeared at his shoulder. 'He's here.'

Taking a moment to finish the story, Dom closed the newspaper, folding it in half, before placing it next to the beer bottle. Leaning against the bar, he looked past his business partner, towards the guy flanked by the minder with the gun in his pocket and the pneumatic black woman.

'Tuco,' Dom said cheerily, 'can I buy you a drink?'

Tuco Martinez looked contemptuously around Zatoichi's. The place was a long way from full but it wasn't empty either. 'We need to talk,' he said. 'Somewhere private.'

'Here is fine,' Dom said airily, plucking the beer from the bar and lifting it to his lips.

Rico took a step closer. 'Our partnership,' he said, lowering his voice, 'is not going as planned.'

'The police raid was unfortunate,' Silver told him. 'But out of my control. This kind of thing is just part of the cost of doing business, as you well know.'

'But we haven't done any damn business!' Tuco

waved an angry finger under Dominic's nose. 'Don't think you can rip me off like this.' Red in the face, his eyes bulged as if they were about to pop out of his head.

'*Calmes-toi*, Tuco.' The woman put a hand on the old man's shoulder.

'I am calm!' Tuco hissed. Pushing her hand away, he turned back to Silver. 'I have told your corrupt flic that he has to return my dope – and my boy.'

Gideon casually pushed himself off the bar and set his stance for action.

'None of this is in our power and control,' Dominic repeated. 'I will, of course, see what I can do. But I would never waste your time with false promises or meaningless guarantees.'

'You have one week,' Tuco threatened him. 'If I have to come back to this stinking city of yours, you will all die.'

Silver watched the French trio leave the bar and turned to Gideon Spanner. 'Well,' he said perkily, 'I think that went well.' Finishing his beer, he signalled to Michela for another bottle.

As usual, Gideon kept his own counsel.

The first floor of Honeymann's Finsbury Square offices was busier than the middle of Oxford Street in the January sales. Young, animated professionals descended from all directions on the open-plan canteen. All around were screens showing the current output of Honeymann TV. The place hummed with excitement and activity.

Baseer Yazdani contemplated the inspector with wry amusement as he took it all in. 'The offices are designed to create what's called "pandemonium with a purpose" – loads of technology, lots of activity and...' he smiled at an attractive Asian girl who was headed for the drinks machine, 'lots of babes. What more could you want?'

'Bloody hell!' Carlyle laughed. 'I want to work here.'

'What you've got to remember,' Baseer explained, 'is that it's a young person's game. The average age here is thirty-one, thirty-two, something like that.'

'Yeah,' Carlyle said, 'I'm past it. I know.'

The journalist held up a hand by way of apology. 'Sorry...'

Carlyle frowned. 'Don't worry. I'm the only person in here with grey hair. I'm not going to take offence.'

'I didn't mean...'

'Not a problem. We all get older.' Carlyle gestured at the scene in front of them. 'Even this lot. Mr Honeymann won't be able to save them from that. Not that they'll be worrying about that right now.'

'It's a working space that is designed for incidental contact and accidental creativity.' Baseer pointed towards the lifts. 'Let's make a move. I've been here for three years now. It's great. Twice I've been offered jobs at the BBC but I'd never move. I think I would die of boredom over there. Too many rules.'

They reached the lifts as the doors of one opened and another splurge of journalistic humanity spilled out, heading for the free muesli and bananas. Once it had emptied, Baseer stepped inside and hit the button for the third floor.

Upstairs, parked in a glass cube of a meeting room, Carlyle watched a presenter interview a suit on the set outside. With some effort, he tried to focus on what the suit was talking about – something about Zimbabwe's latest export plans – before losing interest immediately.

'Here we go.' Baseer dropped a thick blue file onto the desk. Carlyle looked at the file. 'What have you got?'

'These are some of the documents from our investigation into Dino Mottram.'

Carlyle pulled his chair towards the desk and sat up straight.

'We have got a lot of material,' Baseer informed him, 'but so far, nothing I can publish. It is simply not enough to get it past my editors.'

Folding his arms, Carlyle smiled. 'So you want me to help you with some more proof?'

'No. I simply thought you might be interested in the stuff relating to Clifford Blitz and Gavin Swann.'

Carlyle nodded. 'You thought right.'

Baseer tapped the file. 'Much of this stuff is publicly available documentation. Some, however, has come from my sources, whom I cannot reveal.'

'I understand.'

'Okay. The deal is that you can look through this material here and take notes, but you cannot take it away or make copies. Our relationship has to remain confidential. When you have progress in your investigation, you give me a heads-up first.'

'That's fine.' Carlyle produced a notepad and

pen and said, 'Give me the executive summary, please.'

Baseer took a deep breath. 'The top rate of tax has gone up and the expectation is that it will go up further.'

Good, thought Carlyle.

'Footballers and their agents are keener than ever to minimize their tax bill. One tactic that has been used by Blitz is for Swann to take a director's loan from his image rights company.'

Carlyle began to make notes approximating the journalist's briefing. The reality, however, was that the detail was lost on him and the words were just bouncing off his brain with nothing going in.

'As a result, Swann has been able to cut his tax bill by ninety-eight per cent,' Baseer concluded.

Carlyle raised an eyebrow. 'How much?'

'He has borrowed nearly ten million from Monkeyface 286, his image rights company, over the past four years. Had he taken this money as a salary, he would have been liable for more than four million in tax.'

'But this is legal, isn't it?'

Baseer smiled. 'With the taxman, you never really know, do you?'

'I suppose not.'

'Getting into things like this means you are treading a very fine line. You would expect the Revenue to be all over it.'

Carlyle looked the young journalist up and down. 'And you would help HMRC with their enquiries?'

'If I can ... and if I can get some copy out of it.'

'Okay. Let me make a few calls.' Stuffing his

notes in his pocket, Carlyle got to his feet. 'In the meantime, I think I'm gonna have to grab a little snack on the way out.'

Pushing up the half-opened shutter, Umar Sligo stepped inside Everton's and was immediately confronted by a shaven-headed bouncer who was almost as wide as he was tall. In one of his meaty paws was a mug with a Chelsea FC crest on the side.

'Come back later,' the man growled, taking a mouthful of tea. 'We're closed.'

Umar pulled out his warrant card and let the man slowly read the text.

'I'm looking for Clive Martin,' he said.

'Haven't seen him,' the man shrugged, standing aside, 'but he might be in the back.'

Replacing the ID in his pocket, Umar wandered into the club proper. Aside from a delivery man placing boxes of spirits on the bar and an old woman mopping the floor, the place was empty.

'The boss isn't around.'

Umar turned to see the American girl who had whacked the unlucky PC Lea stroll across the room towards him. If anything, she looked even more of an Amazonian goddess with her clothes on, and, without any make-up on her face, he could see that she was definitely on the beautiful side of pretty. Pretending not to recognize her, Umar lifted his gaze to the middle distance.

Christina O'Brien grinned. She was used to making men flustered and the cute cop was not the best when it came to hiding his thoughts. She flashed him a smile, dazzling him with her impossibly white, impossibly perfect American teeth. 'Clive's probably in bed with a couple of the girls and a monster hangover. You won't see him around here until tonight.'

Umar gazed at his shoes. He felt like a deer being circled by a lion; usually it was the other way round and he felt distinctly uncomfortable with this role reversal. 'Where does he live?'

The bouncer appeared by the bar and glared at Christina.

'I don't know,' she shrugged, enjoying the obvious lie, before heading for the door at the back of the stage. When Umar followed, she stopped, turned and tapped him on the chest with an immaculately manicured index finger. 'A bit early for a private dance, isn't it?' she grinned, looking over Umar's shoulder at the bouncer.

Umar felt himself blush but soldiered on. 'Have you met any of his family?' he asked, lowering his voice.

Leading him through the door, Christina closed it behind them before answering. 'He has two sons,' she said quietly. 'Both in their 40s, I think. One of them is an accountant or something – he's never here, which is not surprising seeing as he's gay.' She laughed mirthlessly. 'Clive, being a stupid old bugger, is quite put out about it.'

'The other?' Umar asked.

'A right pig. Never worked a day in his life. He uses the place as if it's his own private knocking shop; I don't know how his wife puts up with it.'

Umar wasn't looking for a middle-aged man. 'What about a grandson?'

Christina gave him a funny look but knew better than to ask any questions herself. 'No idea.'

Umar frowned.

'Anyway, you can ask him yourself. He has a flat in Covent Garden.' She gave him an address on Maiden Lane, off Garrick Street, near the piazza.

'Thanks. I won't let slip where I got the information from.' Umar turned away. He had the door half-open when he felt her hand on his shoulder.

'Where are you going?' she whispered. 'There's no rush. Clive will definitely still be asleep.'

Umar felt an unfamiliar sense of panic as she led him towards one of the back rooms. Pushing him through the nearest door, Christina ran her tongue along her bottom lip. 'I came in early to try out a new routine. You can give me a hand.'

THIRTY-EIGHT

Sitting in the Box Café, Carlyle was enjoying a Coke when a call lit up his mobile. He eyed the machine suspiciously for several seconds before picking it up.

'Carlyle.'

'What the fuck do you think you are playing at?'

Pulling the phone away from his head, it took the inspector a moment to realize that the snarling voice on the other end belonged to Gavin Swann's agent, Clifford Blitz.

Smiling, he put the handset back to his ear.

'What's the problem, Mr Blitz?'

'You know damn well what the problem is!' Blitz screamed at him. 'I've had the Inland Revenue at my house since six o'clock this morning. They are hoovering up every bit of paper they can find and carting it off for forensic investigation, whatever the fuck that is.'

Struggling to keep the amusement from his voice, Carlyle cleared his throat. 'I know nothing about this,' he lied. 'The Inland Revenue is nothing to do with me.'

'Don't fuck with me, Inspector,' Blitz hissed. 'We had a deal.'

'We do, indeed,' Carlyle agreed, 'and as you know, I have been scrupulous in keeping to it. Mr Swann has been kept as far from my investigations as you could have hoped – further, in fact.'

Blitz made a noise that sounded like he was in pain.

'Who is leading the HMRC investigation?' Carlyle asked.

'A woman,' Blitz groaned, as if that somehow added insult to injury. 'I've got a card here... Maria March, Special Investigations Department.'

Carlyle took a few seconds to give the impression of carefully searching through his mental contacts list. 'Never heard of her,' he said finally. The truth was rather different. The inspector had known Maria March for more than ten years. Back in 2004, as an ambitious young investigator for HM Revenue & Customs, she had been investigating a City scam of the type that came along with monotonous regularity. One of the traders caught in the HMRC web had walked in front of a number 19 bus travelling down Charing Cross

Road rather than face the music. Carlyle remembered that his only real surprise at the time was that the bus had been going fast enough to actually kill the bloke, although – if his memory served him correctly – the trader only finally shuffled off this mortal coil after spending a week in a coma.

After his conversation with the Honeymann journalist Baseer Yazdani, the inspector had spent an hour in Maria's tiny office in Somerset House, talking her through the alleged fraud involving Gavin Swann. Sitting in front of a floor-to-ceiling bookcase crammed with files, papers and various tax guides, Maria looked even smaller than her five foot two inches. A pretty, raven-haired woman now well into her forties, she had Italian parents and a French husband, with two kids who were Londoners through and through.

'Okay. I see.' Maria nodded thoughtfully all the way through Carlyle's opening monologue, taking copious notes in a hard-backed A4 notebook.

When he couldn't think of anything else to say, the inspector sat back in his chair, knocking a copy of *Tolley's Tax Guide* from the table behind him.

'Sorry.'

Maria rolled her hazel eyes. 'Don't worry about it.'

Carlyle picked the book off the floor and placed it back in its place. 'So,' he asked, 'what do you think?'

'Well,' Maria looked at her notes, 'this kind of thing is fairly common. I should imagine we know all of this stuff – and more already. It's clearly a grey area; the question is, how actively are we investigating it?'

'I see,' said Carlyle, unable to keep the disappointment from his voice.

'Don't worry,' Maria smiled, 'I'm sure we will be able to give this guy a hard time for you. My boss is a complete media tart. He will love the publicity of such a high-profile target. He would have sex with his grandmother in Selfridges window for a couple of minutes on the *Today* programme.'

'Urgh.'

'His words, not mine.'

'This has to be more than just a publicity stunt.'

She looked at him doubtfully.

'Really.'

'Okay. I understand. I'm sure if we put our minds to it we could probably come up with enough to put Mr Blitz away for a year or two, maybe more.'

'Perfect,' Carlyle smiled. 'That would be great.'

'Never heard of her?' Blitz parroted, sensing that he was being given some flannel but unable to do anything about it.

'No, sorry,' Carlyle replied. 'But let me see what I can find out.'

'Appreciate it,' Blitz said grudgingly.

'Meantime,' Carlyle continued, deciding to yank Blitz's chain a bit more, 'you can do something for me.'

There was a suspicious pause. 'What would that be?'

'I need to get in touch with Paul Groom's agent.'

'Hah!' Blitz laughed. 'Wayne Devine isn't his

agent any more.'

'Oh? Who is?'

'I am.'

Ending the call, Carlyle finished his drink and signalled to the waitress that he would like another. Then he called Baseer, gave him a mobile number for Maria March and told him he could finally write his Gavin Swann story.

'She'll "no comment" it for you,' Carlyle said, 'but she can't deny it. I would have thought that should be enough to get it past your editors.'

'I hope so,' Baseer replied. 'Thanks.'

'No problem.' Carlyle did a thumbs-up as the waitress placed a cold drink in front of him. 'Let's keep in touch.'

Dropping the phone onto the table, the inspector cracked open the can and took a swig of its contents. He was contemplating ordering a sandwich when someone pulled up a chair and sat down beside him. Looking up, he was surprised to see that it was Gideon Spanner.

Dropping a Nike holdall by his feet, Spanner carefully placed a copy of that afternoon's *Standard* on the table, opened at page six and folded in half. Below the fold was a story headlined: *WAR VETERAN KICKED TO DEATH BY THUGS*. He tapped the story with his index finger, saying, 'You were supposed to give me a heads-up on this.'

Picking up the paper, Carlyle scanned down the story. They had Gasparino's name, some details of his service record, along with a quote from Dr Bell. In the last paragraph, a 'Metropolitan Police source' was quoted as saying: '*The attackers left a lot of forensic evidence at the scene. On that basis, we would expect to make good progress in identifying them quite quickly.*' The inspector sighed heavily; it wasn't the worst leak he had ever seen, or the quickest, but it was pretty bad. *If Umar had anything to do with this,* he thought, *I will kick the smug bastard all the way back up to Manchester.* He dropped the paper back onto the table and shrugged. 'This doesn't really help me, but I don't think we'll have too much trouble catching them – they're just a bunch of kids. Idiots like that always get caught.'

Gideon gave him a stony look. '*I* want to deal with them.'

'Don't go all Charles Bronson on me, Gideon,' Carlyle sighed. 'They will get what's coming to them. Leave it alone or I'll end up having to arrest you.'

If the big man was at all perturbed by the prospect, it didn't show as he gazed out of the window. 'Who's Charles Bronson?'

Carlyle suddenly felt very old indeed. 'For God's sake, Gideon, is that what you came over here to hassle me about?'

'Two things,' Gideon said firmly. 'One – be ready to go on a little trip tomorrow night, thirty-six hours or so. Wear old clothes, stuff you don't mind losing. Make sure all your pockets are empty: no cash, no identification, no electronic devices.'

Carlyle looked at him, bemused. 'This is a joke, right?'

'Two.' Gideon reached down, unzipped the holdall, pulled out a Waitrose plastic bag and handed it to Carlyle. 'This is for you. Don't touch anything inside there, it's all clean – no fingerprints.'

Sighing, the inspector peered at a small canvas satchel inside. 'What is it?' Even though he knew the answer, he thought that he might as well ask.

'It's the drugs from the house that your people raided in Docklands.'

'All of them?'

'So I'm told.' Gideon got to his feet. 'Apologies for any inconvenience caused.'

'Thanks a lot,' said Carlyle sarcastically, but the other man was already gone.

Invigorated after an hour with Christina O'Brien and a chicken panini from Carluccio's, Umar felt almost giddy as he climbed the steps to Clive Martin's penthouse apartment on Maiden Lane. Ringing the doorbell, he hopped from foot to foot, humming an approximation of 'Time of My Life' as he waited for a reply. When no one came, he rang the bell again, longer this time, his enthusiasm for the Black-Eyed Peas beginning to wane.

'Come on!' He pressed the buzzer for a third time just as the door swung open.

'There's no need to keep ringing the bloody bell!'

Although it was the middle of the afternoon, the girl in front of him looked like she'd just fallen out of bed. Her long blonde hair was all over the place and her face still bore traces of last night's makeup. Then there was the fact that she was naked, apart from a pair of black lace panties.

Umar slowly looked her up and down. This

truly was his lucky day. *Must remember to buy a lottery ticket tonight,* he told himself.

'Who are you?' the girl demanded, making no effort to cover herself up.

'I'm looking for Clive,' Umar explained.

'He's still in bed.' Her accent was broad Liverpool; she vaguely reminded Umar of some Scouse pop singer or soap star from when he was a kid, whose name, if he had ever known it in the first place, he had long since forgotten.

Umar glanced at his watch. It was after three thirty. 'He can't still be asleep, surely.'

'Nah,' the girl grinned. 'My mate Gemma's giving him a blow job. At least she's trying to. The old bugger often struggles to get it up these days.'

Finally, Umar remembered his warrant card. He pulled out his ID and showed it to the girl. 'Go and tell him I need to talk to him.'

'Okay,' the girl pouted, 'but Clive doesn't like to be disturbed.' She gave Umar an evil grin. 'He gets very pissed off if he can't deliver the money shot, if you know what I mean.'

'Sorry.' Umar watched as she turned and sashayed down the corridor, disappearing somewhere off to the left. Stepping inside, he closed the door behind him and went off to find the living room.

'This police harassment is getting very tiresome. I have already telephoned my lawyer.' Clive Martin shuffled into the lounge in a Bon Jovi T-shirt and a pair of boxer shorts with what looked to Umar very much like a padded crotch. The look on his face suggested that poor old Gemma had not managed to close the deal. Snatching a pair of spectacles from the coffee table, he took a seat on an oversized red fabric sofa.

Umar smiled apologetically. 'This is not about Everton's.'

'No?' Martin allowed himself a leer. 'I hear you were there this morning, screwing one of my girls.'

For a moment, Umar was speechless. The thought of Christina hanging out here with Martin sent a wave of sadness and anger through him. Breaking off eye-contact, he contemplated Rob Ryan's *You Are My Universe* on the wall above Martin's head. The print seemed completely out of place in the strip-club owner's shagpad.

'News travels fast, Sergeant,' Martin laughed. 'Not that it had a long way to come in this instance. Anyway, it's no big deal. I'm certainly not going to hold it against you. I only wish that your boss was as ... interesting.'

'Inspector Carlyle is a really boring straitlaced bastard,' Umar agreed.

'He certainly is.' Martin smiled as a naked, auburn-haired girl, presumably Gemma, appeared with a demitasse which she placed on the coffee table. 'Thanks, sweetie.'

'No problem.' The girl turned to Umar, placing her hands on her hips. 'Would you like one, Officer?'

Umar's mouth was dry and his brain struggled to get any signal to his jaw.

Stepping away from Martin's grasp, the girl scratched a spot-on her right thigh. 'An espresso, that is.'

'Er,' Umar finally managed to hold up a hand. 'I'm fine.'

'Go to the bedroom,' Martin commanded. 'I'll be back in a minute.'

'All right,' the girl pouted.

'Quite a set-up you've got here,' Umar said after Gemma had left.

'It's hard work,' Martin grumbled. Grabbing the demitasse, he downed the espresso in one. 'Especially at my age.'

Umar murmured sympathetically.

'So,' Martin asked, 'what do you want?'

It took Umar more than a moment to remember why he was there. 'I need to speak to your grandson,' he said finally.

'What on earth are you talking about?' Martin got to his feet, theatrically scratching his padded crotch. 'I don't *have* a bloody grandson.'

THIRTY-NINE

Carlyle returned to Charing Cross carrying his plastic Waitrose bag as casually as he could manage. Looking up from behind the desk, Angie Middleton gave him a welcoming grin.

'Been shopping?' she asked, gesturing at the bag with her biro.

'Nah,' Carlyle shook his head. 'Just some odds and ends.' Walking past the desk, he headed through the fire doors and up the stairs.

Up on the third floor, he called Julie Crisp.

'What do you want?' she asked suspiciously. She was outside somewhere, maybe at a playground for he could hear children shouting happily in the background.

'That stuff we missed the other day...'

'Don't go there,' she said immediately. 'I'm a completely busted flush with my superiors after that wild goose chase you sent me on. It's gonna take me ages to get over that.'

'This time it's guaranteed,' Carlyle protested.

'Wasn't it supposed to be "guaranteed" last time?'

'Yes, but–'

'It's no fucking good to me now, John. Even if you came right over and placed the bloody stuff on my desk, it wouldn't undo the damage done. I have enough trouble here dealing with all the normal, day-to-day shit without you making it worse. You can't...' her angry words were carried away on a gust of wind, but he got the message. With a heavy sigh, he ended the call and placed the receiver carefully back on the cradle. Pushing his chair away from his desk, he bent down and rummaged around amongst the pile of boxfiles that he had accumulated over the years. Choosing the largest one, he emptied the papers inside into a bin marked *Confidential Shredding,* replacing them with the package that he had been handed by Gideon Spanner. With the drugs inside, the file didn't quite shut, but it was close enough. Placing the file on his desk, Carlyle switched on his PC and surfed the net aimlessly for ten minutes before heading back downstairs.

The evidence locker was a secure storeroom that took up approximately 600 square feet of the raised ground floor on the William IV Street side of the building. The duty officer, a WPC whose name Carlyle didn't know, buzzed him through the security gates and watched blankly as he signed the visitor's log.

'I just want to look at something from the Cameron case,' he said, trying to look as bored as she did.

This, as it happened, was almost true. Wally Cameron was an accountant who had been found dead in his Dean Street office four months earlier. The autopsy suggested a heart attack but Wally's wife was convinced he had been murdered by an unhappy client. She'd been running a low-intensity media campaign to have the case reopened; Carlyle had happily ignored it until Sonia Cameron had managed to buttonhole one of the Met's more gullible Assistant Commissioners at a public meeting and got him to agree to review the case.

'The bastards at Paddington Green,' Carlyle added, 'have asked me to rewrite my bloody report.' He raised his eyes to the ceiling in mock exasperation.

The WPC couldn't have managed to look more bored if she was dead herself.

'I know where the file is. Only need ten minutes, max.'

'What's in there?' The woman nodded at the boxfile under his arm.

'Just my papers,' Carlyle replied, 'the original report. I want to cross-reference a couple of things.'

The woman gestured at the rows of shelving that stretched out behind her. 'Be my guest.'

I can hardly walk! I hope you've got some more of

those pills – I've got a special surprise for you x

Staring at his iPad, Christian Holyrod re-read the email and winced. His dick felt like it had been rubbed with heavy-duty sandpaper, and every time he moved in his chair a spasm of pain crept through his guts. At least Abigail seemed happy with his new-found stamina. He couldn't remember the last time she had shown any enthusiasm about his lovemaking; then again, he couldn't remember the last time he cared. Dino had given him half-a-dozen of the bloody pills. It would be a while before he was in any state to try another one. All he could hope for was that Abigail's 'surprise', whatever it was, didn't arrive too soon.

'Mr Mayor?'

'Hm?' Holyrod reluctantly looked up from the screen into the enquiring gaze of London Assembly Member Victoria Boffington. Sitting to his right, Rosie Green, Adviser for Economic Affairs, drummed her fingers impatiently on the table. Green was forever complaining that Holyrod needed to up his game when it came to Mayor's Question Time. She seemed to be in denial about the fact that his time at City Hall – and therefore her hundred and eighty grand a year sinecure – was rapidly coming to an end. The thought of Green, a bland party hack, having to try and get a job in the real world caused him to snort with laughter.

'Well,' Boffington demanded, 'what is your stance on this?'

At the last minute, Green saved him by scrawling 'artistic metropolis' on the pad in front of her in letters big enough for him to be able to read.

'This is an incredibly important issue,' the Mayor said pompously as he dragged the relevant script from some backwater in his brain. 'It is essential that we support and work in partnership with a sector that generates over eighteen billion pounds a year, to help ensure that London maintains its position as the "greatest cultural capital of the world".'

Having stashed the unwanted dope in a dusty corner of the evidence locker, Carlyle grabbed a cheese roll and an orange juice from the canteen and went back to his desk, where he wrote the briefest possible update on his various endeavours in an email to Simpson. Hitting Send, he looked up to see Umar sauntering across the floor, a lopsided grin on his face.

The boy looks like he's in even more of a daze than usual, Carlyle observed critically.

'How's it going?' he asked.

'Fine,' Umar replied, slipping into his chair.

Carlyle eyed him suspiciously. 'What have you been up to?'

Umar tried to keep his grin from spreading. 'Nothing much.' He pulled out his mobile and stuck it into a charger he kept plugged into a socket under his desk. 'I spoke to Clive Martin.' After checking that the phone was charging, he dropped it on top of a pile of papers.

'And?' Carlyle asked impatiently.

Sparing all the unnecessary colour, Umar gave the inspector a short précis of what the club owner had told him.

'Shit,' Carlyle said thoughtfully. 'So where does

that leave us?'

'It leaves me going down to Wimbledon tomorrow to see the son.'

'Which one?'

'The straight one, of course.'

'We should speak to both of them, really.'

'The other one has been on a safari in Southern Africa for the last month.'

'Fair enough, that's a decent alibi.'

'Anyway,' Umar mused, 'we're not looking for a middle-aged man, are we?'

'You tell me,' Carlyle shrugged. 'Stranger things have happened.'

'You wanna come along?'

'Nah. I've got other things to do. By the way, did you ever find that girl – Kelly?'

'Kelly Kellaway?' Umar scratched his head. 'Yeah. Sorry, I forgot to mention it. She was photographed in Fifty-Ninth Street.'

Carlyle looked at him uncomprehendingly.

'It's a nightclub in Manchester,' Umar said. 'She was hanging off one of Citeh's new signings.'

'How the mighty have fallen,' Carlyle sneered. 'From threesomes with Gavin Swann to hanging out with your mob in the provinces.'

Umar ignored the barb. 'I got a mate up there to track her down. He spoke to her yesterday, but she was no use whatsoever.'

'What a surprise,' Carlyle grunted.

'Claimed she barely knew Sandy Carroll, that they had only done the one threesome together and she didn't know that Carroll was partying with Swann and Groom the night she got killed.'

'How very convenient.'

'Indeed. As soon as she was pressed, she got all pissy and started talking about a lawyer, so we didn't push it.'

'Fair enough.'

'We can drag her down for questioning,' Umar said, 'but seeing as you haven't even taken a formal statement from Swann yet, it seems a bit premature.'

'Okay,' Carlyle sighed, 'we've got a confession. The rest is just more admin.'

Umar looked at him. 'You still think Swann did it?'

Carlyle picked up a pencil from his desk and started doodling on a report that should have been filed weeks ago. 'It doesn't really matter, does it? It certainly doesn't matter to Sandy Carroll.' He talked Umar through his phone conversation with Blitz. 'The whole thing stinks. Why would Swann's agent want to represent a reserve goalie who is going to jail, for God's sake?'

'So what do we do now?' Umar asked. 'Groom has a hearing scheduled for a fortnight.'

'Sort out the paperwork.'

Umar rolled his eyes to the heavens.

'Get the statements done,' Carlyle said, ignoring his sergeant's reaction. 'Keep it all brisk and official, like we're going through the motions. Make sure everything is on time and in order.'

'Brisk and official,' Umar smiled, 'that's me. What will you be up to, though?'

Carlyle was saved from having to reply by the appearance of a plain-looking blonde girl at Umar's desk. She was wearing a brown leather jacket over a flowery print dress and the inspector was fairly sure he had seen her around.

'Oh, hi Heather,' Umar said sheepishly.

The girl turned to Carlyle. 'WPC Heather Wilson.'

Getting to his feet, so that he could make a quick getaway, Carlyle shook her hand. 'John Carlyle.'

'We all know who you are, Inspector,' Wilson grinned in a rather unsettling manner. She flicked a thumb in Umar's direction. 'I'm here to see if your sergeant is going to deliver on his promise to take me out.'

'Oh yes?' Carlyle enjoyed watching Umar squirm in his seat.

'You see—'

Carlyle held up a hand. 'No need to explain, Umar.' Smiling broadly, he patted Wilson on the shoulder. 'Make sure he takes you somewhere really expensive,' he said mischievously. 'I hear that Nobu on Park Lane is excellent.'

Having caused as much trouble as he could, Carlyle left. Was that the sound of Umar gasping for air as he headed for the lift? He certainly liked to think so.

FORTY

'Want another?'

Carlyle shook his head. There was barely enough whiskey left to cover the bottom of his glass but now was not the time for a refill; he

331

wanted to get home.

Alison Roche took the hint and placed the remains of her Guinness on the table.

Carlyle gestured at her three-quarters empty glass. 'You go for it, if you want another.'

'Nah,' Roche told him. 'I'm fine.'

Carlyle shrugged. 'When did you get into drinking that stuff?'

'Some of the guys I work with like a pint – or ten,' Roche laughed. 'I don't mind the occasional one, now and again.'

'Never got into it myself.' Carlyle looked around the Essex Serpent and wished he had chosen a better venue to meet his former colleague for a quiet drink. The place was heaving, with more people coming through the door all the time.

Sensing his discomfort, Roche finished her drink. 'Alain Costello's preliminary hearing is due next week.'

Carlyle happily got to his feet. 'It should be a formality.'

'You would hope so,' said Roche, hoisting her bag over her shoulder. 'Will you come along?'

'Sorry,' Carlyle smiled, 'I can't. I'll be in Liberia.'

Roche gave him a funny look. 'Where?'

He waited until they were outside, standing on the relative calm of the pavement before he explained his unusual family trip.

'Sounds interesting,' she said doubtfully. 'How are Helen and Alice getting on out there?'

'Fine.' Carlyle stepped into the gutter to allow a gaggle of Chinese tourists to get past. 'To be honest, I haven't heard that much from them so far.'

'No news is good news.'

'Yeah.' Under the yellow glow of the streetlight, he noticed belatedly how tired she looked. 'How are things with you?'

Roche zipped up her coat. 'Not too bad. Things have been a lot better since we nailed that little French bastard. They're still making me go to your shrink, though.'

'He's hardly *my* shrink,' Carlyle protested. As he did so, the uncomfortable recollection hit him that he had an appointment with Dr Wolf the next day.

'You know what I mean.'

'Yeah,' Carlyle groaned. Pulling his BlackBerry from his jacket pocket, he checked the calendar. There it was: 3 p.m. 'I've got to see him tomorrow, as it happens.'

'What do you talk about?'

'As little as possible,' Carlyle said. 'I find him very – I dunno – disengaged.'

'Isn't that how it's supposed to be?'

'Okay, for "disengaged" read "full of shit".'

'At least you manage to say what you think,' Roche grinned. 'You don't bottle it all up inside.'

'That would be unhealthy.' Sticking his hands in his pockets, he started walking towards the piazza, knowing that Roche would be going the other way. 'Good luck with Mr Costello,' he called. 'I'll give you a ring when I get back from Africa.'

Back at the flat, Carlyle retrieved the packet that had been left by Tuco Martinez and padded into the kitchen. Ripping open the envelope, he emptied the contents into the sink. There was a first-class open Eurostar ticket to Brussels, along with an authentic-looking Belgian passport, bearing Alain Costello's photograph but in the name of Sébastien Daerden; then there was the cash: £500 in a mixture of £20 and £50 notes and a much thicker wad of crisp new €50 notes.

Carlyle gave up when he got to €5,000. Placing the cash on the draining board, he considered his options. After a few moments, he pulled open a drawer, rooting around until he found a pre-addressed, freepost envelope for the Supporter Care Department at Avalon, Helen's aid charity. With some reluctance, he stuffed the cash into the envelope, sealing it at both ends with some sellotape before sticking it in his jacket pocket. He then took a box of matches from the drawer and carefully set fire to the ticket, watching it burn before washing the remnants down the plughole. The passport was a tougher proposition; after several unsuccessful attempts to get it to light, Carlyle settled for cutting it up into small pieces with a large pair of scissors. Scooping up the pieces, he placed them back in the envelope and headed for the door.

After dumping the remains of the Daerden passport in three different bins along Drury Lane, Carlyle dropped the cash in a post box on High Holborn, acknowledging just the slightest tinge of regret as he let it slip from his fingers and fall amongst the other first-class mail. To cheer himself up, he headed for the Rock & Sole Plaice, Covent Garden's only fish and chip shop, a block away on Endell Street. After a ten-minute wait behind the usual line of tourists, he retreated back home with his order of skate and chips warming his hands.

FORTY-ONE

Wayne Devine looked like he was overdue a session on the sunbed. The suit he was wearing still looked expensive, but the man himself looked considerably shabbier than the last time they had met. There was no iPad in sight either. Instead, Paul Groom's ex-agent fiddled with a cheap-looking mobile phone of the kind that Carlyle himself might use.

'I don't know what I can really tell you, Inspector,' he sighed, staring into his cappuccino. 'People change agents all the time. In my line of work you have to plan for that. You can't put all your eggs in one basket.'

'No.' Carlyle finished his espresso and waited for Devine to continue.

'You have to develop and maintain a portfolio of clients. I still have a group of quality players on my books.' He reeled off a list of names, none of which Carlyle had ever heard of.

'How long had you worked with Paul?'

Devine blew the air out of his cheeks. 'Going on for eight years. He came all the way through the ranks – county football, Academy, England under-18s, professional contract...' His voice tailed off.

'His career had stalled though,' Carlyle mused, 'even before he found himself in this mess.'

'Hard to say,' Devine said defensively. 'He was

still young, especially for a goalkeeper. He could have ended up dropping down a division, or even two, and still have had plenty of time to make it back to the top.'

'Not now.'

Devine shrugged. 'Plenty of footballers have gone to jail and been able to resume their careers when they've got out.'

'Yeah,' Carlyle spluttered, 'when they've been done for drink driving, not for murder!'

'Manslaughter,' Devine corrected him.

'Whatever.'

'There was the guy – can't remember his name – killed a guy in a car crash and ran off.'

'I remember that,' Carlyle said. 'He was done for Death By Dangerous Driving and got six years.'

'Did three. Which, I suppose, is fair enough.'

'Not if you're the family of the guy he killed,' Carlyle suggested.

'He's done quite well since he came back.' Devine mentioned a lower league club. 'He gets on the scoresheet quite often.'

'I'm sure that makes them feel much better.'

'Paul's lawyer reckons he'll get twelve years, absolute max. If he's out in, say, six, he can still have a decent career.'

'Is that why Blitz took him on?'

Devine said, 'That's got to be a question for him, don't you think?'

'So you were happy to let him go?'

'It comes with the territory.' Devine made an effort to sound philosophical. 'You have to move on. Paul won't be earning anything for the fore-seeable. Maybe Mr Blitz thinks he's doing the right thing by standing by him.'

'Maybe,' said Carlyle, sounding doubtful.

'I'm sure he will get Paul something when he gets out.'

'And what about you?' Carlyle asked.

'Things are looking good,' Devine said, as if reciting a set of lines that he'd been busy learning for public consumption. 'I have just joined forces with Marcus Angelides and will be representing a considerably expanded portfolio of talent.'

Angelides? The name rang a bell. 'Who's he?'

'One of the leading agents in the country,' Devine explained happily. 'Runs an agency based in Mayfair.'

'Nice.'

'Yes, it is.' Leaning across the table, Devine confided, 'That's the great thing about my business, Inspector; there are young lads appearing over the horizon all the time. It's a never-ending conveyor belt of opportunity.'

Sitting outside Dr Wolf's office, Carlyle looked at his watch and sighed. He was due to meet Dom at four thirty and it was already approaching ten past three.

Wolf might not be a particularly engaging fellow but he was usually quite punctual. On the one hand, Carlyle had no desire to sit through another fifty minutes, or rather, forty minutes and counting, of navel gazing. On the other hand, he was here now. Someone was paying for the session, even if it wasn't him, and just to abandon it felt like a waste of sorts.

The doctor's secretary had disappeared on

some unspecified errand. The thought suddenly occurred to Carlyle that Wolf himself might be having an afternoon nap. During their sessions, Carlyle had got used to the doctor nodding off or, at least, giving every impression of having fallen asleep. A couple of boring patients in the morning and a decent lunch – perhaps washed down by a glass or two of Rioja – would probably do the trick quite easily.

Another minute passed and the inspector felt his irritation solidifying in his gut. He couldn't sit here like a lemon forever. Getting to his feet, he stepped stealthily towards the door, on the alert for sounds of snoring. All he could hear, however, was the comforting hum of traffic noise outside. He had started to step away from the door before he realized it was ever so slightly ajar. Giving it the gentlest of pushes, he peered into the room.

Five minutes later, Carlyle finished his call to the station and took one last look at Wolf. The shrink was hanging from a length of black rubber flex that had been attached to the light fitting in the middle of the ceiling. It looked like he had stood on his desk, tied himself up and jumped. Stapled to the left leg of his olive corduroy trousers was a small sheet of paper on which had been written, in blue ink: *This is a suicide note.*

Nice penmanship, Carlyle thought. He wanted to feel some sympathy for the doctor but all that was forthcoming was a kind of generic dismay. Maybe the guy should have had therapy himself. In the distance, he could hear a siren approaching from the direction of the Euston Road. The first uniforms would be here in about a minute, which was just as well; he needed to get going.

FORTY-TWO

'Where are we going?' Carlyle stood shivering on an empty jetty in Brighton Marina. Not dressed for the occasion, he hopped from foot to foot as the biting wind cut through him.

'Here you go.' Dom threw him a pair of black leather gloves. 'Put these on. And keep them on.'

With his fingers going numb, Carlyle clumsily obliged.

Dom gestured in front of them. 'Time to get on board.'

Carlyle looked at the 49-foot vessel with the name *El Nino* emblazoned in blue script on the stern. 'You've got to be fucking kidding.'

'This is a great boat,' said Dom, pulling on his own gloves, 'a tough and no-nonsense long-distance cruiser, with good speed and sail characteristics. The Germans built it with a high ballast-to-weight ratio for safe offshore work,' he gazed up into the light-polluted darkness, 'which will be handy tonight.'

'What did you do,' Carlyle said grumpily, 'swallow the manual?'

'Sailing is one of my passions,' Dom said simply.

'Since when?'

'Since about thirty years ago, when I could first

afford a decent boat.' He gave Carlyle a look. 'You don't know everything about me, Inspector.'

Gideon stuck his head out of the cabin. 'We're good to go.'

'Okay,' Dom gave him a thumbs-up.

Not for the first time, Carlyle cursed his total stupidity. What the fuck was he playing at? 'So we're just going to tootle over to France,' he asked, 'and ... what? Murder Martinez.'

'RIP the Samurai,' Dom grinned.

'But I'm a fucking copper,' Carlyle wailed.

'A copper who is just protecting his family.' Dom gave him a light punch on the shoulder. 'Wake up and grow a pair.'

Carlyle scowled like a ten year old being told it was time for bed. 'What happens if we don't get him?'

Dom threw a comforting arm around him. 'Remember Sol Abramyan?'

'The arms dealer?' Carlyle nodded slowly. 'Yeah, course I do.' Sol was the last man who had tried to kill him. He shuddered at the memory of staring down the barrel of a gun thinking what he truly imagined would be his last ever thoughts in this, or any other, life.

What had those thoughts been? All he could re-member now was the sense of crushing failure; how he had let Helen and Alice down, completely.

It was not the kind of feeling that you ever forgot.

'I stood shoulder to shoulder with you then,' Dom reminded him. 'And we got through it.'

'True.' Feeling more reluctant than he had ever done about anything in his life, Carlyle fell in

340

step with Dom as they edged slowly towards the boat. As he did so, another name from the past came to mind.

'Remember Sam Hooper?'

Silver nodded. 'Sure.'

Hooper had been a member of the Met's Middle Market Drugs Project. Dominic Silver had been in the unit's sights. Carlyle was, at the very least, 90 per cent certain that Hooper had been killed at Dom's insistence. 'What about him?' he asked warily.

'I had to get the job done,' Dom replied, 'and I got the job done. I always get the job done, Johnny boy. Always.'

Stepping on board, Carlyle immediately felt queasy. 'Is this your boat?'

'No,' Dom said brusquely. 'Of course not. It's owned by a Spanish family and was rented out a month ago under a false name using a credit card that will never come back to me. I have it for another two months, with an option to buy,' he grinned, 'which, you won't be surprised to learn, I will not be taking up.'

Carlyle thought about that for a moment. 'So this has been in the works for a while?'

'I'm not slow to admit when I've made a mistake. After hooking up with Tuco in Paris, I knew that it wasn't going to work out.'

Despite his discomfort, Carlyle managed to muster an *I told you so* smirk.

'You were right,' Dom sighed. 'Eva was right. I was a mug for looking to get back into the game at this level.'

'So now you have to take him out?'

'He's a complete nut job. I'm not going to sit around and wait for the next parcel bomb.'

Fair enough, Carlyle thought. *Fair enough.* 'So where are we going?'

'An island called Belle-Île-en-Mer, off the Brittany coast. It's not that far.'

'Great.' Carlyle knew nothing about sailing but he knew that crossing the Channel meant crossing one of the busiest shipping lanes in the world. Images of *El Nino* being mown down by a ferry or an oil tanker flashed across his brain.

'Tuco was born there. He grew up on the island and still has strong links there. His family is descended from Acadian colonists who returned to France after being expelled from Nova Scotia during le Grand Derangement.'

Carlyle didn't have a clue what Dom was talking about.

'He has a farm on the Atlantic side of the island, the Côte Sauvage,' Dom went on. 'It's quite remote. Far better to deal with him there than in Paris or London. I've been waiting for him to put in an appearance on the island, which he finally did four days ago.'

'How do you know he's still there?'

'He normally stays for a week, at least.'

Carlyle wondered where Dom had his intelligence from but knew better than to ask.

'It's a very relaxing spot. The British occupied Belle-Île for a couple of years in the eighteenth century,' Dom informed him. 'I've sailed there a couple of times – it's a great place for a family trip in the summer. I much prefer it to the Ile de

342

Ré; for a start, you're a lot less likely to bump into Johnny Depp and Vanessa Paradis.'

'Fuck me, Dom,' Carlyle grumbled, 'we're not going on a bloody holiday.' A celebrity gossip thought popped into his head. 'Anyway, didn't they get divorced?'

'Yeah, I think so. He was chasing after some hot lesbian, or something like that.'

'Glad we got that sorted out,' said Carlyle, shivering.

'Why don't you go inside?' Dom pointed towards the cockpit. 'There's some Jameson's in the saloon to warm you up a bit.'

As Gideon cranked up the engine, Carlyle stared at the jetty. He should get off the boat while he still had the chance. His brain was screaming at him to get off. Slowly, the boat edged away from its berth and headed out of the marina. Chilled to the bone, he stepped below deck in search of the whiskey.

FORTY-THREE

'Wake up, we're here.'

Carlyle rubbed his eyes. Thanks to the calming effects of a quarter of the bottle of Jameson's, he had enjoyed a surprisingly good sleep as they had crossed the Channel. He swung his feet over the side of the bunk and made his way unsteadily outside.

Standing near the stern, Dom and Gideon were pulling on what looked like black jumpsuits. A

343

third suit lay crumpled at their feet. Seeing Carlyle emerge, Dom kicked at it with his toe.

'Get this on.'

Carlyle nodded as he stepped over to the side of the boat, pulled off his gloves and unzipped his trousers. Careful not to aim into the wind, he sent a stream of urine into the darkness, listening in vain for a splash. As his eyes became accustomed to the night, he could just about make out that they were anchored in a small cove about fifty yards from a beach which was ringed by steep cliffs that rose up maybe two hundred feet.

Try as he might, he couldn't shake off the sensation that he was part of a bunch of kids playing a game of Cowboys and Indians. In some wretched way, it was like being eight again. There was a moment of panic when Carlyle thought that he might be expected to swim to the shore; when he saw Gideon lowering an inflatable dinghy off the stern of the yacht, he let out a sigh of relief. The firm breeze helped him get fully awake. The sea was calm and the air was noticeably warmer than in England. Finishing his business, he turned back to his companions as a beacon of light appeared overhead, briefly illuminated the sky, then disappeared.

'What's that?'

'Le Grand Phare,' Dom explained. 'The lighthouse. Nothing to worry about.' Zipping up his suit, he slipped a pair of plastic covers over his shoes. Together, he and Gideon looked like a couple of the Met's forensic technicians who'd gone over to the dark side. 'Hurry up. Get dressed.'

Once he had struggled into his suit and fixed his shoe coverings, Carlyle pulled his gloves back on, watching nervously as Gideon appeared from the saloon and dropped a large holdall on the deck. Kneeling down, Spanner opened it up to reveal an array of weapons. Carlyle's stomach did a somersault. Appearing at his shoulder, Dom peered inside.

'Give me the K100.'

'Sure.' Gideon threaded a silencer on to the semi-automatic and handed it to Dom. He nodded at Carlyle 'What about him?'

Dom grinned. 'Which is the most idiot-proof?'

Gideon shrugged. 'They're all simple enough – maybe the Beretta?'

'Fine.' Picking a gun out of the bag, Dom tossed it at Carlyle. 'Here.'

Carlyle caught it by the barrel, relieved that it hadn't gone off.

'Silencer?' Gideon asked.

Looking Carlyle up and down, Dom thought about it for a moment. 'Have you ever used a gun before?'

Carlyle shook his head.

'Jesus,' Dom said. 'What kind of a cop are you?'

Carlyle had to resist the urge to throw up. *A British one,* he thought.

'Let's leave it as it is,' Dom sighed, 'otherwise he's bound to miss his target.'

Gideon pulled a couple of handguns out of the bag and stuck them into his pockets. Then he added a couple of spare magazines and another silencer. 'Just as long as he doesn't shoot us,' he grunted, zipping up the bag and stowing it back in the cockpit.

With the wind at their backs, the three men marched in silence through the coarse grass of the flat terrain, Dom and Gideon shoulder to shoulder with Carlyle hanging back half a yard, as if that would somehow absolve him from getting involved when the shooting started. Having left the dinghy on the beach, they had scrambled up a steep path to the top of the cliffs and taken their bearings from the lighthouse, which stood a couple of miles to the south. Overhead, heavy cloud cover obscured the moon, adding to the sense of gloom. Despite everything, however, Carlyle felt invigorated by the exercise and the wind blowing in off the Atlantic. Filling his lungs with the bracing sea air, he felt almost giddy.

Near the lighthouse, Dom pointed to a cluster of lights. 'That's the village of Bangor.' He directed Carlyle's gaze to a single light in a cluster of trees a mile or so to the north. 'And that's where we're going.'

FORTY-FOUR

Carlyle glanced at his wrist, staring at it blankly for several seconds before realizing that he wasn't wearing a watch. Cursing himself, he returned his attention to the farmhouse. The lair of Tuco Martinez was a long, low building that radiated malevolence. It was sitting in darkness, apart from one window at the far end where light leaked through a half-closed shutter.

How long had Dom and Gideon been inside? It had to be five minutes at least. Twice, he had heard what might have been gunshots but, with the noise of the gusting wind, it was impossible to be sure.

Suddenly, there was a burst of light from behind a window and a muzzle flash, followed by another.

Game on.

Hopping from foot to foot, he shivered behind a Toyota Land Cruiser parked twenty or so yards from the house, wondering precisely what he should do. Gripping the Beretta tightly, he kept his finger as far away from the trigger as possible. If ever there was a man who would shoot himself in the foot...

Another minute went by, feeling more like an hour. Carlyle felt an almost overwhelming need to piss but dared not try and release himself from his jumpsuit. He was contemplating the pros and cons of simply going in his pants when a second light went on in the house.

Was that good news? He had no idea.

Finally, he had an epiphany of sorts: the only way he was going to get off this fucking island – other than in a coffin – was if Dom sailed him home; either things were going okay, in which case there was no harm in taking a looksee, or they weren't, in which case he was totally fucked whether he walked through the front door or not.

'Glad we sorted that out,' the inspector murmured to himself as he stepped out from behind the SUV and strode forwards.

Finding the door ajar, he gently kicked it open with the toe of his boot. Creeping inside, his nostrils were assailed by a strong smell of damp and neglect. If anything, the temperature seemed 5 degrees colder than it had been outside. Standing in a long, empty corridor, a mixture of cold and fear began eating into his bones. His hands were shaking so badly he was unable to keep the gun pointed at the door at the far end. As he edged forward, the sole of his shoe stuck to the concrete floor. Looking down, Carlyle saw that he was walking through a trail of blood. With a sinking heart, he moved onwards.

At the end of the corridor, he took a deep breath. Yanking the door open, he jumped into a filthy room, illuminated by a bare bulb hanging from the ceiling. Its weak light flickered off the uneven brick walls, adding to the sense that he had walked into a torture chamber from a snuff movie. The stink made him want to gag.

'About fucking time!' Dom was sitting on the floor, next to Gideon. The two comrades presented a sorry picture; their, hands were taped behind their backs and they had been chained to a metal ring driven into the centre of the floor. Standing over them, grinning like a lunatic, was Tuco Martinez. In his left hand was a machete, its curved blade shining dully in the poor light. If that didn't do the trick, a semi-automatic was stuffed into the belt of his trousers.

'Shoot the fucker!' Dom demanded.

Taking the Beretta in both hands, Carlyle planted his feet apart like they did in the movies,

pointing the gun at a spot he hoped was somewhere near the middle of the Samurai's chest.

Tuco seemed completely unperturbed by the
new arrival. He looked at his blade and then he
looked at Carlyle, shaking his head sadly. Finally,
he turned to Dom: 'So you brought your bastard
flic, too, huh?'

'Put down your weapons, and lie face down on
the floor.' Momentarily forgetting where he was,
Carlyle spoke slowly and firmly. To his own ear,
it almost sounded as if he was a bona fide officer
of the law going about the legal execution of his
duties. Almost.

'Put them down.' His breathing was becoming
more regular and he was no longer aware of his
heart trying to jackhammer out of his chest.
Slowly it dawned on him that he could actually
take control of this situation.

'You're not in London now, you metrosexual
ponce,' Dom hissed angrily, 'Fucking *do* him!'

'Okay, okay, just stay calm.'

Tuco's smile grew wider as he lifted his hands
in the air and took a careful sideways step away
from his prisoners.

'Throw your weapons towards me,' Carlyle
demanded.

'Sure. Anything you say, mister policeman.'
Arching his back, Tuco heaved the machete
towards Carlyle's head. But his throw was wild
and he missed by a good two feet. Standing his
ground, the inspector kept his weapon trained on
the Frenchman.

'I had to try.' Tuco's shrug was almost apologetic. He glanced round the room, as if finally

realizing that it would all end here.

'John, for fuck's sake get on with it!'

Carlyle shot his mate a frayed grin. 'Don't worry,' he rasped, 'I've got it all under control.'

As the words stumbled across his lips, Tuco reached for his gun. A jolt of adrenaline surged through Carlyle's chest. Gripping the gun as tightly as he could, he jerked the trigger of the Beretta as hard as he could.

Nothing happened.

Fuck! What now?

'The safety!' Dom screamed. 'The fucking safety!'

'Shit!' As he fiddled with the switch above the grip, a grinning Tuco aimed for his head. Flinching, Carlyle closed his eyes and yanked the trigger once, twice, three times.

FORTY-FIVE

'Enough, enough – ENOUGH!'

He finally heard Dom over the buzzing in his head. How long had it taken him to realize that Tuco was down?

'Behind you!'

Carlyle swivelled round as the black woman from his apartment stormed through the doorway. Grabbing the machete, she screamed something unintelligible as she lunged towards him. Stumbling backwards, the inspector squeezed off another two rounds, sending her sprawling.

350

Finally, there was silence.

Released from his chains, Dom struggled to his feet. The colour was slowly returning to his face. Trying to fake a smile, he gave Carlyle a hearty pat on the back. 'You don't look too good.'

Carlyle grunted as he watched Gideon reach down and pull the semi-automatic from Tuco's hand.

'There's still one more out there.' Stepping over the corpse, Gideon disappeared through the door.

Feeling the cold sweat pooling at the base of his spine, Carlyle shivered, watching in silence as Dom dragged the woman's body into the middle of the room, letting her drop next to her former lover.

'United in death,' Dom observed breathlessly. 'That's something, I suppose.'

I don't know about that, Carlyle thought. Suddenly, his mind was a jumble of thoughts: regrets, recriminations and relief. What the hell had he done?

He had just admitted double-murder?

Or was it self-defence?

He had no idea. It had all happened so quickly that he felt completely at the mercy of events.

What was he even doing here, with these criminals? The word made him giggle.

'What's so funny?' Dom demanded, distinctly unamused as he wiped the sweat from his forehead with the back of his wrist.

'Nothing.' A wave of euphoria washed over him: he had survived. 'I think I'm going into shock.'

'Save that for later, if you don't mind.'

Somewhere in the house came a shot, then another. A few moments later, they heard footsteps coming down the hall.

'Give me the Beretta.'

Carlyle handed Dom the gun.

'Gideon?'

'Yeah.' Spanner appeared in the doorway, a battered red jerry can in each hand. He gestured back down the hallway. 'The other guy is in the kitchen. Go and get him. Bring him here.'

Carlyle assumed that the guy in the kitchen was Tuco's footsoldier, the man who had pointed a gun at his head back in Covent Garden. It was hard to tell, however, given that most of his face was missing. He was quick to grab the guy's ankles and let Dom take the shoulders as they carried him back to where his erstwhile employer was waiting. With the three bodies lined up in a row, Gideon doused them in the petrol from one of the cans; the fuel from the other was spread liberally around the room. Then he pulled what looked like a miniature bomb – a bunch of wires protruding from an outsized cigarette packet, attached to an old school kitchen-timer – from the breast pocket of his jumpsuit, placing it next to a pool of gasoline, alongside Tuco's right foot.

'Right,' he said, getting to his feet. 'Let's go.' He looked at Dom. 'This place will go up with a bang in three hours.'

'That's fine,' Dom nodded. 'No one's going to find them before then and it gives us plenty of time to get the hell out of here.'

They jogged back to the beach in silence. Carlyle struggled to keep up as Gideon set a punishing pace. Twice he stumbled and had to be helped back up.

Back on the yacht, Dom sniffed the air as Carlyle felt the first few drops of rain on his face.

Dom grinned at Gideon, who was already in the cockpit, pulling up the anchor. 'Good timing. A nice bit of rain is just what the doctor ordered.'

Gideon said nothing as he brought the engine to life and they headed for the open sea.

FORTY-SIX

The whiskey bottle was empty by the time Gideon steered *El Nino* gently into her berth at Brighton Marina. Shoving it under his arm, Carlyle stuck his head out of the cabin and scowled at the grey morning. He had not slept a wink on the return journey. The Jameson's hadn't been able to stop his mind from running in various directions all night, but at least it had helped him forget some of his physical aches and pains. Without waiting for Gideon to tie up the yacht, he scrambled off it as quickly as he could. Jumping onto the jetty, he stumbled, dropping the bottle and, somehow, managing to knock his glasses off the end of his nose. 'Shit!'

While the bottle bounced harmlessly on the wooden planks and rested at his feet, the spectacles went straight over the edge and into the water.

Despair welled up inside him as Carlyle watched three hundred quid disappear beneath a patch of foamy scum. 'Shit, shit, SHIT!'

'They're gone,' said Dom, picking up the bottle and placing it in a black bin liner. 'I'm afraid you'll have to get a new pair.'

They headed to a small lock-up garage on Marina Way. Inside, the space smelled of damp, motor oil and bleach. Feeling faintly nauseous, Carlyle looked around, trying not to imagine what earlier crimes might have occurred within these breezeblock walls.

The garage was empty apart from three black bin liners which sat on a workbench running along one wall.

'Here.' Dom grabbed one of the bin bags and dropped it at Carlyle's feet. 'New clothes. Put the old stuff in there. Everything we were wearing on our little trip gets dumped.'

Dom and Gideon began to strip. Emptying out the contents of his bag, Carlyle contemplated his new outfit. There was a pair of boxer shorts, socks, some cheap trainers, jeans, a red sweat-shirt and a brown parka with a furry hood.

'Hurry up!'

'Okay, okay.' Slowly, he did as he was told.

'Get rid of the new gear when you get home,' Dom instructed him. 'Put the underwear in the rubbish.'

'Not taking any chances, are you?'

'Of course not, you berk.'

Carlyle slipped off his boxers. Shivering against the cold, he dropped them into one of the bin liners. 'Maybe I'll just go commando.'

'Suit yourself,' Dom said gruffly. 'Give the rest of the stuff to Oxfam if you want – but not the one on Drury Lane. Understood?'

'Yes.' Carlyle dressed quickly, stuffing his previous clothes into another bin liner. A thought suddenly crept across his brain. 'What did you do with the guns?'

With one leg stuck in a pair of fresh jeans, Gideon tutted at the stupidity of the question.

'Stripped down and scattered in the middle of the English Channel,' Dom explained as he pulled on a grey T-shirt. 'Nothing to worry about on that score.'

'Nothing to worry about on *any* score,' Gideon muttered.

'No, indeed,' Dom agreed.

Gideon shot Carlyle a threatening look. 'Just make sure you keep your fucking mouth shut.'

'He will.' Smiling, Dom put his arm round Carlyle's shoulder. 'Of course he will.'

They drove back towards London in silence. Pulling in at the Pease Pottage motorway services, Dom donned a West Ham baseball cap, disappearing inside while Gideon stuffed the bin liners containing their soiled clothes into the trash.

Sitting in the back of the SUV, Carlyle rested his forehead against the cold glass of the window. Twenty yards away, a woman was shouting at a screaming child as she dragged the unhappy girl across the car park.

What should he make of the last twenty-four hours? Closing his eyes, the inspector tried to think of something suitably profound but nothing came to mind.

After a while, the car door reopened and Dom placed a tray of coffees on the driver's seat. 'Hungry?' he asked, offering up a bag of doughnuts.

Carlyle thought about it for a moment. 'Nah. Thanks.'

Dom frowned. 'John Carlyle refusing a doughnut! Whatever next? Are you ill?'

'I'm not hungry.'

'Hungover?'

'Amongst other things,' Carlyle replied dolefully.

'It was a tough night,' Dom reflected, 'but it's over now.' He stuck a hand in the bag, pulled out a doughnut and took a large bite, sending raspberry jam all over his chin. Groaning, he grabbed a napkin and dabbed at the mess. 'Job done.'

'Let's hope so.'

'It's over,' Dom repeated. Dropping the remains of the doughnut back into the bag, he began wiping his fingers clean. 'I know you're worried that you've crossed some kind of Rubicon here. Gone over to the dark side. Whatever. But it's not like that. Think of all the shit you've had to deal with over the years. It's all one big grey area. This is no different.'

A very dark shade of grey, Carlyle thought as he watched Gideon reappear from behind the service station.

'In difficult situations you have to make choices.' Handing Carlyle the coffees and the bag of doughnuts, Dom settled in behind the wheel, ready to resume the journey home. 'And you have

356

to live with them.'

Balancing the tray on his knees, Carlyle peeked inside the bag and felt his mouth begin to water. Maybe he could manage a nibble after all.

'We're big boys,' Dom continued. 'We can live with the decisions we make. We *have* to live with them. Above all else, we owe it to our families.'

Amen to that. Carlyle stuck his hand inside the bag and pulled out an iced ring as Gideon opened the car door and slid into the passenger seat.

'All good?' Dom asked.

Gideon nodded. 'Just one thing.'

'What?'

'You've got jam all over your chin.'

FORTY-SEVEN

'Where have you been?' Umar asked.

Hiding behind his plastic cup, Carlyle mumbled something about the flu.

'Simpson's looking for you.' The sergeant grinned.

'She's always looking for me.'

'She's very...'

'...pissed off?'

'No, not at all.'

'Eh? Why not?' Carlyle was stumped.

Umar's grin grew wider. 'She's very pleased that we've wrapped up the Gasparino case.'

Carlyle took a mouthful of orange juice while he slowly recalled the basic points of the

Gasparino case. It seemed a long time ago now. Everything that had happened before he stepped on *El Nino* seemed an extremely long time ago. How the hell did that get solved when he was away? 'We did?'

'Yes,' Umar folded his arms and sat back in his chair triumphantly. 'We – I in other words – tracked down Clive Martin's *granddaughter* and got her to confess and give up all her mates within two hours.'

Carlyle frowned. 'It was a girl who attacked him?'

'Yeah, nasty little character. She was proud of being the ringleader of her little gang. Clive is really cut up about it. More so than her parents, it seems to me.'

Clive? Carlyle thought. So, he's *Clive* now, is he? 'Why did they do it?'

'God!' Umar snorted. 'You don't think there's anything as straightforward as a rational explanation, do you?'

'I suppose not,' Carlyle sighed. 'Anyway, well done.' A cheeky thought popped into his head. 'Have you taken that WPC to Nobu yet? The one who got us,' he corrected himself, 'the one who got *you* the ID?'

'Not yet.' Umar looked around nervously. 'She's stalking me.'

'She seems like a nice girl,' said Carlyle, amused. 'You never know...'

'The thing is,' putting his hands on his knees, Umar leaned forward and lowered his voice, 'I've started going out with someone else.'

'Oh?'

'Yeah.' He hesitated before coughing up a name. 'Christina O'Brien.'

Carlyle looked at him blankly.

'The girl from Everton's.' Umar lowered his voice even more, so it was barely more than a whisper. 'The one who twatted PC Lea.'

After a moment of stunned silence, Carlyle burst out laughing. 'You're kidding!'

Umar shook his head.

The inspector gave his sergeant a nudge on the arm. 'You lucky bastard!'

FORTY-EIGHT

Typing in the PIN number for his credit card, Carlyle felt almost physically ill. Printing off the receipt, Denzil Taleb looked at him with sympathetic glee.

'What time is your flight tomorrow?'

'Eight p.m.,' Carlyle replied. 'I need to be at the airport by six, so I will need to be on the tube about half four.'

'That should give you plenty of time,' the optician agreed. 'I'll make sure that your new glasses are ready by two at the latest.' He handed Carlyle the receipt. Three hundred and fifty-eight fucking pounds. 'Thanks.' Stuffing it in his pocket, he turned and headed for the door.

Out in the street, he paused, unsure where he wanted to head next. When his mobile went off, he answered it immediately.

'Carlyle.'

'John, it's Maria March.'

He smiled. 'And how is Her Majesty's Revenue and Customs today?'

'Fine,' said Maria briskly, suggesting that she didn't have time for small talk. 'I just thought you'd want to hear about Gavin Swann.'

Gavin Swann. It was another name – like Adrian Gasparino – that almost seemed to belong to a past life. All the righteous anger that he'd felt about both men – one probable perpetrator, one definite victim – had evaporated over the last few days, lost at sea. 'What about him?'

'He's been shot.'

'Oh?' Carlyle's first thought was that Maria sounded very matter-of-fact about it. Then again, in his experience, tax inspectors tended to sound very matter-of-fact about most things.

'He's not dead,' Maria explained. 'One of my colleagues was just turning up to interview him as the ambulance arrived.'

Carlyle's mind turned to Wayne Devine and Marcus Angelides. 'I suppose the media will have the story already. It's bound to be a total shit storm.'

'The attackers shot Mr Swann in the leg,' Maria continued, apparently uninterested in the business of the fourth estate. 'I don't know whether that will stop him from playing football in the future...'

'It should certainly give him more time to help you with your enquiries,' Carlyle quipped.

'We'll see,' Maria chuckled. 'Anyway, I've got to go. I just thought I'd let you know.'

'Thanks.' Ending the call, Carlyle dropped the phone into his pocket and decided to head for home.

Back at the flat, he filled a small backpack with some clothes and threw in his passport, travel documents and a copy of the latest Elvis Cole and Joe Pike paperback. He'd been looking forward to reading it for some time, knowing it would be a rollercoaster ride towards an insanely satisfying climax where the two buddies would ruthlessly take out the bad guys using enough weapons to equip a small army.

If only real life was like that.

Closing up the bag, he dropped it in the hall by the front door and headed into the kitchen to make a cup of green tea. The kettle had just boiled when the landline started ringing. He padded into the lounge to pick it up.

'Hello.'

'It's me.' Clear as a bell, Helen's voice came down the line, causing a flutter in his chest.

'How's it going?'

'Fine. It's been quite gruelling and a real eye-opener, especially for Alice, but it was certainly worth coming. How are you?'

'Fine.' Images of the farmhouse in Belle-Île-en-Mer flashed through his brain. It took him a moment to suppress them. 'How is Alice? Can I speak to her?'

'She's doing great. She's just having a shower at the moment. I just wanted to say hi, and check you are okay for the flight tomorrow.'

'I am. I've just finished packing. I'll send you a text before I get on the plane.'

'Good. We're looking forward to seeing you.'

'Me too. I'm really quite up for it.'

'How are things in London?'

'All quiet. Nothing much to report.' The conversation about Harry Ripley could wait till they got back or, at least, until he had worked out what he was going to say about the poor old bugger.

'Okay,' Helen sighed. She sounded tired but happy. 'We'll see you in a couple of days.'

'Yeah.'

'Lots of love.'

'You too. Give Alice a kiss for me.'

'Will do. Bye.'

Putting down the phone, he looked around the room, as if realizing for the first time how empty it was without them. With a sigh, he started back to the kitchen when the phone rang again. Assuming it was Alice, he grabbed the handset.

'Hiya, sweetheart!'

'Hiya to you too,' Umar laughed, *'sweetheart.'*

Carlyle cursed under his breath. 'Sorry, I thought it was my daughter. What is it?'

'I'm waiting for you in a car downstairs. We've gotta get going.'

'Fucking hell, what now?' Carlyle asked grumpily.

'Trust me. You're gonna love this. Hurry up.'

FORTY-NINE

Shielding his eyes against the floodlights, Carlyle watched as Evan Milch strode towards the centre circle, with a couple of forensics technicians in tow. It was bizarre to be standing in the middle of one of London's largest sports stadia, surrounded by empty stands on all sides. Turning to Umar standing beside him, he asked: 'How did we hear about this so quickly?'

'I was at the station,' Umar explained, 'when a call came in for you from a guy called Bas-something.'

'Baseer Yazdani, the wire journalist at Honeymann?'

'Yeah. He gave me the basics. He said you had a deal.'

Carlyle said nothing as he watched Milch approach the plastic sheeting that covered the centre of the pitch.

'I should be selling bloody tickets to this,' the pathologist grumbled. 'Everyone wants a look.' Reaching down, he lifted up a corner of the sheet.

Carlyle and Umar quickly stepped forward to see with their own eyes that the rumours were most emphatically true. Lying on his back along the halfway line, Christian Holyrod gazed vacantly up at them with his lifeless eyes; all the politician's cunning gone from his face. However, it was not his face that caught Carlyle's attention. Naked

363

from the waist down, the dead Mayor still retained a massive erection.

'It looks like he rather overdid it with the Viagra,' Milch smirked.

Carlyle gave a harsh, unsympathetic laugh. 'He died with his hard-on.'

'Will it wear off?' Umar enquired.

'Eventually.'

'Surely,' said Carlyle, 'that wasn't the cause of death?'

'No, no,' Milch replied. 'The excitement of sexual congress was too much for the poor chap. He had a massive heart attack. Dead before he hit the turf.'

'An extreme case of coitus interruptus,' Umar reflected.

'Indeed.' Milch let the sheet fall from his hand.

'Where's the girlfriend?' Carlyle asked.

'I think they took Ms Slater to the boardroom for a cup of tea – and some gentle questioning,' Milch replied.

'Apparently,' said Umar, the glee clear in his voice, 'she paid one of the ground staff five grand to switch on the lights.' He nodded in the direction of the corpse. 'She set it up as a special treat for Holyrod. They found her screaming her head off, wearing nothing but a replica jersey and a strap-on dildo.'

'Outstanding effort. Truly outstanding!' Carlyle knew that he was grinning idiotically – like a kid who'd just managed to lay his hands on his first ever porn mag – but he did not care one jot. 'Abigail Slater, what a woman! Out-fucking-standing.' Starting back towards the main stand, he pulled out his mobile and called Baseer. Waiting patiently for it to go to voicemail, he left a simple message: 'It is, my friend, the story of your dreams. Fill your boots.'

Ending the call, he pulled up Simpson's number. She answered on the third ring.

'You've heard about what's happened, I presume?' Carlyle asked, by way of greeting.

'Dino's in a foul mood,' she said, by way of reply. 'He's stomping around – I've never seen anything like it.' Her voice was cautious, low; a tone that he'd never heard before.

'Are you okay?'

'I'm fine, John.' Simpson audibly bristled at the suggestion that she might not be able to handle her boyfriend's moods. 'Just a bit surprised at Dino's lack of grace under pressure.'

'I'm surprised that Holyrod was that important to his operation,' Carlyle mused. 'After all, he'd only just joined the Board.'

'Holyrod?' Simpson spluttered. 'Dino couldn't give a fig about that self-important buffoon. It's his bloody love-child Gavin Swann that he's exercised about. The people who shot him in the leg knew what they were doing. It looks like his career could be over.'

'Shame.' Signalling to Umar and Milch that he was leaving, Carlyle began walking off the pitch.

'Dino reckons that Mr Swann's premature retirement could end up costing him the best part of a hundred million,' Simpson added, in a tone that suggested she cared as little about it as the inspector did himself.

'Who's investigating the Swann shooting?'

Simpson mentioned the name of a Detective Chief Inspector who they both knew was completely useless.

'I'd offer to help,' Carlyle said sincerely, 'but I'm off tomorrow.' Reaching the tunnel, he headed for an illuminated Exit sign.

'Of course, of course,' Simpson said, not particularly interested in his holiday plans either. 'I hope you have a good time,' she offered half-heartedly. 'Come and see me when you get back.'

Ending the call, Carlyle pushed open a gate marked *NO RE-ENTRY*. Outside the ground, he counted a dozen or so police officers standing around, clearly unsure about what they should be doing. For some reason, two fire engines had turned up. A large group of journalists and TV crews were swarming around an ambulance that had just arrived at the kerb, shouting questions that no one would ever answer.

Feeling a gentle rain on his face, Carlyle lowered his head. 'This bitch of a life,' he mumbled to himself. 'This fucking *bitch* of a life.' Not knowing whether to laugh or cry, he thrust his hands deep into his pockets, moving away from the crowd at a brisk pace.

The publishers hope that this book has given you enjoyable reading. Large Print Books are especially designed to be as easy to see and hold as possible. If you wish a complete list of our books please ask at your local library or write directly to:

Magna Large Print Books
Magna House, Long Preston,
Skipton, North Yorkshire.
BD23 4ND

This Large Print Book for the partially sighted, who cannot read normal print, is published under the auspices of

THE ULVERSCROFT FOUNDATION

THE ULVERSCROFT FOUNDATION

... we hope that you have enjoyed this Large Print Book. Please think for a moment about those people who have worse eyesight problems than you ... and are unable to even read or enjoy Large Print, without great difficulty.

You can help them by sending a donation, large or small to:

**The Ulverscroft Foundation,
1, The Green, Bradgate Road,
Anstey, Leicestershire, LE7 7FU,
England.**
or request a copy of our brochure for more details.

The Foundation will use all your help to assist those people who are handicapped by various sight problems and need special attention.

Thank you very much for your help.